THE
BILLIONAIRES
THE
BOSSES

THE BILLIONAIRES

THE BOSSES

CALISTA FOX

ST. MARTIN'S GRIFFIN
NEW YORK

THE BILLIONAIRES: THE BOSSES. Copyright © 2017 by Calista Fox. All rights reserved. Printed in the United States of America. For information, address St. Martin's Press, 175 Fifth Avenue, New York, N.Y. 10010.

www.stmartins.com

Designed by Omar Chapa

The Library of Congress Cataloging-in-Publication Data is available upon request.

ISBN 978-1-250-09642-5 (trade paperback)
ISBN 978-1-250-09643-2 (e-book)

Our books may be purchased in bulk for promotional, educational, or business use. Please contact your local bookseller or the Macmillan Corporate and Premium Sales Department at 1-800-221-7945, extension 5442, or by e-mail at MacmillanSpecialMarkets@macmillan.com.

First Edition: September 2017

10 9 8 7 6 5 4 3 2 1

To the Art Department at St. Martin's Press.
I can't thank you enough for the beautiful covers
you give me, the mockups when needed, and
the extra graphics for this entire series. Sensational!

ACKNOWLEDGMENTS

Once again, I am so thrilled to partner with my editor, Monique Patterson. I love your high-concept visions and working with you is a dream. I'm feeling quite blessed.

Of course, I owe that initial foot-in-the-door with Monique and St. Martin's Press to my lovely agent, Sarah E. Younger, of the Nancy Yost Literary Agency. Thank you, as always!

For my readers, new and long-standing, I hope you are enjoying this series. After high-speed chases and blowing things up in the Burned Deep series, I had backed off from suspense/thriller elements in *The Billionaires,* but had to add a little danger and intrigue to this one. I couldn't help myself.

Naturally, I'm eternally grateful to my husband and my parents for their unwavering support and love.

All my best to everyone at St. Martin's Press, including my fantastic copyeditor and proofreader, and everyone who is working so hard to promote my books. I appreciate everything you do for me!

THE
BILLIONAIRES

THE
BOSSES

ONE

Bayli Styles had extra pep in her step as she made her way down Lexington Avenue toward Manhattan's hottest new venue, the newly opened steakhouse Davila's NYC. Owned by international restaurateur Christian Davila and his business partner, celebrity chef Rory St. James.

She had an interview for a hostess position. Not the ultimate gig she aspired to, but living in New York City didn't come cheap. Even her crappy apartment in a sketchy neighborhood cost a small fortune in rent. She was willing to pay the price—she'd wanted to live here since she was seventeen. Until recently, however, circumstances beyond her control had precluded her from packing herself up and making the trek from the beautiful wine country of River Cross, California. Tragic circumstances, to be exact.

Yet a decade later, here she was. Starting a new life. One that required her to land several part-time jobs with flexible hours so she could also take on modeling assignments sent her way by the agency that had agreed to rep her when she'd arrived two months ago. The assignments were a bit too few and far between, but at least she was building her portfolio. Perhaps someday soon she'd make a name for herself.

In the meantime, she'd do whatever it took to keep this city from kicking her ass. This vibrant, energetic city that she'd already fallen in love with, even if it did intimidate the hell out of her sometimes with the honking of horns, the hordes of people walking brisk seven-minute miles to and from work, and the infinite number of sights to see.

Luckily, she'd spent a few years living in San Francisco with her friends from high school—Jewel Catalano, a wine heiress, and Scarlet Drake, an insurance fraud investigator. So Bayli didn't feel *too* country bumpkin. Most of the time, at any rate.

Today was a good example. She was treating this interview as she would a modeling job. She wore her favorite sleeveless one-shouldered black mini, believing the manager of Davila's would want to see that she was chic and fashion forward. And could work her shift in five-inch heels. She'd pulled her long dark hair up in a sleek style and added simple accessories. Slim, elongated silver hoops and the sparkly crystal bracelet her mother had given her for Christmas several years ago. It was a costume piece and not worth anything other than sentimental value. A pretty trinket that kept her dearly departed mom close to her in spirit.

Bayli knew her mother would be proud of her for finally breaking free of all the trauma back in California and finding her own path. Even if it was slow going and she had to put in extra effort to make ends meet. Bayli had never lived a charmed life. She had high hopes her luck might change now that she'd ventured east to chase her wildest dreams.

Her stomach fluttered as she approached the tall, arched double doors of the steakhouse.

This could be so *huge.*

The "in" she needed when it came to conquering this city. So much potential lay beyond those doors. It was up to her to seize the opportunity. Reach for her own brass ring.

You can do this, Bay. Just go for it!

The restaurant didn't open until cocktail hour during the week, which meant there'd be little activity, likely a low-key environment, before the hustle and bustle of dinnertime. That helped to minimize her anxiety over really and truly needing to be hired so she could pay her bills.

Although she was borderline in dire financial straits and feeling a tiny bit desperate, exhilaration trilled down her spine. Bayli had an ace in the hole for this interview and wasn't above pulling out her connection to the Davila enterprise, no matter how indirect and distant that connection was. She simply had to get this job.

It wasn't just about the money. As she'd mentioned to Jewel and Scarlet before the restaurant had launched, she considered it a viable springboard for her modeling career. A famous restaurateur and celebrity chef would pack in the people and the press. What a great place for Bayli to be discovered!

The possibility made her more excited. More determined to slay this.

She pulled open one of the doors and entered the softly lit establishment. Standing in the middle of the vast foyer, she inhaled deeply, smelling a wood-burning fire, new leather, and the most tantalizing, mouthwatering aroma coming from the kitchen.

To her right was a wide hallway with a wine cellar and private tasting room. Farther down were the restrooms. To her left was a lounge that looked more like a cozy study, showcasing endless shelves filled with hardback novels, a fireplace, sofas, and coffee and end tables. Being a bookworm who loved libraries, Bayli felt right at home.

It was also all very upscale and gorgeous. As she'd expected.

She walked beyond the large round table in the middle of the entryway with an enormous floral arrangement serving as a centerpiece and a stunning chandelier hanging overhead. Bayli had already looked at the menu online, and that was why she wasn't surprised by the elegant and expensive décor. Anyone who'd lay down a couple hundred dollars for a filet mignon deserved to dine in high style.

The restaurant wasn't a big one—just enough to comfortably accommodate thirty. She'd been forewarned when the manager had contacted her for the interview that reservations were difficult to come by. And, if hired, she'd be turning away more people than she'd be seating. A daunting challenge, but Bayli understood the exclusivity of the place.

What did shock her, however, was that there was a group of four at a table, sampling a trio of soups in miniature artsy bowls. The restaurant served lunch only on the weekends, so she surmised they must be food critics, magazine editors, or bloggers.

She didn't have time to observe their reactions to the food, because a lanky, well-groomed blond in a tuxedo strode toward her with purpose. He extended his hand and swiftly and efficiently shook hers as he announced in a thick French accent, "I am Pierre LaVallier, the manager of Davila's NYC. You must be Miss Styles."

"Yes. And *Bayli* is fine." She smiled politely.

"Tres bien."

Thank God Bayli had taken a year of French in high school. Hopefully nothing would get lost in translation during the interviewing process.

"Come, come," he lightly insisted.

Pierre directed her past the massive bar made of rich, dark wood with intricate scrolled accents and panels and a shiny copper top. The wall behind it was lined with glass shelves and every manner of premium-level alcohol.

"Chef St. James would like to meet you before you and I sit down to chat," Pierre informed her. "He's already reviewed your application. Though you're early, so he'll require you to wait in the kitchen while he finishes his work."

Bayli drew up short and gasped. "Rory St. James is here? *Now?*"

Pierre turned back to face her. *"Oui.* Of course," he said a bit haughtily. "The restaurant has only been open for a month. He stays on-site for the first quarter before making the rounds at the other kitchens. Obviously, that's part of the grand-opening frenzy.

Why our phones ring off the hook for reservations that have to be booked two to three months out. *If* they're lucky," he added with panache and a dramatic hand gesture.

"Right. That makes perfect sense." It also made it incredibly difficult for Bayli to breathe. She was going to meet Rory St. James. The man, the myth, the legend.

The chef who made sure every one of his and Christian Davila's restaurants earned Michelin stars. Putting them on the "best of the best" lists in their respective cities. The chef who reportedly roared like a lion when things didn't go right in his den.

Oh, shit.

Her hands started to shake. She clutched her slim black leather folder, which contained a copy of her résumé and some highlights from her modeling portfolio, to her chest.

Bayli was a research buff by nature, and she'd done her homework before she'd even applied for this position. So she knew what she was getting herself into. Problem was, she'd never worked as a hostess before and, well, the idea of being interviewed by Rory St. James was downright nerve-wracking.

"Are you all right?" Pierre asked with notable concern. "You've gone a bit pale."

"Fine. I'm fine. I just like to be fully prepared when I . . ." *Become someone else.*

Breathe, Bay. Just breathe.

She pulled in several long streams of air. Went to that place in her mind where positivity and optimism reigned supreme. Mentally shook off her tension.

Then she flashed her camera-ready smile.

"Bon Dieu!" Pierre's blond brows shot up. "Liane was right about you. She said you could light up an entire room."

"That's very sweet of her."

Liane was the former main hostess of Davila's. A new friend of a friend Bayli had recently met. And likely the only reason Bayli had scored this opportunity, because according to Liane, there was a foot-high stack of submissions from much more qualified candidates on Pierre's desk.

He said, "It was kind of her to make a recommendation after, unfortunately, we had to let her go."

Bayli's head cocked to the side. "Let her go? I thought she quit in order to start the fall semester at NYU."

"Ah, is that what she claimed? She's a lovely girl, so please don't mention to her that I told you that Chef St. James excused her when she turned away the governor for a table."

"Wow." Bayli's mind reeled. "The governor of New York? Who would be—"

"A man you do *not* shoo away because he doesn't have a reservation. Especially when he shows up with foreign dignitaries he wants to impress. I'll make it all perfectly clear how to accommodate situations such as that . . . provided Chef gives you the head nod."

The head nod.

Oh, fuck.

She inhaled again. Held the breath. Let it out slowly.

Back to your happy place, Bay.

The smile easily returned. "I'm fine," she assured Pierre again, though her heart thundered and her pulse raced.

Okay, desperation was a bit of a scary thing. But she bucked up, because being "on" came naturally to Bayli.

Finally stepping out of the shadows of her past and really being seen was what motivated her, what drove her to succeed no matter the bleak years and pain she'd suffered back in California. Like Jewel had told her, this was Bayli's time to shine.

And shine she would!

Hitching her chin a notch, she said, "Let's go meet Chef St. James."

Oh, dear God, please let him like me!

Rory St. James was already planning the new menu that would roll out in a couple of months. It was his custom to keep changing up the selections that came from his kitchens, not just to ensure loyal patrons didn't feel a sense of repetitiveness but also because there were endless dishes to surprise and enthrall diners. One of the reasons Rory preferred a different style of cuisine for each establishment.

Wine country chic in River Cross, California. Fresh seafood in Boston. Cuban fusion in Miami. Traditional pub-food-taken-to-the-next-level in London. Six courses with wine pairings in Paris . . .

At thirty-two, Rory did not yet feel as though he'd fully explored his culinary genius and therefore continued to study and practice and add to his repertoire. In his mind, there really was no such thing as being at the top of your game in this business, because around every corner there was a new discovery to make and a new direction to take.

The steakhouse was meant to provide a basis for some of the classics with Rory's twist on them. Medium-rare filet mignon cooked at sixteen hundred degrees and drizzled with a decadent crab-béarnaise sauce. Pepper-encrusted New York strips. Beef Wellington. Chateaubriand. Thick, juicy T-bones. All with his own spices incorporated—and all of which he was currently preparing for an elite group of food critics sitting in his dining room. He also prepped samples of Australian rack of lamb and Chilean sea bass for variety.

He'd already offered three different types of specialty soups. Now he plated the salads and arranged them on a serving tray with a bread display and accompaniments. He hadn't requested a server for today's affair. Pierre poured the wine, and the sous and dessert chefs were on hand, but Rory wanted to take a more personable approach with these particular critics as they immersed themselves in his menu, so he chose to be more engaging than usual and deliver the food himself.

He knew his reputation preceded him. Type A, control freak, perfectionist. He'd heard it all—and deserved the labels. He'd lost his temper more than once in his kitchens. It was no secret he could be surly when he was in the zone. Not out of extreme arrogance, though, yes, he was proud of his achievements even as he continued to strive for greater excellence. Rory just wasn't a people person, per se. It was the main reason he stuck to what had been deemed his "den" by the epicurean media and let Christian or Pierre or the front-of-house managers at the other restaurants converse with the customers.

Rory comprehended the importance of circulating throughout the dining room, inquiring as to whether everything had been prepared to guests' satisfaction. But the majority of the time, he was deep in thought, challenging his own knowledge, concocting more creative dishes.

It was hugely helpful that Christian was so charismatic—and women fawned over him. It was also advantageous for both men that they were on the same page when it came to diversity at each of their restaurants. Neither settled for the status quo, and Christian was always open to new innovations.

They'd met at Columbia University and had hit it off instantly.

Ironically, they'd almost *literally* hit each other instantly. At the time they'd met, they'd both been dating the same woman. And hadn't known it.

Turned out to be a fortuitous encounter. Because here they were, twelve years later, still best friends and business partners. Still sharing their women . . .

But that wasn't something for Rory to think about at the moment. He had cutthroat foodies to win over.

He hefted the tray, flattened his palm in the center, and carried it above shoulder height through the kitchen and out the pass-through door. He only made it one step beyond the wide doorframe when he kicked something hard and unyielding. At first. Then the object gave way and a delicate shriek shattered the silence.

Just as Rory tripped—over a body.

"Jesus Christ!" he bellowed.

The tray went flying, slamming into the far wall of the servers' station, the painstakingly chosen china crashing to the tile floor and resonating throughout the narrow space and nearly empty restaurant as Rory fell to his knees. Next to the body.

A very svelte, gorgeous body. One that shouldn't have been squatting anywhere near the entrance to his kitchen.

The woman who was sprawled partially on the floor alongside him blurted, "Oh, my God! I'm so sorry!"

Pierre swooped in to hastily clean the mess while Rory hopped to his feet. His hand shot out in the general direction of the startled woman. He curtly said, "You must be Bayli Styles. Hostess wannabe?" His next words came on a near growl. "You're early."

She stared at him, a little rocked by the incident if he read her stunned expression accurately. Then she seemed to come around and actually glared. "Bayli, yes."

He smirked at how she neither confirmed nor denied the tidbit about whether she now wanted to be a Davila's hostess. Feisty thing that she apparently was.

With her head tilted back to look up at him, Rory got the full effect of her sculpted face, unbelievably long black lashes, and the most tempting crimson-colored mouth he'd ever seen.

He didn't even have time to process the natural sparkle in her tawny eyes, because her palm slipped into his and everything in his brain went haywire. Her touch was warm and velvety and . . . *electrifying*. Jolting Rory.

She gripped his hand tightly, either fearing he might let go and cause her to fall back on her ass or to prove she wasn't intimidated by him. He burned with curiosity to know which was more accurate.

He helped her up, and as Bayli Styles stood before him— almost eye to eye given the tall heels she wore—something even more profound happened to Rory.

A click. In his brain. In his gut.

His gaze slid over her, taking in every glamorous inch but

mostly fixating on legs that didn't quit. Holy hell, she had incredible legs. Bare, sleek, and sexy looking. They'd feel fucking fantastic wrapped around his hips.

But no. That wasn't what the click was about. Not entirely, anyway.

She was insanely beautiful, yes. Poised, even after he'd laid her flat. Squared shoulders. Lifted chin. She was . . . sensational.

Not just in the way that instantly charged him, sexually. Especially as her nipples pebbled beneath her tight black dress. While Rory's groin tightened at her physical response to him, his mind suddenly whirled with other thoughts. Potentially the solution to a professional problem that had plagued him and Christian the past several months. A project that had tanked miserably, with no plausible way in sight to rectify it. Until now. Because a new vision stood right before his very eyes.

But Rory wasn't one to give anything away. He had to further gauge the situation, assess the ebb and flow between Bayli and his sometimes overpowering demeanor before he jumped to any brilliant conclusions about whether he was staring at the Holy Grail he and Christian desperately sought.

First, Rory would have to determine if this woman was a flight-or-fight one.

He sensed it would be the latter. *Hoped* it would be the latter.

"Are you all right?" he demanded, not curbing his annoyance that she'd disrupted his lunch service, had effectively made a calamity of it. He wanted her full-on, unchecked reaction to him not going all soft on her because of her pretty face and haunting eyes.

Bayli ripped her hand from his as though she'd been scalded, and rubbed her shapely left hip where he'd accidentally kicked her. In a husky tone that confirmed she felt the spontaneous chemistry as well, she told him, "Think you'll leave a mark, but I'm sure I'll survive."

There was a tinge of sass to her voice, a flicker of it in her shimmering irises.

Definitely fight.

"Good to hear." That sentiment held dual meaning for him.

She intrigued Rory. He could see quite clearly that he rattled her cage with his brusque disposition, but she was still willing to go toe-to-toe with him. And there was no mistaking the exhilaration and heat in her expression.

All *very* interesting . . .

Rory wasn't thrilled he'd marred her, was irritated at himself as much as he was at her for being in his way. But he was still thinking three steps ahead. Far beyond the hostess position she'd come to see him about . . .

He scooped up her portfolio, along with the papers and pictures that had spilled from it. Then asked her, "Mind telling me why you decided to be a tree stump in front of my swinging kitchen doors?"

Snatching the leather folder from him, she said between clenched teeth, "A couple of photos slipped out and I bent down to retrieve them. I wasn't expecting you to come charging through those doors like a bull in a china shop."

"Ha!" he exploded. More of an admonishment than a jest. "First lesson in a restaurant—expect the unexpected. Second lesson—know these double doors swing both ways and there's *always* someone coming or going."

He spun around, shoved through the right-side door. Went straight to the salad station, where he replated salads, doing his damnedest to banish images blazing in his mind of long, luxurious legs and full, enticing breasts. Those puckered nipples that beckoned him to peel away her clothing and tease the little buds tighter with his tongue . . .

Jesus, man. Get a grip. You're not an animal.

Yet Bayli Styles certainly brought out his primal instincts.

Focus on your work, asshole. There are food critics in your dining room. Remember?

The commotion at the servers' station had no doubt echoed

out front—and in the ears of his special guests—so time was of the
essence to serve them. Distract them from the shattering of china
and the clattering of serving utensils behind the scenes.

But as Rory stared at the dishes before him, he had another
startling revelation. Why the hell had he prepped Caesar salads?
Sure, they were complementary to all meals at a steakhouse. *But
fuck.* He had a list of more colorful, flavorful selections. So he put
away the single-serving plates and reached for the sampler ones
that were specific to a trio of smaller portions.

Out of the corner of his eye, he caught Bayli Styles tentatively
entering his domain, holding her portfolio to her ample chest.

She watched him from afar for a few moments and then took
several strides toward him.

As though she'd read his thoughts earlier and now followed
his every movement, keeping a mental pace with him, she said,
"Very clever. An arugula, pear, and walnut salad. Field of greens
with strawberries. And endive with apple crisps and Gorgonzola.
Fancy, but nothing to overpower whatever the hell it is you're cooking that smells like heaven."

"You know your salads. Where does that come from?" It was
meant to be mindless chatter, but she didn't seem to catch on.

"Well, I'm a model, so lettuce is my best friend. But aside from
that, I pretty much devour books and magazines on every topic.
Including food."

"Devour, eh?" He didn't look up as he made quick work of the
new round of salads.

"Sorry. My brain operates in silos. I compartmentalize, so
when we're discussing meals I—"

"I get it. Now, why don't you tell me why you'd like to be a
hostess at this restaurant, particularly when you have no prior
experience?"

He didn't miss the hitch in her breath at his abrupt change of
subject, even though his focus was on ladling a traditional balsamic
vinaigrette and a lighter white one into dressing boats.

"I enjoy working with the public, have excellent customer service skills, and I'm a fan of yours and Mr. Davila's," she said.

"I see." He spared a glance her way. She was certainly polished. A quick thinker. But she wasn't the right woman for the hostess job. He knew it innately. Having worked in restaurants since he was ten, starting with his uncle's bistro, Rory had a lifetime of expertise tucked under his belt and could easily deduce that Bayli Styles didn't quite grasp the intensity of restaurant work. Yes, he based that assessment primarily on the incident at the servers' station.

Rory, Christian, and their staff had to be seasoned. And even then, there were certain things Rory wouldn't turn a blind eye to—say, telling the governor of the state in which you operated that there was no table for him and his associates. Not recognizing him was even more unforgivable. Christ, would Liane have overlooked Michelle Obama and sent her on her merry way because the First Lady didn't have a reservation?

There were little secrets in Rory's world, and one of them was that a few seats were always held in reserve for VIPs who showed up on the fly.

Yet that wasn't the main issue he had with Miss Styles.

He suspected greeting and seating diners wouldn't challenge her. At least not beyond a week or two. Then she'd move on to something more her speed—likely a coveted modeling job, because a woman who looked like her was meant to be in front of the camera—and they'd be back to square one at Davila's NYC, needing to interview and train someone else.

Conversely, believing she belonged in front of a camera was what solidified in his mind that there could very well be a suitable alternative with this situation. The gnawing sensation grew with every second she lingered close to him. Rory felt an intrinsic pull as her darkly stirring scent wafted under his nose, so very distinct and alluring as it competed with the aromas from the ovens, and something contradictory about her very presence captivated him.

Her beauty was certainly an appealing feature, but Bayli didn't strike him as the sort who'd rely strictly on her looks to get what she wanted, to land her a job such as this. The way she watched him so intently told him she was a woman with a thirst for knowledge and a need to learn new things, see new sights. She seemed to take great interest in everything around her, and Rory found that refreshing.

He only wished Christian were here at the moment to discuss the potential of hiring Bayli for their next joint venture, which was currently in the retooling stage.

Unfortunately, Rory couldn't propose anything to Bayli without consulting his partner—and there was no time for that at present—so he simply told her, "I'll be in touch."

He loaded up his second round of salads, bread, and a cracked pepper mill.

"Wait. I'm sorry," she hastily said. "What does that mean? Should I still sit down with Pierre?"

"No need. You'll hear from me personally." He lifted the tray high. "Thank you for stopping by, Miss Styles." He breezed past her to get on with his business.

Though the image of Bayli was burned into his brain and thoughts of their disastrous, though fortuitous, meeting continued to simmer . . .

Bayli stood outside of Davila's NYC, fuming. She hit the speed dial number on her phone for Scarlet, who conferenced in Jewel.

"You guys are not going to believe this." Bayli jumped right in. "I was kicked in the hip and then dismissed!".

"*What?*" Jewel shrieked. "At your interview?"

"Oh, there was no interview! There was a loud crash and a gruff chef and then an 'I'll be in touch.'" She huffed. "Yeah, right. He'll be in touch when he goes vegan with his next restaurant—which is the equivalent of hell freezing over for this man. Shit!"

It'd all happened so fast. And she'd let it.

What the fuck?

"I don't understand," Scarlet said as Bayli stalked down the crowded sidewalk toward the subway, a bit too far away for a woman in five-inch heels, but she didn't really notice the strain on her feet, in her current agitated state.

Jewel told her, "You're perfect for the job! You're attractive. Friendly. Professional. Smart. What more could they possibly be looking for in a hostess?"

"Beats the hell out of me," she grumbled. "But His Royal Culinary Highness Rory St. James tripped over me, his tray went sailing, and two minutes later he was like, 'Bye-bye, baby.'"

"What an ass," Scarlet scoffed.

"I don't know," Bayli lamented as she came to an abrupt halt, miraculously not interrupting anyone else's flow so that they slammed into her. She whirled around and stared in the direction from which she'd come. She considered marching back into the restaurant and demanding an actual interview. But what good would that do? If Rory and Pierre agreed, it'd only be to humor her. Then they'd promptly toss her application in the trash.

On the other hand, they'd probably already done that, so what the hell?

Except that she still had a hand to play.

And if Rory St. James was the type who wanted an interviewee to "sing for their supper," then by God, she'd start warming up her pipes.

She hadn't come all the way to New York to be stonewalled. She'd put her heart and soul into freeing herself from shackles and heartbreak, and Bayli Styles would not give up so easily!

Her enthusiasm returning, she told the girls, "I have a modeling job of sorts on Saturday night. Some uber-exclusive fundraising event. The organizers had me familiarize myself with the guest list—Christian Davila is on it. I might be able to turn this whole thing around with one good impression."

"You really want to work for angsty chef guy after today's debacle?" This from Jewel.

"It's suddenly become more *personal vindication* than *survival tactic*," Bayli said. "I'll keep you posted."

She disconnected the call. And plotted her next encounter with the famous duo.

TWO

Christian Davila was completely engrossed in Dr. Gene Eckhart's latest research findings on cardiac ablations and advanced technologies that could significantly alter structural heart problems when a flash of red caught his attention.

That flash of red being an insanely short hem of a tight skirt that ended at the tops of tanned and toned thighs.

Glossy, golden skin made Christian's mind instantly shift gears from the scientific discoveries that he'd always found fascinating while catching up with his Columbia University roommate.

With his attention now divided, Christian watched the woman in red out of the corner of his eye as she worked the after-dinner crowd on the expansive terrace of a private estate outside of Manhattan. She offered cigars from a fancy humidor and was followed closely by a twentysomething sandy-haired male in a tux who carried a portable stand he snapped open when the leggy brunette needed to set the box down. Her assistant would then hand her the selections made by the guests of this extravagant event so that she could ceremoniously unveil and prep the cigars.

Christian's interest was instantly piqued. She did more than work the crowd. She engaged fully with each person she spoke to, and left numerous tongues dragging on the ground as she moved on to the next group.

His gaze remained partially on the Bond Girl–esque cigar hostess as she progressed across the terrace, on her way to his intimate conglomeration.

Eckhart injected a bit of humor into his dissertation, amusing the three other men in their cluster. Christian chuckled along, though he really hadn't heard the punch line. There was something wholly enthralling about the woman. And it wasn't just her striking appearance—the bare, mile-long legs, or the itty-bitty off-the-shoulder dress she wore that hugged every luscious curve. The sleeves covered her wrists, one of which was adorned with a glittery bracelet.

Nor was it the shiny, sleek, nearly black hair that was pulled over one shoulder, the ends subtly curling against her tantalizing chest.

He'd say that perhaps it was her vibrant pearl-white smile that held him spellbound. Her tawny irises were also radiant with an inner exuberance that called to Christian. Seriously, the woman burned brighter than a bonfire.

Though that wasn't it, either.

Another zinger from Eckhart had the guys laughing again, and Christian was late joining in.

His old college buddy snickered. "Really, Davila. What has you so out of touch with my impeccable comedic timing and the snappy delivery of my witty repar—*aha. . . .* "

Apparently, Eckhart also caught the flash of red as the woman approached them in what could only be described as the sexiest goddamn walk on the planet. One that caused heart rates to accelerate, adrenaline to pump, and cocks to stiffen.

He could attest from personal experience.

She slowly made her way toward Christian and his friends, crisscrossing one gorgeous leg in front of the other in a seductive stride that showed off her considerable assets and the five-inch black leather stilettos she wore.

Forgetting all about Eckhart and the others, Christian now centered his full attention on this stunning creature.

In a provocative voice that resonated deep within him, she greeted everyone with a courteous, "Good evening, gentlemen." Then her gaze met and held Christian's. "Mr. Davila, it's a pleasure to serve you." She lifted the lid of the humidor with manicured fingers. No ring on that important one of her left hand. Though it could be stashed away at home. A woman who looked the way she did, and in her mid-to-late twenties, couldn't possibly have avoided being snatched up by now.

Yet he found himself hoping she was single.

"May I offer you an Arturo Fuente Opus X 'A'?" she asked him. "Or perhaps a Fuente Don Arturo AnniverXario?"

Her enunciation was above reproach. Damn sensual, even. His brow crooked. "Those are very serious cigars." He noted a wider selection available and wondered if she was pushing the extremely high-end brands to all the guests. Or just to the ones she recognized.

"Indeed," she said of his comment. "They rank in the top five of the most expensive cigars in the world. Not exactly easy to procure, either. But a man of your stature already knows that." There was a sexy, flirtatious lilt to her tone. She continued, expertly pontificating on the merits of her recommendations, as well as discussing their size, shape, and shade. Instantly impressing Christian with her vast knowledge—regardless of where it might have come from: a boyfriend, a book, or a broker of fine cigars.

Then she added, "I also have one HMR Gurkha Black Dragon tucked away." She smiled conspiratorially, letting that little tidbit sink in. Tempt him. Though it wasn't so much the prestigious stogie that enticed him. She was more than capable of doing that all on her own.

With a hint of excitement in her eyes, she told him, "I haven't suggested it to anyone else. I thought you might prefer a celebratory offering in honor of your latest restaurant opening. To rave reviews, no less. Congratulations."

This intrigued him even more. Not only did she know who he was, but she also knew he was a connoisseur of expensive cigars.

Christian said, "There's a three-year wait-list for a box of HMR Black Dragons, and that one stick is worth about eleven hundred dollars."

"They're all complimentary, of course. And . . ." She leaned in close to quietly impart a little pearl of wisdom, saying, "Rumor has it, Matthew McConaughey donated this cigar as part of his charitable contribution for the gala."

Christian kept his tone equally low, private. "I'm more appreciative that you held it back for me, though I'll be sure to thank Matthew personally."

"Very good." She smiled again, beguilingly. Bewitchingly. Christian wasn't sure of the more accurate description. All he knew was that her engaging expression and glowing eyes jarred him, like a physical blow to the midsection.

And told him quite blatantly that he'd just stumbled upon more than an elusive cigar this evening. He was damn certain he'd just put his finger on the pulse of an elusive *success*. He felt it to the depths of his soul—and straight to his groin.

She's the one.

And he suddenly itched to phone Rory to tell him of this amazingly perfect discovery.

This woman just might be the answer to their problems. Both of them. Though he had to temporarily back-burner that second issue. Sure, Rory would find this woman attractive and mesmerizing. Would no doubt feel the same rush of heat through his veins and the same pulsing of his cock that Christian did at the moment. But that wasn't the most important revelation at hand—significant though it was, since both men had been waiting, waiting, waiting for the right woman to enter their lives.

They'd sampled their fair share, yes. But had never found one capable of holding both their interests for more than a few nights. The way his blood turned to magma convinced Christian this one had the potential to be more than a temporary bedmate or a passing fancy. A woman both men would enjoy pleasuring. Repeatedly.

But, again, that wasn't the current pressing matter.

Rather, an incredible idea popped into Christian's head that just might get his and Rory's derailed project back on track.

Christian's testosterone level surged at this unexpected opportunity.

"Who are you?" he inquired. "If you don't mind me asking."

"I don't mind at all," she said, an alluring look on her face that enhanced her artistically crafted features. Her high cheekbones, her sculpted eyebrows, her aristocratic nose. "I'm Bayli Styles. *Bayli* with an *i*. *Styles* with a *y*."

"And you're a model, Bayli with an *i*, Styles with a *y*?"

She laughed at his bit of humor. "Aspiring, mostly," she confessed. "I've only been in New York a couple of months."

Hmm. As of yet undiscovered by anyone else . . .

Yes. Absolutely perfect.

Christian had just found a golden nugget.

Wait till Rory fucking finds out.

Christian's best friend and business partner had been so wrapped up in the launch of their new steakhouse in Manhattan that he couldn't be bothered with a night out at a premier fund-raising gala. Instead, Rory was in the kitchen this evening.

Well, that actually wasn't out of the ordinary. Rory was a bit of a recluse. A famous recluse, but a recluse nonetheless. He made his presence known when necessary, but the man's kitchen was his castle, in the restaurants they jointly owned and in Rory's home.

Christian would have liked to persuade his friend to get out more often, but that was no easy feat. And neither here nor there at present.

Christian had something entirely different to focus on at the moment.

"I will take the Black Dragon," he told Bayli, pleased with the sudden turn of events. "Thank you."

"It's my pleasure," she said, beaming and stealing his breath with her megawatt smile and easy demeanor. There was nothing forced about her conversation or her expressiveness. Nothing contrived or even practiced. She was so natural, so comfortable in her own skin. Confident and yet incredibly friendly and instantly likeable.

For months, Christian had needed a catalyst to spark his creativity. And damned if lightning hadn't just struck!

While his mind buzzed with the sort of activity that always charged him to the core, Bayli's assistant set up the stand and took the humidor from her to locate the coveted cigar she'd mentioned to Christian and opened the individual wooden encasement. A work of art unto itself.

Bayli retrieved the cutter and asked, "May I?"

"Please."

She gingerly held the cigar with two fingers and her thumb and used an elegant, wafer-thin cutter, executing a clean wedge cut of the cap, as though she'd cut an eleven-hundred-dollar cigar a million times before. Christian nodded his approval. He'd actually tensed up for a moment, hoping like hell she wouldn't mutilate such a highly regarded cigar. But Bayli Styles knew what she was doing.

She handed over the Black Dragon and then her assistant provided her with a well-crafted lighter. She held the flame close for Christian, careful to keep it from touching the tip of his cigar as he slowly rotated it, achieving a glowing ring. The whole time, his eyes were locked with hers. He noted the deep-orange color mixed with golden flecks that rimmed the tawny pools. Caught the hitch in her breath that pulled the cords of her neck tight. Felt the nearness of her seep inside him and bunch his muscles.

He wasn't accustomed to reacting so quickly and so vehemently to a woman. Usually, he was more guarded. Assessing the attraction. It was Rory who had the immediate and strong responses to their objects of desire. Though Rory hadn't really been feeling the vibe of late, Christian had sensed. And attributed it to the pressure of last month's grand opening, and the new menu Rory spent all of his spare time working on. Completely understandable.

Hell, they hadn't even found a few minutes over the past couple of days to catch up on business, because Christian had been inundated as well, with travel. They kept missing each other's calls.

When Christian had the cigar going, Bayli snapped the lid of the lighter shut. A server appeared at her elbow with a silver tray holding a crystal tumbler.

She must have caught the movement from her peripheral vision, because Bayli's gaze remained on Christian as she asked him, "Rémy Martin cognac?"

"Certainly," he said.

She lifted the intricately cut Baccarat glass from the tray and graciously handed it over.

He took a sip, then assured her, "A perfect complement to the Black Dragon. You don't miss a beat, do you?"

"I try not to. Enjoy." She batted her long, sooty lashes. His cock twitched. His gut tightened again. Some women just possessed that certain je ne sais quoi. This one possessed it in spades.

Bayli moved on, making recommendations to his friends and lighting their cigars as well.

Just as she had clearly researched him right down to the cognac he preferred, Christian would find out what he could about *her*. Piper and Jackson Rutherford, the owners of the estate and the hosts of this evening's event, would be able to provide the information on the modeling agency that represented Bayli, and Christian could easily track her down that way.

As he contemplated this and his gaze remained on her while she gracefully migrated to a larger group, Christian's brain already churned with a new spin for his and Rory's project. A completely different construct that would capitalize on the raven-haired beauty's radiance and personable demeanor. She'd draw a huge crowd, tons of fans. She just needed a bigger audience than tonight's festivities, a grander stage.

Christian and Rory could give it to her.

If Bayli Styles truly wanted to be a star, Christian was positive he and Rory could make it happen for her.

Bayli felt his gaze on her as she continued to make the rounds. She didn't glance over her shoulder, though of course she'd hoped from the get-go to garner Christian Davila's attention. What she hadn't considered was how *he'd* affect *her*. There was some serious sizzling and crackling going on inside her over having caught his eye— over the fact that she held his interest.

She'd experienced a vibrant spark when she'd first met Rory at the restaurant and he'd unabashedly taken her in from head to toe. But they'd both been irritated with each other and then their introduction had turned into a crazy hot mess and she'd pretty much ignored that he'd lit her up. The way Christian Davila did. So that her clit tingled and her inner thighs flamed.

Like Rory, Christian was ridiculously gorgeous. She'd known this already, had perused plenty of articles on him in *Forbes* and *Time* and a slew of epicurean magazines. He was tall and had thick, luxurious obsidian-colored hair that went well with his tanned skin and his mesmerizing ice-blue eyes. Eyes that were alert and intelligent, even a trifle cunning in a mysterious, intriguing way. As though he were perpetually mulling over his next great success.

And there wasn't a hint of recognition in them, telling her Rory had not mentioned her to Christian. A little disappointing, because that meant she hadn't been the least bit noteworthy to the chef, even though she'd felt the searing heat between them.

But she surmised this gave her the chance she needed to connect with Christian without the dark cloud of her misadventure with Rory looming over her head.

Still, it was kind of odd that the culinary god had looked at her with flames fringing his eyes and had then promptly dismissed her. There'd been something else reflected in those smoldering dark-brown irises of Rory's . . . something undefinable. As though he were running scenarios well beyond her comprehension through his mind. Sexual or otherwise?

A little thrill raced down her spine at the prospect of it being the former.

Admittedly, it'd been a bit challenging to focus on the conversation and searing dynamic with him, because Rory St. James was magnetic with his primal intensity and his overwhelming presence. He was tall and athletic looking, likely riddled with rigid muscles under his chef's jacket. His bronze-colored hair was thick and bushy. Unruly by design, she suspected.

He had rough edges to him, no doubt there. Whereas Christian was much more refined.

They were the perfect complement to each other.

Which made an interesting—though highly lascivious notion—pop into her head regarding the high-profile entrepreneurs. Bayli had seen Rory featured in most of those articles with Christian and they made for a double dose of sexiness. Especially since a beautiful woman usually stood between them, a mischievous expression on her face. As though she had a naughty secret she was dying to tell the world.

Bayli had seen that look before. One of her best friends, Jewel Catalano, wore the expression well when she was out and about with her two lovers, Rogen Angelini and Vin D'Angelo.

At first, the idea of being shared by two men had confused Bayli. Not just the physical mechanics of the situation but also the

emotional aspect. It seemed there'd be a hell of a lot of jealousy
and fragile egos and feelings to work with, not to mention three
hearts were always on the line.

But Rogen and Vin had been best friends since they were kids
and Jewel had always been tangled up with them. First Rogen,
then Vin. Then the two of them at the same time.

At the *same* time.

Another wicked shudder ran through Bayli.

What must that be like?

To have two men devoted to her pleasure, devoted to giving
her whatever she wanted in bed, whatever she needed.

Bayli couldn't help wondering if Christian Davila and Rory
St. James believed in the power of three as well.

An incredibly forbidden and yet highly scintillating fantasy . . .

One that wove a spell on her as she finished making the rounds.
Obviously, she'd had a specific reason for saving the Black Dragon
for Christian and ensuring he knew she'd taken the time to study
up on him. Bayli hoped she'd left that indelible impression she
needed so that Christian would mention her favorably to Rory and
then Bayli could reengage the chef about the hostess position.

The party wound down and she returned the humidor to the
Rutherfords' event planner, Kristin Harding, who told her, "Piper
and Jackson are quite pleased you pulled off your hostess role so
fantastically. Numerous guests commented on your grace and how
inviting you were. Mr. Davila, in particular, expressed his appre-
ciation for your expertise."

Precisely the validation Bayli needed.

Kristin continued. "The Rutherfords will contact your modeling agency to let them know what a fabulous job you did. And
they've added a generous tip to the hours you spent training for the
evening and the time you were here. Their check will be couriered
over on Monday morning."

Ah . . . rent money. A beautiful thing.

"I'm grateful they're so prompt with the payment," Bayli said.

"They're known for that. Say, I have several parties coming up that I'll keep you in mind for, including as cigar hostess. You really pulled it off, Bayli."

"I'm a bit on the obsessive-compulsive side when it comes to things like these," she admitted. "I don't mind studying up or practicing. Maybe it's more neurosis than OCD."

Kristin laughed. "Either way, it works in your favor and is huge for building your reputation."

They said their good-nights and Bayli retrieved her pashmina and handbag. Most of the guests had already departed. She'd planned that, taking her time so that when she eventually reached the valets out front, there was only a small group of guests waiting for their drivers. It'd be a bit embarrassing to have the bright-yellow cab she'd called earlier pull into the circular driveway that was filled with gleaming black limos.

She stood off to the side, partially in the shadows, hoping no one noticed her. Of course, one of the ultra-efficient valets did. He gave her a casual grin and asked, "Would you like me to phone your driver, miss?"

"No, thank you. I've already contacted him. He's not too far away." She mentally crossed her fingers.

"Great. Let me know if there's anything else I can do for you."

She kept her head high as some of the remaining partygoers slid looks her way. Yes, she was part of the hired help—and had forgotten to mention the service entry to the cabbie as a pickup point. So she maintained her distance. And prayed they were all gone before her ride arrived.

At least she didn't spot Christian Davila as a straggler. Thank God he'd already left. She feared her confidence would take a substantial hit if he witnessed her mode of transportation.

She played the waiting game with as much dignity as one could muster when in this sort of situation. Tapped her toe impatiently, though she projected calm with her easy smile and nods when someone glanced her way. Despite there still being tuxedo- and gown-clad guests milling about, she grew anxious over getting the heck out of there and back to Manhattan. Where the hell was her cab?

Nervous energy ran through her. What if he'd blown her off? Picked up a more convenient fare and ditched her in the country? *Shit!* How would she get home? There was no public transit in this remote area, and she didn't have enough cash on her for any other alternative. Not to mention, her credit card was maxed out. She'd needed a bed to sleep in, a sofa to sit on, and a dozen cans of Raid to spray her bug-infested apartment, after all.

Why the hell hadn't she just suffered through a few months with the 1970s lawn furniture that had come with the place and left a reserve on her card?

No . . . instead, Bayli had needed to clean and disinfect every square inch of the place and then paint the dreary, dingy walls. And she simply hadn't been able to bring herself to sleep in the used-by-however-many-hundreds-of-aspiring-stars-before-her futon that'd been tucked into the small alcove off the living room. A glorified closet advertised as an actual bedroom.

But the price on the apartment had been just right, and it was either that or . . . Jersey. Or a borough. Anywhere that wasn't the city proper in her mind. And since Manhattan was her dream, she'd had to suck it up.

Now she was starting to panic because she just might be stranded out here in the Land of the Richies.

She swallowed down a lump of anxiety as she glanced around.

Unfortunately, her current awkward and somewhat heart-wrenching scenario of practically being "last man standing" tonight with three valets shooting glances her way brought back all the insecurities she'd suffered as a child. Fearing her mother was going to be turned away from a few nights in the hospital. Agonizing over where the next meal would come from or whether they'd make rent.

So at this moment, what was she supposed to do? Ask one of the valets if he could drive her into the city, and hand over all the cash she had in her purse? Pray he didn't ask for more payment—of the nonmonetary variety?

Her stomach roiled. This was a nightmare.

She fished her cell out of her clutch and hit the redial number for the cab. It went straight to voice mail.

Bayli's eyes squeezed shut. She suspected that this was something people with money didn't grasp. A strained desperation. The horror of humiliation. That *what the hell am I supposed to do now?* sensation that frazzled her nerves.

She pulled up the Web browser on her phone to find another cab company. She'd call a dozen of them if she had to. Posthaste, because now the valets appeared a bit nervous. For her. The last of the limos was pulling away. With the exception of a silver stretch Jag, shimmering in the glittery moonlight.

She had her cell pressed to her ear when she sensed a commanding presence behind her, felt his heat at her back, and smelled his sinfully delicious cognac-and-cigar-scented breath as he murmured, "If your boyfriend's stuck in traffic, I'd be happy to give you a lift."

Christian Davila.

THREE

Bayli would never mistake his low, deep, intimate tone.

She sucked in a sharp slice of air. Every nerve ending that had been frayed moments earlier now exploded. Her hand fell away from her ear and she hit the disconnect button with her thumb.

In a breathy voice, she said, "I don't have a boyfriend."

Christian made a soft *tsk*ing sound as he stepped around her and they were suddenly face-to-face.

"That's shocking," he told her.

"Not really. I'm new to the city," she reminded him. "And I have my career to focus on."

Plus, Bayli had decided long ago that she'd never settle for flickers of excitement when fireworks might be waiting for her around the corner.

She fought the smile now as she considered that she'd turned that corner this very night. Because her pulse pounded erratically at the sight of Christian and his wildly charismatic grin.

"Well, then. Duly noted," he said, his gorgeous blue eyes penetrating and hypnotic. "Can I drop you somewhere? I had business with Jackson Rutherford while everyone was leaving. That's my limo."

Bayli spared another glance at the Jag.

Christian told her, "I'm on the Upper East Side overlooking

the park, and you can have a drink with me there. Or my driver will take you straight to your apartment. Whatever you want."

Whatever you want . . .

That was such a loaded comment. A double-edged sword, really.

She could take Christian up on his offer and then grab a cab to her place. Easy enough. Except that she was attracted to him in the sort of way that would make vying for the hostess job difficult, because he was a near-impossible-to-resist temptation. And it wasn't in Bayli's nature to sleep with a man to get what she wanted.

Yet if she were to just say to hell with the job . . . ?

She sighed inwardly.

Yeah, if she said to hell with the job, then sleeping with him would be her first order of business. Particularly if that fire in his eyes had anything to do with her. . . .

Still wanting the hostess position, though, made standing her ground imperative. Added to that challenging feat was the fact that there was no goddamn cab coming for her. No one else to rescue her. And honestly, it'd be a fantastic opportunity to chat up Christian and then discuss the possibility of the part-time job in his restaurant.

So she told him, "I guess my driver got lost. I'd love a ride into the city. And thanks for the offer."

Total savior, but she was still a little too embarrassed over being stood up by the cabbie to say that out loud.

Christian gestured for her to precede him toward the limo, where the chauffeur held the back door open for them. Bayli slid across the black leather seat. Christian divested himself of his tuxedo jacket before joining her. He unraveled his bow tie but left the ends resting against his crisp white shirt, which he unbuttoned at the throat.

There was no way she could escape his virility, his magnetism. His very essence seemingly surrounded her. And good Lord, he took up a hell of a lot of space with his broad shoulders and his powerful thigh brushing against her bare leg. Sending a wave of desire rushing through her veins.

He asked, "Where are we off to?"

Every fiber of her being wanted to agree to his apartment. Especially with all the zings he incited homing in on her erogenous zones. Along with the suggestive expression on Christian's too-handsome-for-words face.

Seriously, the man was a masterpiece from head to toe, and Bayli's fingers itched to work the rest of those tiny disks through their holes, sweep back the flaps of his shirt, and just enjoy the sight of all that bronze skin and sinew. Though that'd hardly be enough, and she knew it. She'd want to do so much more than look. She'd want to touch this fantastically built man. *Everywhere*.

Her stomach fluttered as the thought of running her tongue over his hot, hard flesh overruled her more sensible thoughts. Like the fact that in addition to not being able to cave to a "drink" at his place, she also didn't want to tell him where she lived.

Talk about humiliation.

So she forced the tantalizing ruminations from her head—as best as she could, anyway—to focus on the appropriate answer to his query.

And lied through her teeth to Christian Davila.

"Actually, I'm staying at The Cleveland. It's a boutique hotel." She gave the crossroads.

Christian relayed the information to his driver.

Meanwhile, Bayli's heart thudded in her chest, echoed in her ears. Not just because of the highly stimulating man sitting so damn close to her, but because Bayli didn't like bending the truth. But The Cleveland was near enough to her apartment that she could walk the few blocks home. Not exactly a smart thing to do by herself, late at night. Not in that neighborhood. So she hoped she'd be much more successful this time around in securing a cab. At least the hotel's doorman would help her with that.

So okay. It was a viable solution. A safer one than being any-where near a bed when in Christian's company.

She breathed a discreet sigh of relief. She could still play this hand calmly and coolly.

Bayli sat back in her seat and crossed her legs. Christian's gaze followed her movements. Then slid slowly over her thighs to the extremely short hem that stretched taut and just barely covered her red lacy thong.

So much for being calm and cool. His eyes roving her body singed her as though he'd just blazed a trail over her skin with his fingertips.

She was ridiculously turned on and incinerating from the inside out.

And he hadn't even touched her yet!

Yet . . .

Bayli groaned inwardly. She wasn't doing herself any favors by being tucked into the back of a limo with the ultimate sexual lure. Except that at least she now had a ride home.

Christian said, "Since you're off the clock, how about a glass of champagne? Or brandy? Scotch?" He indicated the side bar. "Whatever you'd like." One corner of his mouth lifted in a sexy, inviting way.

There he went, once more putting all sorts of indulgent possi-bilities on the table.

"Champagne would be wonderful."

Christian seemed to have a little trouble tearing his gaze from her to reach for the bottle in the chiller. He eventually did and popped the cork. He poured for both of them and handed over a flute. They clinked rims and he said, "Meeting you was the high-light of my evening."

Bayli laughed softly. "Somehow I find that hard to believe, flattering though it is of you to say. I happen to know you won three coveted silent auction items and the grand finale in the live auction during dessert. Then there's the matter of enjoying a cigar even Bill Clinton has difficulty getting his hands on."

"Best damn stick I've ever smoked, no doubt about it. But the real pleasure was in the presentation." He winked.

Shivers cascaded down her spine. Her gaze dropped to her glass so that he didn't see in her eyes the flash of excitement he'd evoked. It was one thing to be aroused by a photo in a magazine— something entirely different in person. Because Bayli wanted to act on this obviously mutual attraction.

She sipped her bubbly as the limo passed through the tall gates at the entrance of the estate. Hands down, this beat the hell out of a cab and the ominous possibility that existed of her not making it safely back to Manhattan.

Christian said, "I'm curious as to how you know so much about me."

"That's an easy one." Bayli smiled. "I'm a huge fan of your flagship California restaurant."

"Bristol's?" He looked taken aback. "How on earth—"

"I was born in River Cross. I still remember when the restaurant opened. I was seventeen, so it was the year before I went off to San Francisco State University."

"A decade ago," he said with a slight shake of his head. "Sometimes it seems like only yesterday. Sometimes it feels like an entire lifetime ago."

"You've been busy, from what I understand. A new eatery every two years. I'd call that extremely ambitious. Aggressive, even."

"What can I say?" He shot her a determined look, tinged with heat—a look similar to the one Rory had given her when he'd helped her to her feet, his gaze drinking her in from head to toe.

Both men looking at her with lust in their eyes did things to Bayli. Made her breath catch and her heart hammer.

"When I want something," Christian told her with steely conviction in his voice, "I go after it."

The tingling returned between her legs. Actually, it'd never fully gone away. It was just a bit more powerful now. She pressed her thighs together in an attempt to stave off the incessant thrumming.

Christian's gaze dropped to her crossed legs as she squeezed them tight. A low, sexy sound slipped through his parted lips. A soft groan of desire.

He said, "You're incredibly stunning. Damn tempting." His eyes lifted, the pale-blue pools glowing seductively. "But you know that already, don't you?"

"Just because I'm a model, don't think I'm big in the head. I chose this career because I have a really short attention span and I like that every assignment is different. I never know what I'm going to be doing a week from now." She let out a small, self-deprecating laugh. "Which can be thrilling for someone like me, but also nerve-wracking."

"How so?"

"I don't know when I'm going to get paid next," she admitted.

"Ah, yes. There is that." He considered her comment, then added, "What if you had a more permanent job that still offered variety and a steady paycheck? Travel, even."

She instantly perked up. "I'd love to travel. That's another reason I got into the business. But those gigs are hard to come by—I mostly do studio work, nothing really on location. Ironically, that made it easier to, uh, well . . . apply for a hostess position. At Davila's NYC."

Bayli paused a moment so Christian could digest her revelation. He stared at her with an inquisitive look. Was he wondering if she'd intentionally maneuvered the "lost driver," forcing Christian to play knight in shining armor?

Yes or no, she might never figure that out. So she surged on, earnestly saying, "Unfortunately, my invasion of Chef St. James's space didn't go over all that well."

Christian suddenly grinned, surprising her. He had beautiful teeth that were quite brilliant against his bronzed skin. "Rory can be a bit intense. Don't take it personally."

She studied him a moment, then asked, "You're not bothered by the fact that I'm trying to get a job at your restaurant?"

"Why would I be bothered? I'm flattered you'd be interested in working there. And if you saved that cigar to impress me, more power to you."

"I saved that cigar for the exact reasons I stated previously—I thought you deserved it for celebratory purposes. Opening a restaurant in New York City to such an esteemed response is certainly worth commemorating. But of course *you* already know that."

He took a long sip from his glass, clearly weighing options she knew nothing about. Finally, he said, "Will you excuse me for just a second? I don't mean to be rude, but I need to make a quick call."

"Sure." She tried to appear nonchalant, though she eyed him curiously, dying to know what went through his mind when he looked at her. She wondered the same thing about Rory. Which made it particularly unsettling when Christian whipped out his iPhone and hit a number, mere moments later saying, "Rory, did you interview a woman named Bayli Styles?"

Her stomach launched into her throat. She gasped around it.

Oh, fuck!

Bad move mentioning the interview. Bad. Move!

Rory was going to tell Christian what a complete and utter disaster she'd been the other day and then—

"Hmm, yes, that's what I think as well." A short pause. Then: "No, actually, I have a completely different idea now for that project. Just hit me this evening." Christian slid a glance Bayli's way, one dark brow lifting. "Let me run it by you in the morning. New concept, new platform." He listened a while longer, and as he did Christian's gaze dropped to her legs. "Yes, she does." Once more, lust lit his ice-blue eyes. "I'll talk to you later."

Christian disconnected the call and slipped the phone back into his pocket.

Meanwhile, Bayli tried to remember how to breathe.

She'd lost her breath not just over the scorching expression on

Christian's face but also because that had been an extremely favorable-sounding conversation.

She inhaled deeply, strove for as calm a tone as possible, and asked, "What exactly was that all about?"

"You."

Christian refreshed their drinks.

"Could you be a little more specific?"

And could I be a little less breathy?

"Have dinner with us on Tuesday night. At the restaurant. I'll send a car to The Cleveland for you."

Uh–oh.

She swallowed down some champagne. Tried not to sound panicked as she said, "I'd love dinner. No need to send a car. I'm really good with the subway lines and buses. Got them all down pat."

He frowned. "I'd prefer you didn't have to take the subway. Especially if you plan to wear anything that looks remotely like that dress."

"I have one in mind," she said suggestively. Christian Davila easily brought out the flirt in her.

Whereas Rory St. James . . . that man needed to be tamed.

Oh, what an enticing thought!

But not exactly a convenient one at the moment.

"I'll make the arrangements." Christian tapped the rim of his glass to hers again. "And know Rory will enjoy your company as much as I do."

The hint of mischief in Christian's eyes sent goose bumps along her arms. Thoughts of Jewel and her two men popped into Bayli's head again, and a wave of exhilaration washed over her at the mere notion of both Christian and Rory "enjoying her company."

What might *that* lead to?

It was probably all too dangerous a liaison to entertain, especially since she could end up with the door slammed in her face, after she'd just gotten her foot in. But, honestly, it'd been so long since she'd had sex, so long since she'd felt true gratification and satisfaction, that it just might take two men at once to sate her.

She sipped some more as the fantasy continued to blossom in her mind. Christian topped off her champagne, an expensive brand that tasted heavenly. She'd skipped dinner and was buzzing a little from the alcohol and the devilishly handsome man sitting next to her. By the time they'd reached Manhattan, she was regretting not having taken Christian up on his original offer to stop at his apartment. She didn't need another drink, as his invitation had stated. But she was definitely in need of *him*.

It wasn't just virility the man exuded . . . the pheromones were most certainly affecting her.

So, too, was the way he watched her closely. Leaned in when he spoke to her. Got her caught up in the private moments they shared in the back of his limo as he asked more about her and what other modeling jobs she'd had, which consisted of a few photo shoots for book covers and some stock images. Two clothing catalogs.

She told him, "I also did an entire ad campaign for the Wax Museum complex on the Wharf, back in San Francisco. The campaign targeted Japanese tourists. Apparently, I'm fairly popular in Asia. Received a bit of fan mail as a result, in fact."

The majority had been extremely complimentary. Some, however, had been unsavory communiqués. E-mails from men looking for a bride, an adulterous Internet affair, the exchange of nude photos via text messaging, a meet-up when they were in town.

One guy in particular had been persistent enough—and downright lewd, suggesting they masturbate together over a Skype session—that she'd had to change her e-mail address. But Bayli figured that was the nature of the beast in this business. It wasn't difficult to attract unwanted attention. And she wisely deduced that if one put herself out there like that, a few of the crazies were invariably going to make an attempt to get close to her.

Though Bayli had always lived a bit of a sheltered life—with most of her time spent in hospital waiting rooms and libraries where she'd studied up on her mother's congenital heart disease—so she'd never been easily accessible.

Now that she was trying to get her career off the ground, she surmised it'd be advantageous to have more of a social media presence, despite the online stalkers. Her selfie count was tragically low. And she didn't always have time to keep up with Facebook or Twitter. Just when she had news to impart, which she also posted to her Web site. A blog was in her future, she'd decided a few months ago. But nothing exciting had happened to her of late to inspire routine blogging, so she'd shelved the idea for now.

Christian said, "I can certainly see where you'd have an international appeal. That could work in your favor. You just need greater exposure."

"Easier said than done," she lamented. "Let's be honest. I'm practically a dime a dozen in this city, and over-the-hill by global standards. Not to mention with so many actresses, singers, reality TV stars, and female athletes landing product endorsement deals it narrows the playing field for models. Which is why I'm so grateful for people like the Rutherfords who use professionals for various roles at an event."

"You're following your dream, Bayli. That's admirable. And . . ." He grinned again, keeping her insides blazing. "You're much too striking not to make it big. Plus, there's so much more to your look than the physical aspects. You radiate a genuine, palpable sense of charm and grace. Very modern-day Audrey Hepburn." He chuckled, a warm, rich sound that reverberated deep within her. Then he asked, "You do know who that is, right?"

Bayli playfully swatted his arm with her free hand. "Please. First, she's iconic. Second, you're only five years older than me. Which is a little disconcerting."

His brow jumped. "I'm too old for you?"

"No!" She choked on a sip of champagne. Her cheeks flamed.

"That's not what I meant. I was just pointing out the obvious—I'm twenty-seven and trying to launch a modeling career. Since I'm a bookworm, you'd think I was much smarter than that. But what can I say? When the fire's burning inside, you have to do something about it, right?"

Okay, perhaps she'd had a bit too much of the bubbly. She was spewing her guts here. But something about Christian Davila's own inner fire called to her. Yes, he was ambitious and aggressive. And that excited her. Challenged her. Told her that committing to a dream was the only way to achieve it and if she never tried, if she gave up too soon . . . she'd regret it for the rest of her life. Never forgive herself.

Not that she wasn't clever enough to know that sometimes a girl reached that point when it was time to hang up her ballet shoes. Yet Bayli didn't think her time for that was now. She was just getting started, she mentally contended. Even if she was ten years behind in coming to New York. That had been unavoidable with her mother's illness, because Bayli had refused to leave her side.

But in the long run, Bayli hadn't been able to help save her mom's life.

And now . . . here she was.

She intended to seize every moment, every opportunity offered. Take the bull by the horns, as she'd done tonight when she'd reserved that special cigar for Christian. A strategic move that was helping to pave her way with the hostess position she wanted.

For that matter, she wasn't wholly convinced he'd had business with Jackson Rutherford while everyone was leaving, because it seemed pretty coincidental that she and Christian were the only ones left at the valet station.

Or maybe that was the champagne bringing on a delusion of grandeur and a shitload of wishful thinking.

She laughed. The man should intimidate the hell out of her. He was wealthy and affluent—famous in his own right. Had ice-blue eyes that could likely cut through diamonds. A set jaw. Squared shoulders. The whole nine yards. And yet when he looked at her . . . those ice-blue eyes melted a little. His rigid features loosened. His smile brightened.

Unable to stop herself, Bayli let out a dreamy-sounding breath. Then rapidly pressed the tips of two fingers to her lips as her own eyes widened.

Christian gave her a quizzical yet amused look.

"Sorry," she mumbled. "It's the champagne."

"Is it really?" he quietly challenged.

And oh, boy, did that push the door wide open!

FOUR

Christian still had his mind on the prospect of Bayli Styles being exactly what he and Rory needed to turn around their epic failure, a cooking show that had never gotten off the ground—which luckily wasn't public knowledge at present. They'd managed to keep the development of the show under wraps in its infancy. The pilot hadn't even launched, because, quite honestly, they hadn't come up with a fresh, provocative idea.

Well, that and the fact that test audiences had been more terrified than entertained by Rory, because he was a bit too abrasive and forebidding when in chef mode.

A bit being a huge understatement.

But Christian had been toying with the idea of having a friendly face to interact with the audience while Rory did his thing in the background. It'd only been a hint of a concept to nibble on, but it grew by leaps and bounds with every passing second in Bayli's presence.

She'd make a sensational frontwoman.

Yet there really wasn't anything Christian could do about his rampantly running thoughts this evening, prior to first discussing these new ideas invading his brain with Rory. Besides, Christian's body had already moved on to another possibility. Sampling Miss Styles.

Sure, he'd also prefer to do that first with Rory, because they worked extremely well together in arousing and satisfying a woman. And this was one Christian longed to apply their expertise to, provided she was game.

But Rory was at the restaurant and Christian didn't really want to wait until his next rendezvous with Bayli. He wanted her tonight.

When they reached the hotel where she said she was staying, he climbed out of the limo and then offered his hand to assist her. He told her, "I'll walk you inside."

She gave him a small, quirky smile. "That's not necessary. There's a doorman. Thank you, though. And thanks for the ride."

"Anytime," he said. "But I'd still like to walk you to the door. *Your* door, to be precise."

He flattened a palm at her lower back to guide her down the sidewalk, toward the hotel.

Bayli's steps were slow, hesitant.

Gazing down at her, Christian asked, "Something wrong?"

"Um . . . no." She gnawed her lower lip, then shook her head. "Yes, actually."

She stopped and turned to face him, her back to the double doors at the entrance and the man guarding them.

"What is it?" Christian asked.

"It's a little embarrassing."

Several red flags sprang to mind. Perhaps she wasn't single, after all. Or maybe she was perfectly aware of his intentions and it wasn't a good time of the month to act on the mutual attraction.

In a nonassuming tone, he said, "Whatever it is, you can tell me. Nothing to worry about."

Even if it turned out that she did belong to someone else. Though he really didn't think that was the case. She didn't seem like the type who'd flirt and bat her lashes, especially when he'd been forthcoming about his interest in her.

"Bayli," he said while she appeared to contemplate or debate whatever was going on inside her head. "We're adults here. Just tell me—"

"I'm not staying at The Cleveland," she said. Then bit her lip again.

This confused Christian. His gaze narrowed. "I don't understand."

"I just wanted your driver to drop me here. The hotel bar is already closed and the doorman is going to ask to see my key in order to let us in. I don't have one. Nor am I on their reservations list. I have an apartment."

He shook his head. "What am I missing here? Why didn't you just give me your address and I'd have my driver—"

"I really don't want you to see where I live, Christian."

His mind reeled. "Bayli, I—"

"I appreciate the ride. Truly, I do. But I can get home from here. I'm not far and—"

"I'm not going to just let you wander the streets alone at night!" he told her, incredulous.

"It's not exactly wandering," she said with a hint of indignation. "I'm perfectly capable of getting from point A to point B on my own." She let out a long sigh of resignation. "At least, most of the time."

"Bayli, I'm not trying to insult you. I just don't find it necessary to lie about where you live."

"I'm sure you have a gorgeous apartment. It even overlooks Central Park. I, on the other hand, live in a micro-dump that I had to fumigate before I could move furniture into it. Not exactly on-par with what you're accustomed to."

His teeth ground. Then he said, "You don't know what I am or am not accustomed to—and I'm certainly not one to judge. You already told me you were new to town and that you're an aspiring model. I wasn't expecting you to say you were renting a residential suite at The Plaza."

She grimaced. "It's just kind of awkward. You being who you are . . . and me being who I am." She lifted her hands in the air and added, "I'm sorry. I'm not trying to be difficult or complicated. It's just uncomfortable to be driven home to my real place—in a limo, no less."

"For God's sake, please do *not* feel awkward about your address or anything else for that matter. Just tell me where we're going so that I can deliver you safely there."

She stared at him a few moments. He waited patiently until she came around and gave him the appropriate information. Christian led her back to the car, where he simply provided the chauffeur with the new location, no explanation given.

They rode in silence, Christian not attempting to reengage her but rather giving her the opportunity to collect herself.

It didn't take long. When they reached her building, she said, "You might as well come up. See what I've done with the place. Maybe I can leave you with a better impression."

"Trust me," he told her with notable conviction in his tone. "You've made a stellar impression all evening. But I will take you up on your offer."

He wasn't ready to call it a night with Bayli. Not by a long shot.

The whole humiliation on her part about her living situation made him want to reassure her that he wasn't materialistic in a way that would make him look down on her. Sure, he liked the finer things in life and preferred his social and financial status. But his life hadn't always been limousines, private jets, and penthouse suites. He'd endured his own hardships. And felt compelled to share a little something about himself that he'd never told anyone—the press, his friends, or any other woman. Only Rory knew of Christian's humble beginnings.

As Bayli let them into the building and they climbed the stairs to her floor, he said, "I didn't grow up in River Cross."

She glanced at him over her shoulder. "But everything I've read about you says you did."

"Wishful thinking on my part, really. My dad disappeared before I was born. He'd never married my mother, so there was no child support or alimony. She raised me on her own, about ten miles from River Cross town limits. I always felt like the kid on the outside looking in."

Bayli inserted her key into the first of many locks as she said, "That's exactly how I felt—even though I actually did live in River Cross. It can be overwhelming to be surrounded by such elite residents."

"Agreed. My mother encouraged me to derive inspiration from it, though."

Bayli turned to face him. "That's not in any of the articles, either."

He inclined his head to one side and asked, "When *Vanity Fair* or *Vogue* interviews you, are you going to tell them your entire life story, right down to this apartment you tried to keep from me?"

Her hand faltered, the keys jingling in the quiet hallway. Christian didn't say anything further, didn't press.

Eventually, Bayli swallowed hard and said, "I've had plenty of moments in my life when I've been ashamed of my financial circumstances, my address, my clothes. On the other hand, that shame and the fact that my mother always believed in me are what motivated me to dream as big as possible. Whether I make it or not, at least I've tried. At least she'll know I tried." Bayli's eyes misted. "She'd be really disappointed in me if I just gave up and accepted this as my fate."

"Yes, she probably would be. Because you're clearly meant for more than this. But you've got to start somewhere, right? And whether you choose to reveal your struggles when you do make it big, Bayli, depends on the type of image you want to reflect to the public. But in private . . . there's no shame in admitting this is where you live, or that you need a job in order to fund your dream. You're not the first, you know?"

She swiped a wayward tear from her cheek. "That's a really nice thing to say to someone like me."

He let out a frustrated sound. "Don't categorize yourself. I didn't get where I am without a hell of a lot of hard work . . . and help when *I* needed it most."

Bayli gave a fragile smile. "I suppose you might think sharing that with the world would undermine your power. I'm not sure it would."

She turned and pushed open the door.

Christian's gut knotted at her insightfulness, but when he followed her into her apartment he instantly grinned—genuinely, not just for effect or to make her feel better.

"This is fantastic," he assured her.

The entire place sparkled—just like Bayli Styles.

Bayli had been rife with anxiety over foiling her own earlier fabrication and giving Christian all of these personal details of her life.

And then he'd grinned.

Her anxiety faded. Her heart fluttered.

He took the place in with a blatantly assessing eye, nodding, earnestly making it appear as though all the effort she'd put into sprucing the place up was worthwhile.

After the massive bug bombing, which had extended down the hallway to the garbage chute, she'd ensured the place was spic-and-span and then bought several gallons of glossy white paint to slap on the walls and the faux fireplace.

She'd ordered furniture and accessories online—because Target was all she could afford and they'd offered free shipping on the larger items. A chocolate-colored rectangular area rug with golden scrolls covered the scuffed hardwood floor. Battery-operated pillar candles accented the mantle and hearth. She'd also purchased a spa-blue tufted love seat and a white Roman shade with sheers and a draping scarf bordering it to enhance a window that looked out on a boring gray brick wall five or so feet away.

There were framed prints to match the décor and she'd installed alabaster-painted shelves at varying levels for her favorite books and round, squat vases filled with fake blooms.

"This is really very nice," Christian said.

Relief washed over her. "Thank you." She grabbed her casual wear from the armoire and told him, "I'll just be a minute. I need to get out of these shoes."

She ducked into the bathroom and changed into a white T-shirt that slipped off one shoulder and had "Wake Me in Paris" elegantly scrawled across it in shimmering gold. She added white short-shorts and then hung up her dress and put away her high heels.

In the tiny, open kitchen she retrieved a bottle of water, poured two glasses, and handed one to Christian.

She didn't bother giving the five-cent tour of the place. It was all laid out before their eyes.

"Here's to your own little slice of New York," he toasted her.

"It's something I've wanted for a very long time. I'm willing to pay my dues."

"People who are usually find themselves richly rewarded."

Bayli smiled softly. "We'll see if I follow suit."

"I have no doubt."

His sincere look and the admiration in his eyes tugged at her heartstrings. For someone so far out of her league and tax bracket, Christian Davila did not make her feel inferior to him. He made her feel hopeful, optimistic that the efforts she expended to succeed truly would pay off in the end. And that meant a hell of a lot to her.

So much so that another tear welled in her eye and crested the rim.

"Hey." He set his glass on the mantle and then did the same with hers. His thumb swept over her cheek. "I had no intention of making you cry, sweetheart."

"I know. It's just . . ." She gave a small shrug and sniffled. Laughed lightly at her unexpected emotional state. "You've been very kind to me. I appreciate it."

He stared down at her. "And I appreciate it when you're candid with me."

Bayli nodded. She'd keep that in mind.

Christian continued to stand close to her. So close. *Too* close. He seemed to permeate every nook and cranny of her, seep through her veins. Bayli wanted to step away, but that seemed cowardly.

And she wasn't a coward. She was a woman determined to stand her ground with him—and, eventually, Rory St. James.

This moment could be deemed her actual starting point— to hell with what had happened in Rory's kitchen, right?

Christian was interested in meeting with her again, beyond this evening. That was a positive affirmation for her, professionally. But there was no doubt that more hovered on the horizon at this very moment.

She couldn't misconstrue the look he gave her if she tried. And she really didn't want to misconstrue it. She wanted him to be gazing at her the way he did. With heat in his blue eyes, need rimming the mesmerizing irises.

Bayli had no delusions they were about to cross a line. She also had no ability to stop it . . . because it was what she wanted as well.

Christian's head dipped and his warm mouth grazed hers. A whisper of a kiss that sent ripples of anticipation through her.

He murmured against her lips, "You want me to touch you, don't you?"

A soft moan escaped her. Completely unbidden and filled with lust. One corner of his mouth lifted in response. Not too cocky, but the man had no doubt what he did to her.

His fingertips grazed along her neck and then lightly across her collarbone, leaving a burning sensation in their wake.

"Not just here, right?" he said, his tone still low and evocative.

He rotated his wrist and his knuckles brushed over the top of her breast, exposed because of the cut of her tee's neckline.

His free hand rested in the curve of her waist and he gave a gentle squeeze as his mouth sealed with hers, his tongue sweeping over hers, twisting and tangling. Drawing her into a deep, dark kiss filled with erotic promises.

Her fingers curled around his biceps and she held on tight. Let him take her someplace far beyond medical bills that beleaguered her mind, a job in his restaurant that still seemed out of her reach, a career she wasn't sure she'd ever excel at, a tiny apartment she'd been embarrassed to show this man.

All of it fell by the wayside as his kiss intensified and her knees threatened to buckle as shock waves rippled down her legs, making them tremble.

The spell couldn't even be broken when his mouth pulled away just enough for him to mutter, "Here?"

He palmed her breast and massaged with a hint of roughness that caused a flash of excitement to burst against her clit. He captured her moan in his mouth this time. His thumb whisked over her puckered nipple, making it impossibly hard as he stroked her through the thin material. She hadn't bothered with a bra or panties when she'd changed. The crotch of her shorts was already damp. Would be soaked in a matter of seconds if she didn't stop him.

Not that she had the slightest inclination of stopping him. Oh, hell, no.

His kiss alone could transport her to some beautiful, ethereal place where her worries and troubles faded into oblivion and the only thing that registered was how hot his mouth felt on hers, how expertly his tongue led her in a sexy dance. How hard his muscles were as her fingers coiled tighter around them. How badly her body begged for more of his skilled touch, the pebbled nipple not currently receiving his affection aching for it.

And it wasn't just his hands Bayli wanted to feel on her tingly, sizzling skin. She wanted his lips and tongue on every inch of her. Every single inch of her. Driving her wild, pushing her higher. Until she lost all control for him.

He kept up his hungry devouring of her mouth as his hand on her breast slid downward. Slowly. So fucking slowly. She itched to cover his hand with hers and hasten his pace to the destination she knew he sought. But the titillation of his teasing was so captivating, she let herself revel in the anticipation that rapidly mounted and blazed through her.

When his fingers glided over the apex of her legs, she ripped her mouth from his and gasped as the fire ignited deep within her, erupting in her core.

"Definitely here," he whispered smugly. Two fingers glided along her folds, the drenched material providing no barrier against his touch, his heat.

He targeted her clit, setting off all kinds of wicked sparks.

Christian's arm slipped around her waist in a semi-embrace and he pulled her closer to him as he rubbed the knot of nerves between her legs while she burned brighter.

"Have you been wet for me all night?" he asked, his lips brushing her temple as he spoke.

"Yes."

"That makes me even harder."

His erection pressed against her hip. Bayli was dying to wrap her fingers around his shaft and pump heartily, driving him as crazy as he made her. Especially when his hand slipped behind the loose material of her shorts.

She let out a small cry at the skin-on-skin contact. He massaged her clit with more pressure. A quicker, circular motion that had her panting and clasping his biceps in a vise grip to keep herself steady. His mouth was on her neck and he lightly suckled. Her nerve endings jumped.

"Your skin tastes amazing," he said, his voice thick with lust and need. "I bet your pussy tastes even better."

Oh, God . . . His words . . . they sent her soaring. So that all it took was for him to ease two fingers into her and stroke her confidently as the heel of his hand continued rubbing her clit . . . and she erupted.

"Christian!" she called out as the climax raged through her veins and pulsated against every erogenous zone.

Her legs continued to shake, but he had a solid hold on her.

He let out a sharp grunt. "You're so fucking tight," he said. "And so responsive."

Then he kissed her passionately, leaving her light-headed. Dazed.

Her inner muscles clutched his fingers, involuntarily seeking more.

Bayli still feared it might be a horrendous mistake giving in to this man. But her nipples screamed for his touch and her clit and pussy throbbed with fiery need for him.

It might be wrong to cave.

But it was inevitable.

"Christian," she said, a sense of urgency in her quiet tone. Likely reflected in her eyes, too.

His jaw clenched briefly. "We should be naked."

"Yes."

Oh, God, yes!

His fingers withdrew from her and a shudder chased through her as even the tiniest of sensations was magnified by her hyperawareness of him. Jesus, she wanted him. It was a powerful carnal desire, unlike anything she'd ever known before.

All of her sensible reasoning remained scattered in the far recesses of her mind. Only her cravings for Christian resonated, penetrating the sexy haze clouding her brain.

Bayli's fingers deftly released the buttons on his shirt. Christian removed the cuff links at his wrists while his gaze locked with hers. He'd barely shoved the accessories into his pocket when she pushed the material over his shoulders and down his rock-hard arms, yanking the hem from the waist of his pants and tossing the shirt aside.

She sucked in a breath. Stared at his defined pecs and ripped abs. As she'd suspected all along, he was fantastically built, his body as chiseled as his face. She wanted to drag her fingertips and her tongue over every inch of him. But he seemed to have something else in mind. . . .

He didn't hesitate in peeling off her tee. Followed immediately by her shorts, which he slid down her legs as he knelt before her. She stepped out of the garment while his gaze roved her body, taking her in from the tips of her crimson-painted toes to what had to be seductively glowing eyes. Apparently not missing any of the parts in between, because when his gaze held hers it burned. His jaw worked again. She could only imagine what lascivious thoughts filled his mind. And grinned slyly at the endless possibilities.

Christian stood and took her by the hand, leading her to the double bed tucked into the alcove that somehow made this apartment a one bedroom by the landlord's twisted logic.

With her free hand, she reached for the remote on one of the many shelves she'd installed in the cubbyhole, since there was no room for a nightstand. The bed took up the entire space and was pressed against the inner walls, which were also adorned with framed prints featuring spa-blue suede mats to complement her overall color palette.

Bayli hit a couple of buttons on the universal remote and the pillar candles throughout the apartment flickered on, along with the three dimly lit, inexpensive, snowflake-shaped chandeliers strung from the ceiling of the alcove. There were pocket doors for privacy, but all they really did was bring on a massive bout of claustrophobia when closed, so she never bothered with them.

"This is nice," Christian said. "Cozy. Intimate."

A pale-blue duvet with a medium-weight down comforter concealed inside covered the bed and there was a light-gold satin quilted blanket at the foot. Tons of accent pillows.

She told him, "Since it's always just been me sleeping here, it's worked out pretty well. The guys I share a wall with are into the bar scene and don't come home till after four on the weekends—and instantly crash. That's if they're not at their girlfriends' places. So it's usually fairly quiet."

Still, he switched on her alarm clock, set to a classic jazz station. He winked at her as he said, "Just in case they come home early."

Her stomach flipped. "Confident we're going to get loud?"

"Oh, yeah."

Bayli's teeth sank into her lower lip. Her pussy clenched.

Christian guided her down onto the bed, joining her and settling between her parted legs. His weight on her felt heavenly. It'd been forever and a day since she'd had a man's hard angles pressing into her soft curves. His erection nestled against her belly and she desperately wanted to rid him of his pants so she could get the full effect of Christian Davila.

But he twined his fingers with hers and raised their arms over her head, pinning her to the bed as he kissed her.

No. As he *claimed* her.

The searing lip-lock blazed through her, competing with the heat of his skin on hers, the fire that sparked as he shifted just enough to rub his cock against her sex. Bayli slung a long leg over his hips and ground against him.

The attraction that had started with magazine articles and had exploded with their in-person interaction at the gala now rocked her whole fucking world. She couldn't get close enough to him. Grew more and more restless by the moment with the need to have him buried deep inside her, pounding hard, setting her off with a frenetic, mind-blowing orgasm.

Bayli had never been ruled by sexual impulses and erotic desires. Until now.

Christian broke their kiss and his mouth trailed over her throat again, his teeth biting gently yet insistently. As though the craving was just as strong for him, just as relentless.

His head moved lower and he captured her nipple in his mouth, suckling aggressively so that her body would have bowed off the mattress were she not crushed to it with *his* body.

"Yes," she said on a low moan. This was all spiraling out of control. And she didn't care. Wanted the chaos he incited, in fact.

His tongue swept over the inner swells of her breasts and then curled around her other nipple, somehow puckering it even tauter than it was. Jesus, she was sure the peaks had never been harder.

She probably could have come again, just like this. But Christian was on the move once more, nipping and licking his way down her stomach. He released her hands and scooted into position so that his head was between her legs. He inhaled her scent and it caused electric currents to shoot down her spine.

Then he surprised her by quietly ordering, "On your knees."

And damn if she didn't instantly obey. Her chest rested against the mound of pillows and her fingers coiled around the tall scrolls of the wrought-iron headboard. Christian returned to his spot between her parted thighs, this time sprawled on his back. His thumbs swept along her slick folds, heightening her arousal as her mind raced with scintillating thoughts of everything he might do to her.

Then the pad of one thumb circled her clit as he slipped a finger into her wet pussy. Pumped steadily.

"Christian." His name tumbled off her tongue, an octave lower than normal. All sultry and provocative-like, with a tinge of pleading edging the sound.

His thumb stopped rubbing; she felt his hot breath along her highly sensitive flesh, then the tip of his tongue as it flitted against that tiny pearl that pulsed radiantly.

Bayli's hips dropped as she pressed herself to him. Spurred on by her reaction, he drew her clit into his mouth and suckled the way he had her nipple. Jolting her to the core.

"Oh, God," she rasped.

Christian worked a second finger into her pussy. His other hand was on her ass cheek, kneading it as his mouth did wicked things to her, sending her barreling toward another sensational climax.

Her spine arched and her long hair cascaded down her back. Her breaths came in heavy pulls. Heartbeats echoed in her ears.

Christian alternated between the decadent suckling of her clit and the teasing flickers of his tongue while his fingers stroked her inner walls, pushing deeper as she opened further to him, finding that magical spot and massaging with the determination to get her off.

"Yes," she whispered. "Right there. Just like that. Everything you're doing is so amazing, Christian."

Though she'd kill to also have his hands on her breasts, she was losing herself in the way his talented tongue and fingers pleasured her.

She pressed the side of her face against the cool metal she still had a death grip on and it felt good, because she was burning up. All the sensations inside her swelled to a nearly unbearable degree. Then Christian suckled her clit once more and everything within her burst wide open.

Bayli cried out.

He didn't let up as the orgasm crashed over her.

Bayli's hands clutched the metal. Her pussy squeezed Christian's fingers. Shudders of pure euphoria took hold of her.

As her body vibrated from the release, Christian untangled himself from her. She heard the rustling of clothes and then felt his heat again, behind her. Her eyes were closed, little orbs of light still flashing beyond the lids.

His lips skimmed slowly up each vertebra, keeping her shivering. His fingers brushed her hair over one shoulder when he reached her nape. He kissed that tender spot and Bayli wondered how long it'd be before she fell apart for him once more.

"I was right that you'd taste fantastic," he murmured.

Christian's mouth left her for but a moment. She heard him tear open a foil packet and then he was behind her again, sitting on bent legs. The head of his cock nudged her opening. His hands were on her hips and he guided them downward so she straddled his lap. She had to keep her thighs parted wide in order to accommodate him.

As he sank deeper into her, his hands skated up to her breasts. He palmed them and caressed with that dark insistency that got her all fired up—so easily. His mouth wreaked havoc on her nape while his fingers and thumbs rolled and pinched her nipples as she rode his cock, her hands still clutching the wrought iron before her.

This wasn't at all a position she was used to. Bayli wasn't overly experienced. But . . .

"Oh, God," she muttered. She was surrounded by his heat and muscles. His wide shaft filled and stretched her. Her hips rocked and her inner walls clenched him. Little whimpers slipped from her lips. "You feel incredible inside me."

"I love hearing you moan," he whispered against her neck. "And the way you squeeze me so damn tight . . ." He hissed out a breath. "Fuck, Bayli. I'm so goddamn hot for you."

Her pelvis undulated with his thrusts, but it wasn't enough for Bayli. The tension and lust overwhelmed her, and she just wanted more and more of him.

She rose slightly off his lap and then came down hard, his cock slamming into her to the hilt, making them both groan. She sensed it was what they both needed as the pressure mounted between them, within her.

Bayli used her grip on the headboard to leverage an advantageous position and she bounced up and down, Christian's cock sliding along her slick walls with a hint of friction from his size and his full, forceful thrusts that kept stride with her.

Erotic sounds leapt from her throat. Guttural moans she'd never heard from herself. They came from somewhere deep inside.

"Fuck me," she said on a harsh breath. "Oh, God, Christian. Fuck me hard."

She had to sate the desire clawing at her. The surging of her blood in her veins, the staccato pulse that echoed through her body.

"Shit. Bayli." Christian's voice was tight, strained, distant. "Christ." He rose a bit off his knees, too, forcing her forward, giving him an even better angle to drive into her.

"Yes," she sobbed. "Yes. Perfect. Don't stop. Oh, my God, please don't stop." Bayli's biceps flexed almost painfully as she held on to the headboard. "No one has ever fucked me like this. Don't stop, Christian," she repeated. *Demanded.* "Please just make me come."

"Hard," he said on a grunt. "So damn hard." His hips bucked. He kept their bodies moving in perfect sync with each other, pushing them higher and higher.

Bayli couldn't quiet herself. Her jagged breaths filled the small living space. Mingling with Christian's own exertion as he stealthily shifted once more, planting a foot alongside her knee and then pumping into her with such vigor, Bayli wanted to scream for him to *seriously never stop!* But then she shattered.

"Christian!" she cried.

The inferno consumed her. Scorched her skin, her nerve endings, every hypersensitive piece of her.

She milked his cock and Christian erupted inside her, calling her name as his body convulsed and his dick throbbed deep in her pussy, prolonging her climax, the release going on and on while her heart continued to thunder.

And one thought flashed incessantly in her mind.

How the hell will I ever recover from this?

FIVE

Christian had certainly enjoyed moments of triumph in his life-time, no lie there. He was good at reading signals, gauging potential opportunities, acting on instinct. Same as Rory.

This evening, when Christian had spied Bayli Styles at the party and had later learned she'd already met his best friend a few days earlier, there'd been a bit of kismet to get Christian's adrenaline pumping, in addition to her gorgeous legs and unforgettable smile.

He'd sensed there was something significant about Bayli from the second he'd caught a glimpse of her. He had extrapolated that suspicion with each encounter. The limo ride. The sharing of secrets. The phenomenal sex.

No, she hadn't had the best meeting with Rory—who'd vaguely mentioned that they hadn't quite hit it off due to some mishap in the restaurant he didn't elaborate on. But Christian had heard the intrigue in Rory's voice, and he'd known this was still something to pursue.

Christian and Bayli returned to their kneeling position. He had his arms wrapped around her and she was pretty much sitting on his dick and it threatened to expand again within her warm, wet depths.

She was breathing heavily, her cheek pressed to the wrought iron she'd yet to relinquish. Thank God the bed faced an outer brick wall or they just might have brought every neighbor from the floors above and below them to the door.

What fascinated him the most was that tremors still wracked her body. And she let out breathy little laughs or sighs or half sighs that were part laugh. He couldn't fucking discern which and it didn't matter. Because his body absorbed all the tingles and vibrations coming from her and he had a damn good idea what they were all about. He'd moved her in a way she'd never been moved before.

Okay, he'd fucked her in a way she'd never been fucked before. She'd said as much. But he honestly preferred the more poignant notion that he just might have reached deeper within her than anyone else, touched something inside her no one else ever had.

Christian wasn't exactly sure where that summation—desire—came from and certainly couldn't say it was a wise path to follow. He didn't know her, really. And their association was a bit convoluted and twisted, what with her past being somewhat similar to his in River Cross, of all places. And the fact that she'd not landed the job with Rory but done everything in her power to impress Christian at the party.

Yet . . . there was a huge part of him—all related to a huge part of her—that told him she hadn't used a cigar and feminine wiles just to land a job.

They'd sparked. The two of them, from the get-go. And he liked it.

When she eventually came around, she wiggled against his lap and in his arms.

"Your limbs must be falling asleep right now," she said in what sounded to be a sexually satisfied tone. "With my weight on you and your tight embrace."

"Are you kidding? All I really feel is your pussy still clutching and releasing me and all this silky skin. Goddamn, you feel phenomenal." He kissed her neck, a spot that seemed to affect her, because she sighed blissfully.

She said, "You might have to help me pry my hands from the headboard. I'm having trouble letting go."

He chuckled. "If you need something to steady you, just use me."

She tossed a glance over her shoulder. Smiled sweetly, which made his gut clench and his heart trip over itself. *Odd.*

Bayli said, "You really know how to curl a girl's toes."

He eyed her foot, alongside his calf. Her toes were, indeed, tightly curled. "Hmm."

"'*Hmm,*' he says." She laughed quietly. Then she hauled herself up.

Christian hated every second as his cock withdrew from her body. Not a feeling he was at all familiar with, but something about Bayli made him desperate to remain buried inside her.

She gracefully slid under the covers, stretching out next to him. He bent toward her and kissed her. Then climbed off the bed.

"Hey . . . ," she said on a broken breath.

He stared down at her. "Yes?"

"I just . . ." She exhaled long and slow. "Nothing."

Christian's gut coiled. He returned to the spot beside her. "What?"

Bayli gazed at him for several suspended seconds. Her fingertips grazed his temple, pushing back wayward strands of hair. Then she gave a shy smile and said, "You just took me someplace I've never been. And you're going to leave me so quickly?"

"Oh, shit. No. Not at all." He kissed her as his heart constricted. Another peculiar sensation. He said, "I was just going to clean up in your bathroom. Not leave you."

She stared some more and he could see her fight the urge to gnaw her bottom lip.

"Bayli," he said as his fingers twined in her glossy hair. "If you want me to stay . . . just say the word. There isn't anywhere else I'd rather be right now."

She rolled her eyes, likely to break the tension that seemed to suddenly grip her. "Your king-size bed isn't calling your name this very instant?"

He kissed her again. Then whispered, "Nope."

Their gazes locked. She searched his eyes, though he wasn't certain what she hoped to find.

A minute or so passed. Then she simply said, "Stay."

Christian kissed the tip of her nose. "I was planning on it all along."

He slipped from the bed again and tidied up, finding it impossible to keep the grin from his face.

Bayli Styles.

She was something else.

He returned to her, joining her under the covers. He settled on his back and pulled her to him, so that she lay on top of him.

"This definitely can't be comfortable for you," she said.

Christian tucked strands of hair behind her ears to give him a better view of her beautiful face. "I like your skin on mine. And all these luscious curves. Christ, you can get me hard again in a heartbeat."

His hands skimmed over her shoulders, down her back, to her ass. He palmed the cheeks and squeezed. She let out a small cry.

"The way you keep inciting all these sizzling sensations," she murmured against his lips, "I might as well have stuck a bobby pin in a light socket."

He chuckled. "I entertained myself a couple of times as a kid by doing that. The apartment wasn't exactly babyproofed."

"Nor was ours. I was particularly thrilled to discover, around the age of four or five, that all I had to do was open the drawers next to the refrigerator and use them as steps to reach the freezer. I'd grab an ice cube tray and sneak the homemade Popsicles into my room. Keep them in the nightstand drawer, thinking I was quite clever. Then cry a river the next morning when I found they'd melted overnight."

"Sometimes a kid has to learn the hard way. What was your favorite flavor?"

"Wild cherry. Imitation Kool-Aid, of course. It was three cents cheaper per package, my mother always said."

"Ah, yeah, wild cherry. That was a good one."

"But you preferred grape, right? All the boys in the complex preferred grape."

"Not sure what it is about grape Popsicles," he mused. "And shit, I haven't had one in forever."

"Well," she said in a conspiratorial tone, "if you get a craving, my freezer is well stocked with ice cube trays of all flavors. It's how I've been surviving this New York heat and humidity over the summer. I can't wait for the weather to break."

"Any day now . . ."

"Thank God."

His lips brushed her cheek. Then he said, "I can send over ice cream from the restaurant."

"Don't you dare! I'll scarf down every delicious calorie. It's tough enough serving gelato in Central Park two days a week and not setting aside a scoop or ten for myself."

He laughed heartier this time. "Yes, that would be a challenge. What else do you do?"

"I'm at a library fifteen hours a week. It's close to Grand Central Station and the United Nations building. Used to be a church, and it's absolutely gorgeous. But the congregation became so massive that they had to find another facility to accommodate all the people. A private investor came in, bought the building for twice the asking price—his charitable contribution to the parish, I guess—and then turned it into a library. It's positively stunning. I'm quite honored to 'worship' there."

"You like your books," he said, recalling she'd mentioned being a bookworm.

"I *love* my books," she corrected. "Not knocking the Internet or anything, but I'd choose being surrounded by the smell of dusty pages and hearing that cracking of the spine when you open a hardback over the efficiency of Google or Wikipedia any day."

One of his hands remained on her ass. The fingertips of the other grazed along her spine, up to her nape, and then down to the dip at the small of her back. He felt the shivers through her body. Felt the blood rush to his cock as it began to swell again.

Ignoring the intrinsic sexual pull for the moment, he said, "You're a Renaissance woman. Skilled in several areas, fascinated by all manner of subjects, willing to invest time and effort into any task, such as cutting an expensive cigar. And you like the classics, the traditions. Yet one look at you tells me you know how to put a modern spin on traditions."

"Well, I do use Crystal Light or MiO for the Popsicles, instead of Kool-Aid," she quipped.

Christian grinned. "If you're worried about the sugar and calorie content, you should know that I think you're pretty much perfect."

Her tawny eyes glowed. "You're a lot kinder than I expected you to be."

In a swift move, Christian rolled them so she was on her back and he was settled between her parted thighs. "Did you mistake me for some sort of ogre?"

"Not at all." Her arms slid around his neck and her legs tangled with his. "It's just that you and Rory are friends and business partners and so I figure you're both of like minds. And while I definitely sensed there was some chemistry between me and him, there was also palpable tension. And he told me he'd call me. But . . ." Her teeth clamped down on her lip briefly before she seemed to realize she'd self-consciously employed the insecure gesture, then released it. "He never did. He thoroughly dismissed me. Kicked me right out of his kitchen. In more ways than one," she added on a low breath.

Christian's mouth skimmed over her jaw. "Rory has his moods. But he's very much like you—he's a Renaissance man. The two of you will get along fabulously. You just have to find your groove with him. Don't let him scare you off."

Christian kissed her ardently as the mere thought of Bayli and Rory sparking the way Christian and Bayli did charged him, lit him up. Christian's cock throbbed and thickened. The feel of her beneath him, against him, surrounding him, made him hotter than hell. Factor in the notion of Rory partnering with him to bring her the ultimate pleasure . . . Jesus, it was a wonder he didn't just slide right into her and push them both over the brink again.

But there was a big, fat fly in the ointment.

"You don't happen to have a condom handy, do you?" he asked.

Bayli's eyes squeezed shut. "Shit. No." Her lids lifted and she said, "A romantic or even merely a sex life is not something I've actively pursued in . . . wow. A really long time." Her gaze narrowed as she obviously contemplated this further and then she let out a little snicker. "Geez, another embarrassing moment. I probably haven't gotten laid in like . . . two years? I'd like to be more specific, but it really wasn't memorable enough to anchor a time frame to. In fact, it would have pretty much been a waste of a condom *we* could be putting to good use right now. Exceptionally good use."

He kissed her. Then said, "I haven't exactly been active in that arena of late, either. Launching the steakhouse and then trying to fix a colossal business failure—"

"A failure?" Her brows jumped. "All of your restaurants are wildly successful."

"Yes, thankfully. Rory and I have a knack for being in the right market at the right time. But this other project . . ." He snorted at himself and rolled onto his back, pulling Bayli to him so she was nestled alongside him. "I fucked it up badly. It's not even Rory's fault despite him trying to claim some responsibility. My idea was completely uninspired and I didn't take into account his, uh . . . disposition."

"You mean that gruff exterior and sharp tongue that makes a person want to fade into oblivion when he stares them down?"

"Yeah, that. Except Rory told me on the phone earlier that he tried that with you . . . and you still walked into his kitchen. Which impressed him."

"Wait." She sat up suddenly, her long black hair tumbling over her bare shoulders. She stared at Christian. "I *impressed* him? Because that is *not* the way I saw it. By any stretch of the imagination. And I assure you, I am incredibly good at creating my own little Emerald City in my mind over things like blowing an interview. Yet there wasn't one decent takeaway from the entire debacle, aside from the fact that I restrained myself from marching back into the restaurant after he'd shooed me from it to demand an actual interview with the man."

"That must've taken some willpower on your part." Christian had no doubt the woman had steely resolve. And, from the moment he'd laid eyes on her, he'd not missed the determination exuding from her.

Coaxing her bac down beside him and draping an arm around her shoulders as her head rested on his chest, Christian told her, "Rory is a perfectionist. He wants everything to be precisely the way he wants it. But there's another side to him. A very . . . giving . . . side. And I truly believe the two of you will get along incredibly well. Once we've settled the professional aspect of things."

"Still leaving me in the dark with that one," she lightly scolded.

Christian's fingers stroked her skin, drawing lazy circles on her upper arm as he considered how much to divulge at this point. He hadn't fully fleshed out the new idea in his mind, much less run it by Rory. But then again, when it came to conceptualizing, that was Christian's forte and Rory left him to it while capitalizing on his own strength behind the scenes.

So giving Bayli a little preview wouldn't hurt anything, Christian surmised.

He said, "I'm envisioning you in front of TV cameras, not digital ones. Traveling with Rory to off-the-beaten-path places where you use your research skills to unearth interesting local cultural and scenic tidbits and Rory explores the culinary genius of up-and-coming chefs in the area and incorporates their favorite ingredients into a menu he can whip up during the show. While you host it. That way, Rory's focused on what he does best and doesn't have to scare the living hell out of the audience because he neither speaks in layman's terms when in chef mode nor does he interact well with the natives. Any native."

Bayli was instantly back to her sitting position. "A cooking show?"

"Of sorts. When I say 'natives' I even mean a studio audience here in New York. He's much too intense, much too tunnel-visioned. Apparently extremely—"

"Off-putting," she said for Christian. "Yeah, I can see that. Except . . ."

Bayli shifted on the bed so she could look directly at Christian. She'd switched off the chandeliers earlier when he'd popped into the bathroom, but there were still some pillars flickering throughout the apartment, casting shadows and warm glows, softly illuminating her striking features.

She said, "I really didn't consider him pompous or anything. That wasn't the response I had to him. Yes, he set me completely on edge, but it was in sort of a challenging way. And when I just observed him at work, absorbed the entire atmosphere he'd created in that special space of his, I really felt that the all-encompassing surliness isn't so much that; rather, it's . . . passion. Zest. Pride in ownership when it comes to everything he creates."

Christian didn't miss the excitement in her eyes when she spoke of Rory. Nor did Christian miss the admiration in her tone. It convinced him even more that he was on the right track this time. And not just with the show . . .

He told her, "The static—and stagnant—studio concept was all wrong for us. But cooking live on location, on the beach, on a cliff overlooking the ocean, on a balcony, under a thatched *palapa*, whatever . . . I think that will not only give us a more inviting, engaging feel, but it'll focus on more than just discussing ingredients and how to prep the meal. We can make this rich with history, as well as traditional and current flavors. A local flair that's dynamic, interactive, educational, and entertaining all at the same time. Starring you and Rory."

She blinked a few times, looking a little stunned.

He said, "You'd be the hostess, historian, buffer. Rory would be in the background. Where he prefers to be. That way he doesn't have to get aggravated when people can't keep up with him over complicated instructions. You can serve as the liaison. You'll intermingle with the audience and simply relay Rory's instructions with humor and grace . . . and that amazing fucking smile of yours."

She didn't speak as she clearly tried to process it all.

Had she really not known this was the direction in which Christian was headed? Or was he overwhelming her, this concept coming out of the blue since he'd just tapped into it this very evening?

Christian didn't know. All he could focus on was how her eyes bulged a bit and her chest rose and fell more quickly behind the sheet and duvet she pressed against her bare breasts.

"Everything okay over there?" he asked.

Her jaw worked as though she had something to say but couldn't quite find her voice.

He said, "You did a hell of a job with the cigars tonight, sweetheart. Imagine all the research you'll get to do on various locations around the globe? All the travel you can possibly dream of if this show takes off. And damn it, my gut tells me it will. You'll be an international celebrity. Japan will love you even more than they already do."

She let out a strangled laugh. "They've long since forgotten about me. That ad campaign was years ago. But everything you're putting on the table, Christian . . ." Her grip on the bedcovers tightened. "Is it all real? Are you serious? And will Rory even consent? I mean to me? He's—"

"Already thinking along the same lines." Christian rested a hand on her bent knee peeking out from the duvet and said, "Yes, he told me you weren't right for the in-house hostess job. I'm sorry about that, and I do stand behind him. Rory knows the intimate operational details of running a restaurant. I'm the corporate guy, the visionary, the *location, location, location* guy. So I won't override his decision. But he was already trying to work through his mind how to get you involved with the show."

A long breath fell from her luscious lips. "Why didn't he just tell me that? Why keep me in suspense? Why make me feel so damn incompetent?" She flushed as she got a bit riled up over her botched interview with Rory.

"Hey." Christian sat up. His fingers whisked over her cheek. "You didn't seriously feel like that. Or you never would have approached me at the party. Not as boldly as you did."

She gave a reluctant nod. "That's true. Maybe *incompetent* isn't the right word. I just felt so easily dismissed. And it probably wouldn't have mattered so much to me if I didn't really need the job. Or if he hadn't looked at me the way he did. I could tell he had some sort of interest in me. I just wish he would have come right out and told me what it was."

"He was in the middle of a very important lunch service, Bayli. Rory has trouble compartmentalizing."

"Ah . . ." Now she nodded enthusiastically. "That I fully understand, because I *do* compartmentalize. And it can be very confusing to people who don't understand silos. I put everything into buckets to keep all my thoughts neat and orderly. Rory likely sees the bigger picture all at once."

"Don't be offended that he didn't call. He wanted to speak with me first. We've just had trouble connecting the past couple of days. I've been in meetings and negotiations, and he's been holding down the fort."

"I'm not trying to make this all about me, Christian. I'm just not used to screwing up so badly. Yes, I've had plenty of doors slammed in my face. I always try to do the best I can, though, and I just didn't stand out with Rory."

Christian's lips swept over hers. "And I told you that you did. So don't worry so much, hmm?"

He lay back down, bringing her with him, so they were snuggled up once more. Her cheek rested on his pecs and her hand splayed over his abs. Christian was still rock-hard, but he tried not to fantasize about Bayli's palm sliding lower, under the sheet to his cock. He couldn't help but will it, though. He was pulsating with an insatiable need for her. Something far beyond what he was accustomed to feeling with a woman. This one easily held his attention, garnered his lasting interest. And he couldn't help wondering if Rory would experience the same deep-seated need and craving for her that didn't go away with one quick fix.

Breaking into his thoughts, Bayli said, "I'm a bit mind boggled over your business proposal. But how would you feel if I told you the orgasms you give me are even more earth-shattering?"

He smirked. "This platform could launch your career and make you an international star."

"True. But let me tell you where you *really* launched me. . . ." Her hand grazed his lower abdomen to his groin. Teasingly skirting his erection. Her fingernails skated along his inner thigh; then one long finger stroked his balls.

Christian grunted. "It's not exactly fair to get me all revved when we've already established there are no more condoms at our disposal."

"Doesn't mean I can't be a *little* wicked. . . ."

"So you're just going to get me more worked up and then leave me high and dry?"

"Not dry," she said suggestively. And licked her lips.

His pulse surged. "You're going to suck my dick."

"You inspire me to do all kinds of sexy things to this magnificent body of yours."

"And I was grumbling about what, exactly?"

She laughed quietly. "I have no idea."

Her hand drifted upward and her fingers encircled his shaft. Her palm glided to his tip, slid slowly back down to his root. She repeated the gesture and Christian's eyelids dropped.

She squeezed him, then pumped.

"Fuck, yes," he ground out.

Her warm lips swept over his chest. Her tongue swirled around one of his small nipples before she tenderly bit it, jolting him. All the while, she worked his cock, setting a sensual pace to jerk him off. Then she licked the palm of her free hand and rubbed it over the head of his erection as she continued to stroke him.

"Bayli." The word tore from his lips. "Jesus."

She licked again. Set an even sexier, vigorous pace. Pumping, stroking, rubbing . . . Fuck, he couldn't catalog it all. Especially when her head dipped and her tongue replaced her palm at his tip. She lapped at him, then suckled. Tauntingly at first. Then her hand slipped down to the base of his cock and she held him firmly as she took him deep in her mouth. So fucking deep.

"Like that," he groaned. "Just like that."

She sucked him hard.

His body jerked. "Christ!" The orgasm built, fast and furious.

While she held him with one hand and continued to suckle, her other hand shifted to his balls. She cupped them. Rolled them gently. Tugged a little.

"Bayli," he said again, knowing this woman was going to be his undoing. To the depths of his soul. "Make me come. Suck me harder and make me come."

She feverishly did as he bade. Christian's gut clenched; his groin blazed. His cock throbbed in wild beats, keeping time with his hammering heart and pulse.

Instinctively, he placed a hand at the back of her head, keeping her in place as her mouth widened and his hips lifted so that he fucked her mouth. Her fingers worked their magic on his sac until every fiber of his being pulled taut and his breath caught.

She drew him even deeper into her mouth and Christian lost it.

"Yes!" he all but growled. "Fuck, yes. Take it all. Swallow me down."

She didn't let up. A heartbeat later he exploded in her mouth.

She kept perfect pace with him. Sucking him dry. Leaving him convulsing and groaning . . .

And wanting so much more from her.

SIX

Bayli stirred when a crimp in her neck pinched too tight. She didn't have to open her eyes to know she was huddled against the mound of pillows that lined the wall separating her apartment from the guys' next door. Nor did she need to crack an eye open to know she was alone.

She felt the void instantly. A frigid air that had nothing to do with the actual external climate and everything to do with an inner sense of loss. She flopped onto her other side and stared at the vacant space before her. This set of pillows still held the indentation of Christian Davila's head. The sheets were tossed back and rumpled. His enticing scent still lingered.

But none of this chased away the chill in her bones.

Because Christian was gone.

Hugging the bedding to her bare chest, she sat up and shoved a hand through her disheveled hair, pushing the strands off her forehead and cheeks and sweeping the mass over one shoulder.

It wasn't a huge deal that he'd slipped out while she slept, right? In the land of one-night stands, this was pretty much on-par with devastating dating folklore.

So it probably wasn't even wrong that he'd spouted all sorts of fairy-tale lines about how he and Rory St. James were going to change her life. Make all her dreams come true. How they were going to hire her to host a travel/cooking/discovery/whatever show and she was going to be a superstar and would never, ever have to stress out about paying all the bills that flooded her mailbox, because Bayli had filled out credit and financial applications in her own name in an attempt to get her mother the best care possible above and beyond government programs and whatever Disability inadequately covered.

Bayli had never even appealed to her father for aid, because that would mean facing a man who had split as soon as he'd learned of her impending entrance into the world. A man who'd decided long before he'd even met his daughter that she wasn't worth his time, love, or help.

Emotion roiled through her, but Bayli knew she couldn't afford to give in to it. She'd been going it on her own for so damn long that she'd really been foolish to believe last night that Christian Davila had designed a relaunch of his failed cooking show based around her.

Yeah.

Right.

And there's oceanfront property for sale in fucking Arizona.

She sighed and threw off the covers.

Bayli blamed herself for the sting of naïveté. She'd had a reasonable mental conversation with herself when Christian had offered her a ride and a drink at his apartment. That inner voice had told her sleeping with him was a bad idea because she was vying for a job at his restaurant.

And what had she done, despite laying down her own law?

"Idiot," she said with a shake of her head.

What had she expected in the grand scheme of things? That he would somehow see beyond her lapse in moral values and find it endearing that she'd fucked him and gone down on him within hours of meeting him? So that he would hire her in a professional capacity?

Not unless it involves the word porn.

Bayli let out a small shriek. Would have pulled the covers over her head if they weren't strewn everywhere.

Jesus Christ!

She'd just proven that she would go to any lengths in order to get what she wanted!

Who the hell had she become—so damn fast and all over two devilishly handsome men?

Fallen angel to the extreme!

"Well, you're not exactly a whore," she mumbled. Because there'd been no money left on the bedside table.

Then again . . . there *was no bedside table*.

"Urg!" She buried her face in her hands as shame rushed through her.

Why'd I have to do it?

Why'd I have to do him?

What the hell is wrong with me?

As the thought festered in her head, the bathroom door swung open. Bayli jumped, her heart thudding heavily against her ribs.

"Morning," said a fully clothed Christian Davila. "I didn't wake you, did I?" He crossed the studio in a few long strides and rested a knee on the edge of the bed. He kissed the tip of her nose and grinned. "I borrowed your mouthwash and a hairbrush. Not sure I used the right one. You really need four different types? I'm talking about the hairbrush, not the mouthwash." He winked.

"Depends on the style," she absently said as she took him in, all fresh and minty smelling and with dark stubble lining his prominent jaw. He was damn sexy.

Excitement shot through her, making her forget about the tramp she'd been the night before.

"So, I have a ten a.m. brunch," he explained. "But you go back to sleep. It's only a quarter to seven."

"I thought you'd left already."

"Not a chance." His gaze slid over her naked body. "And believe me, I'd crawl right back into bed with you, except that I have some business to attend to. Then I need to stop into the restaurant to speak with Rory. What's on your agenda today?"

"I have a four-hour shift at the library, starting at eleven."

"Such a beautiful bookworm." He kissed her. One of his searing lip-locks that made her practically melt into the mattress.

When he pulled away, she was breathless.

He said, "Have a fantastic day. And don't forget to lock the door behind me."

"Are you kidding?" she quietly quipped. "I've pretty much forgotten my own name at this point."

Christian chuckled. "That's flattering. Now why don't you cover up all that gorgeousness of yours so I can find the willpower to get on with my day? Before I say to hell with it all and call a courier service to deliver a couple boxes of condoms to us."

"There's someone who will actually deliver condoms on a Sunday morning?"

"Sounds a little sacrilegious, sure. But this is New York." He kissed her again, then shifted off the bed. "My driver's waiting downstairs. I've gotta get a move on."

"Of course. No worries. Go be productive. And I shall immerse myself in the beauty of the written word."

"God, I adore that about you." He swooped in to steal yet another kiss, catching Bayli by surprise. "Sexy *and* smart. Trust me, audiences are going to love you. Fuck." He whistled under his breath before whirling around and heading toward the door with a purposeful gait. "Rory and I need to hash out this new platform immediately. I want you in front of a test audience as soon as possible. I'll contact your agent first thing tomorrow morning."

"I'm with the—"

"Polenski Agency." He tossed her a sly look over his shoulder. "That was what my business with Jackson Rutherford was last night when I was still at the party while everyone else was departing. I already knew I had to see you again. Yet there you were, waiting for your driver—and perfect timing for me."

She sighed. "Christian, I wasn't waiting for a driver. I was waiting for a cab. Plain and simple. Nothing fancy, not even an executive town car."

He pulled up short of the door and turned back to her. "Bayli. Sweetheart. That doesn't matter. Whether you were waiting for a cab or a helicopter, it doesn't change the fact that you are sensational. And soon the whole goddamn world is going to see what I see when they look at you. Because they actually *will* get a chance to look at you. No more hiding out in the stacks at the library. You're going to be a celebrity. I'm going to make sure of it."

His brows wagged enthusiastically, making her giggle. Then he ducked out the door. Bayli stared at the empty space where he'd just stood, finding it next to impossible to believe that not only had Christian Davila spent the night in her apartment, but he also was bound and determined to give her the big break she was desperate for.

She felt guilty for having doubted him. But nothing ever came easily for Bayli.

It took a good five minutes of trying to school her breathing and slow the quivering of her body before she slipped from the bed and locked up. Then she returned to the warmth and comfort of her thick bedcovers, pulling them up to her ears. She couldn't contain her ridiculous smile, so she didn't even try.

It was a long shot to hang her hopes and dreams on something of this nature. Not just the TV show that could flop, like their first iteration evidently had. This time, however, it could very well be Bayli's fault if the program didn't make the grade. But beyond that, there was the crystal-clear reality that she'd just slept with a man who'd be her boss.

Bayli would have to accept the fact that she'd been seduced by the casting director. *Willingly* seduced.

Like her crummy apartment, she wouldn't be sharing that tidbit with social media or in *Vanity Fair*.

But Bayli would always know it.

So would her guardian angel, her mother.

Bayli inhaled deeply. Gave herself another mental pep talk.

It's the twenty-first century, Bay. In this day and age, I'm sure it's perfectly acceptable to fuck your boss.

Right?

Bayli sighed. How the hell would she know?

She closed her eyes and tried hard not to fantasize about working so closely with both Christian and Rory. Tried not to conjure delusions of what this project might actually be like. Again, she was wary of getting her hopes up. But it was damn difficult not to build the fairy tale in her mind.

Luckily, she was still a bit exhausted from the night before and all the unexpected twists and turns. And was out minutes later.

The main-door buzzer woke Bayli around nine. She grumbled as she scooped up her discarded clothes and quickly dressed. Then pressed the button on the intercom, suspecting it was a wrong number.

"Yes?" she asked.

"Breakfast delivery for Miss Styles."

She frowned. "I didn't order breakfast." She couldn't afford a delivery fee and a tip! She always grabbed a bagel at the shop on the corner if she was out of them in her own kitchen.

"Compliments of Mr. Davila. May I bring it up?"

Bayli was taken aback. She hadn't anticipated this. But who was she to turn down breakfast from Christian? "Sure." She buzzed in the deliveryman.

Except that when she opened her door for him, it wasn't a mere deliveryman standing before her. It was a fully uniformed Davila's NYC waiter. He swept in with a flourish, the way Pierre LaVallier would have done, and went straight to her tiny counter space, where he set down the box he'd carried in his arms. Then he began unpacking stuff. A lot of stuff.

His head inclined to the round glass table that sat two in the far corner of her studio. "Would you like it over there?"

"Sure." This said a bit more tentatively.

"I'm Denny, by the way."

"Bayli."

"A pleasure to meet you." He crossed to her table and briefly removed the vase of faux flowers. He snapped open a crisp wrinkle-free full-length white tablecloth and covered the glass top with it. Then he returned the vase to its proper place.

Next, Denny prepped hot tea and coffee service with individual-sized pots and accompaniments. He carefully placed a china cup on a saucer, then set the table for one, complete with gleaming flatware and a linen napkin. The food had been stored in warmers and he arranged each dish on a serving platter and indicated the offerings as he laid them out in the remaining space at her table.

"Eggs Benedict with Chef's special hollandaise sauce; steak and eggs with breakfast potatoes; and egg-white frittata with spinach, mushrooms, heirloom tomatoes, and a side of asparagus spears." He added slices of toast and little jars of jams and jelly. Then asked, "May I pour coffee or tea for you? I have a box of popular selections for the tea . . . honey and lemon as well."

A bit mind-blown, Bayli barely eked out, "Coffee is fine, thanks," before Denny was pouring for her.

"Cream and sugar?"

"I take it black."

"Very good." He added utensils to the platters. "I'm happy to serve you. What would you like to start with?"

"Oh, um . . ." *Awkward!* She shook her head and told him, "That's not necessary. I can manage on my own. Can someone just come back later to pick everything up?" She eyed him with hope that he'd be perfectly happy leaving her to her own devices.

He hedged a moment. Then said, "Chef St. James would like me to serve you."

"Oh, well . . . I don't really need you to serve me, so . . . you can just tell him whatever you need to in order to keep him from yelling at you and I'll serve myself. Sound okay with you?"

Denny grinned. "He does seem to enjoy doing that. But I guess what he doesn't know won't kill him, right? I mean, it's probably a bit uncomfortable having a stranger in your apartment, breathing down your neck while you eat."

"That is true. And I'd be eternally grateful."

"Fine. I have your number. I'll check back with you. Just don't feel obligated to clean anything. Of course we'll take care of that at the restaurant."

"Wonderful. And please thank Mr. Davila and Chef St. James for me. And—oh!" She rushed over to the armoire where she'd stashed her handbag the previous night and whipped out some of the cash for the cab that had never come for her. She thrust a twenty at the server for his effort and his discretion.

He only grinned at her. "Thank you, really. But Mr. Davila already took care of my tip."

"It's not like I'm going to tell him or anything," she said, still offering Denny the money.

"I appreciate it, Miss Styles. I'm covered, though. Mr. Davila tends to be a little over-the-top. Not that I'm complaining." He chuckled amiably.

Bayli's stomach fluttered. "Yes, I agree." Her gaze slid to her small table, every inch of it covered. "Apparently, Chef St. James shares his philosophy."

"Indeed." Another friendly laugh. "He can be prickly, I won't lie. But I respect how hard he works, how serious he is about running his kitchen. I'm hoping to someday graduate to prep cook." He clapped his hands together—and possibly his impeccably polished heels, too—and said, "Now. Enjoy this meal before it gets cold. I'll check in with you later."

Bayli smiled. "You can be assured I'll give you a favorable evaluation."

"That's very kind of you. I'll see myself out."

Bayli was glad she hadn't taken a sip of coffee at that moment, or she would have spewed it over his formality. And the fact that "seeing himself out" required all of three seconds of Denny's time.

She locked the door behind him and then settled into a comfy spa-blue chair at the table. Draped her napkin in her lap. Eyed the food that all looked sinfully delicious—and which filled her apartment with a rich aroma she was certain had never permeated this space before, not in its gazillion years of existence.

In fact, Bayli simply pulled in long breaths for a few minutes, savoring the scent and the vision sprawled over the white linen cloth. She wasn't one to indulge in this nature. For one thing, she needed to fit into her clothes and not be ten pounds heavier than what her stats claimed she weighed. Two, she couldn't afford to eat like this, financially, even if she wasn't in need of constantly keeping an eye on the scale.

Yet this was one hell of a treat. Knowing Christian had arranged breakfast for her upped the ante on devouring everything in sight. But what really encouraged her to dig in was that Rory St. James had prepared this feast for her. And he'd done an astounding job. Her first taste of the eggs Benedict had her eyes rolling into the back of her head. Then she sliced through tender medium-rare beef that melted like butter on her tongue. Even the uber-healthy frittata was divine, the asparagus spears lightly sautéed so they remained crisp.

While Bayli sipped her coffee and contemplated her next round of sampling, her phone rang. She squealed in delight as she connected the videoconference call with Jewel and Scarlet.

"You guys are *not* going to believe this!"

Bayli panned the phone over the tabletop so the camera caught every tiny bit of her breakfast service.

Then she turned the phone toward herself and said, "Look at this spread! I am in culinary heaven right this very moment!"

"What the hell, Bay?" Scarlet asked with a laugh. "I've never seen that much food in front of you. Like, *ever*."

"I know, right?" She beamed. "Christian and Rory had it sent over from their restaurant. *Sent over*. With my own personal waiter, by the way. Whom I had to kick out, because that's just plain creepy to have someone hovering when you're still in your jammies. I'm just sayin'."

"I'll let Jewel field that one. She's used to house staff seeing her in her pj's."

"Whatever," Jewel chimed in. "How'd this all happen, Bay? A couple of days ago angsty chef guy was tossing you out on your ear. Scarlet and I were just calling to see if you'd turned things around with Davila last night."

"Things were *definitely* turned around." Literally. Bayli was sure her face flushed as she thought of how Christian had fucked her, with her back to him, straddling his lap, gripping the headboard and holding it tight as he took her on the ride of her life.

"So, you clearly got his attention," Jewel said.

"I did more than that." Bayli paused to shovel in another bite of eggs Benedict and chewed vigorously. Then added, "Apparently, Christian and Rory had an idea for a cooking show that went nowhere, and they want to launch version 2.0—starring me. Can you fucking believe that? Christian took one look at me and suddenly the new concept hit him like a ton of a bricks. I'm going to be famous. *Famous*, you guys!"

"Well, we already knew that," Scarlet said with a sisterly scoff. "But wow . . . this all came out of left field. I thought you were just trying to land a hostess job at the restaurant. What on earth did you do to get that amazing-looking breakfast and a TV—*oh*." Her eyes widened. "I see."

Bayli groaned. Set aside her fork. "Yes, I slept with Christian Davila. I'm not going to lie. But that's not *exactly* what happened between us. . . . That's not what this is all about."

"What *is* it all about?" Scarlet asked with a glint in her eyes.

Bayli briefly told them about the party and how she and Christian had instantly hit it off. Then the missing-cab debacle—she didn't bother tempering the panic she'd felt over being stranded in the country, since both Jewel and Scarlet were well aware of her depressing financial state—and the limo ride to her apartment.

"All well and good," Scarlet mused, "but *then* what happened?"

Bayli laughed. "Let me just say that the man knows what he's doing in and out of the bedroom. There are tremors still randomly running through my body. And what's continuing to happen between my legs . . . good Lord." She let out a long breath. "Downright scandalous. He's incredible."

"Rave reviews for the restaurateur," Jewel said with a soft laugh. "So glad to hear you finally got laid, Bay."

"Yeah," Scarlet added in a mockingly churlish tone. "So glad. At least the two of you are seeing some action."

Bayli gave a sympathetic smile. "Sorry, dear friend. I couldn't help myself even when I tried. I mean, I really *did* try to resist him. But what can I say? The man is steel and I am but a magnet."

"And what about the surly chef?" Jewel inquired.

"Oh, well . . . jury's still out on him. Christian seems to think I made a better impression than I believe I did. He's convinced Rory's going to be as taken by me as Christian claims to be. We shall see about that, and whether this idea of theirs ever gets off the ground. He seemed fairly nonplussed over the first iteration falling apart."

"What makes him think this next edition will be successful?"

Bayli couldn't help but beam. "Because of me. That's his opinion, at any rate."

"Ah, then I'd concur," Scarlet said. "You'd be fantastic in front of TV cameras. Extremely charismatic."

"Apparently, Rory scared the bejesus out of the test audiences," Bayli admitted. "So chances are we'll have a more positive encounter with me as a shield."

"Provided you can put up with him," Jewel reasoned.

"Yes, there is that," Bayli said. "Though . . . really, I just think he's a bit misunderstood. Like he doesn't quite know how to channel his passion for cooking when he's not in front of the stove. Seems like all this creativity builds inside him and then he erupts. I don't know. I'm totally taking a stab in the dark here. But it makes me more and more curious to dissect him."

"See how many licks it takes to get to the chewy center?" Scarlet teased.

"Ha-ha." Bayli smirked at her. "But then again . . ." Her inner muscles squeezed tight at the naughty suggestion. "Yes."

Jewel squealed. "Now we're getting somewhere!"

"No, we're not," Bayli was quick to say. "I slept with one boss. Sleeping with the other one would just be . . . so not right. *Right?*"

"Don't knock it till you try it." Jewel waggled a brow.

Exhilaration trilled down Bayli's spine. But she wouldn't go in the direction of a ménage à trois with this conversation. Even if she was dying to pick Jewel's brain about it. That would be getting way ahead of herself—she didn't even know if Rory wanted her in the way she was thinking of him. Let alone if both men would be interested in a threesome.

It was just such a decadent, delectable notion that it was damn near impossible to shove it under the rug and pretend she'd never considered getting it on with two men at the same time.

So she changed the topic entirely. Safer that way. "Hey, I've got to wrap up now and finish breakfast so I can get to the library."

"I demand you keep us up-to-date on these latest developments," Scarlet told her. "I'm currently living vicariously through you both, and the juicier the details the better!"

"So no luck catching up with your Wolf of Wall Street, Mr. Michael Vandenberg?" Bayli asked her.

"Still successfully evading me. Though, come on, ladies," Scarlet said. "He might be hotter than hell, but don't get any ideas there. . . . I'm not looking to hook up with the man in the way you're thinking. I'm looking to question him about millions of dollars' worth of artwork that went missing from his estate. The family scored on the insurance policy, but the art collection was never fenced and has never hit the black market. Not one single painting. That leads me to believe someone who likely cashed in on the claim is still secretly enjoying the pieces privately on display somewhere. Such as behind locked doors within their mansion."

"I'm shocked he's been able to skirt you," Bayli said. "I know how tenacious you can be."

"Well, to tell you the truth, he hasn't been my sole focus. I had another fraudulent case to chase and some court time on two indictments I helped to bring about. Oh, and here's a kicker. . . . Vandenberg has a stepbrother who was living in the Hamptons mansion at the same time the entire collection disappeared. But he's even harder to track down than Wolfie. So, I'm trying to hunt them both in between all my other cases."

"Jesus, it's no wonder you're not getting laid," Jewel joked. "When would you ever have the time?"

"Trust me, I am reaching the point where I will *make* time," Scarlet assured them. "I'm bordering on full-on torture here."

"So hit a club in SF," Jewel recommended. "Find some anonymous hottie for a one-night stand and then get back to stalking your wolf and stepbrother so that you can stop obsessing over this cold case and maybe meet someone you can actually have a meaningful relationship with."

" 'Cuz that's happened to me before." Scarlet snickered. "Men who want a 'meaningful relationship' have been beating down my door my entire life, just waiting for me to answer. *Not.*"

"Technically, you don't know that," Jewel said. "You're a workaholic—you can't deny it any more than you can deny Bay usually has her nose stuck in a book instead of checking out the talent around her."

"Hey," she snapped, "I'm on this call, too! And I just had the best sex of my life—off-the-charts sex! So there!"

"Way to rub it in," Scarlet lamented. Then added, "I'm dropping off before I need professional help for my sexual repression."

"Bay has to run, too," Jewel said. "So let's chat as soon as there's more to talk about when it comes to angsty-chef guy. Can't wait to hear how *that* goes down!"

"Neither can I," Bayli jested with a hint of lasciviousness in her tone over the double meaning of Jewel's *goes down* comment.

Bayli ended the call with her friends, devoured more of Rory's sensational breakfast, and then put the rest in her fridge for leftovers and packed everything up after cleaning it, regardless of Denny's instructions. The OCD in her couldn't help it. Then she left the box with the super, who'd been awesome from the beginning about storing her deliveries when she wasn't available to receive them. If she ever did make it big, the sweet older gentleman was at the top of her list for a huge tip.

She phoned the restaurant and connected with Denny to let him know he could pick up all the personal catering items.

Bayli then took a bus, followed by the subway, to Grand Central Station. It was a part of town that she loved, teeming with all sorts of activity. The station itself was like nothing she'd ever expected when she'd first arrived in New York. Sure, San Francisco had some underground transportation and BART, but she'd never come across a station that looked like Grand Central— enormous, packed with people and restaurants, gleaming and pulsating with energy.

Farther south was the small but immaculate former church where she worked.

Bayli's favorite sanctuary . . .

"Mission accomplished?" Christian asked as he sauntered into Rory's kitchen around noon.

Rory looked up from the perfectly cut filets mignons laid out on large metal trays that he was inspecting for this evening's dinner crowd. It would include, among others, two movie stars, a rock star, and a famous author, along with a TV producer and a half-dozen politicians. All at separate tables.

"Well, I didn't exactly serve her breakfast in bed," Rory told his friend, "but I did send Denny over to cater to her."

"Excellent."

"This is the first time you've asked me to do this," Rory casually commented.

"You've made breakfast for numerous women the morning after," Christian reminded him.

"That's because I'm usually in their apartment and it seems like the polite thing to do after they've sucked my dick. So I'll amend my statement and say this is the first time I've made breakfast for a woman I didn't even get the pleasure of sleeping with."

With a devilish grin, Christian said, "Trust me, you would have gotten a hell of a lot of pleasure out of sleeping with Bayli Styles."

"Then you should have invited me over." Rory moved on to the rib eyes and the strips, ensuring they were trimmed to his specifications.

"The thought certainly crossed my mind." They were the only ones in the kitchen at present. The prep cook was taking inventory and the chefs would begin trickling in over the next hour or so. Christian added, "She's phenomenal, Rory. It's next to impossible not to offer her the hostess job out front, because she'd rock our customers' worlds when they come through the door. But she's—"

"Destined for more than that," Rory finished his sentence.

"Yes, she is. And we need to talk about a reboot of the show. I'm thinking we do a webcast of a half-dozen episodes for a test run. Then we go back to the network with a full season planned out. I'm talking tucked-away gems, undiscovered beaches, Mediterranean seaports—rather than meccas. Asian villages, African safaris, places difficult to find on a map that are brimming with the potential for culinary brilliance."

"Authentic all the way," Rory concurred. "Nothing commercialized, no overrun destinations. I like it. But who the hell has time to pick these places and fully research them?"

"That's where Miss Styles comes in, initially. She's a book hound. Even works part-time at a library. We'll start paying her a salary as soon I negotiate with her agent, and she can research her heart out." Christian flashed his confident grin. The one that had likely scored him an invitation into Bayli's bed last night.

Rory felt the sting of not having been a part of his friend's discovery of every erogenous zone the raven-haired beauty possessed. He'd fantasized about her several times since meeting her, and Rory was more than interested in stripping her bare and worshiping her gorgeous body. While Christian did the same. Until they both had her so worked up, she came harder than ever before.

Rory's groin tightened at the thought. It was all he could do not to grill Christian over how she tasted, how he'd fucked her, what sort of sexy sounds she made when she was aroused. But Rory tamped down the urge, because he wanted to discover all of those things firsthand.

But there was still business to focus on.

He said, "She's also going to need to spend time with me in the kitchen. So she knows how to work around me, not get in my way. Assimilate to my style. Understand what I'm doing so she can seamlessly interact with both me and the audience."

"Agreed. How do you think she'll pull that off?"

"I'll run her over a few times before she figures out how to move with me."

Christian smirked. "Try to be gentle."

"It won't be intentional, for Christ's sake. But if I'm not operating in my normal mode, then the show will be stilted and appear scripted. That's what fucked us last time. We don't want it technical to the point of being tedious or frustrating, and we sure as hell don't need it to be a procedural how-to. This show needs to be more cutting-edge. More on the fly and—"

"*Sam the Cooking Guy,* not *Hell's Kitchen.*"

"A combination of both, actually," Rory said. "But not a bumbling mess because beauty and the beast are tripping all over each

other. We need to be in sync and she needs to anticipate my movements and recognize when I begin improvising because a better
idea has popped into my head."

"Rory," Christian said with exasperation in his tone. "Let's not
set her up for failure by expecting the impossible from her. The
two of you barely know each other."

"Then I guess we'll have to spend some time together." He
grinned. "Not exactly torture, right?"

SEVEN

The library was meticulously laid out and Bayli spent half of her time shelving books and the other half on a special project for the curator, who was searching for information on an Italian vase presumed to be from the sixteenth century that his husband, the curator of a museum, wanted to get his hands on to display with a similar collection.

Bayli loved searching for lost treasures. She'd spent a couple of weeks scouring books and making phone calls to see what kind of authentic documentation she could unearth related to the missing piece. She'd fallen down a few rabbit holes with misguidance but was quick enough to recover and head in a different direction.

Today, her diligence paid off.

At a little after three, she collected the books she'd checked out earlier and added her pièce de résistance to the pile. She crossed the expanse of the main floor and knocked on Dr. Phillip Holdsworth's partially opened door.

"Come in!" he called from inside. "I'm at the conference table."

She bypassed his desk and walked to the back of the large room where the wiry blond was bent over a half-dozen books spread open on the table. Phillip was an interesting character with a slight British accent, though he'd only studied abroad—he'd actually been born in Ohio. He was married to his work as much as he was to his life partner—who followed the same pattern. They were both petite, almost delicate-looking men with contradictory boisterous personalities and a quirky sense of humor.

Bayli had clicked with Phillip instantly, and when he'd invited her to lunch with Colin Holdsworth during Bayli's first week at the library, she'd felt honored. And had been amused by all their tales of wayward travel where pretty much anything that could possibly go wrong for the couple always did.

Yet they never told their misadventures in a negative light—in fact, it seemed to please them to have such unintentionally eccentric escapades. And their stories captivated Bayli, which might have been the reason why Christian's new idea of a travel/cooking show got her so jazzed. Because what he was contemplating was off-the-beaten-path journeys meant to be both entertaining and educational. Bayli could draw upon some of the Holdsworths' reactions to excursions-gone-awry as color commentary.

Not that she should be thinking so far ahead. She knew it wasn't wise to put all her eggs in one basket. And without the cooking-show basket, she'd be right back to square one. Only she would have lost significant time chasing her tail with that prospect when she could have been looking for another job—since even Christian had confirmed they wouldn't be offering her the hostess position at Davila's NYC. Had likely already filled it.

Her optimism didn't dim, however. Because after this morning she really did believe in Christian's confidence about the project and his interest in her being his and Rory's shooting star. Plus, she was with Phillip and that man was nothing but pure sunshine.

He ardently said, "Colin located a much better rendition of the vase than you and I have previously been working with." Colin was also Dr. Holdsworth. Both PhDs. Phillip explained, "He lost the trail around the early twentieth century, though." Philip handed over the drawing. It was quite similar to the one he'd provided when Bayli had first joined the staff and he'd singled her out for this special procurement. But the new image was colored in with oil paints. Vibrant splashes of red, orange, gold, green, and purple. A little overwhelming visually, but once she got past that, the vase was quite stunning.

Bayli carefully set her pile of books on the table and snatched the one on top, placing it before Phillip where he was still hunched over his designated space. "I've finally found more than a mere mention of the vase. For the past two months, I've been digging a deep hole to China with no concrete leads to follow. Then, suddenly, I hit upon this." She flipped the hardback open to the section she'd flagged with a torn piece of paper and said, "I'm pretty sure this is the same piece."

She held his rendering to the one in the book. The pattern was identical upon first inspection.

"Unfortunately," she continued, "with my version being in sepia tones and yours being so vivid . . ." She frowned. "Does Colin know for sure this is an accurate depiction? I mean, we've all only come across a couple of images and they've never been in color. So how do we confirm these jewel tones are true to life?"

"We can't, of course. Not until we find a solid description in a narrative or caption."

Bayli nodded. "I remember taking the Amtrak from San Francisco to Albuquerque for a college research trip"—before she'd had to drop out because she could no longer afford tuition—"and we stopped in Flagstaff, Arizona, along the way. The freight depot was built in 1886 and the main Atchison, Topeka and Santa Fe railroad depot in 1926. Then they morphed it into a Tudor Revival style that's really beautiful in mostly brick, but there's some bright-turquoise trim that's kind of out of character with the rustic elegance of the mountain town—lumberjack land, as they consider it. Rumor has it, when it came time to spruce the place up in the 1990s someone convinced the City Council that was the original color of the depot."

"That does sound a bit off," Phillip said.

"It's no sore thumb or anything. I just found it amusing that apparently someone of influence sold these people on turquoise paint when the original freight depot was red sandstone, and I just can't imagine paint coming in bright turquoise in the early 1900s. Or, more appropriately, I don't know how they would have pegged the color from black-and-white photos."

"Good point." Phillip gazed at the colorful picture of the vase and said, "I'm a wee leery of the purple. But the pattern is a fabulous match."

Bayli gave him the highlights of what she'd discovered from the text, then said, "My friend Scarlet is an independent insurance fraud investigator. We can ask her to try to authenticate your more modern depiction. With the information I have here, she can also check with her global connections to see if there's a trail to pick up regarding the vase's whereabouts."

"Clever girl."

"You have no idea. Her business is booming and really, I think she's beyond brilliant and—"

"Bayli," he said with a dry look. "I was talking about you."

"Oh." She grinned. "Right. Well, then. Here's plenty for you and Colin to pore over during cocktail hour." She indicated the book. "And I'll just be on my way."

"Why don't you join us?" Phillip offered. "Colin's two roommates from Oxford are in town and he's cooking an enormous feast at the apartment. Come over for really bad food, bottomless bottles of wine, and lots of laughs."

"Phillip! Colin is an excel—"

"Oh, bloody hell, Bay. If you dare say Colin's an excellent cook, I'll be forced to lie and say you're an excellent karaoke singer. And really, I do hate to shine on people I adore."

She snorted. "That was oh, so delicate, *friend* of mine. But I get your point. So I'm *not* bringing my personally crafted, bejeweled mic over this evening. Your loss."

He gaped for a moment, then said, "You don't really have—"

"Of course not!" She laughed. "So gullible. Geez, Oxford will give anyone a PhD, won't they?"

"Keep applying and we'll find out," he joked.

"Sure, like I want to hang out with a bunch of snobby Brits who would dare challenge my knowledge of Shakespeare."

"So predictable," he said with a *tsk*. "Talk to me about a creative genius other than Shakespeare this evening, *please*."

"That sounded downright boorish," she playfully chided.

"Well, you did insult my alma mater."

"You insulted my singing."

"I had to put a stop to your madness over Colin's cooking, didn't I?"

"I'll be kind enough not to mention it to him. Now, what time am I coming over?"

Phillip consulted his Rolex, a recent birthday gift from Colin. "Seven. That will give us sufficient time to get the smell of burnt Chicken Kiev from the apartment."

"Appetizing, Phillip." She crinkled her nose. "Really."

"Be forewarned. You've only sampled Colin's staples on picnics, like fish-and-chips. When he actually tries something new, it can be quite horrifying."

"I'm sure it'll be just fine. What shall I bring this evening?"

"That gorgeous smile of yours, love. And that's all." He gave her a stern look. "I'm serious, Bay."

She hedged. It was hardly polite to show up empty-handed, the only reason she typically turned down in-home dinner invitations. But this was Phillip and Colin. They knew she was a struggling model.

Bayli also remembered she had a nice bottle of merlot her agent had given her upon her first assignment. She would gift it to Phillip and Colin this evening.

That decided, she told Phillip she'd be there at seven and then she hefted her stack of books in her arms again and headed out of his office. She made her way through the library and to the front doors. She juggled the hardbacks as she reached for the handle on one door and pushed it open. Though it didn't take any effort on her part, because someone on the other side jerked the tall wooden-and-stained-glass door open, pulling her along for the ride.

Bayli stumbled forward, her books went flying, and then she fell into a strong embrace, her body slamming against a hard and hunky one.

"*Ooof!*" she cried out at the solid impact. She would have bounced off the brick wall of a chest if two strong hands hadn't immediately gripped her biceps to hold her steady.

"Holy shit!" a familiar voice roared.

Her head snapped back and Bayli stared up at chiseled facial features, dark-chocolate eyes, and disheveled bronze hair.

Her jaw fell slack for all of two seconds. Then she said on an unchecked outburst, "My books!"

She wriggled out of Rory's embrace—only finding the self-control to do so because her beloved hardbacks were scattered on the steps. Good Lord, he was a mountain of muscles and rigidity. And one sturdy-ass pillar of a man.

Bayli sank to her knees to scoop up the pile. He knelt beside her to help.

"What are you doing here?" she demanded.

"I'm here to see you," he retorted in his gruff tone.

Bayli took the books from him and hugged them to her chest. "Christian sent you?"

"No." He stood in one fluid move and offered his hand. She resisted the urge to sigh.

This again.

Her palm slipped into his and she felt the same high-voltage spark as last time, outside his kitchen. She got to her feet and was determined to rip her hand from his, *just like last time.* But Rory St. James was having none of it. He held fast to his grip on her. Not hurting her in any way, but his clasp on her hand left no doubt that he wasn't going to let her make a hasty retreat.

That wasn't exactly on her mind. Though, damn, it'd be nice if just once she could be prepared for a run-in with him. Because he always caught her off-guard. And that was nerve-wracking as hell.

Especially when she eyed him, looking devastatingly handsome, dressed all in black. He wore jeans and boots. A vee-necked T-shirt and sleek leather jacket. Rory wasn't the *GQ* variety that Christian was. The chef was fashionable, no question there, but he had a more reserved style that complemented, not overpowered, his intense demeanor. He was edgy and sexy, and Bayli was drawn to him as fervently as she was to his business partner.

Not exactly wise, she knew. But then again . . . human beings possessed feral instincts, whether it was in their best interests or not to act on them.

Rory said, "I thought we should talk about Christian's plans. Why don't you let me cook you an early dinner this evening?"

His offer took her by surprise. But she had a feeling it'd be a good idea to wait and hear from her agent tomorrow after Christian spoke with her before she got too caught up in this new world—and Rory St. James.

So she wrenched her hand from his and told him, "I have a previous engagement, thank you anyway."

Rory's squared jaw clenched briefly. As though she tried his patience. Probably a true assessment.

He asked, "Any chance you can take a rain check? It's kind of important."

"Related to the show?"

"Yes."

Her belly quivered—because of Rory or the potential job? She had no idea, but strove for nonchalance regardless of the actual truth, whatever it might be. And went against her better judgment of keeping her distance from the man until all the dust had settled.

Sadly, she wasn't quite sure she achieved a calm demeanor as she caustically said, "Fine, then. I'll cancel with my friends."

Phillip and Colin would understand, particularly when she

told them who she was now dining with. Hell, they'd be ecstatic for Bayli. Rory St. James was one hell of a looker. And, again, there was that possibility of a TV show.

Bayli knew she ought to be more thrilled about the latter, rather than how hot Rory was—how hot Rory made her. But she was literally incapable of dismissing or skipping over those pertinent facts. He got her juices flowing in record time and had her mind whirling with all sorts of sexy thoughts centered on how *he* might pleasure her.

Christian had delivered several earth-shattering orgasms. She wondered about Rory doing the same, wondered just how talented *his* tongue might be, how aggressively *he'd* fuck her.

Bayli pressed her bare thighs together as erotic pinpricks targeted her clit. Such bad timing. And much too taunting to ignore. But not at all convenient when she was trying to keep her wits about her around this man.

Rory pried the books from her hands to carry them as his other palm pressed to the small of her back. Surprising her *and* heightening her arousal. He guided her down the stairs and along the busy sidewalk.

He said, "We'll shop first."

"Shouldn't you be at the restaurant?"

"I like to throw my executive chefs for a loop every now and then," he revealed in a conspiratorial tone. "Put them in charge when they least expect it. That way I find out how prepared they are to take over when I'm gone."

"What if it all goes to hell in a handbag because Rory St. James isn't there to rule the roost?"

He chuckled. A low rumbling sound that reverberated deep inside her.

"I know before I hire them whether they're going to crack under the pressure. Still, it doesn't hurt to test the staff from time to time. And to also demonstrate my faith in their abilities."

Bayli gazed at him. "So you're not so much tossing them into the deep end to see if they'll sink or swim. You're proving you trust them."

His head dipped and he whispered in her ear, "Shh. Don't tell anyone."

Her heart did an odd little flip. In a breathy voice, she said, "Far be it from me to give away your secrets."

Rory grinned. "Sometimes being an asshole garners the best responses—and work—from others."

"Sometimes honey catches more flies than vinegar."

"In certain situations," he agreed. "But I'm not interested in catching flies. I'm interested in stars."

She nodded. "Of the Michelin variety." Bayli mulled this over a moment, then added, "But come on, Rory—may I call you Rory?"

"Of course." He stared down at her as though completely taken aback by her inquiry. "What were you planning on calling me?"

"I don't think you want to know." She flashed a sassy smile that made him laugh. Then she said, "Just kidding. Anyway, I do appreciate your devotion to your profession and your commitment to protecting your business assets. I don't even mind that you're intimidating as hell in your kitchen. Well, in life in general." She swallowed hard.

Rory stopped walking, effectively pulling her up short with him. "I'm not trying to intimidate you, Bayli. This is just who I am."

"I know." She smiled again. "Which is one of the reasons why I hoped to make a good impression with Christian at the fund-raiser, so that I could come back to the restaurant and maybe get a *real* interview with you. I'll admit that, at first, I considered the position a foothold for my modeling career. But after I met you . . ." Her head cocked to the side as she took in his six-foot-two- or three-inch stature and his imposing build. "My mind started to whirl with all sorts of possibilities about who you really are and what you're really trying to accomplish. It isn't *just* about the stars, right?"

Rory let out a sigh that could have been part dejection, part frustration. Part agitation? She couldn't be sure.

He continued walking, leading her to a gunmetal-gray sports car parallel parked alongside the walkway. His hand slipped away and she felt the void in the way she had when Christian had withdrawn from her body the night before. Foreign sensations, because Bayli was used to being a loner when it came to male companionship.

She had her "sisterly" love with Jewel and Scarlet. But physical affection had always been lacking in Bayli's life. Until she'd met both Rory and Christian she hadn't noticed the deficiency—or perhaps she just hadn't acknowledged it before this point. But these two men . . . they did something to her. Made her feel a part of something, made her feel a sense of belonging. So much so that when the physical contact was broken she felt empty and cold inside.

It was a little scary to own up to all of that. But also inevitable.

Yet she tried not to dwell on it or, God forbid, dissect its meaning.

Rory said, "The ratings and reviews our restaurants receive are critical to me, yes. But you're right. It's not just about the stars. It's the overall customer experience and what we do as a team to make each dinner service the best it can possibly be . . . night after night. Everyone has 'off' days. And people in every profession strive for greatness yet oftentimes fall short. Not every movie is a blockbuster; not every novel makes the *New York Times* bestseller list; not every baseball player hits a grand slam to win the World Series and become a national hero."

He gestured toward the car to indicate it was his. Then continued. "Sometimes, something comes out of my kitchen that just doesn't make the grade. Is it intentional? Hell, no. Forgivable by the consumer?" He shrugged. "It depends. Does it personally affect everyone in my kitchen, including me? Absolutely. Because those are the kind of conscientious people I hire and because I take it all to heart, too. I don't want to disappoint my diners. But sometimes, Bayli, I do."

Her heart melted a little. "Because you're human, Rory. No one's infallible. Including you."

"And doesn't that just piss me off." He hit a button on the remote and yanked open the passenger door for her.

Bayli didn't immediately slide onto the dove-gray leather seat. Instead, she gazed up at Rory and said, "You can beat yourself up all you want when something goes awry in your kitchen. But I don't think for a second it would have anything to do with slacking off on the job, not putting your heart and soul into it, not doing everything in your power to deliver nothing short of excellence."

"But it does happen. I have difficulty digesting that."

"Rory." Her brow furrowed. "Overachievers are not only under a lot of pressure by society standards, but they put a huge amount of stress on themselves. It's admirable and disheartening at the same time. You don't want to let anyone down. But reasonably speaking, even the best batting average can tank. Because behind that bat is a human being."

Impulsively she kissed him on the cheek. Then slipped inside the car.

It took Rory a few suspended seconds to recover. Then he handed over her books, closed her door, and rounded the front of the vehicle.

All the while, Bayli's pulse raced. She'd kissed him, and maybe it had been a bit on the chaste side but still. She'd demonstrated affection. With angsty chef guy.

The corners of her mouth quivered.

Yes, he was sharp-tongued and surly and all that. But she could see so much more. Could see so far beyond his abrasiveness.

He had a lot on the line every single day, a lot to lose, not just monetarily but reputation-wise. There was a heavy weight on this man's broad shoulders, and Bayli sensed it wasn't just about his own success or failure but that he likely put a shitload of pressure on himself because Christian Davila's name, reputation, and capital were riding on each endeavor as well.

As the car sprang to life and Rory pulled away from the curb, Bayli studied his prominent profile.

She'd been wrong about him at that first meeting. She'd been fuming when she'd left the restaurant and she'd wanted nothing more than to march inside and tell him exactly what she thought of his quick dismissal of her. Something had held her back, though. Bayli now suspected that *something* was the spark of kindred spirit. She was nowhere near as brilliant as Rory. But Bayli had pride and she did her best no matter what the circumstances. And didn't believe in status quo or giving up.

So she found it particularly amazing that she was somehow being aligned with two men who shared her beliefs and did everything to encourage her to continue down her chosen path.

"Where are we off to, exactly?" she asked.

"Farmers' market."

Her eyes popped. "In Manhattan?"

"On Sundays, yes. So we're in luck. There's one on Columbus Avenue not far from my apartment."

"Let me guess." Her tone turned sardonic. "You overlook Central Park."

"As a matter of fact, I do."

Bayli whistled under her breath. Maybe someday she'd have a real-live, honest-to-God one-bedroom with sensational views, instead of a tiny alcove and a dreary brick wall a stone's throw away from her one and only window.

As they drove, Rory told her a little about the 79th Street Greenmarket and mentioned there were two others he frequented. Bayli made a mental note of the locations, because veggies were always at the top of her grocery list.

She asked, "What are you making for dinner?"

"That'd be what are *we* making for dinner? And the answer is . . . depends on what we find."

She stared at Rory a few moments, then gently broke her bad

news to him. "Sorry to disappoint, Chef, but you definitely don't want me in your kitchen. I burn boiling water."

He chuckled good-naturedly. Surprise, surprise. "You'll just be assisting. It'll be fine."

"But I'll be in your way." Was that a hint of panic in her voice? *Why, yes, it is.*

Rory told her, "Christian is moving full-steam ahead with the new design for the show. Granted, it's going to take some time to develop and there are various negotiations to partake in, including with you and your agent, but we can get this concept off the ground before the end of the year. And that means you and I need to find a harmonious rhythm while we're doing cooking exhibitions so that I don't mow you down while I'm moving about and end up—"

"Yelling at me?" She eyed him with a crooked brow.

He smirked. "I was going to say so that I don't end up hurting you again. But that, too."

The yelling part.

She would have been amused that they could lightly tease each other—pleased, even—except that behind this new levity between them was an underlying current that gnawed at Bayli.

She could be totally off base, but it didn't feel that way in her gut, so she ventured to guess, "You weren't just annoyed with me for being at the wrong place at the wrong time when you came barreling through those kitchen doors, right? You were irritated because you'd knocked me over. Even though, admittedly, it was all my fault for being in your way."

Rory expertly wove through traffic, not glancing at her. But Bayli could see from the way his jaw worked that her assumption was right on the money.

When they finally stopped at a light, he slid his gaze her way. "I'm used to being surrounded by people who are lightning quick on their feet and bend and flex with the fast-paced environment. It's not always smooth sailing, of course, and we go through our

fair share of broken glasses and dishes. But yes . . . I was mostly
pissed off because I'd likely left a bruise on that amazingly beautiful body of yours. And will be even more furious if it's still there."

The light turned green. Rory eased the car forward. Bayli
continued to stare at him, her mind blank, her voice vanishing
completely.

But the rest of her . . . Holy hell. Bayli's heart thumped might-
ily in her chest. Excitement rippled through her stomach and down
to the apex of her legs, making her clit tingle and her pussy throb.

Once more, she was breathless and filled with exhilaration.

Not that Rory St. James had come right out and said he wanted
to see her naked and inspect that spot on her hip himself—or
that he wanted her the way Christian had wanted her last night.
Still . . . Rory's tone had lowered a notch and was tinged with a
mixture of lust and torment. An extremely sexy combination. One
that did a number on her insides, igniting every nerve ending.

She'd contend that it was crazy or greedy or selfish to be attracted to two men at the same time. To eagerly want to get to know
them in every way possible—undisputedly in the carnal sense. But
even if she was all of those aforementioned things, it didn't matter.
Because this was yet another part of life Bayli had never lived to
the fullest.

She'd had one boyfriend, her senior year of high school. Other
than that, there'd never been time, or she hadn't had the energy to
date while taking care of her mother, or she was just too afraid to
get attached to someone while watching someone else she cared
for so deeply wither away before her very eyes—and there'd been
absolutely nothing Bayli could do to improve her mother's health
so that she could have had just one more surgery that might have
added a few more years to her existence.

But now was not the time to dwell on Bayli's painful past.
Now was the time for her to wrap her arms around the future and
see just how far she could go. . . .

Finally getting a grip on her racing pulse—to an extent, anyway, because there was something powerful and alluring about the man sitting next to her that crawled under her skin and kept her body charged—she managed to say to Rory, "I haven't checked of late, but I'm pretty sure that all evidence of our little run-in is long gone."

"And Christian would have asked you about it if he'd noticed a mark."

She gaped. Okay, way for Rory to get right to the point.

"Christian didn't exactly do an inch-by-inch visual assessment," she boldly said. Praying like hell her voice wouldn't crack as she added, "He was a bit more singularly focused."

"I know Christian well. Trust me. He didn't miss a thing. Nor would I." Rory flashed her a wicked grin.

Bayli all but incinerated in her seat.

Oh, boy.

She was playing with some serious fire here. Burning both ends of the wick. Or fuse. Take your pick. Either would be equally explosive in the end, she was sure.

Her fingers curled around the stack in her lap. Her inner muscles clenched and released in an attempt to stave off the thrumming deep in her core . . . or the craving still clawing at her, centered wholly around that incredible fulfillment she'd experienced the previous evening.

Yes, Christian had fucked her hard and she'd loved every second of it. Had been sated by how passionately he'd taken her. But in the light of day, and sitting in such close proximity to Rory, with his innuendoes clouding her judgement and the intoxicating scent of his expensive cologne and male heat infiltrating her mind and senses, she was right back to wanting—needing—another highly intense, fantastically arousing fuck.

Plain and simple.

She wouldn't even be apologetic for the naughty thought. Or blush.

Maybe.

As she fought the warmth creeping up her neck and threatening to flood her face, Bayli dared to ask, "Christian told you we slept together?"

"Yes." Rory stopped the car behind one that was pulling out of a space on Columbus Avenue and then expertly maneuvered into the tight spot and shut off the engine. He shifted in his seat and partially faced Bayli. "The verdict was that you're phenomenal. But I'd already assumed that."

He tossed off his seat belt and exited the car in a swift, stealthy move. While Bayli's mind reeled and her nipples tightened.

Rory had to step over the slight vee of his bumper in order to get to the sidewalk and then he opened her door for her. Bayli's fingers shook as she unlatched the belt. Rory took the books from her so she could climb out. He set them carefully on the seat and locked the car.

She searched her brain for something to say that would help to distract her from the zings ricocheting within her but came up empty-handed. Not a common occurrence, except when she was in the company of one of two extremely gorgeous, successful, and enigmatic men.

Rory's fingers twined with hers and he tugged her along beside him. "You're okay walking for a little while in those shoes?"

"Of course." She wore four-inch navy-colored heels that matched her short skirt. A cream-colored blouse completed the ensemble. She'd pulled her long hair up in a high ponytail and added simple earrings and her bracelet. A small purse crossed her chest and rested at her hip.

"It'll be a damn shame when autumn rolls around and you'll have to cover up those sensational legs of yours," he told her.

Bayli's cheeks were going to be burning from grinning after this outing, she had no doubt. "Maybe Christian will choose tropical locales for our shoots."

"I'm sure he's already envisioning you in a string bikini."

With a soft laugh, she said, "No one will take me seriously if I wear a string bikini during your cooking demos."

"To hell with the demos. He's thinking strictly off camera as much as I am." He winked.

Bayli gazed up at him, her chest rising and falling much more quickly than normal. "Are you hitting on me, Chef St. James?"

He let out a mock groan. "Oh, so formal."

"I thought you enjoyed being revered. Treated like a culinary god," she jested.

"Naturally," he shot back. Then he leaned in and whispered sexily in her ear, "Just be sure to call me *Rory*, or *stud muffin*, or something equally endearing when I make you come . . . over and over."

Bayli stumbled. Rory was quick to catch her and steady her so they could continue on to the white-tented vendor tables.

"Jesus," she muttered. "You're both a bit full-throttle."

"That's how we get what we want."

It probably wasn't wise to do so, but Bayli couldn't stop herself from brazenly inquiring, "And do you two typically woo the same woman at the same time?"

His brow jumped. *"Woo?"* He let out a hearty laugh.

"Fine," she huffed. "Flirt with, stare suggestively at, insinuate that you actually do possess the ability to make me come over and over?"

"Do you doubt it?"

"Hmm." *No.*

Another guffaw that echoed down the busy street. No one even bothered to look their way. Until they joined the conglomeration of browsers and shoppers and Rory was instantly recognized.

Bayli rolled her eyes as the women fawned over Angsty Chef, as she now officially—albeit secretly—dubbed him. But Rory was a bit of a man's man, too, and some of the guys on the street wanted grilling tips and his renowned recipe for chili.

Standing off to the side, letting Rory have his much-deserved moments in the sun, Bayli nibbled her lower lip. Partially to keep from smiling from ear to ear because she was the one he'd been holding hands with before he'd been spotted by fans and partially because she was stuck in tortuous suspense awaiting his answer to her question.

Jewel had once explained about the complication of her re-union with both Rogen and Vin when they'd all returned to River Cross after so many years of separation. Yet when all the cards had been laid on the table, she'd said it'd been a huge relief that each man knew she was attracted—as emotionally as she was physically—to him and that she was having sex with the other.

So nothing was shady, nothing needed to be hidden, noth-ing slipped that shouldn't slip, and therefore feelings and egos were spared. As much as could be expected, at any rate. The guys had apparently thrown a few punches when Jewel's back was turned, but really, that was just toe-curling romantic for a girl to learn about.

All in all, with everyone being up-front about their intentions and Jewel not lying about whether she'd been with one man or the other, it'd been much easier for the trio to begin building their re-lationship. Not that they hadn't suffered setbacks, including with their families and some members of the exclusive California wine community, but Jewel swore that keeping everything aboveboard and in the open was the best way to manage the dynamic of a mé-nage à trois. Not just in the sexual connotation, but as a household as well.

No lie, Bayli found the entire arrangement intriguing. Scarlet did, too. And they'd never seen their lifelong friends so happy. Which was likely why Bayli wasn't quite so timid about broaching the subject of currently being the object of both Christian's *and* Rory's desire.

Not that she had any delusions that she'd hold their interest. She did not take either man as being the type to settle down, not when their stars were burning so brightly and there were still many business ventures for them to spearhead and conquer. Bayli felt something similar.

What she was really experiencing at the moment was the rush of having caught both men's attention and the fact that, with each of them, something new seemed to leap out at her around every bend. Bayli loved that. Thrived on the titillation of the unexpected, because it was a huge contrast to her past and easily inspired hope for what tomorrow might bring.

Hell, she had high hopes for what the next couple of hours with Rory St. James might bring!

He eventually worked his way free of the crowd, shaking his head slightly as he eyed her, as though he were exasperated by his adoring fans. But the glimmer in his dark-chocolate irises suggested otherwise. He was just good at keeping up his tough-guy image.

"Sorry about that," he said.

"No worries at all."

"They'll be swarming you someday soon. And won't even notice me."

She beamed up at him and playfully said, "Here's hoping."

Rory snickered amiably.

From his back pocket, he whipped out a folded-up cloth tote, then took her hand again—which thrilled her endlessly—and said, "Let's shop. Little Miss Catches Flies with Honey."

She knew he was referring to himself as one of them.

EIGHT

Rory directed her from table to table, and Bayli carefully surveyed the offerings and either looked disgusted, shrugged nonchalantly, or nodded zealously. He quickly picked up on the nonverbal signals and deduced that she stuck mostly with the standard fare of vegetables, not too fond of cauliflower, turnips, oca, and the like. But zucchini, heirloom tomatoes, and carrots earned high marks, so he snatched a bit of each, along with some other accompaniments, as they worked their way down the tree-lined street.

"How often do you actually get to cook at home, Rory?"

"Not frequently. Just when friends are in town at the same time I am."

"Lady friends?" she asked as she inspected a crown of broccoli and then handed it to him to add to their collection.

Rory wasn't quite sure what the hell he was going to do with that—the broccoli. Given her other selections, he was headed in a specific direction, rather than a hodgepodge one. But seriously . . . he was going to deny her anything? Not a chance.

There were already some extremely unfamiliar and even a tad unsettling feelings centered around this woman that began taking root deep in his gut. Okay, a little higher than that. And lower. Something about her big, soulful eyes tugged at his heart. She wavered between flirty and lost in thought. Not always pleasant thoughts, he could tell. Sometimes she got mired in a murkiness that had nothing to do with whatever topic of conversation they were on or what was happening between them or around them.

And then there was the matter of his cock twitching at the mere sight of her. Threatening to stiffen when she laughed, smiled, gazed up at him. Fuck, it was worse while their fingers were entwined and, on occasion, her breasts brushed against his arm or chest.

The woman who had initially irritated him—for being in his way, for causing him to maim her, for not being the front-of-house hostess he needed—now easily ensnared him. She was beautiful, and sure, that held plenty of appeal for him. But his attraction to Bayli Styles went well beyond surface beauty. He couldn't keep himself from watching her closely and trying to learn every facet of her personality, no matter their environment, whether they were engaging in witty banter or she was pushing his buttons. Honestly, he liked both. She was sweet and feisty. Hesitant at times, audacious at others. Never, ever boring.

Rory wasn't quite sure what would come out of her mouth next. Didn't know how she might react to anything he'd say or do—and that was exciting as hell. He wasn't used to balancing on a tightrope with a woman, but this one had him jonesing for each thrilling second with her.

All of which made it difficult to answer her question. Because, yes, he did entertain "lady friends." He was no saint. But not all of his female acquaintances were lovers. Many were colleagues. Professional chefs he hung out with during downtimes—few and far between, but he managed to fit in special get-togethers whenever possible.

Really, though . . . Rory knew what she was getting at. So he said, "I'm not currently sleeping with anyone."

They checked out the mounds of various potatoes but bypassed the starch. Bayli mused, "And you don't mind that I am? Well . . .

it could've just been a onetime thing. I don't really know if Christian is looking for anything beyond last night."

Rory's hand tenderly squeezed hers. "You want to know if I'm okay with you and Christian, when I want you just as much as he does?"

"Or *did*." She halted abruptly and asked, "Is that true, though?"

Since there were people milling about, who certainly noted their presence, she obviously didn't want to repeat what Rory had said verbatim. It wasn't the most appropriate time and place for this discussion, but Rory didn't want to leave her hanging any longer.

So he coaxed her to fall back into step with him and quietly said, "We do have work to focus on if we're going to get this revamped show off the ground. But both Christian and I are interested in you in more than a professional capacity. Nor would he have mentioned to me how your evening ended if he was just looking to scratch an itch."

"And what are *you* looking to do?"

Rory chuckled, though it was a bit strained. Like his cock against the zipper of his inky jeans. "Thought I'd already made that abundantly clear."

"So I'm not misreading signals."

He told her, "I saw how you reacted to me when we met. I felt the jolt, too. I continue to feel it. And goddamn, Bayli . . . You felt so fucking good when you fell into my arms at the library."

A strangled sound lodged in her throat. "I'm supposed to concentrate now on . . . anything?"

"We're almost done here. I need duck." He greeted the butcher he normally called on for his personal meats, poultries, and fish, giving him a hearty handshake. "Meet Miss Bayli Styles. Bayli, this is Josgue, from Santiago, Chile."

"It's a pleasure, Josgue," she said, nailing the correct enunciation, not "Jose" but "Ho-sway."

The older gentleman whistled under his breath and told Rory, "She's much too pretty for you, my friend."

"Agreed. But I dragged her along for shopping and she's humored me every step of the way."

Bayli laughed. "Who's humored who? You haven't made a single mention of all the veggies I refuse to eat. Carrots, Rory? Really? You'll be happy to serve carrots with your duck breast this evening?"

"Wait'll we spruce 'em up," he said.

Her smile brightened.

And Rory had the sudden overwhelming urge to kiss her. So he did.

Right there at the 79th Street Greenmarket. In front of God, fans, and Josgue the butcher.

Rory's mouth sealed to hers. She was so caught off-guard that when she gasped Rory's tongue swept inside to tangle with hers. It was a hot, intense, possessive kiss. A quick kiss. But when he pulled away he could see she was as stunned as he was by the electric current that had arced between them. Zapped all the interesting places that lit him up—her as well. He could see it in her eyes.

She was even breathless.

Okay, so was he.

There was a round of applause for the impromptu display of public affection. In the back of his mind, Rory knew he'd regret losing his head over this woman and spontaneously demonstrating precisely how easily she enticed him. At the moment, however . . . he just didn't give a rat's ass. He'd wanted to kiss her. And there wasn't a damn thing under the sun that could have held him back.

So he grinned at her. In return, she looked . . . dazed. Swept away.

In that instant, he decided he wouldn't regret showing her just how taken by her he was. And to hell with the audience that had gathered.

He told his butcher, "Duck breast. Best you've got."

"Of course, Chef St. James. *Only* the best for you."

Rory's gaze slid to Bayli, still fluttering her lashes and looking as though she were trying to remember her name, recall where they were, *why* they were here.

While Josgue packaged up the breast, Bayli appeared to fight for a solid breath and her golden skin held a tinge of pink that made her even lovelier. Made Rory want to call upon every trick in the book to keep her brimming with excitement. To keep that shimmer of exhilaration in her tawny eyes and the vibrations visibly humming through her body.

Rory exchanged cash for the duck and said good-bye to his butcher. Bayli finally came around.

She linked her arm through Rory's and said, "Flats are definitely in order if you plan to kiss me like that again. I might topple over."

"I'm just warming up."

"Oh, my." She let out a long breath. "My knees are pretty much knocking together."

"I was hoping to do better than that."

"You did," she assured him. "I was just being tactful amidst polite society."

"So," he said with a devious grin, "what my kiss did to your other body parts is considered unmentionable 'amidst polite society'?"

"Suffice it to say, you don't leave a dry thong in your wake, Chef St. James."

He groaned. "Now I'm hard." Thankfully, his leather jacket was zipped and long enough to cover most of the bulge between his legs.

Bayli said, "Serves you right. What the hell were you thinking kissing me like that in front of all these people?"

"I don't fucking know," he earnestly told her. "Not my style at all. I don't know what the hell you're doing to me, Bayli, but . . .

I'm dying to kiss you like that again. With or without the audience."

"Rory." She stopped walking. "This could be bad publicity for the show."

"First of all, honey, there's no such thing as bad publicity. I yell at people in my kitchen all the time, and that's never resulted in bad publicity. Second, it could actually intrigue viewers if there's speculation about what goes on between us when the cameras *aren't* rolling."

She shook her head. "There's nothing going on between us. Not presently. Not really. And that's not what I'm getting at. I'm thinking in terms of all the female fans—even some of the guys— who will hate me if there's evidence you're into me. Beyond that, what about Christian? And beyond that . . ." She pulled in another deep breath. Let it out slowly. "What am I talking about? What am I trying to say?"

He chuckled.

"It's not funny," she insisted in a haughty tone as she swatted at his arm. "I am a very smart woman who has very collected and highly organized thoughts. Yet at the moment . . . I can't latch on to a single sane one. What did you do to me with just a kiss?"

Rory's lips whisked over hers and he murmured, "Beats the hell out of me. But you being all flustered like this is driving me wild. Let's get going."

"No! Wait!"

She didn't budge when he tried to get her moving toward the car.

"Bayli." He stared her down. "Not the best time for a battle of wills. I've got fresh duck that needs to be in an oven soon and we still have a lot of curious eyes on us."

The woman he'd so rapidly become enthralled with gave him a sassy look. "You're forgetting one thing, Mr. Perfect Chef."

"I never forget *anything* when it comes to cooking."

She pointed at his bag and said, "Where's your French baguette?"

"My wha—"

"The baguette," she repeated. "Every romantic comedy the world over that features any sort of meal being prepared *always* has a scene in it with a French baguette poking out of the paper bag. You don't have a paper bag because you are clearly environmentally friendly with your reusable cloth tote, but still. Point being—"

"Point *taken*," he gruffly interjected, "but I make my own bread."

"Of course you do." She sighed. "Because you really are perfect."

"Hardly," he grumbled. Then stalked over to a vendor who displayed an array of baked goods, slapped down two bucks on the table, and stuffed a baguette into his overcrowded bag. He turned back to Bayli. "All good here?"

She smiled prettily. "Rob Reiner would approve."

"Fabulous."

They returned to the car. As they merged with slow-moving traffic, Rory said, "I read on your application that you've only been in the city a couple of months. And you're from River Cross, California."

"If you're wondering if I knew Christian back in the day, the answer is no."

"Well, we're both five years older than you. But also, he lived outside of town."

"He told me."

"Really?" Rory was taken by surprise. "That's something he rarely shares."

"It's not mentioned in features about him, I know. He didn't go to my schools. I never heard his name until he became famous and was linked to Bristol's. It's my favorite restaurant. Incredibly elegant, yet so comfortable. But you're well aware of that."

Rory said, "Our first restaurant. Christian's vision, my menu."

"And your money?"

He gave her a sideways glance. "Not all of it. Christian had an insurance check after his mom passed and he'd been saving up, investing the funds to gain a little more capital. He went to Columbia mostly on academic scholarships and three jobs he worked in between classes and studying. Made the rest of us look like slackers."

"He said he didn't come from money."

"Yeah, but the rest of us did." Rory let out a puff of air. "Funny how we all felt so privileged. Then Christian Davila appeared on campus, making a mockery of our GPAs, hitting the books harder than we did. . . . Hell, even in his worn jeans and sweatshirts he looked smarter than all of us combined. The man has a steel trap of a mind and anyone who might have doubted he'd succeed big-time in the world was just one more person for Christian to prove wrong."

Bayli fell silent. Rory knew exactly what she was thinking. For as diligent as Rory had been in building his reputation and the reputation of Davila's in every city in which they opened a restaurant and creating a more impressive menu than the last, he'd had a safety net all along. Christian never had.

That was one of the things that had always impressed Rory when it came to his friend. Christian had been balls to the wall from the start, truly leaving footprints worth following. He wasn't the type to let obstacles stand in his way. Not that Christian had skated through school or his first business ventures. Rory knew that firsthand. But his friend was a force with which to be reckoned. Always had been. Always would be. And Rory not only respected him for that, but he also admired Christian for the free yet determined spirit that he was.

Rory told Bayli, "Christian should have been born a Kennedy or a Bush, or something. He could change the world if he had the right last name and financial backing. He has the uncanny ability to see things in black and white—yet, Jesus Christ, he never misses the gray matter in between. I don't know anyone whose brain churns twenty-four-seven like this guy's. Well. Maybe yours does."

Bayli gave a small, pained chortle. "Sort of goes—or I should say *went*—with the territory. I spent many, many hours in hospital waiting rooms, and even more time studying medical terminology so that I had some semblance of an idea as to what the surgeons were trying to explain to me in their words, versus layman's terms, when my mother was ill. My first glassed-over-eyes experience when I was twelve—after my grandmother died and she wasn't there to field all the questions and information from the cardiothoracic staff—convinced me that I needed to truly understand what was happening with my mother's heart condition."

Rory didn't say anything until he pulled into his reserved spot in the underground parking garage of his complex. He went to the passenger's side to collect Bayli, taking her books and carrying their grocery bag.

But before he led her to the elevators, he asked, "What was happening with your mother's heart?"

Bayli blinked a couple of times—to keep tears from her eyes?

That just plain killed him.

But he tried to remain focused on the conversation at hand.

She said, "Mom was born with heart disease. It worsened over time. Having me was . . . hard on her. She shouldn't have done it. Shouldn't have gotten pregnant."

Rory's own heart wrenched. A world without the beautiful Bayli Styles . . .

Inconceivable.

Since Wednesday at his restaurant, Rory hadn't been able to imagine a brighter New York without this woman's smile to light it. Julia Roberts had nothing on her.

With unmistakable remorse in her tone, Bayli said, "I can't begin to fathom why it was so important to my mother to have a child if it meant she was cutting her own life short. But according to Grams, it meant everything to Mom. So she went for it—with her high school boyfriend. And it was all good for her, health-wise, in the beginning. A couple of years later . . . not so much." She used her hip to close the car door and sniffled. "I don't really want to say anything more about that, okay?"

Rory kissed her forehead. "Okay."

When they were in his apartment, Bayli perked up again, as he'd suspected she would. The foyer was a rounded sitting room with floor-to-ceiling bookshelves and equally tall windows featuring city and park views. Chairs and sofas with accent tables were scattered about.

"Look at all of this. . . ." Bayli circled the room with an expression of awe on her face, her fingertips lovingly grazing over spines of classic literature, some first-edition works, numerous biographies and memoirs. She met Rory at the entrance where she'd started and said, "Please tell me you actually read these books."

"That's sort of the point of owning them."

"Not just to impress bookworms such as myself?"

He set her own bundle on an end table. "I don't know women who'd go all soft on me just because I had a personal library."

"I'm not going all soft on you," she insisted.

"You're not?" His arms slipped around her waist. "Because you seem much less annoyed with me than the first time we met."

"Well, the *second* time we met you gave up on teaching me the merits of oca—which I'd never even heard of until today—and settled for carrots instead. So I figure we're even."

His head lowered to hers. "We're nowhere close to even."

NINE

Bayli's breath caught. She gazed into warm, seductive brown eyes that made her body blaze and her inner thighs flare with heat and desire.

It was bizarre that she reacted just as vehemently to Rory as she did to Christian. Both men enticed her; both men made her blood sing. Both left her with the unyielding need to be stripped bare and ravaged. Until she was limp and boneless and deliriously happy. No dismal thoughts consuming her mind. No doubts and misgivings holding her back.

She wanted to be left in a blissful, mind-numbing state. Christian had started her down that path the previous evening, giving her what she'd needed, what they'd both wanted.

Now she burned for Rory to do the same. To pick up where Christian had left off.

Against his lips, she asked, "Can the duck wait an hour or so?"

A sexy growl escaped him. Exciting her even more.

"Some question to ask a chef. If you were any other woman, I'd say no."

Bayli wound her arms around his neck. Pressed her body to his. Reveled in his flexed muscles and delicious scent. Her lips skimmed along his jaw as she whispered, "Show me I'm not just 'any other woman.' . . ."

"Bayli." The tote dropped to the floor and his arms snaked around her waist. Clasping her tight. But then he let out another growl, this one a bit on the frustrated side. He said, "Fuck." Released her. Grabbed the bag and stalked into the apartment.

She sighed. Tried to get her bearings. Eventually followed him in. The man was so close to blowing his top—she sensed it, felt it. But he was Mr. Perfect who was also Mr. Responsible, it seemed.

Rory shoved the bag into the fridge and then raked his hands through his messy hair. He turned back to Bayli, who watched him with curiosity and anticipation.

He read her well. Read her innate need for him. He sauntered toward her in a predatory way and lifted her up, forcing her to wrap her legs around his waist as her skirt hitched a couple inches.

Another sensual sound fell from his lips. "I imagined these long legs circling my hips the moment I got a glimpse of them."

"I really didn't think you'd noticed anything beyond salads scattered on the floor."

"You are impossible to overlook."

He carried her toward the living area, which stretched between the entryway/library and the vast open kitchen and dining combo. Tall windows showcased the park, but Bayli couldn't be bothered with admiring that particular view when she was staring at such a gorgeous man. And instantly fantasizing about all the things he might do to her now that he had her alone in his apartment.

He set her on her feet before the sofa and reached for a remote to flip on the gas fireplace and a little mood music.

"Mm, romantic," she murmured as her lips grazed his neck.

His head dropped and he kissed her with the same reckless abandon as when they'd been at the market. His arms wound around her and he crushed her to him, her breasts pressing below his hard pecs, her belly cradling his erection.

Her fingers curled into his rock-hard biceps and she let him control the searing kiss, his tongue doing crazy-wicked things to hers that made her pulse soar and her insides sizzle.

One of his hands shifted and slid down to her ass. He cupped a cheek and squeezed roughly, causing her to rub against the powerful thigh wedged between her parted legs. And sending bolts of excitement through her.

That wasn't enough for her and he seemed to know it—or perhaps it wasn't enough for him, either. He jerked the side of her skirt up farther and then went back to kneading her ass, now it being her bare skin under his fingers. Her clit continued to grind against his leg. Her soaked thong no doubt dampened the denim he wore.

His fingers slipped behind the strand of her thong, nestled in her cleft. He stroked the sensitive skin, his touch scorching hot and forbidden as he rimmed the small hole with the pad of his thumb while caressing her opening with a finger.

Her body tensed involuntarily at the not-so-subtle probing.

She broke the kiss. "Rory—"

"Shh." His mouth sealed hers again.

His long finger eased into her pussy from behind, and it felt incredibly good. A second one followed. He explored her wet depths and she opened to him. He pumped slowly but steadily within her and the tension began to mount, pulling taut.

He deepened their kiss. And Bayli knew she was about to lose it completely.

His thumb pressed in and she jumped in his tight embrace. He dragged his mouth from hers and she gasped for a breath.

"You're close . . . ," Rory said.

"*So* close." Her hands tightened around his arms.

"Don't fight it," he whispered against her temple. "Don't fight me."

She knew what he meant. That foreign, slightly burning sensation of her backside had her on high alert for what he might have planned for her. But as his fingers stroked and his warm lips skimmed over her cheek and across her lips, she couldn't deny the need swelling within her.

"I want to feel you fall apart for me," he said. "Then I want to taste your pussy."

A low whimper tumbled from her gaping mouth. A shudder ran through her.

He pumped harder and her head buzzed with lustful thoughts while her body flamed from his nearness, his ministrations, his words.

"Rory."

He kissed her again, so feverishly, so desperately, that everything building within her instantly collided and erupted. She tore her mouth from his and cried out as the orgasm blazed through her, setting every inch of her on fire.

"Oh, God," she moaned on a broken breath. "Oh, my God." Her body quaked. Her inner walls held fast to his fingers, squeezing tight as she savored every second of the climax, prolonging it as much as possible.

"Fuck," he muttered. "You make me so damn hot."

She was still recovering from the sizzle through her veins as he withdrew his fingers, unzipped her skirt, and shoved it down her legs. He had her out of her blouse just as quickly. Then he eased her down onto the sofa, where she sprawled out, her shoulders and head propped against a mound of pillows in the corner.

Rory's hungry gaze roved over her, leaving her with an insistent need to feel his hands and mouth on her.

He didn't waste any time, or give her more than a moment of wishful thinking. He knelt alongside the sofa and peeled her thong down her legs.

"Sexy as this is, it has to go." He tossed the scant material onto her pile of clothing. Then he reached around her to unclasp her bra and he whisked it off as well. "Jesus, you really are sensational."

"Stop admiring and start touching," she urged, her heart pounding, every fiber of her being yearning for him.

"*Tasting*," he reminded her. He whipped his tee over his head and discarded it, then spread her thighs and settled between them.

His head dipped and he inhaled her scent. Let out a guttural, primal sound that turned her on even more, flooding her body with heat.

Rory's tongue swept slowly over her slick folds, the intimate touch jarring her. Possibly because Christian's head had been between her legs the night before and it was an enticing thought to speculate over how different their techniques might be. But more than that, it was thrilling to know this man wanted to pleasure her this way—as Christian had. And that Rory wanted to sample her cream, revel in the very essence of her.

He licked languidly, making her squirm with anticipation. But she did nothing to hurry him along. Let him tug gently on her pussy lips with his mouth, let him tease her swollen clit with the tip of his tongue as it swirled and pressed, then fluttered.

Oh, Christ, the fluttering . . .

A long stream of air blew through her teeth.

This really was different from Christian. He'd been purposeful and determined. Aggressive. He'd eaten her pussy with fervor and the need to get her off. It had been fucking fantastic.

But this . . . Jesus. Rory was taking his time. Torturing her in the absolute sexiest way as his tongue circled the knot of nerves, then toyed with her dewy folds, then lapped over her opening, before tracing the flesh. Slightly penetrating, retreating, penetrating.

"Rory," she said on a sharp murmur. "You're driving me wild."

"Good." His hot breath on her moist flesh lit her up even more. He draped one of her legs over his shoulder, the crook behind her knee resting on his traps. "You taste like heaven. I'm just going to spend a little more time here, if you don't mind."

She nearly choked on a sob. "This could very well be the death of me."

"I think you can handle it." His lips grazed her lower ones as he spoke. Teasing her senseless.

"Don't be too sure." The scintillating sensations were boiling once again.

Rory's tongue swiped over her labia with more pressure this time. The tip flicked her clit—with more pressure this time. Then he suckled the little pearl, his teeth grazing, the suctioning pulling at the tiny bud.

"Shit," she ground out. "Rory, that's just . . . That's so . . . Oh, fuck." One of her hands threaded through his thick, lush hair. The other slid under her hip, spreading wide the leg not draped over his shoulder. "Do that again."

He repeated the sequence.

"Yes," she practically wailed as her body writhed and excitement ripped through her. "Again," she quietly demanded.

He didn't hesitate. Added a little to his repertoire at the end, licking her with fervor, his tongue really stroking with the intent to make her come again. His hand slipped under her thigh to tangle with hers just below her hip and he held on. Suckled all her tingly flesh and pushed her higher and higher.

As he returned to licking, two fingers from his free hand plunged into her and he stroked her quickly, the pace and the force sending her barreling toward another orgasm. One that would have her screaming his name, she had no doubt.

Her hand clasped his tighter beneath her leg. Rory worked a third finger into her. Twisted them just as he drew her clit against his teeth.

"Oh, Christ—Rory!" She did scream. And climaxed with such intensity, her body bowed off the cushion beneath her and her pussy clamped around his fingers, milking them, bringing her even more pleasure.

"Yes," he muttered, his mouth hovering over her. "Come for me. Come all over my fingers."

She could feel they were coated as they still slid along her inner walls. Pushing just a bit deeper to keep her free-falling into sexual bliss.

"Goddamn, you're tight. And so fucking responsive."

Christian had said the same thing. They apparently cataloged similar feminine traits with their women.

Rory released the hand he was holding and deftly unfastened his belt and jeans, jamming the material—along with his boxer briefs—down his hips. Then he withdrew his fingers from her and stroked his cock with her juices.

"Jesus, Rory," she said on a harsh breath as another blaze sparked between her legs. He fisted his cock and pumped while his gaze locked with hers. Bayli's chest heaved. She couldn't quite get a grip on herself but knew exactly what she wanted to do for him.

"Let me," she simply said. And slipped from the couch to kneel before him.

Her hand replaced his on his shaft and she held him firmly as her head lowered and her tongue slid over his hot, slick skin. She tasted herself, mixed with his distinct flavor . . . and the combination was a heady one.

Bayli's mouth closed around his tip and she slowly drew him in, his cock heavy against her tongue. His fingers plowed through her hair, which was already a tangled mess as the strands escaped the ponytail.

She took him as deep as she could while her fingers remained around his root. She sucked him hard and his body jolted.

"Fuck, yes," he murmured. "Like that."

She repeated the gesture, sucking with a bit more force.

Perhaps too much force, because he jerked her head up.

"Don't make me come. Not yet." He gently set her away from him and stood. He whisked off the rest of his clothes and pulled a condom from his wallet. "I need to be inside you when I come. *Really* deep inside you, honey."

His prominent features had turned to stone, need etching every chiseled-to-perfection inch of him.

Bayli was breathless, captivated. Dripping wet from the desire and raw intensity exuding from him. Hell, it practically rolled off him in waves. Exciting her to the point of fear. *The good kind of fear*, she mentally contended. The kind that told her she was in for something far beyond her comprehension.

Even Christian's mad skills in the bedroom had come with a certain level of understanding on his part that she was fragile in a sense, sexually. He'd known she hadn't been with anyone in a long while—and he'd learned a great deal about her emotional state before they'd become intimately involved.

Rory didn't know quite so much about her. And she wasn't inclined to explain it all. Because she wanted him feasting on her the way he did with his smoldering irises and she wanted him exuding that silent demand that she surrender to him . . . somehow knowing he would do the same.

She eased back onto the sofa. Spread her legs. "Fuck me." Her chest rose and fell rapidly again. She had no control over her pounding heart and erratic pulse. "I want to feel you hot and hard inside me, Rory. I want you to fuck me hard. Until you can't take it anymore. Until you *have* to come."

His jaw clenched.

She said, "I want to feel every inch of you, and I don't want you holding back the tiniest bit. Unleash all of your passion on me. You haven't been in a kitchen since this morning, right? That has to have you teeming with the need for some sort of release. Make *me* your release."

"Bayli—"

"Do it." She hadn't missed the warning in his tone. Nor did she care about it. "Do *me*."

He was sheathed moments later. His gaze continued to hold hers as he moved in close, spiking her adrenaline, keeping her juices flowing.

Her fingers grazed over his sculpted cheeks and set jaw. Down his thick, corded throat to his collarbone. Lower to his chest. One nail scraped his small, pebbled nipple. He smirked.

"Careful there, beauty queen. Payback can be a real bitch."

"Promise?"

He nipped at the corner of her mouth. "You didn't tease Christian like this, did you?"

"He's more the sort to be direct with, you know? Like . . . 'let's get down to brass tacks.'"

"Isn't that what *we're* doing?"

"Well, yes. I did tell you to fuck me."

He gently bit her jaw, her neck. "Say it again."

"Seriously?" she asked, breathy and wiggling beneath him. Her hand skated down his heavily muscled back to his bare ass. "Are you worried I might change my mind once you're inside me?"

"I don't make love," he told her as he stared into her eyes. "Just so you know."

Everything inside her went haywire. "Rory. The way you just—"

"I don't," he insisted. Not even wanting to hear that the way he'd just set her off had been all about his extreme attention to detail. Using every single one of her whimpers, moans, and sighs as it had escaped her parted lips as a guide.

But . . . okay. She'd play along.

"Say it," he commanded.

Her gaze didn't waver. "Fuck me. Like you really and truly can't get enough of me."

His strong forearm hooked under her leg, at the bend in her knee, and he lifted it, widening her for his entry. The head of his cock nudged her opening. His eyes didn't leave hers. There were questions and answers not necessarily correlating with each other in his dark gaze. She had no delusions she was in over her head. Maybe he felt the same way.

All she knew at the moment was that she needed him inside her, wanted him to take everything *he* needed from her.

His lips swept over hers and he said, "You really do bring out the animal in me."

He thrust into her.

So very fucking deep into her.

Bayli cried out. Not from pain—from sheer and utter ecstasy.

He recognized the difference. And instantly retreated and plunged with the sort of diligence that pushed the air from her lungs and had her hips lifting off the sofa to meet every assertive thrust.

His mouth was on her throat and he bit her with each stroke, sending shock waves through her. The sensual assault was frenetic and electrifying.

Rory slipped a hand under her ass and tilted her hips, giving him a better angle, better leverage to drive into her. Bayli clutched at him. With her fingernails digging into his shoulders, with her pussy contracting around his cock.

Jesus, he was thick and wide . . . and filled her so beautifully.

His hips bucked and he jarred her with his fervent movements— she loved every second of it.

"You feel so damn good," he told her. "So fucking good."

Bayli couldn't get a word out. Couldn't speak around the *oh, hell, yes, please keep doing this to me!* lodged in her throat.

He was hammering into her, the head of his cock hitting that precious spot that made unfamiliar and untamed sounds lurch from low in her throat. Made her mind swim in a sea of erotic thoughts. Made her body quiver and her insides home in on every sensation that expanded and coalesced and then once again erupted.

"Rory!" she called out. "*Oh!* Oh, God!"

"Bayli," he grunted. "Honey . . . not so tight. Don't squeeze me so damn . . . Ah, hell!" He pumped into her. "Not so fucking tight . . ."

But she knew it was too late. *He* knew it was too late.

She couldn't stop. Neither could he.

His hips continued to surge; his cock swelled. She felt the throbbing within her, even as she succumbed to her own orgasm. And sensed another building behind it.

Rory's hand on her ass clasped her cheek tightly, kept her

angled just right. His mouth was on her neck, tugging at the skin with his teeth, soothing the bites with his tongue.

"Shit . . . ," he said on a rough sigh. Then, "Oh, hell, yes."

He gave a final thrust. His body convulsed, his cock exploded deep within her.

"Oh, God, Rory!" She came again on a rush of heat and a wave of euphoria. "Oh, fuck."

She held him to her as they both lost themselves in the heat of the moment, in the electrifying release.

Bayli had absolutely no desire to move. To return to reality. To face the fact that she was drowning in a sexual abyss created by two unbelievably sensual, talented men . . . and she didn't want anything or anyone to encroach on the most incredible fantasy/fairy tale any woman could ever wish for. . . .

TEN

"I'm crushing you," was the first thing out of Rory's mouth when he eventually came around. How long that took him he had no fucking clue.

"I'm okay," Bayli said in a soft, languorous tone. "No need to move just yet."

"This can't be comfortable."

"It's fantastic," she assured him. "You on top of me, inside me, breathing quite heavily on my neck. All amazingly fantastic."

He chuckled, low and just as lazy as her voice was. "Well, you did pretty much blow my mind."

"Impossible."

"Says you." He shifted slightly and she groaned in protest. "Just trying to alleviate some of the weight on you."

"I did just say that it's fantastic, right? Are you hard of hearing?"

"No, I am not hard of hearing. Smart-ass." His lips skimmed the long column of her neck down to her collarbone. She shivered from the touch. So he continued on. His tongue swept over the top of one breast. Then his head dipped so that he could curl his tongue around her puckered nipple. Her perfectly pink puckered nipple, to be exact.

She writhed beneath him. Sighed contentedly.

"That'll lead to all kinds of crazy things happening between us again," she said.

"I didn't think you'd complain."

"I'm clearly *not* complaining." Her leg was draped over his lower back. Her fingers were tangled in his hair. Well, one hand, anyway. The other gripped his ass cheek. It'd been there for some time. She'd pressed him into her as he'd fucked her, telling him in no uncertain terms that she wanted more and more of what he had to offer. Without even saying a word.

He suckled her nipple and she moaned. A sound he loved hearing.

Rory murmured, "I could completely lose myself in this body of yours." He kissed the underside of her breast, then down her rib cage to her belly. She had to let go of his ass, but it was a price he was willing to pay. Because he was headed south again to that incredibly delectable spot between her legs where—

"Hey," she said as his cock started to pull out of her to accommodate the new position. "Where are you going? You were getting hard again."

He gave her a self-assured grin. "I'll get there even faster while I'm licking your pussy."

"Oooh," she said on a long breath. And smiled.

Rory sat back just long enough to whip off the condom and set it on top of the wrapper. Then found one more in his wallet, thank God.

The mere thought of pleasuring her again with his mouth had his cock stiffening. But it was more the prospect of being buried to the hilt in her tight, wet pussy that really turned him on.

"Shit." He marveled as he stared at the bounty before him. "You honestly do have the most tempting pink parts. Small, glistening, looking as though they really, really need my mouth on them."

She combed a hand through his hair once more. "All well and good . . . stud muffin. . . ."

He chuckled at her joke.

"But I'd rather have you inside me."

"You're just sassy enough for me to oblige." He shifted slightly. Slid into her heat and moisture. Let out a low groan of pleasure.

"Such a nice spot . . . ," she mused.

"You like it like this?"

"Just like this."

Their hips rocked together. But Rory wanted, needed, more.

His hand swept around to her backside and his index finger rimmed her anus. She jerked against him.

"Not there," she murmured.

"Yes, here," he quietly insisted. "You're wet enough that I can lube up my finger and ease it inside."

"No. . . ." Her eyes widened.

"Yes." He nipped at her bottom lip, then kissed her passionately until she was melting beneath him and he knew she'd give him whatever he wanted. Breaking their kiss, he told her, "I'm going to fuck this tight, gorgeous ass of yours."

The thought sent violent tremors through his body. He thrust vigorously into her until she was panting and he was heaving.

But she fought the lure—fought him. Her palms pressed to his chest.

"No, Rory. That's not something I can do."

"I'll teach you. We'll take it slow and easy." Though that was hardly what he was doing at the moment as he drove into her slick pussy.

"Rory, I'm not kidding. . . ."

He heard the panic in her voice. That was definitely a warning to be heeded.

He shifted slightly and they both lost their balance on the edge of the sofa. Bayli's body twisted in some sort of auto-correct move, and the next thing he knew Rory was flat on his back on the hardwood floor and she was lying on top of him.

"Whoa, holy hell," she said on a dazed breath.

"Yeah. Holy hell, indeed." It wasn't a bad position to be in by any stretch of the imagination. His hands gripped her hips and he pressed her down against his pelvis as his butt clenched and he thrust up into her.

"Wait." The panic returned. Her hands splayed across his pecs. Her messy hair fell over one bare shoulder and she stared down at him with a hint of uncertainty in her eyes.

"Why? I'm not doing anything you said you didn't want me to do." She was straddling his hips and his dick was deep inside her. All he had to do was coax her into a slow and steady rhythm that would morph into a wild and wicked one and they'd both be coming again.

But Bayli's fingertips curled into his skin, the nails digging in. "This isn't something . . ." She shook her head. "This isn't . . ." She swore under her breath. "I'm not exactly sure what to do. . . ."

Rory sat up suddenly and that startled her all the more.

"Whoa!" she called out again. Gasped as his arms wrapped around her waist. "Rory!"

"What?"

Her gaze locked with his. "Jesus Christ. You're . . . huge to begin with. So much bigger this way."

His eyes narrowed on her. "Bayli. Honey. You've never done it like this before?"

She stared at him, her mouth working as though she had something to say but couldn't quite get the words to form.

"Bayli . . ." His arms tightened around her. "You've never been on top?"

"I—" She swallowed hard.

"Son of a bitch," he whispered. Something incredibly unsettling was clicking into place. "Bayli, you weren't a virgin before Christian, were you?"

This seemed to bring her around. A little too quickly and a little too volatilely—like a splash of cold water to the face.

The heels of her hands slammed against Rory's shoulders to push him back and make him release her as she climbed off him and stood. She snatched up her thong and agitatedly jerked it on before reaching for her bra.

"Bayli—"

"I was *not* a virgin before Christian," she angrily told Rory. She yanked her skirt up her long legs. "You really think that? Just because I don't know every sexual position under the sun and have never had a dick in my ass, I'm some sort of country bump—" She shook her head. Pulled on her blouse and buttoned it while Rory got to his feet.

His brain lacked sufficient blood, admittedly, but he knew he'd struck a sour chord. He just wasn't sure how he'd done it.

"Look, honey—"

"Christian told you, didn't he?" she demanded as she searched for her small purse. "He told you all about my shitty-ass apartment and how I lied about where I lived so that he wouldn't have to see it. How I was almost stranded out in the country because I don't have a limo or a driver or any other fucking person to pick me up. He told you about the library, and probably about my job in Central Park, and how I'm broke and was so, so desperate for the hostess job at your restaurant."

She stalked from the room, heading into the foyer.

"Hey!" he called after her. But he had to make a quick pit stop to rid himself of the condom and then grab his jeans. She was already out the door.

"Bayli, for fuck's sake!" he yelled. And raced after her.

She was in the elevator when he threw open his apartment doors. "What the hell?" he all but roared. "What the fuck did I say . . . *do*?"

There were tears in her eyes. "I am just some naïve idiot trying to start a life too late in the game. And all this time . . . you really were just humoring me."

He stalked toward her. "I didn't call you after the interview, and I know that upset you. But you're wrong about the reasons."

"I can't be an inside joke between the two of you." She jammed her finger onto the button that made the elevator doors *whoosh* closed. Before he could lurch forward and stop them—stop her from leaving him.

His hands fisted at his sides.

"Son of a bitch!"

Bayli rushed from the elevator and out the revolving door at the entrance of Rory's apartment building. A uniformed man with a cap and white gloves smiled politely and asked, "May I get you a taxi, miss?"

"Yes, please. Quickly." She feared Rory was just two steps behind her. She continued to glance over her shoulder as the doorman used his whistle to hail a passing cab. Bayli fished a couple of bucks from her purse and handed the cash over. Then slid into the backseat, gave an address, and buried her face in her hands.

What. The. Hell?

Jesus, Bay. Just . . . Jesus!

She'd freaked.

About what?

A finger in her ass?

Possibly a cock?

Urg!

Like it was *such* a big deal!

Rory had been into the moment. *She'd* been into the moment. His comment about *fucking her tight, gorgeous ass* hadn't turned her off—it'd sent a wave of heat through her. Had jolted her in a *good* way. But the reality of the situation . . .

He didn't do it, *Bay.*

Yeah. There was that. He'd seemed perfectly content to get it on with her again while she was on top. Had said he wasn't doing anything she'd asked him not to do.

And he'd been right.

It was just that the whole scenario had thrown her. And then when he'd sat up and she could feel every single, solid inch of him filling her . . .

Good Lord.

It'd felt spectacular. He'd felt spectacular. And she'd thrilled over how big and wide and so scorching hot he was inside her.

But it'd been too late. She'd already been jilted off course and instantly felt like she had no idea what the hell she was doing and, really, that had just sent her into a mental tailspin.

For him to think she'd been a virgin before Christian . . .

Well, didn't that just scream hick from the sticks? Small-town girl in the big city who had no fucking clue whatsoever about what awaited her around every corner—no fucking clue as to how *real* men wanted to be satisfied.

Rory wanted to fuck her ass.

Well, gee, Bay. What had you expected? Polite, civil sex from a man who actually yells *at people for a living?*

She lifted her head. Rolled her eyes at her own idiocy.

Yanked out more money from her purse to pay the fare, since Phillip and Colin's loft wasn't far from Rory's neighborhood and they'd just arrived.

She paid and then carted her books up the short steps that led to a double door. She pressed the buzzer and waited for one of the guys to let her in. They were expecting her, since she'd forgotten to cancel. Because she'd been too swept away by Rory St. James taking her to the farmers' market, wanting to cook dinner with her, kissing her, fucking her . . .

Unfortunately, she was early, but Bayli didn't intend to stay long. Just make apologies for bowing out in person. Well, and get one big, fat hug from Colin. She desperately needed it.

When the lock sprang free, she entered the large foyer and headed to the door straight ahead, one of five in the conglomeration. She rang that buzzer as well and announced herself. Another lock released. Bayli deposited her stack on a chair in the entryway and climbed the polished wooden stairs with a stylish runner down the middle and crested the landing.

Phillip greeted her with a friendly smile and a glass of wine.

"I'm so sorry to be stopping by early," she immediately said. And accepted the wine. She sipped, then hurriedly told him, "I don't mean to interrupt all your prepping for your dinner party. I just . . . I just . . ."

Oh, crap.

Emotion welled within her. Tears burned the backs of her eyes.

"Bayli, what—"

"Who's here, darling?" Colin in his extreme loveliness—mocha skin, neatly trimmed hair, manicured nails, and impeccable attire of pressed dark-blue slacks and ecru-colored sweater—came from the kitchen. He drew up short at the sight of Bayli and clapped his hands together. In a British accent thicker than Phillip's, because he'd been born in London, he said, "Perfect! It's the angel heaven is missing!"

He squeezed her tight and she laughed as she tried to blink away the tears.

It was a joke amongst the three of them. They'd been at a bar together when some NYU dolt had used the line on her. Phillip and Colin had gaped at the trite pickup attempt. Then Colin had shooed away the student with a dismissive wave of his hand and a sharp *tsk*ing sound that had probably left College Joe rethinking his level of cleverness and originality.

Colin did the European double-cheek air-kiss thing with Bayli, then said, "This is excellent timing on your part, young lady." Colin was only a year older than her. "You can entertain Phillip while I finish the Kiev and put it in the oven. Otherwise, he'll stand over my shoulder and question whether I have the right temperature and the right timer setting."

"Careful," Phillip drolly warned, "or I'll make sure Bayli and

I *both* stand over your shoulder and question whether you have the right temperature and the right timer setting."

"Oh, *pshaw*." Colin did his trademark hand wave. "I know perfectly well what I'm doing in the kitchen, so stay the hell out."

"Gladly. I'll just be sure to keep the fire extinguisher easily accessible."

"We never replaced it after the last fire."

Bayli nearly spewed her sip of wine. "The last—"

"Oh, we most certainly did," Phillip assured him. "But then you left a candle burning in the guest bathroom too close to a hanging hand towel."

"Oh, right." Colin sighed. "That."

"What's the deal, Colin?" Bayli tentatively asked, jesting without being snarky.

He shrugged a delicate shoulder. "I like flames?"

"They *are* pretty," she conceded. Then finally snickered, her consternation over yet another Rory St. James debacle ebbing now that she was in the joyful presence of these two men.

Colin mockingly grumbled, "Anyhoo, back to the kitchen I go."

"Hey, wait," she said as she caught his arm with her free hand. "I'm not staying. I should have called earlier, but I got sidetracked."

By a really, really hot chef and even hotter sex.

You had to go there?

No, she did not need the memory taking up permanent residence in her brain. But it was likely inevitable.

"What do you mean you're not staying?" Phillip asked. "I very efficiently talked you into coming to dinner when we were at the library this afternoon."

"Yes, you did. But then something else came up and, well . . . I need a little breather at the moment. I did something incredibly stupid from the time I left the library until now." And that incredibly stupid thing wasn't begging Rory to fuck her. It was everything that had happened *after* the ass reference.

"Come sit down," Colin instructed as he led her to a sofa in their fabulously adult loft. Everyone she knew had a *fabulously adult* loft or apartment. And they all had a mortgage and a cleaning service. Didn't even need an exterminator, she surmised.

All except for Bayli.

With a shake of her head so she didn't get mired in that mental drudgery, she told the guys, "I'm not inviting you to my pity party. Suffice it to say that this past week I have repeatedly been slapped in the face by the glaring reality that I am just now getting started in life while everyone else my age is already immersed in theirs. It makes me feel foolish—and apparently, it makes me act foolishly."

"Bay." Phillip directed her to sit, despite her words. "Love, we know about your past and your mother. Since you were a kid you were caring for someone else. When, exactly, were you supposed to start this life of yours?"

This choked her up, but she tried to keep herself in check.

"You had two good years," Colin chimed in as he sat on the other side of her. "Your freshman and sophomore terms at San Francisco State. Smart enough to get scholarships and you also worked."

"And shared an apartment with two dear friends who refused to let me pay my full share of rent and utilities," she pointed out. "I had plenty of help along the way."

"But you also had to give up college when your mother's health took another bad turn."

"I couldn't afford twenty-four-seven live-in care for her," Bayli agreed. "I had to be that live-in care."

"So there you go. . . ." This from Phillip in his matter-of-fact tone. "You made every attempt when you had the chance to better your situation, to 'start your life.' Unfortunately, there were dire circumstances keeping you from progressing further."

"Until now." Colin gingerly patted her knee. "You have your own place, angel. You have two adoring friends . . . probably others, but I'm sure they're nowhere near as brilliant and wonderful as Phillip and me."

She let out a soft laugh as a tear crested her eye.

Colin added, "And for fuck's sake, you clearly have a man in your life you have *yet* to tell us about."

Her head snapped up and she stared at him. "How the hell do you know that?"

Phillip snorted beside her. Colin rolled his light-brown eyes. "The love bites, angel. The love bites."

"The *what*?"

She jumped up and crossed to a mirror hanging over a beautifully decorated table. And gaped. One side of her neck was black-and-blue. Hickeys scattered from her jaw to her collarbone.

Her stomach flipped excitedly when it should have roiled from the markings. The *branding*.

"Oh, shit." She turned back to her friends.

They both flashed Cheshire cat grins.

"Spill, already," Colin sweetly demanded.

"I—" She shook her head. "I—"

"Phillip, be a dear and get this lovely lady who obviously got laid earlier this evening another glass of wine."

Bayli knew better than to protest. A half hour later the three were in the kitchen while the chicken rested and Colin fussed over the side dishes. Bayli continued to provide every juicy detail. Talk about singing for her supper . . .

She decided to stay for dinner after all, since Colin had planned on her being there and Phillip insisted she stick around to meet their Oxford pals. That turned into a lively affair that had her less agitated about her encounter with Rory, though Colin could be counted on to throw out a few zingers here and there to bring to mind exactly what Rory had done to her—and exactly what he wanted to do to her. Which wove an enchanting spell on her that both thrilled and worried her.

Granted, the percentage of worry diminished greatly as the party raged on. So that by the end of the evening she was wondering yet again why she'd made such a big deal out of anal sex and why the hell she'd let her vulnerabilities get the best of her.

Of course, that very well could have been the wine clouding her judgement. Phillip and Colin had to practically pour her into a cab. They'd wanted her to stay overnight for safekeeping, but she'd assured them she'd be fine. And she was.

Would continue to be.

If she could just get her feet steadily beneath her and figure out what the hell she really wanted with, or from, the sexy restaurateur and the angsty chef . . .

ELEVEN

Christian had paperwork sprawled before him at a table in the dining room of Davila's NYC on Monday afternoon when Lily Madison swept in, dressed to the nines as was her custom and cloaked in her signature Chanel No. 5 scent.

"Special delivery," she announced with the grand gesture of handing over a sealed nine-by-thirteen-inch envelope. "You said you wanted it immediately."

"Yes, thank you." He took the thick packet from his assistant, an attractive blonde with siren-red nails and a flair for the dramatic. A woman he'd engaged in recreational sex with, though Lily tended to substitute "monogamous" for "recreational" when it came to him. Regardless of Christian having never led her to believe they were an exclusive item.

She'd come on to him at a Christmas party three years ago in their Miami office. The orgasms had been great and he'd enjoyed the extra attention to detail she'd exhibited thereafter with corporate affairs, while she'd liked all the perks that came with sleeping with the boss, including traveling by private jet when he needed her and being put up in five-star hotels with a hefty expense account. Her bonuses typically had an extra zero tacked on to them as well.

She slid gracefully into the seat across from him, her pale-green eyes flitting over the documents he'd been studying when she'd sauntered in. "What's all this?" she asked. "I don't recall making copies of any of it for you."

"No, I printed everything at home from my computer," he said, slightly distracted now that he had the contract from Bayli's agency in hand. The packet Lily had brought with her had arrived at his office quicker than he'd anticipated. Then again, the terms he'd negotiated for Bayli's services were astoundingly in favor of the model, so it wasn't a tremendous surprise her legal representation had jumped on the formalities to ensure the deal was sealed before anything went awry that might make the verbal agreement implode.

Lily gave him a brief run-down of office happenings, but there was nothing pressing to contend with at the moment, aside from this cooking-show idea that was burning a hole in his brain. He wanted to get things under way. No, it wasn't the be-all-end-all concept, but that didn't actually matter this time around, and he suspected the premise would evolve into something even greater along the way. Perhaps incorporating a competition among local chefs. Currently, it was the gregarious personality who would appear before audiences that was driving him to get the ball rolling.

Bayli was going to be an overnight sensation. He could feel it in his bones. And Christian had the very powerful desire and prodigious opportunity to be the one to deliver her to the masses.

He wanted his and Rory's business venture to soar, sure. But a more potent aspiration had become introducing Bayli Styles to the world—launching her career and seeing just how far she'd go.

Across from him, Lily leaned forward and whisked her slender fingers over his hand. She smiled seductively and said, "We haven't seen much of each other lately. You've been a very busy boy." Her crimson lips dipped in a perfectly practiced and executed pout. "I hate it when you get all tangled up in double-booked scheduling and back-to-back travel. In fact . . ." Her fingertip caressed his skin. "I was expecting you at my apartment on Saturday night. After the fund-raiser."

"We didn't have a date, did we?" He did a mental rewind. Was positive he hadn't mentioned anything to her about stopping by, because he typically didn't pencil her into his calendar. As a rule, they got together when they were both at the right place, at the right/same time. Nothing premeditated. At least, not on his part.

"No," she said, "but since you were in the city and the gala wasn't a business event, per se, I figured you'd be in the mood for—"

"Damn, I'm sorry, Lil. There actually was business to take care of." Specifically, finding out more about Bayli from Jackson Rutherford. And yes, Christian had been in the mood. For Bayli. But that wasn't anything he needed to share with his assistant and occasional lover.

Former occasional lover.

Because his interests had definitely shifted elsewhere.

But Lily was still a trusted and valued employee. So he had to play this hand carefully. Christian wasn't into leaving scorned hearts in his wake. Did it happen? Of course. But he put significant effort into severing romantic ties while keeping professional or friendly ones intact.

Lily might be a more complex situation to manage than usual, though. Christian would typically ease into the "breakup" scenario, not just drop the axe, even when it wasn't actually a breakup since there'd never been the insinuation of a relationship on his part. He wasn't good with relationships that didn't involve Rory. And those never had a long-running shelf life because it was difficult to find a woman who could hold both their attention for any serious duration.

With Lily, Christian had made the mistake of dipping his quill in the company ink. He didn't want to lose her as an assistant. She'd been with him for nearly six years. Knew all the ins and outs of his and Rory's enterprise, knew all of Christian's professional and personal preferences, right down to ensuring that when he was on the road, a fresh pot of gourmet coffee and a continental breakfast arrived on his hotel room doorstep at precisely 6:45 without a single knock on the door.

She was an asset. Just not girlfriend material. Not for him.

Christian didn't know if Lily understood that or not—they'd never had a heart-to-heart. She'd followed his lead, and while she'd dropped hints that she thought she was the only one he was sleeping with, he'd never confirmed that as fact. Had never really thought he'd had to because, in all honesty, they spent such little time together outside of the office that it seemed a bit inconceivable for her to think they were more than convenient sexual companions.

But that really was neither here nor there at the moment. He was ready to move forward with his plans now that he had a contract to take one more look at before it went to Bayli for her signature.

Lily asked in a provocative voice, "Is there anything else I can do for you, boss?"

He recognized the suggestive tone for what it was. Gently said, "Thanks, but no. I need to wrap all of this up." He indicated the files spread before him.

"You're usually not so secretive."

He didn't miss her disappointment that he wasn't relying on her for all of the administrative detail related to this new quest. Christian told her, "I'm still working through all the nuances. Why don't you go back to the office? I'm keeping you from your other responsibilities. If something crops up, I'll give you a call. Otherwise, expect me back in the office tomorrow."

She stared at him a few moments, likely trying to read his thoughts. Then shrugged and said, "Okay. Just give a holler."

Lily put extra sway in her hips as she sashayed out. Christian chuckled under his breath. She wasn't exactly the type to give up. Nor was she the type to be denied. By most men. But Christian had another woman on his mind.

He unclasped the envelope Lily had delivered just as Rory sank into the chair she'd vacated.

"We have a small problem," Rory announced. "And by *small*, I mean huge."

Eyeing him over the top of the package, Christian asked, "What the fuck happened with Bayli yesterday?"

"Funny how you just immediately knew that I screwed everything up."

"Well, it does seem to be the pattern between the two of you." Christian let out a long hiss of breath as he set aside the contract. "And that's really the only facet of your life involving me that I don't have some control over, so . . . Easy deduction, Watson."

"Wait." Rory stood, flipped his chair around, and straddled it. "Why do you get to be Sherlock?"

"Because I'm smarter than you."

"Well, we all fucking know that," he scoffed. "Though not by much. I graduated with . . . some . . . honors."

"I graduated with *all* honors. And who the hell cares?" He speared his friend with a hard look. "What did you *do*?"

"I'm not exactly sure," Rory confessed. "I mean, you and I agreed I needed to spend more time with Bayli in order to find a groove that'll work for the show. So I surprised her at the library— that was a bit of a disaster, not that anyone is shocked by this. Then we went to the farmers' market and things were going well. *Really* well."

Christian's gaze narrowed. "How well?"

"I kissed her."

"You . . . what?" His mind reeled.

"Kissed her."

"In front of . . . ?"

"Everyone."

"Oh, goddamn it." Christian whipped out his iPhone and searched for *Rory St. James* on Google, and lo and behold, there was a video already posted on YouTube of his friend and . . . Bayli.

Christian tossed the phone on the table and it skidded to a halt before Rory. "Nice going. She's supposed to be our secret weapon.

You know, we spring her on the unsuspecting world and take everyone's fucking breath away?"

Rory didn't even bother glancing at the screen. "What can I say? She took mine away. I couldn't help myself. And who are you to talk? You nailed her Saturday night."

"I did not *nail* her," he insisted. Then shook his head. "Jesus. Yes. I nailed her. She was just so vulnerable and sexy and willing . . . *so* willing."

His groin tightened. He said, "Damn, I wanted her. From the moment I saw her. And, granted, it took a little while for her to warm up to me because she was interested in the job you aren't going to give her and she had some other things going on, but once we cut through all that minutiae, it was downright electrifying."

"Yeah." Rory clenched his fist and rapped his knuckles on the table. "I can identify with the electrifying part. Problem is, we never actually cut through any minutiae. We somehow created all that *after* we'd had sex. And then she just . . . left. *Stormed out* is more like it, but what's the difference, right? She couldn't get out of my apartment fast enough."

Christian's gut clenched. Was that the reason the Polenski Agency had been so amenable with his legal team, so that they could hash out terms this quickly and have contracts drawn up this afternoon? Had Bayli said something to her agent, mentioned the possibility of pulling out of the show because of whatever altercation had happened with Rory yesterday, and so her agent had jumped on the negotiations to execute the deal before Bayli backed out?

"Oh, goddamn." He yelled out, "Pierre! Scotch on the rocks, please!"

"*Oui, monsieur,*" came the curt reply.

Pinning Rory with yet another unyielding look, Christian said in a measured tone, "Please tell me you did *not* run her off on purpose."

Rory glared. Then very bluntly said, "*You* fucked her. Tell me you didn't completely lose your mind over her. She's unbelievable,

Christian. More than beautiful. More than sexy. More than charming. There is something about that woman that grabs you by the balls and doesn't let go. But here's the problem—"

"No, Rory," he interjected. "There *was* no problem. Not when I left her Sunday morning. Not after I met with you Sunday afternoon. There was no problem!"

"Would you calm down for two seconds?"

Pierre delivered the entire decanter of scotch, two glasses, and a small ice bucket. He served both men before discreetly wandering off to do whatever else it was that needed to be done before dinner service.

Rory said, "Bayli and I were getting along great. Enough so that I kissed her in public—you've seen the video. I was completely and totally into her, and I was convinced she was feeling the same way. We went back to my place to make dinner but got all tangled up with each other instead, and it was worth every diverted moment."

"So why the hell did she walk out on you?"

"Because I don't know who she is!" Rory exploded. "Because Bayli Styles is some gorgeous femme fatale one moment and some fragile flower the next—who isn't even really a fragile flower. Oh, no! She's got some serious wind in her sails and she isn't afraid to unleash the tempest."

Christian sat back in his seat. Sipped his drink. Felt infinitely calmer. Even grinned. "You fucking idiot."

Rory glared again. "As if you're telling me something new."

Christian sighed. "I had a feeling when I watched her act out cigar hostess at the gala that there was something special about her—something that would intrigue both of us. When I slept with her, that feeling only intensified. But, Rory, she's not a full-on femme fatale. And you're right; she's no fragile flower. She's got some issues, a past. Not pleasant stuff. And being thrown into *our* mix? Can you even doubt for a second that it would make someone from very humble beginnings and a shitload of hardships falter?"

Rory's jaw tightened. "Hardships." He shoved away from the

chair and paced. "We talked a little about her mom. I know her cross streets because you gave the info to Denny while I was making breakfast. But goddamn it, Christian, what went haywire with Bayli and me yesterday wasn't about her financial situation or where she came from."

"Then what was it about, Rory?"

He stopped pacing. Planted his hands on his waist and said, "It was about how intense the sex got between us, the fact that my back and my ass look like I went a round with a lion defending her cubs—and she might as well have been a vampire snack, in turn. Her neck . . ." He let out a harsh breath. "I bit the hell out of it. I couldn't help myself. Didn't even really know I was doing it. And all I wanted was *more.* I knew she did, too. But the more I offered . . . the more I mentioned what I wanted . . . the more she tried to digest it all or whatever . . . It was too much for her. She bolted."

"Interesting." Christian stood as well. He drained his glass and poured another. Then restlessly prowled the space between their table and the fireplace.

"I knew exactly what I wanted from her," Rory told him. "But, truthfully, I didn't care if I got *exactly what I wanted from her.* I just *wanted* her."

"She's different from our other women," Christian said.

"She's not *our* woman, Christian. She's attracted to both of us and we're both attracted to her. Always, *always,* though, we know what we're looking to get out of the situation and so does the woman we hook up with. Everything about Bayli is a total one-eighty for us. A complete crapshoot. Does she even know what we're looking for? Did you give her any clue? And for that matter . . . is she a woman we just separately have? Or is she a woman we could jointly have?"

"Rory, slow down, man. You're upset about the two of you hitting a glitch. Don't stress so much. No, I haven't alluded to anything with her. But she didn't have any reservations letting me know there was chemistry between the two of you."

Rory shoved a hand through his hair. "We were open about

the fact that I knew she'd slept with you Saturday night. Neither of us was fazed."

"And none of us are hiding anything." Christian had always contended that Rory was the one to have the initial strong responses to the women they might want to share. In this instance, Christian had been the one to make that very first connection. But he seriously doubted that Bayli would have had sex with Rory just for the sake of having sex. Especially after sleeping with Christian the night before. There had to be a deeper meaning to it all.

He fully believed she was into both of them. And it was mutual on their end. So now they just needed to find some common ground. The show offered a perfect platform for that.

He told Rory, "Let me talk to her. See what's really up. We both could have come on a bit too strong."

"She thinks she's some sort of inside joke between us. That she's naïve and we're viewing her as a small-town girl."

"What *exactly* did you say to her?"

"I might have asked her if she was a virgin before you. . . ."

Christian's lids squeezed tight. Then flew open. He polished off his second drink, snatched up the envelope Lily had delivered, and thrust it in Rory's face. "You are the one who knows when we've found a woman we'll both enjoy. And you never, *ever* fuck it up. So the fact that this one has you so turned around speaks volumes."

"Yeah. I know."

Christian whirled around and stalked toward the entryway, calling out, "I'm moving our dinner with Bayli to Thursday. Ought to give you enough time to get your bearings, lover boy." He pushed open the door and stepped into the late-summer sunlight, already plotting his next move with Bayli Styles.

"What flavors do you have?"

Bayli stared at the girl before her, all blond and perky and staring at the large chalkboard propped on an easel that declared in bold font the day's gelato selections.

But this was nothing new for Bayli, so she politely read, "'Mango, pineapple, chocolate-vanilla swirl, and tiramisu.'"

"Hmm." The girl's lips pressed together. "And that's all?"

"That's all."

There was a line forming behind the girl dragging her feet to commit to a flavor. Luckily, Ken Brooks was there to relieve Bayli at the end of her shift, so he jumped in to start helping the others. The blonde still couldn't make up her mind.

"Would you like to try some samples?" Bayli offered.

"No. I'm just . . . not really sure I'm going to like gelato. It's not really ice cream, right?"

"It's Italian ice cream." Bayli started to explain the difference, but then someone called out the girl's name and her attention span disintegrated into a vapor trail and she wandered off while Bayli was in mid-sentence.

She stared at the blonde's retreating back and then shrugged. It wasn't the craziest thing to happen to Bayli while serving gelato in Central Park.

She turned to the back portion of the makeshift "shoppe" that was fully transportable and came equipped with a vibrantly colored umbrella, removed her apron, folded it, and stuffed it into a cubbyhole before grabbing her purse and slipping the strap across her body.

"Perfect timing," came a deep, familiar voice from behind her. "Looks like you're done for the day."

Bayli's nipples instantly puckered beneath her bra and the lime-green T-shirt that was pulled tight and knotted at her lower back, exposing a bit of skin between the hem and the waist of her faded low-rise jeans. Her hair was piled on top of her head in a messy updo that left long, wavy strands cascading along her temples.

She slid on her gold-rimmed aviator sunglasses and turned to face Christian. Instantly losing her breath at the sight of him, wearing black suit pants and a crisp white shirt, the sleeves rolled up to reveal his strong, sinewy forearms. He'd obviously left his cuff links, tie, and jacket in his car. His limo?

With a shake of her head, she tried not to fixate on the class difference between them. She'd gone off on Rory because he'd made her feel inferior, and she regretted it today. She knew that hadn't been his intention. And Bayli usually wasn't so sensitive. In fact, she was normally quite comfortable in her own skin. What Phillip and Colin had reiterated last night was the absolute truth: Bayli had done whatever was necessary to survive when growing up and taking care of her mother. She was proud of that.

The reason she'd been so off-kilter following her explosive encounter with Rory, however, had more to do with being thrust into both his and Christian's world without having a solid understanding of what her purpose in it was. She wasn't quite sure where the sexual relationships were going, because they were intense and significant to her—but was Bayli just another notch on their bedposts? And really, was that even a question to ponder after she'd once again botched it so badly with Rory?

Stepping around the gelato stand, she lightly teased Christian by asking, "Are you stalking me? Not that I'd mind, since it's you. As long as you don't request we Skype naked. I have to draw the line somewhere with today's advanced technology. You never know who might be recording you on the other end."

He gave a half snort. "Funny you should mention that. You're currently on YouTube with Rory."

Her pulse jumped. Not in the good way. "You're shitting me."

"Nope. That kiss at the farmers' market already has several thousand views. Mostly, all you see is Rory swooping in. Whoever shot the video was behind you."

"A good thing, I suspect." As they started walking through the park, she stuffed her hands into her front pockets to keep from fidgeting as her nerves twisted. Or maybe it was to keep from grabbing Christian and kissing *him* the way Rory had done to her.

"Fastest way to become the world's most hated woman—caught kissing a hotter-than-hell celebrity bachelor in public."

"Clearly, he made the move on you."

She gazed up at Christian. "I didn't stop him. Responded, in fact."

"Yes." He nodded. "That was made quite evident in the video as well."

Bayli sighed. "Are you mad?"

"At what?"

She knew instantly he was testing her.

First, she said, "Because I might eventually be ID'd as the woman Rory St. James spontaneously kissed and TMZ will break the story—perhaps before the cooking show gets off the ground?"

He was quiet a moment, then asked, "So you're still interested?"

"Why wouldn't I still be interested?" Anxiety crept in on her. Was Christian here to cut her out of the show before she'd even officially signed on? Because of that PDA circulating on YouTube?

"Rory told me you were upset when you left his apartment last night."

"That's putting the whole scenario mildly, so I'll assume you're paraphrasing. Which does bring me to my next point. Does Rory kissing me have any bearing on *us*?"

"From what I heard, he did a hell of a lot more than just kiss you."

Bayli stopped walking before they reached the crowded sidewalk at the south entrance of the park. "That's true. And apparently he wanted to do a hell of a lot more. But I wasn't ready for that."

Christian's teeth gritted for a moment. Bayli waited patiently for him to decide on whatever it was he wanted to say to her. A warm breeze ruffled his dark hair. The lines around his ice-blue eyes crinkled as he squinted against the late-afternoon sun. His hands were also in his pockets, and it felt somehow cold and awkward that they stood so close to each other but were clearly disinclined to engage in any sort of physical contact.

Bayli wondered if that was because they both needed to put new terms on the table—ones that distinctly defined the love triangle that had formed between them and Rory.

Finally, Christian told her, "I'd like to move our dinner from tomorrow night to Thursday, if you're available."

"I am."

"In the meantime, I have your contract in the car. I want you to look it over once more before you sign. I know you've already discussed the high points with your agent and you'll want to read the fine print. I'll give you time to do that."

"You know me well enough to know I'll read it line by line."

He grinned. "Twice."

"Yes."

They stared at each other a bit longer. She was dying to ask how he felt about her being with Rory the night before, what his reaction was to seeing that video of his friend and business partner kissing her on the street. What was really going through his mind now that he knew that Rory had fucked her?

But it felt too vain or too premature. She wasn't sure which. She wasn't sure if there was any sort of issue with either man regarding her becoming romantically involved with both of them.

And was she really romantically involved? She'd never even gotten around to cooking dinner with Rory.

Bayli nervously rocked back and forth on the soles of her Skechers before biting the bullet and asking, "By signing, am I committing to more than just a cooking show?"

He let out a low, strained laugh. "Whatever happens when the cameras aren't rolling, Bayli, is your own business."

"Just *my* business?" She dragged a hand from her pocket and pulled off her sunglasses. Brazenly looked him in the eye. "Was that just a one-night stand with us?"

"No," he was quick to say.

Her breath caught.

"At least, not from my perspective," he added.

Her skin tingled at his heated gaze, his pointed expression.

She swallowed hard and pushed a bit more. "What about Rory? Was he just curious about me because you'd had me before him?"

"You'd have to ask Rory that question."

Her gaze didn't waver. She sensed it was imperative she stand her ground and not withdraw the inquiry or sweep it under the rug. She was already waist-deep in murky waters. Best to know what the undertow might be like, because the current continued to tug at her.

Yet Christian didn't appear as though he was going to cave.

So she prompted him by saying, "I thought he was interested in me when we first met. The way he looked at me was . . . fiery. Exciting."

Christian nodded. "He did mention your incredibly sexy legs when I was on the phone with him on our drive back into the city Saturday night."

"So you knew from the beginning that he was attracted to me."

"Of course."

"And there's no sort of . . . competition . . . between you two? Where I'm concerned."

Christian let out a long breath. He wrapped an arm around her waist and directed her down the sidewalk. The intimate gesture sent a sizzle along her spine. There was no denying she'd become addicted to both men's touch from the onset.

"It's not a competition," Christian told her. "We tend to share an interest in the same women. Granted, it's been a while, what with all the work it took to launch the steakhouse."

"And by *share*, you mean . . . ?"

His head dipped and he whispered in her ear, "You know exactly what I mean."

"Yeah. I do." Still, she had to clarify a few things. "So, given how busy the two of you have been lately, you don't currently share a . . . girlfriend? Is that the right word?"

He grinned again. "Yes, that's the right word. No, we aren't simultaneously involved with anyone. Except you."

"But you're not really involved with me," she stated the obvious that had popped into her head minutes before. "Not by the standards you've defined. Just . . . individually. And even that's debatable, especially after last night with Rory." She huffed a little. "God, he must think I'm such a twit."

"Hardly."

"I walked out on him, Christian."

"That's between the two of you. Fixable," he insisted. "If you want it to be."

If I want it to be . . .

A shiver chased through her. On the one hand, yes, she wanted to make amends with Rory. To prove she actually wasn't naïve. To prove that she'd been as into the sex as he'd been; she was just behind the curve experience-wise.

Bayli had been enticed by the idea of a threesome from the time she'd met Christian. Now that she'd been with both men, she was even more intrigued. What had happened with Rory was a setback, a bit of an embarrassment, admittedly. But when she'd woken this morning—around ten because she'd been sleeping off a hangover—she'd had a distinct vision of what she really wanted.

It was perfectly in line with what Christian described when it came to his and Rory's sexual preferences. They liked to pleasure the same woman. *She* wanted to be that woman.

An extremely easy scenario in her mind.

The reality of it, however, was a bit more complex.

First there was the fact that she was on the outs with Rory. Yet again.

Then she had to dig a bit deeper to accept what the ménage would entail. She couldn't delude herself into believing it would have nothing to do with anal sex.

Perhaps it was time to have a graphic conversation with Jewel.

Provided what Christian had said was accurate—was the situation with Rory *fixable*?

He had to be pissed at her. And she didn't blame him for it. He'd been open and honest. He'd even said he'd teach her, that they'd take it slow. He hadn't forced anything; he hadn't ribbed her because she'd balked. Instead, when they'd ended up sprawled on the floor with him still inside her he'd taken a liking to that position and was fine with it.

She would have been, too. If she hadn't been such a spaz.

She and Christian reached the stretch Jag and the chauffeur opened the back door. Christian indicated for her to slide in before him. She settled in the seat while he extracted a large envelope from his laptop bag and handed it over.

"The contract. Actually, there are multiple copies to sign. Obviously your agent can answer any questions, but if you want me to specifically clarify anything, just call me. Anytime, day or night. All of my numbers are in the packet." His jaw tightened again. "Just call my cell. I'll pick up immediately."

"You don't have to do that."

"I *want* to do that." He leaned in close and kissed her. Softly, sweetly. As though he was testing the waters after all that had happened. So much of which had gone awry.

But then his tongue delved deep, sweeping over hers, and Bayli forgot all about the contracts and the astronomical salary that had been proposed and the fact that all of her professional dreams were about to come true.

All she could think about was how wonderful Christian tasted—like expensive scotch. He'd had a drink with lunch? Perhaps he'd needed a stiff cocktail when Rory had told him of their fallout.

She didn't know. Didn't care at the moment. Her arms slipped around Christian's neck and she pressed her chest to his, loving the feeling of his rigid muscles against her, reveling in the way he embraced her so tightly. Again, with that feverish intensity, like he couldn't get close enough to her. Couldn't *get* enough of her.

Only now there was more of an edge to his kiss, to his touch.

He shifted and pulled her into his lap, so she straddled him. This time, Bayli did not freak. Granted, he wasn't inside her, but still.

His hands gripped her ass and he ground his cock against the apex of her legs, the seam of her jeans rubbing her clit, making her restless.

Her fingers practically yanked the buttons of his shirt from their holes, and then she tore her mouth away and kissed his throat, his collarbone, his pecs. His skin was hot. She was hotter.

Her palms flattened against the grooves of his abs and she thrilled over his sculpted perfection. His cut muscles were longer and leaner than Rory's bulky, chiseled physique. The contrast was an exciting one and she thought of how amazing it would be if she were sandwiched between them, her front pressed to Christian's, Rory at her back. Their hands and mouths all over her body. Christian kissing her so deeply, the way he expertly did. Rory biting his way along her neck, marking her as he'd done last night.

Christ, when she'd seen those hickeys in the mirror after Colin had teased her about them she'd felt a jolt in her core as though Rory had been with her at that very moment to darken the marks by sucking harder.

She moaned at the memory, at the sensation that sparked in her pussy over the thought of Rory branding her while Christian's tongue tangled with hers. It would rock her world. No doubt about it.

Christian gently tugged at the pins in her hair so that the thick mass tumbled around her shoulders and across his chest. She vaguely felt the smooth easing away of the limo from the curb. She didn't know if the driver was just arbitrarily taking a spin to give them privacy or if he had a specific destination previously provided by Christian. It didn't matter. Bayli was caught up in the moment, and the only thing that could make it better was if they were both naked.

Well, that and if Rory were there with them.

Her crotch rubbed a bit more aggressively against Christian's as she let her mind wander, let the fantasy take hold. Her lips skated over his rippling flesh, feeling the flexing and releasing beneath her touch. She flicked her tongue over his nipple and then suckled it. Christian's fingers plowed through her hair, tightening around the long strands.

"I want to feel that tongue on my cock," he told her in a low, hoarse tone. "But when I come, it's going to be inside you."

Bayli slipped between his parted thighs. Unfastened his pants. Slid the zipper down its track. Her hand cupped the bulge straining against his boxer briefs, the heel tenderly rubbing his sac.

He groaned. "I knew exactly what Rory was trying to tell me when he said he'd fucked things up with you."

She glanced up at him. "He said *he* fucked things up?"

"Yes." Christian's fingertips tenderly caressed her scalp, her hair still twisted around his fingers so that they pulled lightly in an arousing way. Every fiber of her being was aroused.

"How does he figure?" she asked as she worked the briefs and his pants down Christian's lifted hips so that his cock sprang free of the confining material. His beautiful, thick cock that she instantly craved to taste, to devour.

"He wanted too much from you, too soon."

Bayli let that tidbit simmer in the back of her head as she succumbed to the temptation of silky skin covering steel. She slowly grazed Christian's shaft with her tongue from root to tip. Felt the jarring deep within him at her wicked touch. Her tongue swirled around the slight indentation of his cockhead and then whisked lower to trace the groove underneath.

He hissed out a breath.

She closed her mouth over him and suckled. Not taking him in any farther than his very tip. Using her tongue to stroke languidly.

"He didn't say you liked to tease."

Bayli didn't take the bait. Kept up her playful toying with him. Christian knew she was good for follow-through; she'd already proven that to him. At the moment, she was mostly enthralled with the pulsing of his cock and the staccato beats of his breath.

"Why do you think you know exactly what Rory was trying to tell you when he said he wanted too much from me, too soon?" She blew softly against Christian's skin that was deepening in color with his arousal. His hips bucked. She couldn't resist licking him from base to tip again.

"Fuck." His tone was jagged—as though Bayli were actually working some sort of magic on him, revving him with her simple tonguing, her light breaths on his throbbing cock. In a cagey tone, he said, "Because when I was buried inside you, I was thinking of a dozen other ways I wanted you. All wrapped around making you come, making you scream my name. Making us come together . . . Damn."

Her hand stroked his cock as she peered at him from under her lashes. "Making us *all* come?"

The primal sound that slipped through his lips ignited her insides.

"Christian," she said on a heavy breath. "That's hot."

She took him deep in her mouth. Sucked him hard while fisting him at the root with one hand and carefully rolling his balls with the other. A technique that had Christian's hips jerking and his breaths coming in sharper pulls. A technique she'd not had the opportunity to share with Rory; he'd put a stop to her foreplay much too soon.

Because he'd wanted her.

With erotic thoughts bursting anew in her brain, she sucked one more time—fiercely enough to evoke a violent tremble from Christian—and then released him.

"Goddamn," he growled.

She sat back on the seat across from him. Every bit of her vibrated from a new empowerment coursing through her.

"That's not a look I'm used to seeing from you," Christian commented as he eyed her closely. "What's on your mind?"

Her inner walls were doing some sort of eclectic dance that had them clenching and releasing in a heated frenzy, and her chest heaved of its own accord, giving her away. Damn that part of her body that couldn't control itself.

She said, "I really want to give you a 'happy ending,' Mr. Davila."

He smirked at her sassiness.

"But the thing is . . ." She glided the pad of her finger along the corner of her mouth to whisk away any lip gloss that had smeared. "You and Chef St. James got the chance to weave your little web. Quite a sticky one, I might add."

She made a bold move for the phone tucked into the sidewall, and when the driver came on the line she told him, "You can pull over now, please."

Bayli replaced the receiver as Christian watched her with a crooked brow at her sudden take-charge attitude.

She said, "You've hooked me, clearly." She snatched the envelope he'd brought with him. The car came to a halt. Bayli reached for the handle and shoved the door open. Over her shoulder, she told Christian, "Now it's my turn to do the same."

TWELVE

"You did *not* say that!" Jewel erupted—thankfully before taking a sip of wine.

"Yep. Then I just slipped from the limo and strode off. As though I didn't have a care in the world."

Bayli had played it cool with Christian on Monday afternoon. Unfortunately, her insides had been a rioting mess as she'd briskly wound her way through foot traffic on the sidewalk, wondering if he was going to come after her and foil her little power play.

Though instinct had told her that he would understand she'd needed to bring the ball into her court. Not that it fully and truly was there—she knew damn well two men of Christian's and Rory's influence and experience were the ones in control. But Bayli needed to possess some of it herself. So she'd made the split-second executive decision not to give Christian exactly what he'd wanted from her in the back of that limo.

If she was going to run with the big dogs, she was going to have to get her ass off the porch and go for it.

Which reminded her . . .

"Hey," she said as Jewel did a quick survey of the apartment and nodded encouragingly, good friend that she was. "Can I ask you some questions about your relationship with Rogen and Vin? They might be a bit delicate. . . . Just a heads-up."

"Sure." Jewel was a statuesque blonde who'd worked as a Senior Vice President of Acquisitions for her family's empire before she dove into her own project of building an inn and winery in River Cross. She inspected the large floral arrangement in the center of the glass-topped table with the thick scrolled wrought-iron legs in the corner. "This is so pretty." Her gaze swept over the entire place and she added, "Really, Bay. It's all so pretty, what you've done with the place. I was a little worried when you first moved in."

"Liar. You were a *lot* worried."

"That's because I love you."

"I love you, too. Now . . ." Bay took a long sip of the merlot she'd uncorked for Jewel's surprise visit on Wednesday evening— the very bottle she'd intended to take to Phillip and Colin's dinner party. "I seem to have found myself in the extremely fortuitous position of having two men who are close friends and accustomed to sharing women find me . . ."

Jewel's brow jerked up. "Worthy of sharing?"

"Yes."

Jewel set her glass on the small coffee table in front of the love seat, then grabbed Bayli's hand and pulled her over to sit. "From one lucky girl to another, let me just say—"

"Wait." Bayli took another deep sip before setting her glass next to Jewel's. "I'm not a *lucky girl* yet. Well, in many respects, yes. But not in that ultimate way you're thinking of. We haven't done it yet. I mean we have. Just not—"

"All together. The three of you. At one time."

"At one time." Bayli reached for her wine and swallowed down another big gulp. Not exactly classy, but hell . . . she was dealing with some heavy shit here.

Jewel rested a hand on Bayli's knee and said, "Dear friend of mine, I completely get the nervousness and the reservations. I experienced all of that myself. It's totally natural. More than that, it's warranted. Just thinking back to that first time in my living room when I kissed Rogen and then Vin." Her lovely features softened, but Jewel's sapphire eyes lit with fire. "Rogen stripped his shirt off. And I popped every single button on Vin's—shredded the flap. I couldn't help myself." She sighed dreamily. "God, they were so incredible to look at. And they both wanted me. It was in their eyes, on their faces. Their muscles bunched. Their breaths grew heavier. . . ."

Jewel had to reach for her wine, too. She sipped, then continued. "I knew I'd reached a point of no return. I'd sort of instigated it, to be honest. I'd heard whispers of their secret ways with women. I wanted to be one of those women. No." She licked her bottom lip and gave Bayli a sly look. "I wanted to be their *only* woman."

"Yeah, there is that." Bayli fidgeted with the hem of her skirt. She'd come from the library when Jewel had texted her that she was in town for a quick stop before hopping the pond for a work thing and would meet her at the apartment.

"It's a very fascinating situation," Jewel told her. "Learning that two men actually get more turned on, get even harder, when they're working together to satisfy a woman."

"What it's like?" Bayli asked with bated breath. "Really. Don't hold anything back. Please, Jewel."

Okay, so she was a bit eager beaver. A bit desperate.

Jewel smiled. "Well, to be perfectly honest, I can't tell you *exactly* what it's like. That's all up to Christian and Rory. And you. But with Rogen, Vin, and me . . ." Her grin brightened. "It's a flood of sensations and emotions. I feel every little thing they do to me, only it's magnified by a million. My skin is more sensitive. My pulse soars. My body is infinitely more responsive. All because of how I feel about them and how much they cherish me. How their biggest concern is making me feel good, making me happy."

"And how do they do that? Make you happy? One at a time or . . . ?"

"Together?"

Another long sip. Bayli's cheeks flushed and she hated that she still struggled with what to fully expect.

Jewel said, "Together. And believe me, it's nothing short of volcanic. You just have to be open to it, understand that they're focused on you and what pleases you. They're sort of a different breed, you know?"

"Hmm. Yes. I'm starting to see that. Except . . ." *Crap.* Here came the delicate. "What am I supposed to do when they're into something I know absolutely nothing about?"

Jewel frowned. "Such as?"

"Such as!" Her eyes bulged. "Jesus, Jewel! Were you the one to write *Everything You Always Wanted to Know About Sex* but Were Afraid to Ask?*"

"I could have been a coauthor." She winked.

"Oh, for fuck's sake." Wineglass in hand, Bayli paced her tiny living room.

"Come on . . . joking." Jewel laughed softly. "But you have to remember that Rogen and I were having sex from the time we were sixteen. Then Vin and I got together when I was eighteen, and let me just say . . . he'd been dating an older woman—a twenty-eight-year-old divorcée—so he had plenty of experience under his belt. I learned fairly young."

"But you couldn't have known *everything.*"

"No. But what I didn't know they taught me. And that, my friend, is the absolute *best* way to learn new tricks."

"Great. That's oh so helpful. Thanks."

Jewel stood. She clasped Bayli's shoulders and said, "Whatever you're stressing over, don't. These two gorgeous and prominent men seem very into you, Bay. They've done this before, so let them lead. They'll ease your mind. All they'll want is for you to enjoy yourself. That means doing whatever they can to acclimate you and make you comfortable."

"*Acclimate* me. Sounds like a science project."

"To you, sure. Stop thinking scientifically or metaphysically or any other kind of 'ically.' Just give yourself to them, Bayli. I swear to God, men who thrive on this type of sexual relationship have a certain level of understanding when it comes to making a woman climax that other guys just don't get. It's worth whatever fretting you're doing right now. But in the end, you'll realize you wigged for no good reason, because they're going to get you through this. *They're* going to take care of *you*. And you of all people deserve that, my friend." She kissed Bayli on the cheek.

"You're going to make me cry," Bayli said around a sniffle. "And for God's sake, I've done enough of that already this week. I'm like some hormonal teenager trying to figure out what the hell I'm going to do if no one asks me to the prom."

"Three guys asked you to the prom, silly."

"And I told Billy Geyser that I'd go with him."

"Ah, yes. Captain of the football team. God, he was good looking. What a frame-worthy photo that would have made."

"Except that I ended up in ICU with my mom an hour before he was supposed to pick me up for dinner."

"That totally sucked." Jewel sighed. "On the plus side, that particular emergency surgery was hugely helpful for your mother. A success."

"Her last one, but yes. That was the biggie that made it possible for me to go to college for a couple of years, because she had an excellent recovery. For a while."

"I'm sorry you missed prom." Jewel gave her a quick squeeze. Then said, "But I know the extra time with your mom was infinitely more important."

Bayli choked down the emotion in her throat. She didn't want to get all weepy yet again.

Luckily, Jewel knew her well enough not to let her dwell or mire. She cheerfully said, "I guess all of this is just excellent timing on my part."

"What are you talking about?" Bayli asked.

"Well . . ." Turning to the kitchen counter, Jewel said, "I sort of lied when I said I was on my way to London and that I carted around this big box because I didn't trust my driver with it while he's looking for a place to park and wait for me." Her manicured hand swept over the large white package with the silver bow on top.

"Jewel . . ." Bayli eyed her friend speculatively. "What have you done?"

"Nothing that will have you scolding me, I promise." She held her hands up in surrender for good measure. "It's just that you told me about this dinner date with your two men tomorrow night and how it could be the start of your new business venture with them, but that it could also be the start of something so much more . . ." She waggled a brow. "And I thought you needed a lucky dress to bring it all together. *My* lucky dress."

"Your lucky—"

"Yep! Dress." Jewel lifted the lid and peeled back the glittery tissue.

Bayli leaned in and gasped. "Oh, you did not!"

"But I did!" Jewel carefully extracted the garment, a stunning, shimmery silver ruched strapless mini. "I wore this when Rogen, Vin, and I signed the papers on the land for the new inn and winery. I'm not saying it's been nothing but sunshine and roses since that day—there's a shitload of construction underway with tons of mishaps—but it's been pretty damn close. Close enough for me, anyway."

"Aw, Jewel." Bayli gave her a huge hug. "I am so proud of you for taking on your parents—and Rogen's—in order to secure that property and do something with it that means so much to you both. And to Vin."

"To *all* of us," Jewel said with a tinge of emotion. "It was the catalyst that brought our families back together. And Bayli," she said as she pulled slightly away. "I know a pretty dress can't make you feel any better about your mom, but damn it, she'll light up all of heaven with her smile when she sees you in it."

"Jewel." Tears flooded Bayli's eyes. She hugged her friend

again. "You're supposed to be talking raunchy about my two men. Not making me cry."

"A little crying helps sometimes, Bay. Best to let it out rather than keep it bottled up."

Bayli couldn't disagree, despite her earlier ruminations that she'd been weepy enough of late. So she shed a few tears for all the tension and hopelessness she'd been feeling that she'd never wanted to burden anyone with. And then wiped her cheeks and lifted her chin.

"Mom would frown over this sort of self-indulgence," she said.

"Yeah, well, something tells me that Dori Styles—*that's* Dori *with an* i *and* Styles *with a* y"—Jewel perfectly imitated Bayli's feisty mother—"won't be frowning upon her beautiful daughter landing a TV show and two famous and highly eligible, hot-hot-*hot* bachelors."

"Let's hope she's not the only one," Bayli mumbled.

"What are you talking about?"

With a sigh, Bayli said, "Apparently, Rory and I have gone viral, although I have yet to be identified as the woman he laid a huge kiss on at the Seventy-ninth Street Greenmarket on Sunday. Soon as that cat's out of the bag, I'm sure my in-box will be flooded with an endless stream of nastygrams from all of his admirers."

"Great publicity for the show," Jewel said. "And one delish tidbit about you and Chef St. James. I'll have to check it out."

"Traitor."

"Hey, no nastygrams coming from me. I just want to see how the guy kisses. Make damn certain he's worthy of you. Especially in my dress."

"How'd I know it would all eventually come back to your dress?"

"Because it's always all about the dress. Just make sure no one comes on it."

"Jewel!"

"Teasing!" She nudged Bayli with her shoulder. "It was a joke, girlfriend."

"Why do I suddenly feel queasy?"

"Oh, shut up." Jewel laughed. "Try this baby on and we'll decide whether your hair will be up or down. I have shoes and accessories. A wrap. Not that Christian Davila and Rory St. James are going to notice any of that. They might not even feed you before they cart you off to their bed."

"Jewel!"

"Again with the verbal outburst. Come on, now. Off to the bathroom you go. If I have to call someone in to nip and tuck, be damn sure I will."

"We're the same size," Bayli retorted.

"Yes, and please post that on Facebook, Miss Model. Better yet, send a selfie to Rogen and Vin in the dress so they can see my clothes fit your soon-to-be-famous figure. Wait—" She shook her head. "Scratch that last one. You're much too gorgeous. Don't send selfies to my men. Just . . . don't."

Bayli laughed. "I'll try to control myself. Really, it'll be difficult, what with wanting to steal them away and all that." She snickered. Then frowned. "Well, to be honest, if I were still in River Cross and had never met Christian and Rory, I just might want to steal away at least one of them. I mean, seriously, Jewel. To keep such smart and sexy men all to yourself."

Jewel twirled her around and said, "Go. Now. I know where your interests lie, and it isn't with Rogen and Vin."

"Ah, so true." She headed to the bathroom but stopped just before pushing the door open. She turned back to Jewel. "Thanks for flying all the way across the country to bring me a special dress for a special evening." Emotion tickled her nose, misted her eyes. But she kept herself in check this time.

Jewel nodded. "Only for the very best of friends."

Christian was in the dining room of Davila's NYC, making the rounds with the customers when she walked in.

As it happened, his Columbia roommate, Gene Eckhart, was

in the middle of another dissertation when Christian's attention was instantly snagged. Gene's gaze apparently followed Christian's and he snickered.

"Jesus, Davila," he said in a friendly, chiding tone. "I think you're being stalked. And that makes you one lucky son of a bitch."

"Don't I know it?" Christian briefly clasped his buddy on the shoulder, then said, "Enjoy the crème brûlée. I have a date."

Christian started to move away. But stopped in his tracks when Bayli did the same, just beyond the round table in the foyer. Her gaze swept through the bar area and then the dining room. She spotted him. Smiled radiantly.

His insides pulled taut. She easily took his breath away, wearing a tiny silver dress that showed off her glamorous legs and all that golden skin of hers. Her sleek raven hair was pulled back into intricate knots at her nape with a low ponytail on the side that left angled strands at her collarbone. A silver wrap rested in the crooks of her arms and she held a matching clutch in her hand. Her sandals were strappy, delicate-looking things that sparkled almost as vibrantly as the woman herself. Though not quite as much.

He waited for her to make a move. Knew precisely what she was thinking as she dragged her gaze from his and glanced in the direction of the kitchen. Christian's jaw worked. As much as he wanted Bayli to come straight to him, he also wanted her to smooth the wrinkles with Rory.

She hedged a few moments more, then strolled through the bar to where Pierre was giving instructions to a server. When the manager saw Bayli he grinned and led her to the inner sanctum of the restaurant.

To Rory.

"Where's my rack of lamb and my lobster tails?" Rory called out as he reached for a plate of jumbo prawns and whipped mash and another with a rib eye and baked potato. "I need the rest of my order, guys!" he urged as he expedited the food for a VIP table.

Hell, this early in the launch of the restaurant the only customers who could get in were VIPs.

"Right here, Chef," his sous said.

Rory completed his arrangement of the food on a large oval tray, adding the appropriate accompaniments just as the runner returned from serving the last order.

"Table twenty-two," Rory told the kid. "Make sure you deliver the lobsters to the right place settings. One's paired with—" A flash of silver caught his eye. Quickly followed by silky legs that he now knew felt like heaven wrapped around him. "Read the ticket," he said to the runner. Then stepped away.

The kitchen was filled with noise—the clattering of plates, the banter of the chefs as they worked together to get the orders out on time, the occasional outburst when something went awry. Servers came and went; bussers breezed through with trays piled high from tables they'd cleaned. It was hot and chaotic and also smelled like a gourmet grillfest. Rory thrived on the atmosphere, the aroma, the energy bouncing off the walls.

But all of that faded into the background as he turned to fully face Bayli. Standing off to the side, out of the way. Staring at him. Looking so fucking beautiful that his cock instantly throbbed and micromanaging his staff became the absolute last thing on his mind.

When the path cleared, she stepped toward him. Gave him a tentative smile. "I just stopped in to say hi. I won't take any of your time."

"Too late," he ground out, all the blood rushing to his groin. "Let's go to my office."

He took her by the hand and led her through the maze of his employees and the various workstations. He and Bayli traveled a short hallway and Rory unlocked the door. Closed it behind them after they passed through.

Bayli surveyed the space and said, "This is really nice."

"You don't have to make small talk." His gaze slid over her

from head to toe. "Goddamn . . ." He let out a harsh breath. "You're perfect."

"Nowhere close. But thanks anyway."

He yanked open the snaps of his jacket at the neck, feeling much too hot under the collar at the sight of her. "Why aren't you out front with Christian?"

"I haven't signed the contract," she said on a rush of air, taking him aback, as she duly noted. She explained, "If this was just about Christian, I would have signed days ago. But it's not just about Christian."

His heart constricted. *Odd.* But he couldn't fight the sensation. "Still pissed at me, I see."

"I was never pissed at you," she said without missing a beat. "Not at all. Not even the tiniest bit."

"Then, what—"

"I was pissed at me, Rory. For being so . . . I don't know. For *not* being so . . ." She gave a sharp shake of her head. Draped her wrap over a chair in front of his desk and set her small bag on the seat. She took a few deep breaths, then told him, "I acted like an imbecile, Rory. And I'm very sorry about that."

"No, Bayli, you didn't. You have nothing to be sorry for, I swear. Just . . . don't apologize, okay?" His gut coiled. The strain on his heart intensified, catching him off-guard, but maybe he shouldn't be so surprised. After all, he'd spent the past couple of days replaying in his mind what had gone wrong from the time she'd fallen into his arms at the library to the time he'd stood on the other side of the elevator doors when they'd closed with her inside.

He'd wondered as he'd stood there trying to figure out what the hell had just happened if he should go after her. Had wanted to more than he'd wanted just about anything else in life. But something had held him back. A voice in his head that had told him she'd skipped out on him for a reason. And he had to let her process that reason and come around, not hound her in the insistent way that was a natural part of his personality.

Even now, it was pure torture to not push her a little. He needed answers. He needed to know that he hadn't screwed everything up between them. And he wasn't just thinking of the show.

Planting his hands at his waist, he said, "Look, honey—"

"Can I just tell you something first?" she asked with imploring eyes. The tawny irises glimmered in the dim lighting of his desk lamp and there was a hint of mist at the corners. Tugging at his heartstrings even more.

"Sure," he said with a nod. "Whatever you want."

Unfortunately for him, she stood a bit too far away. Almost across the office. He could still catch the faint hint of her darkly alluring scent, though, and it drove him wild. Made him restless that there were several feet separating them when he wanted her body brushing against his. Wanted his arms around her. Wanted to kiss her until she forgot all about the crap that had unfolded in his apartment after they'd made love.

He groaned inwardly. They hadn't made love. He'd fucked her. *Right?*

Or . . . not?

Maybe that was what the tightening in his chest was all about. It hadn't just been a causal lay. It'd been so much more. Christian had felt the same way when he'd been with her. Bayli meant something to them both, far beyond their professional goal. Rory knew it to the depths of his soul.

But Rory couldn't put any of that into words without freaking the hell out of her again. He was certain of it. So he tried to rein in his emotions and his desires. No easy task.

She folded her arms at her stomach and said, "I'm having this really bizarre dilemma of knowing exactly what I want, but not knowing exactly what to do about it."

They stared at each other as a few tense seconds stretched between them. Then she said, "I know about you and Christian. I know you both want me. *Wanted* me . . ."

"We still want you. We *both* still want you, Bayli."

She pulled in a sharp breath.

Rory raked a hand through his hair. "Does that scare you?"

Her mouth opened, but no words materialized. Her arms dropped. She turned away. Propped her hands on her hips. Stared up at the ceiling.

She said, "I'm not afraid of you, if that's what you're thinking."

He couldn't take the distance a moment longer. He closed the gap in two wide strides and placed his hands at the dip of her waist, above hers. His head lowered and he murmured against her bare neck, "If you're not afraid of me, honey, then what are you afraid of? The way I make you feel?"

"Yes," she whispered.

His fingers curled into her, gripping her firmly. He felt the shudder run through her. "You want me doing things to you no one else has ever done, right?"

She nodded.

"And you want Christian to be with us when I do. You want him touching you when I'm inside you."

"Yes."

Rory's cock now pulsed in wicked beats. His heart hammered. Adrenaline roared through his veins.

"That's what Christian and I want, too."

She let out a small, strangled sound. "I don't know how—"

He released her. Turned her to face him. Stared deep into her eyes. "Stop saying you don't know *how*. We'll show you how. You don't have to know everything, Bayli, *understand* everything. I get that's a part of who you are, but not when it comes to something like this. You're not going to find the answer in your books. You have to trust us to lead the way. And—hell. It's not even us leading, really. It's you giving in to us and letting us make you feel good. It's you commanding us in that sense. Do you see what I'm saying?"

He lifted a hand to her face, desperately needing to touch her, to whisk his thumb over her furrowed brow, brush his fingertips across her cheek. He also craved kissing her. But he didn't want to smudge all of her expertly applied makeup. He couldn't even palm the side of her neck, because he could see she'd blended powder along her throat to cover the marks he'd left behind.

His hand returned to her waist and he pulled her tightly to him, felt the quick rise and fall of her chest against his. Her hands clutched his biceps as she gazed up at him.

He said, "Christian and I have had other women, yes. But none that affected us this way. I've been going crazy this week, dying to see you. But knowing I had to wait for you to come to me. I'm sorry if I hurt you in any way. I never would. I—"

"You didn't, Rory. I've been struggling with this whole time continuum thing, thinking I should be so much further along in life than I am."

"It's not a contest, babe."

"Says the man who opens a new restaurant every two years." She didn't say this flippantly; it was more insistent. "Look at all that you've achieved. And you're only thirty-two."

"You're only twenty-seven. Where's the fire?"

She laughed softly, helping to alleviate some of his tension. "I don't expect you to fully grasp all this. But, Rory . . ." Her tone turned serious and the mist coated her glowing eyes again. "I don't want to be the girl hiding in the stacks anymore. I want to *be* someone. I want my mother to know that she didn't have me in vain. That there was a purpose to her putting her life on the line for mine. Whatever possessed her to have me when it put her own health in such extreme danger—it has to mean *something*. I can't let her regret it or let it all be for naught."

"Bayli." *Fuck*. His heart wrenched once more. "You talked about me being an overachiever and all the pressure that brings, without taking your own damn advice. You don't have to conquer the world by the time you're thirty—you don't have to prove anything to anyone. Sure as hell not your mom. Because even if your face never graced the cover of a magazine or your name never became a household one, she'd still be proud of you and she'd still stand by her decision to have you. Come on . . . even *I* know that. Neanderthal chef that I am."

She sniffled. He had to catch the tears with his thumb and sweep them away before they tumbled down her cheeks.

"Stop thinking you have to be everything to everyone, Bayli." He stared hard into her eyes. "Just be you. Swear to God, you won't go wrong."

She smiled again. It wasn't the megawatt one he'd hoped for. In fact, it was a bit shaky. But he'd take what he could get at the moment.

Bayli said, "Who would have guessed Angsty Chef could be so sensitive? Not a Neanderthal at all."

"Angsty Chef, huh?"

"Mm." She shrugged. "If the jacket fits . . ."

"Ha. Ha." He very lightly kissed her cheek. "Remember that you promised to keep my secrets."

"Wise on my part. Less competition for me that way." She winked.

Rory was about to tell her there was no competition for her, but she was already collecting her things and heading to the door.

Still, he felt compelled to call after her. "Bayli . . ."

She glanced at him over a bare shoulder and said, "I'll sign. And not just because I want to be famous."

She disappeared into the hallway while Rory worked to get his dick—and his heart—under control.

THIRTEEN

Bayli took a few moments to collect herself in the servers' station, inhaling deeply in hopes of getting her racing pulse and raging hormones under control. For as much as Rory had tripped something profound and emotional within her, he also got her hot and bothered.

And Bayli knew Christian would have the same effect on her when she saw him again.

She stepped into the bar and was greeted once more by Pierre, who escorted her to a curved booth tucked into a far corner by a fireplace. It was a seductively lit area and the shape of the booth was cozy and intimate, offering a bit of privacy.

"Monsieur Davila will be right with you. May I pour champagne?"

"*Oui. Merci.*"

He smiled appreciatively at her enunciation of his native language. Then he popped the cork on a bottle of private-reserve Dom Perignon that Bayli suspected cost more than her rent. He splashed a little into a glass for her to sample. As if she'd know whether it was substandard. But she sipped anyway. Decided it was time to play *fake it until you make it* if she was going to pull off this new venture. *Both* of these new ventures.

Her toes curled as she recalled what Rory had said about him and Christian still wanting her. And damn . . . Rory had been so amazing. Not at all mocking, not trivializing what she was going through. No, he'd just let her work through it while he helped her. Solid as oak.

She gave a nod for Pierre to pour.

The spark between her legs when she caught sight of Christian heading her way undermined her more valiant ruminations. Because her brain was suddenly overrun with thoughts of his cock in her mouth in the back of the limo. His mouth on her when they'd been in her apartment. The way he'd fucked her . . .

Heat crept up her neck. She couldn't stop the blush.

Christian slid into the seat beside her, his leg brushing hers and making her flush deeper.

He leaned in and whispered, "That shade of pink on your cheeks is stunning. You were just thinking of my hands on your body, weren't you?"

"Not just your hands," she corrected. And sipped. The crisp champagne did nothing to douse the flames inside her, flickering brighter than those in the hearth.

He draped an arm around her shoulders and said, "You look much more relaxed than earlier. Is it the bubbly or did you and Rory work things out?"

"This is my first glass."

"Then you and Rory worked things out. Good." He waited for Pierre to serve him a glass as well before continuing. "I had a feeling you'd help him set the record straight."

"I didn't have to help him. He did it all on his own." She gazed at Christian and said, "As much as I agonized over what had happened in his apartment, I think he agonized even more."

"I wouldn't be surprised. He tends to keep things bottled up. Probably why he's so explosive in the kitchen."

"Because he can control that environment a bit more than his emotions?"

"That's an intelligent conjecture."

"Hmm." She sipped again. Then asked, "And what about you? Do you always just say what's on your mind?"

"Pretty much." He grinned devilishly.

"Well, that creates a very enticing dynamic between the two of you."

"A little contrast to keep us from being too boring."

"Oh, come on now. Neither of you could ever be boring." She placed her hand on his thigh. "And you both know it."

His voice dropped again as he asked, "Are you flirting with me, Miss Styles?"

"Oh, hell, yes," she said on a lusty breath.

Christian chuckled. A deep, rumbling sound that echoed through her body and made all her erogenous zones pulse erratically. She loved how she responded to something as simple as his laugh as much as she reacted to something as evocative as the way his ice-blue irises seemed to melt when he looked at her and how his fingertips sweeping over her skin made her tingle all over.

Bayli realized it was a damn good thing she was becoming accustomed to these two men separately, because as a whole . . . *Holy cow*. She already knew she was in for sensory overload.

The thought had her squirming in her seat. Christian eyed her curiously.

She crossed her legs and pressed her thighs together. "Just a few fireworks *down there*."

"That's hot, sweetheart." His warm breath tickled the shell of her ear, not helping her to get a grip on the riotous sensations one little bit.

"Behave."

"You started it. Flirting with me and wearing that sexy dress."

"I borrowed it from a friend."

"Who can't possibly look as fine in it as you do."

"She does, actually. But she's already spoken for, so don't get any ideas."

He laughed low and sensuously again. "Think I have my hands full with you. Luckily, I have help."

Damn all those pinpricks targeting her pussy. "Ironically enough, her Boyfriend Number One-A has help from her Boyfriend Number One-B." She gave him a pointed look.

"Aha." Christian gave a slow nod. "Gotcha."

"I hope you don't mind, but I had some questions. And since Jewel is the only woman on the planet I know who is even more fortunate than me . . . I sort of picked her brain."

Christian let out a low groan.

Bayli shifted in her seat again as the zings ensued. "That is one of the sexiest sounds you make," she told him. "It causes everything to go haywire inside me."

His fingers curled around her biceps as he tucked her tighter under his arm and murmured, "This is a conversation I'd prefer to have in private. While you're naked."

"Then let's put it on hold until later." Her heart jumped. Was she being too presumptuous? "Unless you have other plans, of course."

"I do, actually." He loosened his grip on her and put an inch of space between them as the server approached. But under his breath, Christian added, "They involve you, me, and Rory . . . at my apartment. Naked, in case I haven't made that perfectly clear. Okay by you?"

Her entire body lit up like a bonfire. She had to duck her head as the fire ignited on her cheeks. "You're going to have to order for me," she said, all breathy and deeply aroused. Christ, she couldn't speak in her normal voice, let alone look the server in the eye when she made a selection. And who the fuck was she kidding? She wouldn't even be able to concentrate on the menu!

Christian said, "No worries. Rory is whipping something up for the three of us. He just needs to know how you like your steak, or if you want sea bass, cedar-plank salmon, or lamb instead."

"Steak. Medium rare."

"Perfect." Christian relayed the information.

Bayli reached for her champagne and drained the glass. "I'm going to need a refill. Jesus, it's suddenly so hot in here."

Christian gestured for Pierre to return to their table as he said to Bayli, "Everyone else appears to be quite comfortable with the temperature."

"So humorous," she said with a smirk. "It's only because they're not sitting next to a gorgeous, dark-haired, blue-eyed man who can electrically charge the air with little more than a suggestive chuckle and a few wicked words."

"Not really looking to charge the air, sweetheart." He grinned. "Just you."

"Well, you're doing a stellar job of it."

"I sort of suspected that."

Pierre refreshed their champagne and left them.

Christian clinked the rim of his glass against Bayli's and said, "Here's to a successful affair."

"Business or pleasure?"

"Both, of course." He sipped, then added, "Unless there's something I'm missing." One corner of his mouth dipped. "I highly doubt you could conceal a packet of contracts somewhere in that dress."

"I didn't bring them," she affirmed. "They're not signed."

"Bayli." He set aside his glass. Got deathly serious. "Whatever you're worrying about when it comes to me and Rory, however much time you need with that, I completely understand. No one's pressuring you there. But don't let anything related to our personal relationships hold you back from a great professional opportunity. Rory and I would never want you to pass up a chance to fulfill an aspiration because of anything happening with us behind closed doors. These are sole and separate enterprises."

"*Enterprises?*"

He sighed. "You know what I'm getting at—you compartmentalize. Work is one thing. Private affairs are something altogether different."

"Agreed."

"So what's keeping you from signing?"

She took another long drink, then said, "I needed to see Rory first. And now that I have . . . I'm ready to move forward with the show."

"The two of you truly hashed it all out?"

"I needed to feel less moronic and he set me straight."

Christian's gaze narrowed. "Bayli."

"My words, Christian," she told him. "Don't read anything into my insecurity."

He didn't lighten up on the scrutiny. "Rory can be—"

"Intimidating, a lot to handle all at once, difficult to dissect . . . yes. Absolutely. And I fell prey to all of that. My own doing. I got sidetracked and thought I *couldn't* compartmentalize. When it comes to you, Rory, and the show, I'm not fully convinced that I can put it all into my convenient silos. So it threw me a little. But after speaking with Rory"—she shrugged—"I now feel as though I don't want everything in my life to be convenient and easily stacked."

"That's not anything I expected to hear you say."

She laughed softly. "I'm just telling you that I will sign the contract and I'm absolutely thrilled about the show. And I want whatever could happen with you, me, and Rory to actually . . . happen."

There. She'd said it. Put the desire for her own ménage into the universe.

And smiled at the new wave of flames that danced along her skin.

Christian was having a hell of a time concentrating on the conversation. Bayli was animatedly discussing some of the places she'd like him and Rory to consider for the test audience/webcast portion of the show while Rory was still in the kitchen prepping their meal.

Her cheeks were rosy, her hands were gesturing about—so much so that Christian discreetly moved her glass of champagne out of the way twice—and she was as radiant as he'd known she'd be when he'd first envisioned her in front of TV cameras.

No two ways about it, Christian wasn't just lusting after her. It was quickly becoming so much more. She'd said the other day that she wanted to weave her own web to hook him and Rory. What she didn't know was that she'd already done just that. And Christian and his friend only got more tangled up with every passing moment in her presence.

Christian knew that Rory would take the blame for his bungled afternoon with her on Sunday only if he was truly, deeply, passionately interested in her. Otherwise, he would have been dismissive, because Rory didn't have the time or the patience for calming unsettled waters. When things got complicated romantically, Rory was the first to walk away.

Not so when it came to Bayli Styles.

And it was evident that she felt the rift had been mended, because she was reaching all-new levels of vibrancy with her brilliant smile and contagious laugh.

She told Christian, "So there were Phillip and Colin, stranded in the Dominican Republic with no luggage after like twenty hours of traveling and three different airline connections, and the resort restaurants had strict dress codes and wouldn't let them in for dinner because they were in shorts and flip-flops—Abercrombie and Fitch, but whatever, apparently the labels got them nowhere—and there was no on-site shop to buy pants. They were *starving*, and even Colin's incredible charisma and Phillip's increasingly huge bribe couldn't get them past the maître d' since the management didn't want any precedents being set on his watch. They were about to tear each other's hair out—or gnaw on each other's legs—when the bartender told them of a men's clothing shop in town. Well . . ."

She reached for her champagne, her head cocking to the side

briefly as she seemed to ponder if she'd really put it that far out of reach. She shrugged again and sipped. Christian grinned.

"What happened?" he asked, already liking her friends because, from what he'd gleaned from the past two stories she'd told of the couple, they were highly protective of Bayli and adored her to pieces.

Returning her glass to the table—and visibly noting where she'd set it—Bayli said, "The bartender was getting off in ten minutes and offered to take them into town. Only"—she snickered affably—"Phillip and Colin assumed he'd drive them in his car."

"But he didn't have a car?"

"He had a scooter! So both Phillip and Colin were on the back, holding on to each other and the bartender for dear life while he whizzed through rush-hour traffic, zipping right down the road between vehicles so that they were literally flanked by cars and Colin was screaming—*screaming*—bloody murder."

"Now that'd make a great YouTube video."

"Indeed. If only Phillip was coordinated enough to hold on and film at the same time."

"But they bought new clothes and had a wonderful dinner."

"Not even close. The bartender wigged from all the girlish screeching and clinging and at the first available U-ey took them right back to the hotel. They were so traumatized by the 'harrowing' experience, they refused to leave their room that night and raided the minibar. This incredibly classy Lord & Taylor and Harrods couple devoured Pringles and M&M's and sucked down every champagne and wine split and tiny bottle of booze in the fridge. They were plastered and ridiculously hungover in the morning."

Christian chuckled. "Who hasn't been there before?"

"Apparently, Drs. Phillip and Colin Holdsworth. It was quite the rude awakening for them both."

"See, that's the problem with Oxford," Christian humorously

mused. "They don't teach their grad students how to successfully conquer the minibar."

"Or how to not let out more bloodcurdling screams when they see the bill at checkout."

He nodded. "Now *that* was probably a harrowing experience."

"The upcharge alone. Not to mention the service fee and taxation."

Christian *tsk*ed. "Likely would have been cheaper to buy suits in town than hunker down in their room."

"Sure, but you simply cannot convince them it would have been worth the Freddy Krueger scooter incident."

Christian said, "You're a very enthralling storyteller."

"Just relaying their epic vacation disasters."

"Well, we're not going to have to worry about any of that on our travels."

Her brow crooked. "How can you be so sure? The airline could easily lose our luggage and we'll all be fucked."

"Hard for them to lose our luggage when we're not flying commercial. I'm chartering a jet. Your clothes will be safely stored onboard, never to be separated from you."

She stared at him for endless moments. Christian wasn't quite sure in which direction her thoughts ran, so he sipped his champagne while she gaped.

Eventually, she came around and said, "We're flying on a private jet?"

"Gulfstream. Very well appointed. You'll like it. No miniature bottles of hooch, though. All full-size."

"Wow." She reached for her own glass and sipped much more gingerly than before. As though she was suddenly wary of getting tipsy. Like her glittery vision of a private plane would turn into a pumpkin if she didn't keep her wits about her.

Christian said, "I'll take care of all the details. You just have to narrow down your thoughts on locales. You're a bit all over the place. No problem there, but you haven't really hit upon anything that lights *you* up. So far, these are all destinations your friends have told you about."

"That's because I've never been anywhere, Christian."

"Not true. You lived in San Francisco and are now in Manhattan, Bayli. Top global destinations. Ask anyone. Ask the Japanese."

She laughed. "You just had to bring that up." Though she couldn't disagree, and he knew it. "Put that way, I do feel a bit worldlier than I did five seconds ago."

"Perspective is everything, sweetheart."

Bayli leaned in close and said, "Thank you for not judging, Christian Davila."

He kissed the tip of her nose. "Never."

FOURTEEN

Rory felt a surge of excitement when he crossed the dining room, spying Christian and Bayli in a private moment. Sort of lost in each other's eyes. That was Christian and his romantic nature.

Typically, Rory would have smirked over such sappiness. But not this time. He found it riveting that Bayli looked so taken . . . and so did Christian.

Something brewed amongst the three of them that wasn't Rory and Christian's norm. Because Bayli Styles wasn't their norm.

She was striking in ways that went well beyond physical attractiveness. And all that inner vibrancy called to Rory. Along with the way Christian was in tune with her as well.

A server trailed behind Rory with a loaded tray as he made his way down the short line of steps to the back corner where Christian and Bayli were huddled in a booth. Rory had showered in the private bathroom adjacent to his office and changed into a suit and tie. It was edging toward half past ten and the kitchen would be closing at eleven. While the food orders were still pouring in and would continue to, Rory's competent staff had everything under control. So he was joining Christian and Bayli for dinner.

Another unique moment when it came to the two men and a woman they were both interested in. Christian didn't believe in tying up a table for romantic purposes, and neither did Rory. If they ever occupied a coveted seat during business hours, it was to hobnob with, impress, or influence someone.

Clearly, Christian was still working every angle with Bayli. Then again, so was Rory. He'd already sent out meaty sea scallops with a sweet-and-spicy chili sauce. Caesar salads with a newly concocted, decadent anchovy dressing. Lobster bisque with succulent chunks of lobster meat in the center and drizzled with crème fraîche and cognac. Dinner was a surf and turf sampler. More aphrodisiacs.

Bayli tore her gaze from Christian as Rory approached their table. She smiled brightly, making his pulse jump.

Rory stood to the side as the server delivered the food, starting with the lady, of course.

Who instantly scooted out of the small booth and leapt to her feet. "Oh, my God, Rory!" she hissed under her breath. Pointing to her plate, she said, "Those prawns still have their heads and legs attached and those long, curly antenna things. Their beady little eyes are staring at me."

Christian laughed. "Really, Bayli, Phillip and Colin would be so proud of your 'girlish screeching.'"

She shot him a feisty look. "I don't eat food that can actually see me about to devour it."

"Well, in the prawns' defense," Rory lightly jested, "they are dead. And who are Phillip and Colin?"

"Friends of mine," she said, "who basically find themselves in every whacky travel or dining scenario imaginable, excluding, I believe, still having the heads on their crustaceans."

"Sit," Rory instructed. "I'll show you how to eat them."

"I don't know," she hedged. "They already got a good look at me. They'll remember me; I'm sure of it. And come back to haunt me at a later date."

"I was the one who chose them for this esteemed sacrifice," Rory told her. "I promise they'll be too busy haunting me to bother with you. Now. Sit."

She slid back into the booth. Christian grinned at him. Rory chuckled. Then he eased into the booth on the other side of Bayli. The server left them and Rory said, "Damn good thing I only laid out the lobster tails instead of the whole lobster. And, thankfully, the cow stopped mooing before I cooked each filet mignon."

"Rory," she scolded. "You could be insulting vegetarians at this very moment."

"Not in this restaurant." He glanced around. Returned his gaze to her. "We're in a steakhouse, honey."

"Right." She sighed. "Good point."

"I will concede that we've found New Yorkers aren't overwhelmingly receptive to eating their prawns with the heads on," Christian said. "They're not big on getting down and dirty, which you have to in order to enjoy this delicacy."

Bayli blanched. "Did you just say that you *eat* the heads?"

While she stared at her plate, aghast, Rory explained, "It's an eclectic flavor explosion. I'd give you all the technical terms of what you're actually eating, but then you might not try it."

"Oh, fuck, I'm not trying it even without the graphic description!" she blurted.

Rory said, "It's more of a southern thing, I'll admit. And big in Asia, not to mention shrimping towns the world over. But, Bayli, the culinary experience isn't just about eating your typical, everyday fare. Diversity goes a long way. Like soft-shell crab. You can eat the shell."

"Rory, that's disgusting."

He gently squeezed her thigh under the table. "Variety is the spice of life, or haven't you heard?"

"Hey, I got all kinds of adventurous the other day at the salad bar and tried beets for the very first time."

God, he wanted to kiss her! In that full-on, who-gives-a-rip-that-there's-an-audience sort of way. Like at the farmers' market.

Christian said, "Just let him demonstrate with the prawns."

"You can snap the heads off if you want," Rory told her. "Or take a bite. I recommend doing it quickly. There's a burst of . . . liquid. Don't be surprised."

"What kind of liquid?" Her pretty face screwed into a semi-tortured look. "And by *burst*, do you mean it's going to squirt all over the place and I'm going to gag?"

Rory reached for one of his prawns and bit into it. Chewed, savored. Swallowed. "No gagging involved. It's really very good. And you'll love the fire-roasted lemon aioli."

"Oh, good Lord." She slid her glance to Christian. "Well? What are *you* waiting for?"

"For *him* to be the one to gross you out. Now that we have that out of the way . . ." He reached for a prawn and chomped down.

"Jesus Christ!" she quietly squealed. "Oh, that's just so, so wrong!"

Rory finished off his first prawn and went for another. "At least try one," he insisted. "It'll give you your first color commentary for the show."

"Sure," she dryly said. "I'll get tons of mileage out of heaving in a fancy steakhouse owned by the two men who hired me to host their cooking show."

Rory told her, "No one's currently watching. Do it before someone whips out a camera and you've got yet another YouTube video to go viral."

"That's *your* vid," she corrected. "No one knows it's me you're kissing."

"Just a matter of time," he assured her.

She looked at Christian again, who said, "If you're hoping I'm going to bail you out on this one, you're wrong. Try it."

Rory saw her work down a lump of fear or disgust or angst—he wasn't sure which was more accurate.

Then she followed suit and took a healthy bite out of her prawn.

Her eyes popped.

Her hand flew to her mouth.

But she chewed. Swallowed. Tawny eyes still outrageously wide.

"See, not so bad . . . ," Christian slyly coaxed.

"Oh, for fuck's sake." Rory laughed. "She didn't spit it into her napkin. She likes it."

Bayli chewed some more, then slowly nodded. "It's . . . sweet. Like, unexpectedly sweet. And you're right. There's a huge burst of flavor. Holy cow. It just floods the mouth and it's so deliciously sweet. . . ." She shook her head. "I need better adjectives. I can't just say something's *sweet*. I need to be able to target all the nuances and really describe what something tastes like."

"Don't expect it to just happen overnight," Rory told her. "We'll work on it."

"Wow, Rory," she said as she peeled away the shell and dipped the prawn into the lemon aioli. "You do have a knack for goading me into things."

"I prefer to think of it as broadening your horizons."

She stared contemplatively at him, and Rory wondered if she was mulling over what he'd said to her when he'd been deep inside her on Sunday. About what he really wanted to do to her. That thought spiked his testosterone and he tore his gaze from her and glanced at Christian over her head. His friend wore an intense expression, as though considering all the sexual possibilities as well.

Rory's eyes dropped to meet Bayli's once more. "Try the oysters."

"Not a chance," she said without so much as blinking.

He grinned. "I promise you'll enjoy it."

"I know you're all about me trying new things, but I'm not going to cave to *everything*."

"We'll see about that." And he knew his grin turned mischievous. "Start with the oysters."

"They're slimy."

"They're not slimy. Let Christian show you how to shoot 'em."

She shifted slightly in her seat. "Fine. If you'll eat one, so will I."

"That's not much of a challenge you're issuing," Christian told her. "I like them." He reached for one and used the seafood fork to loosen the shucked oyster away from the shell. Then he spooned on a bit of the red wine and shallot vinaigrette, put the shell to his bottom lip, tilted back his head, and sucked down the oyster.

Bayli squirmed a little in her seat. "What if mine doesn't go down that smoothly?"

"Give it a whirl," Rory said as he prepped one for her. "Just let it slide down your throat."

She inhaled deeply. Took the shell from him. Let out a stream of air, then perfectly imitated Christian.

Rory didn't miss the shiver down her spine. Nor did Christian, he was sure.

"Oh . . . ," Bayli said on a long sigh. "That was . . . I . . . That was . . . so exhilarating."

Her thighs pressed together. Rory's cock instantly swelled.

She reached for another, only this time sprinkling his special hot-sauce creation on the oyster. She shivered again as it went down.

"Kind of a rush," she said, her eyes sparkling.

Rory's head lowered and he whispered, "I won't steer you wrong."

Her gaze locked with his again. "You're mistaking my hesitation for lack of trust. That's not it at all. I'm just not used to all of this, you know? The five-star dining experience, the exotic food, the heat that's radiating from the two of you . . ."

She shifted her attention to Christian. "I'm really not hungry for food anymore."

"Fine by me." He snatched the napkin from his lap and set it on the table. "Rory?"

"Pierre will package up the untouched food for the homeless. I think that's his favorite closing chore."

Rory stood and offered his hand to Bayli.

"I need to step into the restroom to wash my hands," she said.

"Same with us. We'll meet you in the foyer."

She collected her wrap and clutch, ascended the three steps that led up to the main floor, and then wound her way through tables and the bar before disappearing from sight.

Rory said to Christian, "This isn't going to be anything like our past affairs. She's—"

"Everything we've ever wanted in a woman?" Christian joined Rory and buttoned his suit jacket. "And you're wondering if she really knows what she's getting herself into."

"You aren't?"

Christian's jaw clenched. Then he said, "We're both good at sensing what's not enough, what's too much. That's why we work so well together. That's why we'll both make sure she gets *exactly* what she needs."

Rory grinned. "Many, *many* orgasms."

Bayli stared at her reflection in the mirror and saw one hell of an excited woman staring back at her. Well, she looked nervous, too. Not overly nervous, just that sort of *oh, shit, do I really know what I'm doing?* sort of nervous.

But yes. She really did know what she was doing. Mostly.

Okay, there was still a hint of the unknown lingering in the far recesses of her mind. Yet nothing powerful enough to over-shadow the excitement. Christian Davila and Rory St. James were going to take her to one of their apartments and do incredibly wicked things to her.

Anticipation shot through her, igniting against her clit and deep in her core.

"Fuck," she whispered, though she was the only one presently in the ladies' room.

Her knees weakened and her inner thighs burned. And the trio wasn't even out of the restaurant yet!

She tidied up, used an individually packaged toothbrush and paste, then swilled some mouthwash. Tried to collect herself as best as possible, but Bayli was teeming with eagerness and a blazing euphoria wrapped around two absurdly sexy men she had no doubt would go to any length to pleasure her.

And oh, dear God, how she wanted them both!

With the excitement rushing through her, she met her men in the entryway and preceded them out into the crisp late-summer air. Not brisk enough to be considered fall, but wonderfully refreshing on her hot, tingling skin. For Christ's sake, she could break out in a sweat in an igloo when Christian and Rory flanked her and she inhaled each of their distinct yet complementary scents.

Was that somehow planned? Did they shop for cologne together to make sure they both created the perfect aroma to seduce a woman's olfactory neurons?

She stifled a giggle. Now she was getting giddy with expectations, innately knowing each one would be exceeded this evening.

Christian's stretch Jag arrived curbside and he slipped in first, then Bayli, followed by Rory.

Could they tell how thrilled she was? How anxious in a really good way? In fact, she wondered how she'd survive the ride to Christian's building. The ride in the elevator up to his apartment. The ride of her life they were about to take her on . . .

Bayli swallowed down the lump of enthusiasm in her throat and forced herself to sit still when, in actuality, her body was already beginning to vibrate. She was practically desperate for them. Wanted to lose herself in their touch, their kisses, their sinful words.

"You okay?" Rory asked in a low tone.

She was wiggling a bit between them. Couldn't help herself.

"Sure," she said. "Contrary to everything I've told you from the moment you met me, I'm completely used to being on my way to some den of iniquity with two incredibly gorgeous men who are likely mentally plotting even as I speak how they're going to make me come."

Rory chuckled.

Christian snickered. "It might not be the penthouse suite, but my apartment is in one of the most prestigious buildings in Manhattan. Hardly a den."

"Ah," she said with a small laugh. "You take offense to *den* but not *iniquity*."

"Not while Rory and I are mentally plotting how we're going to make you come."

"Oh, Lord," she muttered. Even mild flirting with these two got her juices flowing. She *so* was not in their league. But Bayli didn't care. Not anymore.

Especially not when she was wedged between them on the seat, on each side one of their legs pressing to the outside of hers. Christian draped an arm around her bare shoulders. Rory rested a hand on her thigh, a mere breath from the short hem. The partition separating them from the driver was up, and they had all the privacy they could possibly want. Yet Bayli buzzed with the knowledge that there was, indeed, someone else on the other side of that window. Someone who might know exactly what these three were up to.

"I'd say we're not the only ones mentally plotting," Rory teased as his fingers swept lightly over her skin. Dipping between the gap in her legs to lazily whisk along her inner thigh. Heading north, under her dress.

She didn't stop him.

Christian placed a hand on her other leg. Gave a titillating squeeze. Bayli sucked in a sharp slice of air.

Rory's warm, minty breath tickled the shell of her ear as he said, "So it's not the food that has you trembling."

"I'll admit that your culinary combinations sparked something inside me, but you both already know what really gets me hot."

"And wet," Rory added as his fingertips grazed the thin satin covering the heart of her.

On the other side of her, Christian's lips skimmed along her neck. His hand on her thigh tugged gently so that she spread her legs. In doing so, her skirt hitched up.

Rory languidly rubbed her clit through her thong while Christian kissed her throat. Bayli's head fell back on the top of the seat and her eyelids fluttered closed. Her hands skated across the material of their suit pants, into their laps, and Bayli massaged their cocks. Rory's fingers slipped beyond her thong and he stroked her clit more feverishly, instantly sending her arousal skyrocketing.

Christian's mouth sealed hers and he kissed her as erotic sensations began to build deep within her.

But neither man seemed content with his current position. Christian broke their kiss and eased the hidden zipper of her dress down her side. He peeled away the structured bodice to bare her breasts. At the same time, Rory shifted and knelt on the floor before her. His fingers hooked in the thin strands at her hips and he stripped away the skimpy lingerie. Then his hands slid under her ass and he tilted her hips just so. A heartbeat later his mouth was on her.

Bayli let out a small cry.

Christian palmed one of her breasts and his thumb flicked over her puckered nipple, tightening it further. His tongue toyed with her other pebbled bead. One of her hands plowed through his hair. The other threaded through Rory's as he licked her pussy.

Bayli had never known such pleasure. It was all so different from anything she'd experienced with this duo separately. Because it was both of them—*at the same time*—pleasuring her. To have one tongue fervently fluttering over that swollen knot of nerves that seemed more sensitive this evening than ever before and another tongue flitting against her nipple . . . it was almost a bit overwhelming. But so glorious.

One mouth suckled her clit. The other suckled the taut center of her breast.

Rory's finger eased inside her pussy and stroked with purpose.

Christian's fingers and thumb pinched and rolled the nipple his mouth wasn't devouring.

The wealth of sensations multiplied, intensified. Pushed her right to the edge.

And they seemed to know it, wanted to get her off explosively.

Rory moved slightly as he worked a second finger into her tight canal and fucked her assertively while Christian's hand left her breast and he used the pads of two fingers to massage her clit with an equally aggressive touch. His tongue still teased her nipple; his mouth still suckled. Rory nipped at her inner thigh, making the flesh quiver.

Bayli's pulse hammered in her head. Her heart pounded. Whimpers fell from her parted lips. Her hips undulated and her inner muscles squeezed, taking everything both men gave her. Her fingers coiled tighter around the strands of hair she held.

"Oh, God," she moaned. "*Yes*. Make me come. Oh, God, please make me come." Her lids drifted open and she watched them work in tandem to push her higher and higher. It was the sexiest damn thing she'd ever seen.

Two men dedicated strictly to her pleasure. Both determined to set her off.

Rory shifted once again, coming up on his knees so that he hovered above her, and kissed her passionately as he added a third finger to fuck her pussy. Nerve endings jumped and she clutched at his fingers as he deepened their kiss, and Christian hit just the right pace and pressure on that sensitive pearl between her legs to send her spiraling out of control. Everything erupted inside her. She ripped her mouth from Rory's and cried out.

Her head fell back again and he bit her neck as sheer ecstasy burned through her veins.

Her body shook. Her pussy contracted around his fingers and she didn't relinquish them, loving the feeling of being filled as she stole every ounce of pleasure from the fiery climax.

And simply reveled in the nearness of Christian and Rory. Luxuriated in the way their entire focus had been on her.

Thank God Jewel had not kept this forbidden romantic scenario a secret from her. Because Bayli knew she'd just tapped into the ultimate in sexual decadence!

FIFTEEN

Christian's apartment was nothing short of spectacular, as Bayli had expected all along.

She barely had a memory of her two lovers disentangling from her, zipping her up, sliding her thong into place, and pouring a brandy to share.

The stroll through the enormous and opulent lobby was pretty much a blur, too. Inside the elevator, she'd stared at the shiny doors and thrilled over the reflection of the three of them, looking quite devilish. Then they'd stepped through the double entrance to Christian's apartment and she'd taken in the wide-open, gorgeously decorated space with bulging eyes and a slack jaw.

While Christian and Rory divested themselves of their jackets and cuff links and Christian fixed drinks, she wandered through the vast living room with its tall corner fireplace and all the plush furniture facing the floor-to-second-level windows that showcased Central Park. Sprawled right before them. From the south end to as far as the eye could see. Which was pretty damn far from this vantage point.

As Christian lit the multiple fires and dimly set chandeliers, she passed through glass doors to the terrace. Rory followed closely behind.

"He has a swimming pool," she drolly commented. "Why am I not surprised?"

"And a spa."

All sleek and stylish, with water features made of flat, polished obsidian stone, all artistically lit. Bayli stood at the railing and took in the scene once more.

"Not too shabby, eh?" Rory said from beside her.

"Your apartment is incredible, too. Remind me to *never* show you mine."

"Bayli."

"Shh." She kissed him. It was meant to be a quick kiss, but of course Rory took charge of it. His arms slid around her waist and he hauled her up against him.

Where Christian's kisses were intense and all-consuming, Rory's held the playful promise of wicked things to come, making her toes curl.

When she finally pulled away, she breathlessly said, "I had a point to make."

He grinned deviously. "So did I."

Unraveling from him—and fanning her flushed face with a hand—she took a couple of steps back so that she didn't fall into his embrace again.

She told him, "This is all extremely nice," gesturing toward the terrace and Christian's apartment in general, "but it's not the reason I'm here. Yes, I want to someday be someone and maybe have my own swimming pool, too. You know this about me already, and it's one hundred percent true. I want more for myself than I've ever had—I'm sure that's also how Christian felt from the time he was a kid. But . . . there's something much more enticing and poignant about all of this that has nothing to do with material desires."

Rory crossed his arms over his chest. Cocked his head to the side. "Tell me."

"It's like when you read a novel and the character has painted himself into a corner and, as the reader, you're wondering how the hell he'll ever free himself. How he'll escape whatever drudgery or peril or cage he's facing with no obvious route in sight or in mind. And then something mysterious happens—he discovers a secret or accidentally flips a switch that reveals a private passage through the walls or he finds a trapdoor. Whatever. And suddenly a slew of new opportunities are laid out before him. It's a very heady sensation for the reader as much as for the character."

"You might be losing me on this one, babe."

She laughed softly. "Think about it. When I came to your restaurant it was because I needed a job. Would I have been content coming in three nights a week to seat people who'd look right through me—a nobody—because they're more interested in *seeing and being seen* in a roomful of VIPs?"

"Likely not. One of the reasons I didn't hire you."

"Smart of you. But I faced a corner because you turned me away. Luckily, I had the gig at the fund-raiser with the opportunity to impress Christian. He was my trapdoor . . . Except." She held up her finger as Rory started to speak. "Not in the way I'd anticipated. The show will be a fantastic break for me, and I'm eternally grateful for the chance to prove I can do this, for being chosen. But I got painted right back into the corner, because I came full circle with you."

"I'm your corner?"

She grinned. "*You're* my trapdoor, too."

"Why am I not getting that logic?"

With another laugh, Bayli said, "Because I'm high on champagne and aphrodisiacs and a really amazing orgasm. But, Rory, what I'm telling you is that I was living in fear of not landing the hostess job—because I really need the steady paycheck. And while I was all tangled up in that fear, the two of you were already working out my escape route. And the truth is, I don't care about this amazing view of Central Park. I mean, it *is* amazing . . . but my point is, for the first time in my life I'm understanding that what I want isn't just about *being* special in the eyes of strangers. It's about *feeling* special, and worthy, when I'm with people I care about. Who care about me." She got a little teary-eyed, but Rory didn't seem to mind.

He brushed his fingers over her cheek. His breath blew against her temple as he said, "Beautiful Bayli. Sometimes you're just too much in your head, honey." His finger and thumb gingerly pinched her chin and lifted it so that she stared him in the eyes. "Christian and I aren't *your* escape route. You're ours. From the moment we saw you, even though it was separately, we both knew you were the answer to our problem with the show. And that we both wanted you. That you are what we *both* want."

His mouth claimed hers and he kissed her with the sort of hunger that always clawed at her when it came to Christian and Rory. She was instantly restless. Craved carnal pleasures she knew little about but was more than eager to learn. With them.

Bayli unraveled Rory's tie as the kiss went on and on. She shoved the buttons of his shirt through their holes. Yanked the hem from his pants. Then her hands splayed over his ridged abs and she got even hotter.

Breaking the kiss, Rory took her by the hand and slowly backed into the apartment, his burning gaze still on her. She tried to breathe normally, but that proved impossible. They entered the living room, the atmosphere warm and inviting.

Bayli gently pulled her hand from Rory's and crossed to where Christian watched them, a sexy grin on his face.

"What are you smiling at?" she asked before her lips swept over his.

"The two of you. I was getting worried that you were arguing again. But . . . clearly not."

"Definitely not. Though don't count on us to always be so well behaved with each other. He gets so easily agitated."

From behind her, Rory gave a half snort. Bayli laughed quietly.

She told Christian, "He seems to think I have some complexities as well."

"Don't we all?" Christian offered.

"Indeed. Currently, yours is being too buttoned up." She had him out of his tie and shirt in record time, then admired his chest and the long grooves of his obliques. Sighed dreamily. "You make me want to lick every single inch of you."

"Maybe we'll get to that later. At the moment, I think you're the one wearing too much clothing."

Rory was suddenly at her back. He slid the side zipper of her dress down its track, the slow zinging of metal filling the otherwise quiet room.

Christian's head dipped and he pulled her into one of his soul-stirring kisses that snagged her from reality. Meanwhile, Rory eased the silver material down her body and then knelt behind her. He dragged her thong away and palmed her ass, spreading her cheeks. His mouth was on her pussy in the next instant and she moaned into Christian's mouth.

Christian's arm wound around her waist to hold her steady. His other hand cupped her breast and kneaded a bit roughly, insistently, as Rory tongued her clit and then her opening. He suckled her slit and then pressed his tongue inside.

Bayli had to end her blazing kiss with Christian in order to suck in some much-needed oxygen. And because her entire being was on fire.

She twisted slightly at the waist and combed her hand through Rory's hair. Christian drew her puckered nipple into his mouth while Rory continued to lick her pussy. The compounded sensations were scintillating and had her deeply aroused again. And stepping further away from the restrictive confines of a conventional sexual relationship.

When she was on the verge of coming, Rory stood. Her mind whirled. "Hey. I was about to come."

He gave her his cocky grin. "Not just yet," he told her. "You weren't begging for it." He gave her a quick, sexy kiss.

"Not verbally," she complained. "But trust me, my body is screaming for another release."

"We'll make it scream louder," Christian assured her.

And an entire Fourth of July full of fireworks went off inside her.

Rory took her hand and led her across the room, toward the elevated entryway and curving staircase. But they didn't make it that far. There was an ebony credenza that stretched along the short wall at the foyer and was partially tucked into a corner. Its purpose was primarily bar service, with fancy decanters and glasses set out. Along with a silver-plated ice bucket with a lid. Though a large portion of the surface was devoid of items.

Christian stopped here and said, "This'll do nicely."

"Care to elaborate?" Bayli asked.

"You'll enjoy what I have in mind." He shot a look toward Rory. "What *we* have in mind."

"I can certainly improvise and make this work," Rory said. And freed the fastenings of his pants.

Bayli's fingers were at Christian's waist, loosening his belt, then unbuttoning and unzipping him. She shoved his pants and briefs down his legs while he toed off his shoes. She admired him as he stepped out of the clothing and his socks. His cock was rock-hard and his muscles were bunched.

Oysters and lobster bisque be damned, Christian and Rory were the *ultimate* aphrodisiacs.

She turned to Rory, who was naked as well. Her heart skipped some necessary beats.

For a few suspended seconds, Bayli wasn't the least bit sure what she should do. What she should do *with these two men*, to be exact.

They were several steps ahead of her, though.

Christian took her hand, garnering her attention. He perched himself on the edge of the credenza and she stood between the vee of his parted legs. He kissed her as he wrapped her fingers around his steel erection.

Behind her, Rory lifted her leg and draped it over Christian's thigh, opening her to them both. Rory's fingers slid into her moisture and heat from behind. Christian's rubbed her clit.

It was nearly impossible to keep up their sizzling kiss and slowly pump his cock while he and Rory were sending her into that blissful state again.

So Bayli decided to change things up. Take charge this time.

She broke her kiss with Christian and released his cock from her tight fist. She grabbed Rory's free hand and pulled it around her side, forcing him to coil his fingers around Christian's throbbing dick.

"Bayli," both men said in unison. With the same distinct edge of *oh, hell no!* in their voices.

"Do this for me," she said. "So I can concentrate on what you're doing to me. And, because . . . well, it's making me absolutely crazy, Rory, to see your hand on Christian's cock."

"This isn't what we do," Christian said in a strained voice.

Her brow crooked. "But for me . . . ?"

Rory let out a low growl. "That's a two-way street, honey."

Excitement rippled through her. When it really shouldn't, since she knew exactly what flitted through Rory's mind at that very moment.

The ass reference. Though unspoken this time.

She said, "Just give me this right now." Because good Lord, it was riveting to watch Rory's strong hand encircle Christian's thick shaft. And pump heartily.

Her mouth was all over Christian's chest, her tongue fluttering over his small nipples, her teeth lightly nipping his flesh, her lips dragging along his smooth skin. All the while he rubbed her clit with a fervor that screamed *payback*. And she loved every second of it.

Rory's fingers withdrew from her and he grabbed a condom from the strip he'd set on the ledge of the divider wall. He was sheathed in seconds and his cock teased her opening for a few moments.

Bayli studied Christian's face as Rory fisted him again, just as Rory was about to enter her.

The air was thick with sexual tension. With denial of what both men believed in, and the silent acceptance that they would do whatever Bayli asked of them. She was in control. Even as her body tightened and she wanted them both with a voracious appetite she'd never before imagined, let alone experienced, she understood that everything she didn't know and wasn't accustomed to didn't matter in the slightest.

They would give her whatever she wanted. Whatever she asked for.

Rory thrust into her and Bayli cried out. Her fingernails dug into Christian's chest as she held on to him while Rory fucked her. Hard.

Rory's hand clasped one of hers, using it to replace his on Christian's cock. She squeezed tight. Christian groaned.

Rory's fingers took over between her legs with a heated, intense rhythm as he thrust wildly into her.

Christian kissed her while Rory drove deep into her. Christian's hands were on her breasts now, alternately caressing and toying with her nipples, pinching lightly and sending bolts of lightning to all her erogenous zones.

Bayli was moments away from losing it. Rory kissed her neck as he hammered into her. She felt his cock swell. Knew he was damn close to exploding, too.

Tearing her mouth from Christian's, she said, "Make me come."

"Yes," Christian ground out. "Fuck her harder, Rory."

He thrust into her and Bayli felt that disassociation from the tangible wash over her as she let go and gave in to the frenetic sensations seizing her.

Her body tensed and then everything ignited and she screamed her pleasure.

"Goddamn," Rory rumbled from behind her. "Oh, Jesus, Bayli."

His cock pushed deeper and she felt the surging and the erupting and it kept her coming. She clutched him firmly with her inner muscles. He panted heavily.

"Fuck," Christian said on a low groan. "Bayli, don't squeeze me so tight, sweetheart."

Rory was quick to pry her fist from Christian's shaft. "Don't make him come just yet," he said. "Let him fuck you."

Rory pulled out of her and swiftly hoisted her up. Just as Christian lay back against the top of the credenza. Bayli straddled his lap as Christian rolled on a condom. Then he plunged into her and the frenzy of sensation started all over again.

Only this time, Rory was poised behind them and he cupped her ass, then nipped at the cheeks.

She was trying to fall into a rhythm with Christian and getting sidetracked by Rory. It was a little chaotic yet so damn thrilling. Christian palmed her breasts and massaged. Rory held her hips and made them gyrate against Christian's pelvis as he fucked her. It turned into another melee of erotic feelings coursing through her.

"This is almost perfect," Rory said.

Propping herself up on Christian's wide chest with her forearms, she watched Rory round the credenza and whip off the lid of the ice bucket. One corner of his mouth lifted.

He held up a crystal-clear square cube with a hole in the center and said, "Cocktail ice." Then he snatched a crescent-shaped cube from the small pocket separated by a divider and his grin turned downright sinful. "And then there's ice for more practical purposes."

Bayli had no idea what he meant. Until Rory inched closer to her and rubbed the cube against one of her nipples, then the other. The ice instantly started to melt against her heated flesh. And her nipples beaded tight.

"Rory," she ground out as the fever burned within her.

He rounded the credenza. She glanced down at Christian, whose eyes were a stunning, glittery blue.

"You know what he's up to, don't you?" she asked.

"Not this time." And he used a hand on the small of her back to press her more firmly against him as he plunged deeper into her.

"Oh, God, Christian." His cock slid smoothly along her slick walls and she was just about to tune out everything but him. Until Rory's hands were on her ass again and he spread her cheeks.

She felt the edge of the ice cube along her cleft and knew the cube was in his mouth. She gasped.

Christian's strong features darkened. "Oh, fuck."

He must have felt the cool rush of liquid as the ice melted against her skin and dripped onto him, because Christian's ass clenched, his hips lifted, and he pistoned rapidly into her.

Bayli couldn't catch her breath, let alone process Rory's next move. She felt the tip of the crescent rim her anus. Then penetrate. Ever so slightly. Ever so slowly.

"Oh, God." The ice inched in farther. She felt Rory's lips against her skin. Then suddenly— "Oh, my God!" The cube literally popped into her. More like there was a suctioning action within her that drew it in. Either way, it filled her with a crisp sensation surrounded by her body heat and it felt . . . so fucking fantastic.

Her forehead dropped to Christian's chest. His grip on her hips tightened. Rory's hands pushed her cheeks together, holding in the cube. Not that it was going anywhere, because Bayli clenched it and felt the deliciously chilly burst along with the corresponding tantalizing trickle down the inside of her leg.

"I'm going to come," she said on a ragged breath. "I'm going to come so damn hard."

"Yes," Rory all but growled from behind her.

Her palms pressed to Christian's pecs, her spine arched. Christian thrust up into her as Rory's teeth nipped at her ass.

"Fuck!" she cried. "Christian." She was on the precipice and nothing could stop her from falling. But she still needed more. Her fingertips curled. She tried to straighten them.

"It's okay," Christian said. "Do it. Whatever you want, whatever you need."

Her fingers dug in. He fucked her harder, apparently feeding off her arousal. She wanted to hold on to the searing intensity consuming her, but it was all too overwhelming, too exhilarating.

"Oh, God," she said on a broken breath. All of the sensations collided and burst wide open, and Bayli screamed even louder this time.

"Yes," Christian growled as she milked his cock. "Fuck, yes." A heartbeat later he exploded inside her, keeping Bayli's body quaking and every inch of her sizzling.

"Now that was hot," Rory said.

Bayli collapsed against Christian's chest and he stroked her spine while she tried to return to herself.

Wondering if that would ever happen.

Because she was no longer the Bayli Styles she used to be . . .

SIXTEEN

Rory eased her off of Christian sometime later. Bayli had no idea how many minutes had ticked by—dozens?—while she'd clung to Christian and he'd kept up his sensual, languid sweeping of his fingers up and down her spine. Tremors still ran through her. Her pussy throbbed from being filled and stretched, and perhaps because Bayli still yearned for more from these men.

But she was spent. Couldn't even open her eyes as Rory maneuvered her into his arms. She snuggled against him, her face buried in the crook of his neck. He carried her upstairs and presumably into Christian's bedroom, because he slipped her between crisp, cool sheets. He climbed in next to her. She surmised he'd removed his condom and tidied up while she'd been huddled on top of Christian.

Now her body curled into Rory's as they lay on their sides. Christian joined them and he spooned her from behind. She twined her fingers with Christian's and rested their hands against Rory's chest.

"Are you all right?" Christian murmured.

"Never better." Her voice was weak, raspy from screaming in sheer ecstasy.

Rory's hand was on her hip and his thumb absently grazed her

still-sensitive flesh, keeping her charged. He said, "You did extremely well for a first-timer."

She grimaced. "You're trying to bait me and it's not going to
work. I am literally Zenned out. Completely boneless and mindless.
It is absolutely fantastic. The most incredible feeling in the world."

"Well, not *the* most incredible feeling," Rory grumbled. "Right?"

Bayli barely had the energy to laugh. It came out a wisp of air.
"Of course not. Winning the lottery would be the most incredible
feeling in the world."

Christian snickered. "Now who's baiting whom?"

"He started it."

"And you just can't resist prodding."

"You do recall what he did to me downstairs, yes?"

"Hmm, yes. That."

"How's your ass?" Rory asked in a playful tone.

"Ha-ha," she muttered. Then smiled. "Actually, it's really a
very interesting sensation. Like there's a fresh, cool breeze trilling
through me."

"Ah, the gift that keeps on giving." Rory chuckled. She felt the
low rumbling straight to her core.

"You really shouldn't have done that without my permission."

"But you enjoyed it. And what about what you did without my
permission?"

"Your hand on Christian's cock?" She moaned. Her eyelids
fluttered open. "That was damn hot." She twisted slightly so she
could look at Christian over her shoulder. "So unbelievably hot. I
could come just by watching you two." She kissed him.

His lips tangled with hers for a few moments. Then he whispered against them, "Don't get any ideas."

"Too late."

She turned back to Rory. Kissed him as well. Asked, "What's
the big deal, anyway? It's impossible to keep your bodies from
touching when you're with one woman."

"Totally different," Rory adamantly said. "Yeah, body parts

are going to bump and rub from time to time, but it's not something blatant or intentional."

Christian added, "It's not something that registers as direct contact; it's just part of the overall experience."

"But it enhances the overall experience, right?" she asked.

"Don't confuse it as something we're interested in," Rory was quick to say.

"Hmm. All well and good, I guess. It's not like I'd want to share either of you, even if it was with each other."

"The primary focus is supposed to be you," Christian pointed out.

"How can I complain about that?" She yawned. Snuggled a little closer to Rory, with her head under his chin. Christian's chiseled chest was pressed to her back, his entire body melding to her, really. It was beautiful to be surrounded by their heat and muscles, wrapped in their embrace. As her lids dipped, she quietly asked, "Is it always like this with the women you share?"

Neither of her lovers responded. Endless moments stretched out in the ensuing silence. Bayli was about to nod off when both men said just one significant, powerful word, almost simultaneously.

"No."

Her hand was on his cock as sleep ebbed and realization dawned on Christian. Her tongue swept over his chest and she licked his nipples. All the while, she stroked his erect shaft with a firm grip.

They'd shifted in the middle of the night, Bayli curling into him while Rory spooned her. Christian had yet to open an eye, but he knew Rory was still in bed with them. And was fingering her pussy while her leg tangled with Christian's and her clit and slick folds rubbed against his thigh. Her little pants of air blew across his skin, stimulating him further. Everything about her excited him, including the fact that Rory was so taken with her.

The tip of Bayli's tongue flickered over a pebbled bead and Christian groaned. "That'll get you into lots of trouble."

"Oh, yay," she murmured. "You're awake."

"Or having a stellar dream."

"It's no dream."

"Wonderful. And so happy to know Rory's able to keep his hands off me after he's sampled the goods."

"Asshole," Rory retorted.

"Ah, come on," Christian goaded, his voice a bit strained as Bayli picked up the pace, stroking him with just the right amount of pressure. "You wish you had a cock as big as mine."

"Boys," she chided. "I'm trying to get Christian off here."

She moved down his body and took him deep in her mouth. Sucked him hard. So fucking hard. He let out a low growl. Got lost in the moment until he heard Rory rummage in the nightstand drawer, since he knew where Christian's condom stashes were located.

Then Rory told Bayli, "Come up on your knees, honey."

A few seconds later she released Christian's dick to draw in a breath of air as Rory entered her. Then she returned to her task, expertly teasing Christian with her tongue, her lips. Her fingers massaging and gently tugging on his sac.

"Yes," he said. "That's so fucking good. You have one seriously wicked mouth, Miss Styles."

Naturally, she didn't bother replying. Except to suck him fervently, making his pulse jump.

He could feel the jarring in her body as Rory moved forcefully inside her. Christian finally opened his eyes and watched while she took him deep again. His hips jerked as he fucked her mouth. Then his gaze panned to get the full effect of Rory buried in her pussy, his hips bucking, his muscles pulling taut as he worked her good, his fingers on her clit.

Christian used one hand to brush away strands of hair from her face. The other palmed her breast, then rolled her taut nipple between his finger and thumb. But he wanted to help Rory really send her soaring. So Christian reached for the nightstand on his side of the bed and whipped open the door. Fumbled around for the lube. He squirted some on his middle finger and then rimmed her anus.

"Do it," Rory demanded. "It'll make me even harder and she'll come with both of us."

Obviously, Bayli knew what he was up to—and didn't stop him.

Christian very carefully penetrated the small hole with just the tip of his finger. Bayli's head popped up again and she let out an erotic cry.

"Yes," Rory ground out as she apparently squeezed his cock.

Christian pressed in a little farther and stroked slightly.

"Oh, my God," she whimpered. And then she put an incredible amount of effort into jerking Christian off, her fingers coiling with a steel grip. Christian drizzled some of the lube at the tip of his cock and her hand glided fiercely up and down his shaft. He went barreling toward orgasm as she pumped him and Rory fucked her.

"Yes," she murmured. "God, yes. Like that."

"Make her come, Rory."

"You're both going to make me come," she said. "Oh, Christ, it's *too* much. But don't you dare stop!"

She was panting heavily, her chest heaving. They both plunged into her as Rory rubbed her clit and seconds later her hand contracted even more firmly around Christian's cock and he felt the release build to the boiling point.

"Come now, sweetheart," Christian urged. "Come for us."

"Yes. *Yes!*"

Her body tensed and then quaked violently as she cried once more.

"Oh, goddamn!" Rory roared as he erupted.

Christian crested the edge and told Bayli, "Suck my dick. Swallow my cum."

Her mouth closed around him as her body continued to shake,

the orgasm still blazing through her. She sucked just as her fingers rolled his balls and Christian's booming, "Hell, yes!" echoed in the quiet room as his pulse raged in his head.

He hit a high he wasn't quite sure he'd ever come down from.

Rory was in Christian's gourmet kitchen grilling vegetables to load the omelets with when Bayli stole behind him and wrapped her arms around his waist. He wore nothing but his suit pants, zipped but not buttoned. She'd put on Christian's dress shirt, but it was also unbuttoned. Rory loved the feel of her bare breasts and hard nipples against his skin.

"You should be severely punished for encouraging Christian to do such naughty things to me." Her warm lips grazed his shoulder blades, sending the blood to his cock.

"You could have said no, honey."

"Sure. But after the ice cube incident, I—"

"Is that what we're calling it now?"

She bit him. And damn if that didn't get him hard in a heartbeat.

"Behave," she lightly scolded. "Now, given that I have never imagined or fantasized it was possible to come as powerfully as I do with the two of you, I have no choice but to concede that the tricks you both have up your sleeves are worth allowing some experimentation on my part."

"Is that a roundabout way of saying you're giving us carte blanche with your body?" He peered at her over his shoulder. "Because you were trying to confuse me there, babe. I could tell."

She smiled, all pretty and perky like. Fresh-faced and with her damp hair tumbling in waves down her back, she made Rory want to drag her off to bed again. His gaze lifted and he searched the open dining room/great room combo for Christian.

Apparently knowing the direction in which Rory's thoughts ran, Bayli informed him, "Christian's on the phone about a scheduling conflict, it sounded like when I left him."

"Too bad. I was thinking another go at you was in order before breakfast."

"Not that I'd mind, believe me." Her cheek rubbed against his back and she all but purred. "Unfortunately, I'm famished and I only have a little time before I have to get home, get dressed, and get to the library for my shift."

Rory frowned. "Honey, you don't have to work at the library anymore. I happen to know what Christian and I are paying you, remember?" Tension suddenly gripped him. "Unless you've changed your mind about the show—"

"Of course not! Oh, my God!" Her arms tightened around him. "God, no. Are you crazy? Opportunity of a lifetime. I am beyond excited."

Relief washed over him. "Okay, good. I just didn't want anything that happened last night or this morning to—"

"It's not that at all, Rory. In fact, Christian and I had a conversation about this and the job being two very separate enterprises."

"Enterprises. Sounds like something he'd say."

"Yeah, I kind of rolled my eyes at the term as well. But he does have a point. And, Rory . . ."

Her arms slipped away. He groaned in protest. Turned to her.

She said, "We all have to agree that there will be zero weirdness amongst us if this doesn't work."

"*This* being the three of us."

"Yes. And the same goes for the show. If it doesn't launch the way you and Christian are so convinced it will, I don't want it to affect us personally."

Rory set aside his spatula and cupped her face in his hands. "Zero weirdness, I promise. But don't go planning for imminent failure for either *enterprise*. These are one-day-at-a-time endeavors. Lots of intricate nuances to consider and wade through. Both take an open mind, a thick skin, and some creativity. Okay?" He kissed her forehead.

"Okay." She flashed her pearly whites again. "I hear you."

"Good. Now, about the library—"

"Rory." She stepped out of his reach. "I haven't signed the contract yet and that means I have no check in hand. Still need to
make ends meet, you know? So after breakfast and a wardrobe
change, I'm going to work at the library."

"Fine. I know better than to argue with you. But at least give
your notice to the gelato stand. I'm concerned about you being so
easily accessible when news starts to break of your involvement
with the show. I don't want you getting swarmed in Central Park."

"That's a good point. I'm only there ten hours a week, anyway.
No biggie to bow out."

"You do realize Christian is planning press releases and promo
to get a buzz going about the show? Your name and face are going
to be *everywhere,* babe. People will recognize you on the street.
Even follow you into the bathroom from time to time." He shuddered.

That'd been a bizarre reality to accept the first few times it'd
happened to him. Especially since it'd been female fans following
him into the john. And they hadn't stopped talking, either. So he'd
whipped it out and figured as long as they weren't snapping photos
it wasn't an issue. If they were offended, they only had themselves
to blame. Unfortunately, none of them had been. So perhaps not
the best strategy to employ . . .

Bayli said, "No worries. I've had a stalker or two in my time.
I can handle it."

"That's good to hear," came another female voice.

Rory's head snapped up and he shot a look over Bayli's head
toward Lily Madison as she strutted through the apartment. He
fought the scowl. She was a bit too pretentious and overly done up
in that *Dynasty* way for his liking. But she was efficient and took
good care of business affairs. Too bad she was a woman willing to
do whatever necessary to get her hooks into Christian.

Bayli quickly tugged Christian's shirt around her body, wrapping her arms about her waist to secure the material, and turned to the unexpected intruder.

Rory said, "Doesn't the doorman typically announce you?"

"Not when Christian knows I'm on my way over. I have paperwork for him to sign." She held up a slim dark-brown leather portfolio. "Besides, he doesn't usually have company so early in the morning. That I'm aware of." Her smile was a tight, forced one as her gaze landed on Bayli.

"We also have business with Christian," Rory simply said.

"So it would appear." Lily seemed to take a few moments to get her bearings. Then she squared her shoulders and said, "I'm Lily Madison. Christian's assistant."

"Oh, how nice to meet you," Bayli said congenially. "Bayli Styles."

"Bayli Styles." Lily's eyes widened as she said the name. "The plot thickens."

"I'm sorry?" Bayli spared a glance at Rory, who merely shrugged.

Lily explained, "I just immediately assumed you were the woman in the YouTube video with Rory—given the hair color and the fact that you're here with him this morning . . . not fully clothed. But apparently you're more than just Rory's new flame. You're the model Christian selected for the relaunch of the cooking show. I recognize your name from some messages that have come in from your agent."

Bayli's chin hitched. "Yes, as a matter of fact, I am that Bayli Styles. It all happened rather quickly."

"Indeed." Lily shifted her weight from one six-inch stiletto to another.

Rory asked her, "What did you mean when you told Bayli it was good she'd had a stalker or two in her time?"

"Oh." Lily seemed to come around from whatever thoughts she'd been momentarily lost in. Which Rory could easily deduce were centered around Bayli being half-naked in Christian's apartment. Rory knew all about his friend's occasional sleepovers with Lily. She said, "I guess neither of you has read the comments on the video. Some not so pleasant. But, hey, that's showbiz. *Haters are gonna hate*, according to Taylor Swift, right?"

Rory draped an arm around Bayli's shoulders out of instinct. A peculiar protectiveness? The need to comfort her? Though she really didn't look fazed by Lily's news.

Bayli said, "I've collected some crazies along the way. Nothing too worrisome. I changed my e-mail once, but other than that, I'm not exactly noteworthy enough to hate on. At least, not for any length of time."

Rory said, "That'll change, honey. But, so far, no one actually knows it's Bayli associated with me, right?" He directed the question to Lily.

"That'd be my guess. I mean, of the comments I perused for PR purposes I didn't see an actual mention of her name. And there isn't a clear shot of her in that video. Like I said, I just put it all together because the pieces were laid out in front of me. But once the PR and marketing materials roll out, then sure, the dots will be connected by the masses. And, Rory, you really do have a huge following—"

"I'm heeding the warning," he assured her. To Bayli, he said, "Definitely no more work in Central Park. The library's safe enough, I'm sure. But we should invest in bodyguards for you."

"Bodyguards!" She jumped out of his semi-embrace. "Rory St. James, I am not going to be shadowed by retired Secret Servicemen when all I'm doing is a cooking show. *I'm* not the celebrity— you are! Do *you* have bodyguards?"

"No," he scoffed. "I'm not afraid of the women who follow me into the men's room. And I know martial arts."

"It's not a bad idea, Miss Styles. Or may I call you Bayli?"

"*Bayli*'s fine," she told Lily. "And . . . please, both of you. You're suddenly making a big deal out of nothing. I haven't even signed the contract, for God's sake." Her head whipped in Rory's direction. "And don't you dare mention any of this to Christian. Not a word, Rory. Don't stress him out over nothing."

Rory rubbed his jaw. He knew better than to keep anything from Christian. That was how they'd stayed such close friends over the past decade. But Rory also knew that Christian would pretty much come apart at the seams if there were already fans creating a backlash against Bayli—all because of that goddamn YouTube video.

It was Rory's fault, and he knew it. He'd told himself it was a bad move to kiss her at the market. But he hadn't been able to stop himself. Hadn't regretted it, either. Until now.

Though . . . it was one video and so there were evidently some comments that might be a little snarky toward Bayli. Once the show launched and audiences and fans got sucked in with that contagious smile and rich, good-natured laugh of hers, the haters wouldn't be hating anymore. They'd adore her. Totally fall for her the way Rory was.

Whoa. Wait.

Rewind.

Fall for her?

Rory's brow furrowed.

He was *falling* for Bayli Styles? The woman he'd kicked outside his kitchen. The woman he wouldn't hire as a hostess in his restaurant. The woman who loved to push his buttons and playfully mock him at every turn.

A woman unlike any he'd ever met before.

A woman Christian was equally smitten with, he had no doubt.

Bayli captivated them both. And it wasn't a fleeting desire they each held for her.

Rory might not have been well versed in love and romance, but he wasn't a total dolt. He recognized something significant when it came his way. And last night when she'd asked if what they'd experienced with her was the norm for them, both he and Christian had been in agreement.

It was not.

Something to ponder. But not at the moment, because Rory needed to finish the omelets and Bayli had to get to the library.

So Rory told Lily, "Christian was on the phone last I heard. That means he's in his study."

Rory turned back to the stove and resumed his cooking.

Lily said, "I'll just drop these off and be on my way. Nice to meet you, Bayli. If there's anything you need, don't hesitate to call Christian's office. I'm happy to help in any way."

"That's very kind of you, thanks. And nice to meet you, too."

Lily left them, and Bayli went about exploring the kitchen, collecting three plates, glasses, and flatware.

"Which seating area should I set?" she asked. "The island, the breakfast nook, the formal dining table?"

"How about the table on the terrace?"

"Right. Even better." She grabbed some napkins and disappeared outside.

Rory finished prepping the food while some of what Lily had said festered in his brain and in his gut. What if his fans actually did take a disliking to Bayli, strictly because they'd know she was more than just a cohost?

What sort of problems might that bring on for the show? For her?

He rubbed the back of his neck as a knot of tension formed.

Damn him for kissing her on the street.

Talk about a stupid, impulsive, selfish move that just might come back to bite them all in the butt.

Christian was just disconnecting a call when Lily entered his study at the back of the apartment. She crossed the room with long, confident strides, which always astounded Christian given the skyscraping heels she wore.

Lily set the portfolio she carried on his desk and filled him in on a few corporate issues. Then she said, "So, I've met Miss Styles. She mentioned contracts for the cooking show. That was what was in the packet I gave you from the Polenski Agency, right?"

"Yes." He flipped open the leather folder and retrieved the documents inside.

Lily asked, "And she's going to be some sort of cohost on the show with Rory?"

"Actually, she's going to provide commentary on local culture and flavor—travel-documentary style, with flair—and then, yes, she'll host the cooking portion as Rory and a local up-and-coming chef provide the demo. She'll interact with the chefs and the audience. It ought to be a very informative and engaging hour. She's extremely charismatic."

"I can see that."

Christian glanced up from his paperwork. "Lily . . ."

"You didn't even audition anyone, Christian. That's not like you to do something so spontaneous when it comes to business."

"I didn't need to audition anyone, Lil. I saw her at work—live and in person. She's sensational. She'll be perfect for this role."

"But if you were thinking of going in this direction . . . ," Lily said, then let out a long breath.

Christian recognized the disappointment in her tone. He asked, "Is there something wrong with this direction?"

"I'd just think that you would consider all the options. I mean . . . You could have even given me the chance to audition."

He stared at her a moment. Lily wasn't one to get wrapped around the axle about anything, really. She was paid extremely well, had a very elegant lifestyle, could get into the best of restaurants around the globe because of Christian's and Rory's names, enjoyed the freedom of being able to take a half day off here and there to spend at the spa—and still get paid. There were plenty of other fringe benefits she took advantage of, though sleeping with Christian was one perk he had to take off the table now.

Despite that, Lily had a pretty cushy existence with his company. It'd never occurred to him that she might want to be involved with the cooking show. He knew for a fact Lily Madison had never connected the stove in her apartment to the gas line and instead used it to store paper and toner for her laser printer.

So Christian closed the folder and gave her his full attention. "Why are you interested in auditioning, Lil?"

"It'd be nice to get out from behind my desk and step in front of the cameras. Who wouldn't want that?"

"You've never mentioned anything like this before. I thought you liked being my assistant."

"I love being your assistant," she was quick to say. "But with this traveling cooking show, you're going to be out of the office more now than ever, Christian. You'll need me less and I'll hardly see you." Panic tinged her voice.

This was a facet of Lily he'd never seen before. But Christian could understand that his new plans might throw her. He said, "Look, Lil. I'm going to be on the road more, initially, that's true. But business still needs to be taken care of, and I need you managing the office the way you always have. I can't do any of this without you."

"There are a million assistants in the world who can do what I do, Christian." Now she sounded exasperated, borderline agitated.

"No." He grinned, hoping to placate her. "Not the way you handle everything, Lil. I need you to continue doing what you do best."

"Sit behind a desk."

He sighed. "If it's more travel you want, I'll figure something out, all right? I don't want to lose you, Lil. You're invaluable to the company."

She didn't appear completely convinced this would all work out in her favor but didn't push further. Except to say, "I suppose my time with you outside of business hours will become less and less as well, correct? Bayli Styles obviously spent the night here, and Rory is clearly fascinated by her. I have no doubt you are as well."

"Lil, you and I never discussed mutual exclusivity."

"No, we didn't. I assumed the only reason for that was because Rory isn't attracted to me. If he were . . . things might be different with the three of us."

"I can't say for sure. But you know I adore you. And I've enjoyed the time we've spent together."

"But that's all over now."

He stood. "Lil—"

She raised a manicured hand to stop him. "I have plenty of work to do, Christian. I need to get back to the office."

She whirled around and sauntered out, leaving the lingering scent of Chanel No. 5 and a distinct chill in the air.

Christian sighed. She was pissed. But she had to have known this day was coming. Christian had never given her the impression that they were more than part-time lovers. He'd never asked for more, never offered more. She'd been accepting of the arrangement.

Now he'd have to figure out how to keep her happy and content as his assistant *only*. Finding a way for her to be involved with the show that allowed her to tag along from time to time might be paramount to proving how much he really did count on her and appreciated her hard work.

He let the thought percolate as he left his study. Rory had breakfast ready and he and Bayli were carting out serving dishes to the patio when Christian joined them.

As the trio sat around the table, Christian read the *Wall Street Journal*, Rory checked his e-mails on his iPhone, and Bayli stared out at the park with a smile on her face.

Then she took off for home and the library. Rory headed to the restaurant. Christian went to the office.

It was an easy transition to this new paradigm. They'd all fallen into step with one another and he found it enticing, exciting.

Perhaps he and Rory had finally achieved just the right balance in their personal lives. And as soon as the show started to take shape, they just might end up with everything they'd always wanted.

SEVENTEEN

A frenzy of activity ensued. Once Bayli signed the contracts and a check was delivered to her agency, Christian dove right into setting up a traveling production crew and secured modes of transportation. Rory was secretive about destinations on his list but was also plotting his culinary strategy, determining ingredients he'd capitalize on and recipes to invent.

All the while, Bayli was being "prepped." Polished to within an inch of her life with spa treatments that went well beyond your basic massage, facial, mani/pedi. No, she was wrapped and buffed and soaked.

She now had a full-time hairstylist who'd lopped off three inches of her hair and left it sleek and shiny with long bangs swept to one side and the ends angled in at her collarbone. A makeup artist who'd mastered neutral tones that made Bayli dewy and fresh-faced with just the right contouring of her high cheekbones and pop of her tawny eyes.

A fashion consultant whisked her off to Barneys, Bloomingdale's, and Bergdorf's—*oh, my!* Bayli was in awe. In shock. In heaven. All at once.

The whirlwind adventure left her with little time to catch Jewel and Scarlet up on the happenings and even less time to spend an evening with Phillip and Colin. Though Bayli squeezed in a quick meet-and-greet lunch that included Christian and Rory. Her friends were a little tongue-tied over the famous duo. Perhaps not so much that they were famous but that they were so damn good looking.

Bayli had felt a surge of pride at Phillip and Colin fawning over her male companions. And her lovers were charming and witty, as charismatic as ever. Even Rory.

Above that, however, she was getting pulled deeper into Christian and Rory's world. Reveled in it. They spent most of their evenings at Christian's apartment as they mapped out business strategies . . . then got tangled up with one another in bed. Mornings were fairly routine with Rory cooking, Bayli assisting, and Christian yakking on the phone. But still so exciting.

Things were progressing nicely.

Bayli's name had leaked to the public and entertainment channels and bloggers before the official press releases had even been approved, and her Japanese stalker had returned, sending e-mails to her new address. She made another change but decided that was her last. She wanted to be able to hear from fans . . . if she ever got some who didn't call her a whore or a flash in the pan.

Rory had one seriously loyal following, she'd discovered, and it seemed a lot of those women thought of him as theirs.

This wasn't a news flash for Bayli. And it didn't undermine her confidence or throw her for a loop. It was to be expected, really. She was cutting in on their turf, these devotees who e-mailed Rory regularly, blogged, tweeted, and posted Facebook messages about and to him. It was only natural they'd be nonplussed to have Bayli suddenly appear on the scene.

Likely it wouldn't have been such a big deal if the trio had just launched the cooking show with no up-front drama. But with her and Rory's kiss going viral, feathers had been ruffled.

Bayli spent a lot of mental energy trying to figure how to mitigate the damage done. Meanwhile, she also studied up on locales

Rory discarded because he felt they held no potential. Mostly, he was moody because he was in chef mode, thinking a million steps ahead to what he might prepare on the show. So she dug deeper when he got sidetracked or just plain frustrated.

Christian, she discovered, was about as unflappable as one could ever be, nimbly hurdling every obstacle that came their way. She admired his professionalism, his intelligence, his dry wit. Sometimes, she couldn't even tell he was jesting. Until she caught the sparkle in his ice-blue eyes. Then her stomach would flip and she'd let out an unchecked laugh, even as he tried to remain serious.

Despite the stoicism he sometimes demonstrated, she could see he got a kick out of her vivaciousness. So she didn't temper it, even when he was in serious business mode.

The same went for Rory. Because the more she didn't cave to his angsty side, the flirtier he got. And that was downright lethal to a girl's heart.

Honestly, both men had her wrapped up in a decadent bliss that created double the exhilaration, double the desire, double the emotions blooming within her. She couldn't say which man entertained her, thrilled her, pleased her more. They were equals in every way, especially where she was concerned. And Bayli was surprised to find she not only more than held their interest, but she seemed to bring out different sides to each of them also.

Bayli paid close attention to the emerging personalities. The protectiveness. The tenderness. The intensity. Christian and Rory not only worked together to take Bayli to all-new heights of sexual ecstasy, but they also were both in tune emotionally with each other and her. It was uncanny. And so damn alluring.

The reason she studied them so closely as they all interacted was because Bayli felt a gnawing deep within her that hinted at the need to be just as forthcoming and evolving in this nontraditional relationship as the guys were. But there was always something holding her back. She wanted to dissect herself and fix her glitch in the system. Yet all she had time to fully concentrate on was the speeding train that was her career and new life. . . .

"What's all this?" Rory asked on a rainy weekend. He stared over Bayli's shoulder as she slid a silver-plated letter opener under the flap of an envelope. She was sitting on a high-backed upholstered barstool at the kitchen island, where he usually found her in the morning, waiting for him.

Rory's latest fetish was breakfast with a creole flair. He was thinking the first few stops for the webcasts should be in the Deep South. New Orleans and Kentucky were both on his short list for future restaurants, and this might make a great immersion into the local flavor.

Bayli said, "I haven't had time to stop by my apartment in a while. I just grabbed all my mail in one fell swoop yesterday afternoon. I've basically been living here."

"Well, don't think for a second that Christian minds."

As Rory leaned in, she kissed him, then said, "You've basically been living here, too."

"That's because I know he can't satisfy you the way I can, so I'm here as backup." He winked.

"I'll be sure and let him know you said so."

Rory chuckled. He rounded the island and reached for a frying pan from the overhead rack.

Bayli's new iPhone—a "signing bonus" from Rory and Christian—buzzed. She eyed the screen and yelped, "Holy shit! I have to take this! I think Scarlet has finally trapped her elusive wolf!"

Rory's brow knitted. "Do I even want to know what that means?"

"She's tracking a potential art thief. I'll tell you about it later." She slipped off the stool. "Back in ten!" She headed out to the terrace.

Rory whistled under his breath. "She's a zany one."

"Who?" Christian asked as he came from his study, stuffing his phone in his pocket. His gaze darted around the room, not seeing any signs of Bayli so clearly wondering to whom Rory referred.

Rory jested back, "Our Beauty, Beastly."

"Oh, yeah, right. I'm the beast."

Rory snorted. "Just because I have a temper I'm the beast?"

"If the roar fits . . ."

"Ha-ha." Rory recalled Bayli saying something similar to him when they'd first met. So maybe he did have an unruly side. She didn't seem to mind.

"Anyway," Christian said, "the good news is that we have our traveling production crew in place. Of course, we have no idea where we're traveling to at present, but—"

"Climb off my back, dude. I'm still investigating."

"Well, maybe you could speed it up a little, so that we don't lose our crew to some other project."

"Yeah, yeah. I hear you."

Christian slid onto the stool Bayli had just vacated and sifted through the paperwork laid out. "Doing your taxes while whipping up breakfast? Impressive skill set you possess."

"It's Bayli's stuff."

Christian eyed one slip of paper, then another. "Holy shit."

"What?" Rory tore his attention from the stove and joined Christian, snatching a sheet from his hand. Rory's gaze homed in on a very lofty figure—boldly denoted as a *balance*—and his jaw clenched. "What the fuck?" he amended.

"She said she had medical expenses—her mother's."

"So why hasn't she paid this off? For God's sake, we gave her a check to get the ball rolling with research and so that she could leave her other jobs to work full-time on the development of the show."

Christian scanned a few more sheets and let out a sharp grunt. "Because that's not the only astronomical bill to pay off. She owes cardiothoracic surgeons, anesthesiologists, hospitals . . . fuck. She has credit card debt, too. For basic living expenses and medical supplies. Pills . . . lots of pills." He sighed.

Rory did quick mental calculations and said, "It doesn't make sense that she's still living under this dark cloud. Damn it, Christian. I could just pay all of this off and—"

"And *what*, Rory?" he challenged with a stern look. "Tell her all of her problems are solved? There's a reason she's still making minimum payments on her bills when she's deposited a sufficient enough amount in her checking account to make a bigger dent in these balances."

Rory stared at him, perplexed. But not for long. "Ah, shit." He tossed the papers back on the countertop.

Christian said, "Right. You know the story. It was the same way I felt when I cashed my first big check after Bristol's took off. It's one check. It's a well that can easily dry up. So you hoard the money. Keep making the minimum payments so you feel as though you have a safety net in the bank in the event there's no second, or third, or fourth check. You can still survive if everything goes to hell for you."

"But she wouldn't be stressing over any of that if the bills were all taken care of."

"True. But she'd never find any personal pride in one or the two of us paying off these expenses. They're Bayli's to deal with. And she will deal with them. She's going to make more than enough money to cover her mother's surgeries and still have plenty left in the bank. It's just going to take some time. And you're going to have to let it all unfold at the pace that keeps Bayli on her even keel. From what I've learned, she's been opening these envelopes for many, many years. She knows what she owes every month. Eventually, she'll take a look at her bank statement and realize she can pay this all off *and* comfortably exist."

Rory tried to rationalize all this. But his surly disposition reared its head and he quietly demanded, "What's so wrong with letting someone help you? This is like pocket change to us, Christian. Why *wouldn't* we do this for her?"

Christian stared at him for several moments, then grinned. "You want to rescue her. I get that. Don't think for a second that I don't want to as well. But we're talking about a woman who, when physically stranded in Upstate New York, still lied to me about where she lived because she didn't want to be embarrassed about her struggles, nor did she want anyone to feel bad for her or pity her. She's a strong, independent woman, Rory. She wants to stay that way. We want her to stay that way—it's one of the things that makes her so attractive to us. If we have the opportunity to help her, then hell, yes, we'll both jump on it. But Bayli has to come to us. She has to ask us. We can't just circumvent her in trying to solve all of her problems."

"Because then she'll resent us." Rory tossed aside the towel he'd used to dry his hands.

"Exactly. And she'll feel inferior, and she'll likely pull away. Let her breathe, Rory. Let her be who she's always been."

"Yeah, but, Christian. Even you took on a partner when you knew it was the only way to get what you wanted."

"And she signed on with this show to get what *she* wanted, Rory." Christian pinned him with a serious look. "I'm thrilled that you want to help her so desperately. That she means that much to you. She means that much to me, too. Therefore, we can't suffocate her or take over her life. It'd be incredibly easy to do. That's not the kind of woman we're involved with, though. We could crush her with our need to help her. She's done so much for herself . . . that proves she'll be okay without us force-feeding her. Let her be Bayli, man. If she needs us, she'll tell us."

"Right."

Rory didn't like that answer. Nor could he deny it as fact.

So he went back to cooking.

Several days later, Bayli strolled into the apartment from the terrace and smiled at Christian, who was sitting at the kitchen island, chatting with Rory.

"Hey, look who's off his cell phone," she mused.

"Funny," Christian said with a smirk. "Do you want a job or not?"

She flattened her palms on his thighs, wedged herself into the vee his parted legs created, and kissed him. Then she said, "Of course I do."

Her attention turned to Rory. "Whatever the hell you're cooking smells absolutely to die for."

"Cantonese this time."

"Huh," she said. "Didn't see that one coming."

"What has you in such a good mood?" Christian asked. "On a really dreary day?"

She took a quick peek at the gray weather and said, "We're in Manhattan. There is no such thing as a dreary day."

"Fine," Christian said. "Your optimism trumps all."

"Yes, it does." She kissed him again. "And damn it, Rory, I'm suddenly starving. Your food is as irresistible as the both of you, and I'm putting in more time on Christian's elliptical machine than he is. There's some bizarre irony in all of this."

Rory said, "Well, I did once read that having sex burns about two hundred calories, so if you're having sex with two men at the same time wouldn't that double the burn and up you to four hundred?"

"I like that logic," she told him with a nod. "I really do. I'm just not sure—"

Christian's cell phone rang with the specific jingle that alerted him to the doorman contacting him about the arrival of a visitor or a delivery. It turned out to be a delivery that Christian told him to bring up.

Bayli shoved away from Christian and headed across the apartment.

"Miranda can get the door!" Rory called out.

"She's upstairs making the bed and cleaning."

"You will never get used to having staff, will you?" he quipped.

"She's not *my* staff. And I'm perfectly capable of answering the door."

Bayli trotted up the short set of steps to the entryway. She made it to the foyer just as the bell chimed.

Pulling open the double doors, she gave the Building Manager a bright smile. Tom was the one who typically made special deliveries directly to Christian's floor and the four-story penthouse above him.

"This just came for you, Miss Styles."

Her eyes fixated on the long, narrow gold box with a red ribbon and bow. "Roses. So old-school Hollywood." Christian all the way. She accepted the box and Tom closed the doors for her. Feeling a little like Hollywood royalty—though she clearly wasn't by any stretch of the imagination, but perhaps someday—Bayli tugged at the bow. The velvety ribbon unraveled and she whisked off the lid.

A million tiny spiders suddenly raced over hands and up her arms.

Bayli screamed bloody murder.

À la Phillip and Colin style.

Rory dropped a bowl of rice, ignored the shattering of the glass, and rushed through the apartment, Christian by his side. They both took the steps to the foyer two at a time.

"Get them off of me!" Bayli screeched.

"Son of a bitch!" Rory exploded as he stomped on the spiders scattering about while Christian lunged forward and brushed the arachnids from Bayli's body.

Having no great luck, Christian dragged her into the hallway bathroom and Rory heard the instant spray of the shower while Bayli still wailed.

Tom barreled back into the apartment, apparently having heard Bayli's screams. "Jesus Christ!" he bellowed.

"Just stomp," Rory demanded in a tight voice.

Tom did just that but also grabbed his cell and contacted the Facilities Manager to alert him to the situation. Then told Rory, "An exterminator will be here ASAP."

"Who the hell delivered this box?"

"A courier with a business card. Martin at the front desk accepted it."

"Then you and Martin need to figure out who would bring a box of spiders to Christian Davila's guest, at his *apartment*."

"Yes, sir. Of course. Right away."

Rory tried to dial down his fury. "I know this isn't your fault. But it scared the hell out of the woman who opened the box."

"Whatever we can do to find out who made that delivery, Mr. St. James, we'll do it."

"Thank you." Rory tried to get his temper under control. "We appreciate your assistance."

The Facilities Manager appeared minutes later with the in-house emergency exterminating canister and he sprayed the box, then the entryway, though Rory was pretty certain he and Tom had squashed every spider in sight at that point. Miranda had heard the commotion and hastily cleaned up, not even batting a lash. Making Rory wonder just how much Christian paid the housekeeper.

When the entryway was back to normal, the building management departed, as did Miranda. Christian and Bayli emerged from the bathroom, him soaking wet in his clothes, her wrapped in a towel that she hugged tight to her chest, though she was still dripping from head to toe. Shaking, too.

And, goddamn it, Rory thought, it wasn't the good kind of shaking that she did after he and Christian had just made her come.

No, this was shaking of the terrified kind.

But she wore a brave face, tried to appear natural. Rory didn't buy it, and from the look on Christian's face that basically said he was ready to throttle someone, Christian wasn't buying it, either. He had his arm around her shoulders and she was tucked close to him.

Christian said, "They were all over her. Even in her hair."

"Yeah, they had scampering down pat." Rory's fists clenched at his sides.

"Someone did a very nice job of freaking the hell out of her," Christian said, not the least bit successful at masking his fury.

Bayli told them, "It wasn't a female fan. No woman would *ever* send a box of spiders to another woman, no matter how pissed off she was. The mere thought would make her skin crawl as much as the recipient's. Trust me on this one."

"So your stalker from Japan . . . ?" Christian ventured.

"Best guess," she said with a nod. "All he has to do is set a Google Alert and whenever my name pops up he's privy to everything mentioned or written about me. Easy enough for him to track me down since I'm now associated with Davila–St. James Enterprises."

"Fuck," Rory raged. "All because of that kiss. I never should have—"

"Rory." Bayli placed a hand on his forearm. "You don't know it's about that kiss. My name was linked to the show recently, ahead of official press releases. Anyone can be annoyed with me at this point."

"Your name wasn't out there when the video went viral and comments got nasty," he reminded her.

Christian said, "He's right. This isn't about the show. It's about someone—male or female, your fan or Rory's—not happy to see the two of you together."

Rory could spit nails. He needed air—and answers. He marched past them and grabbed his leather jacket from the coatrack, then stormed out, with Bayli calling after him.

He took the elevator downstairs and grilled Martin himself. The courier had indeed provided a business card, but it was a flimsy, poorly designed one that had clearly come out of a desktop printer, not professionally generated.

"Whoever sent that box," Rory said to the front deskman and Tom, "could have easily hired someone off the street to bring it in and provide the business card, knowing you'd need credentials before you'd deliver. There's no way we're going to figure out who the 'courier' or the sender is. Damn it."

Rory strode past the two men on his way out. Another building employee pulled open one of the tall doors for him and a gust of wind blew in. And sent a small white envelope skittering across the marble floor, from under the edge of one decorative tree planter to another. Rory scooped it up.

He stared at the name neatly printed in bold caps:

MISS BAYLI STYLES

"Son of a bitch," he groaned. Though he was glad to have found the note that evidently had fallen from the box, probably due to the stiff breeze and the vacuum it created when the door was opened.

He tore at the tiny flap and removed the card inside.

And bit back a litany of curse words at the message printed in the exact same way as her name:

STAY AWAY FROM HIM

Rory did an abrupt about-face and went back to the elevator. Returned to the apartment.

Christian and Bayli were standing by the fireplace. He'd changed into a pair of black drawstring pants and nothing more. She wore one of Rory's sweaters and socks, the tops bunched at her ankles.

Christian took one look at him and visibly steeled himself for this next attack on Bayli.

Rory thrust the card at Christian, who snatched it away and then yelled, "Goddamn it!"

"Yeah," Rory barked. "It *is* that fucking YouTube video!"

EIGHTEEN

Bayli took another shower. Then soaked in the tub with both Rory and Christian.

She needed the water rushing over her skin to chase away the lingering sensation of a gazillion legs crawling all over her. The guys needed something to relax them. Bring the blood pressure down a few notches. Make them a little less ready to wrap their bare hands around someone's neck for terrorizing her.

She saw it all in their tense muscles and hooded eyes.

Unfortunately, Rory was doubly pissed off because he blamed himself for the whole mess. Bayli tried to convince him it wasn't his fault.

She sat between Christian's parted legs, her back to his chest as he cupped his hands on each side of her, filled them with water, and poured the streams over her shoulders and down her arms to keep her from being so damn creeped out. But her gaze was on Rory across from them in the giant tub.

"This'll blow over," she said. "The men who e-mailed me suggesting Internet affairs and swapping nude photos got bored with my lack of a reply and quietly went away. My more persistent stalker hung in there until I closed my e-mail account. He didn't bother to track down the new one. Until recently, that is. When you don't engage, they go away. That's been my experience."

"I'm not discounting that," Rory said between clenched teeth. "On the other hand, has anyone ever sent you a box of spiders?"

"Well . . . no. Of course not." Okay, so he had her on that one.

"This isn't the same as annoying or lewd e-mails, Bayli," he said.

"I understand that, Rory. And from here on out, I won't accept any deliveries I'm not expecting. But what else am I supposed to do? What does this nutjob think I'm going to do? Back out of the show or my relationship with you and Christian just because he did something menacing to warn me off?"

"It scared the shit out of you," Rory said with an unwavering look.

"Yes." She sighed. "No lie. It did. But not enough for me to cower in a corner. I'm not walking away from everything we're all currently building because someone thinks in their deluded mind they have a claim on you—or even me, if it's my guy who's all amped up."

"Sweetheart," Christian said in his low, sensual tone, ever the voice of reason. And extreme stimulation. "Rory's just saying that it's infuriating to see something so insidious happen to you, and I'm with him on that. The video is likely the catalyst. Whether it is or not is actually irrelevant." He paused and she could tell Christian was staring at Rory over her head, making his own point. "We'll have to deal with this, because chances are very good it's not the last attempt this person will make in their quest to be heard. And there will no doubt be plenty of other fans who will get out of hand. Comes with the territory. Rory already knows this."

"So we ought to talk about security measures," Rory said.

Bayli gave a sharp shake of her head. "Do not go there, Rory."

"Go where?" Christian asked.

"Bodyguards. She needs one."

"Rory, I do not—"

"You're right," Christian said.

"Hey." She shifted slightly to glare at him. "Don't I get a say in the matter?"

Christian's brow furrowed. "You don't want a bodyguard?"

"Would you like someone shadowing *you* twenty-four-seven?" she demanded.

From behind her, Rory caustically said, "Well, it wouldn't be twenty-four-seven. I mean, you won't need a bodyguard when you're with us."

She slumped back against Christian's chest and grumbled under her breath.

"It's pretty standard operating procedure for celebrities," Rory contended. "Hell, even Kris Kardashian has bodyguards. Can't imagine who'd stalk her, but I guess there are rabid fans who want to touch her as she's making the rounds from one designer to another at Fashion Week, just to say they did."

"I'm not a celebrity, Rory," she reminded him.

"Depends on who you ask is my guess."

She climbed out of the tub and reached for a towel.

"Thank God," Rory quipped. "This was getting too girly for me."

"I did bring you brandy," she shot back.

"Enough," Christian said as he stood and wrapped a towel around his waist, then used another to rub the dark strands of his damp hair. "We can bypass the bodyguard for now, if you want," he told Bayli. "But let's all be on our toes. Keep our private affairs private." He turned his gaze on Rory again. "No kissing her in public. You're working together. Maintain some professionalism and this will likely die off."

Bayli used the blow-dryer while the men settled in bed. She slipped in between them, under the covers, and said, "Sorry for the theatrics." Her head rolled on the pillow and she stared at Rory. "Didn't mean to get all girly on you."

He smirked. "I suppose I can let it slide this time."

"Awfully big of you."

She gazed over at Christian. "And I know your brain is churning with every scenario imaginable, so hopefully we can all distract one another enough that we can actually sleep tonight."

One corner of his mouth lifted. "What'd you have in mind?"

"As it happens, I have a surprise for you two." She sat up and shifted so she could look back at both of them. "Jewel was in Paris on business recently and she sent me a gift. A toy, to be exact. One she thought I ought to have, given that I'm sleeping with two impossible-to-resist men at the same time."

"And this gift—"

"Is what will allow me to *have* you both at the same time." She waggled a brow. "After the ice cube incident, I realized I needed to expand my repertoire. Or my acceptance of yours. Whatever." She shrugged.

Christian and Rory eyed her curiously. She kissed one, then the other. And explained, "I want to feel you inside me. At the same time."

Christian grinned. Rory's gaze smoldered. Bayli's stomach fluttered.

"You think you're ready for that?" Rory asked.

"Yes. I do." She leaned into him and kissed him again, her tongue twisting with his, her hands skating over his wide chest.

She could hear Christian sifting through the nightstand drawer, retrieving the condoms and lubricant. Then he swept the covers away from her. His lips skimmed up her spine, sending shivers cascading along each vertebra. Bayli straddled Rory's lap and she propped herself up on her knees, her forearms resting on Rory's well-defined pecs. Christian's fingers grazed her cleft, then rubbed her opening. She was already wet. His other hand covered her mound and his fingertips massaged her clit and slick folds.

Rory palmed her breasts and caressed aggressively. Then puckered her nipples with the pads of his thumbs whisking over the hypersensitive beads while Christian's pace picked up between her legs and he stroked her quickly, two of his long fingers plunging into her. A moan lodged in her throat.

She dragged her mouth from Rory's and whispered, "You both make me so hot, so fast."

"Well, you did utter magic words, honey."

She smiled against his lips. "I've been fantasizing about this. What it'd feel like to have you both inside me."

Her words seemed to excite Christian, because he stroked a bit more forcefully, pushing her right to the brink.

"Get her good and wet," Rory told him. "So fucking wet."

He kissed her again. Bayli's body sizzled and her heart pounded. A tremor ran through her.

Recognizing the sign for what it was, Christian said, "She's going to come. All over my fingers."

Bayli trailed her hand down Rory's abs and teased his balls. Then she reached for the lube and squirted it on his skin before she encircled his cock. Pumped feverishly, making his hips buck.

She smiled down at him. "You want to be thrusting into me, don't you?"

His eyes blazed. "Hard."

"And you know what I want, right?" Her gaze slid to Christian's erection.

"Jesus, Bayli," Rory all but growled. But after she dribbled lube onto his palm Rory fisted Christian's cock and matched her pace on his.

"Fuck," Christian said in a strained tone.

Their heavy breaths filled the room, over the crackle of the fire and the pinging of the rain on the windowpanes. There was a low rumble of thunder in the distance and an occasional flash of lightning. Bayli loved the moody weather, loved the scent of rainwater mixed with arousal.

Christian worked her a bit more fervently, and her pulse echoed in her ears.

"Yes," she mumbled. "Oh, God, yes. I'm going to come."

Rory drew her nipple into his mouth and suckled.

"Oh, God!" She panted in short breaths. Felt the tingles skate over her skin and the tremors move through her body. Her gaze was on Rory's hand pumping Christian's cock, a drop of pre-cum forming on the tip. "Yes," she said on a sliver of air. "Oh, fuck, yes!" She lost it completely and cried out as the orgasm shot through her, stealing her breath, setting every inch of her on fire.

"Shit." Rory released Christian, gripped Bayli's hips, and just as Christian's hands slid away from her Rory pushed her pelvis down and he thrust up into her and fucked her.

"Yes," she sobbed. "Oh, God, yes. Rory, that is so good. You feel *so* good." She could barely get the words out. But managed to say, "Christian, now. Fuck me now."

He sheathed and lubed himself and then the tip of his cock pressed against her small hole. She whimpered in anticipation. And from the intensity of Rory plunging into her, blatantly excited by this next level of lovemaking they'd reached.

His hands shifted and he spread her ass cheeks to help accommodate Christian's entry.

"Do it," she insisted. "I have to feel you, too. Do it, Christian. Fuck me. Both of you fuck me."

She was crazed. Her hips rocked and undulated as she opened further to Rory and took his cock deeper inside, eliciting sexy, desire-roughened sounds from him.

Christian's cockhead penetrated so slowly and so deliciously. It was a completely different sensation from ice or a finger or the toy Jewel had given her. The smooth, lubricated tip popped in the way the ice did, but it was thicker, fuller. And felt a million times better.

"Oh, Christ," she whispered as her fingers clenched around the sheet beneath Rory. She purposely avoided his shoulders, knowing her nails would tear him up at this point. Because she was completely out of control, clutching at his cock with her inner walls even as Christian warned her not to squeeze, not to tense up. She couldn't help it. Couldn't stop herself.

Christian had a firm hold on her hips and he tried to slow her movements as he eased farther into her. But Rory was losing it, too, fucking her ferociously, and all Bayli wanted to do was give in to the heat and moisture within her and surrounding their cocks.

Christian abandoned his attempt at being careful and let her meet Rory's thrusts while Christian pumped slowly.

"Yes!" she wailed. "Like that. Oh, God. Just like that!"

She demanded more, the erotic pleas tumbling unbidden from her lips as Bayli slipped into some blissful realm where all that registered was how both men felt inside her, how Rory's mouth felt on her nipple, his tongue flickering madly in time with the way he fucked her.

The sensations intensified. Magnified. Amplified.

And then it was just all too much. The climax hit her hard and fast and Bayli screamed. Her body jerked, then quaked.

"Damn," Christian said. "I'm going to come."

He shuddered and she felt the throbbing of his dick—and it added to the sensations consuming her.

"Rory," she begged, "come inside me, too. Please come inside me. Let me feel you. Now."

"Are you sure?"

"I'm on the pill."

"Oh, fuck." He erupted and his seed flooded her pussy, sparking another orgasm.

Christian withdrew from her, and she was able to contract around Rory's shaft, the squeezing and releasing drawing out both their climaxes. She couldn't stop it, actually. The involuntary action was completely primal and self-gratifying. Though Rory reaped the benefit, too, as he continued to thrust into her until they were both drained, completely spent.

"Lord," she mumbled as she collapsed against his chest. "That was so far beyond what I'd expected. Christ, that was so good."

She wasn't sure she'd ever get her breath back.

And she didn't care.

Christian was in the middle of a conference call the next afternoon when Bayli let out a squeal.

His heart launched into his throat and he immediately said, "Gentlemen, I have to drop off. I'll reschedule."

He hung up, jumped to his feet, and rounded his desk. He stalked from the study and demanded, "What happened? Are you okay?"

She was bouncing up and down in her tennis shoes, clapping her hands together.

Christian frowned. "Bayli, what the hell just happened?"

"Good news!" She lunged for him and threw her arms around his neck.

Christian held on tight, his heart returning to its proper place, though his pulse still pounded harshly. "You scared the crap out of me," he told her as he held her tight.

"Sorry, didn't mean to shriek like that. But sometimes I just can't control myself. You should know this about me already."

"Now's hardly the time to flirt. You sent my blood pressure through the roof."

"Everything's fine," she assured him. "No spiders or disgusting e-mails today. This is exuberance, not horror."

"Glad to hear that." He released her and carefully set her away from him before he forgot all about whatever had made her so cheerful and took her upstairs to bed instead. With or without Rory, wherever the hell he was. Apparently not in earshot, or he would have come running, too, when she'd cried out. "So what's all the excitement over?"

"I have the *perfect* locations for our test run with the webcasts. Breathtaking views, intimate villages, and flavor explosions for Rory. He'll love this, I swear."

"Where is he?"

"At the restaurant. He'll be back after the dinner service. But I don't know if I can wait that long to tell you—"

Rory suddenly came bounding down the entryway steps and into the apartment.

Bayli clapped again, clearly riding a high. She said, "You're not supposed to be here yet!"

"Am I interrupting something?"

"Yes," she told him. "I was trying to figure out how to keep from sharing my awesome news with Christian until you got here. Now I don't have to wait!" She gave Rory a hug and a kiss. "You're going to love this. But . . . why are you here?"

"The restaurant is completely mobbed with media," Rory said as he whipped off his jacket and tossed it on the sofa. "They're all asking questions about the cooking show. I fed them some sound bites, but I couldn't get anything accomplished in the kitchen with Pierre constantly coming to get me. So I decided to be elusive. That ought to leave tongues wagging."

"Most likely," Christian agreed. "And besides, there's only so much you can say, since we haven't selected destinations yet."

"Which is where my happy-happy-joy-joy moment comes into play!" Bayli interjected. "Notice the vibrant smile," she said as she swirled her hand in front of her face. "Note the flushed cheeks and the glittery eyes." She leaned in close to Rory. "My eyes *are* glittery, right?"

Christian snickered as Rory's surly demeanor instantly softened. "More than usual. What gives?"

"Come sit with me." She latched on to their hands and tugged. She led them to the breakfast nook where books, papers, and folders were sprawled across the smoky, glass-topped, counter-height table. She slid onto a stool and they each took one as well.

Christian reached for a computer printout of a beach, but she gently slapped his hand away.

"They're all perfectly arranged. Silos, remember?" she said.

"Sure, sweetheart," he humored her. "We'll try to compartmentalize right along with you."

"Smart-ass. Now," she said, "I have a huge list of incredible places that will work for the show. But I want to save some of the more eclectic ones for when we get picked up by the network. *If* we get picked up."

"That's not going to be a problem in the long run," Christian told her.

"How so?" Rory asked.

"Because most of my phone conversations of late have been threefold. One, we do have serious network interest—you're a huge name, Rory. And Bayli is intriguing. Two, not only do we have traditional networks wanting to negotiate, but we also have interest from Netflix and Amazon, who are looking for original productions."

"And third?" Bayli asked with bated breath.

"There's absolutely nothing keeping us from producing the show on our own and streaming via the Web."

Bayli bit her bottom lip.

Rory grinned. "Honey, he *is* saying exactly what you're thinking. The show's happening no matter the platform. Not just the test run, but a full season. Two, three, four. You get the picture. The *big* picture."

She released her lip. Shoved back her stool and stood. "I'm going to need a drink."

"Break out the champagne," Rory told her as she went to the wet bar and the wine chiller. Then he said to Christian, "You'll do anything to make her a star, won't you?"

"It's what she wants. And let's face it: She's not meant to be hanging out here or in the library doing endless amounts of research. She should be in front of cameras and entertaining audiences."

"And you'd pay whatever price you had to in order to make that happen?"

Christian speared him with an honest look. "And you wouldn't?"

Rory clenched his jaw a moment, fighting the grin. Then he caved and said, "Of course. But with network interest . . ."

Christian nodded. "I want the largest medium and platform for this show. But Bayli also needs to know that this is happening any way it can. She has to buy into this, Rory. She has to understand that it's real and long-lasting and—"

"That it's okay to pay off all of those bills, because that fucking well is going to runneth over."

"Damn straight."

"Christian, buddy. You're one hell of a man."

"With a bigger cock than you."

Rory let out a rumble of laughter. "Still living the dream, I see. Whatever. All that matters at the moment is that we're a go regardless of how we . . . go. So, good news. Now . . . why don't you pop the cork on that really expensive bottle of champagne she's bringing our way? Not sure our girl knows that a private reserve such as that costs about six hundred dollars, but what the hell? Let's celebrate."

Christian took the bottle from Bayli and she set out the three glasses. Then she settled back on her stool and got down to business.

"So, I understand that we should be thinking exotic locales," she said, "and, again, I have a lengthy list. But one thing that occurred to me when I was researching cultures and sights and local fare is that it seems as though lesser-known destinations hold a greater appeal. Like when Gordon Ramsay is visiting kitchens in England I'm more enthralled with the cozy, coastal towns than I would be if he stuck to London proper. I learn more about the country, the denizens, the customs that way. For example, I'd like us to explore Canada, particularly Nova Scotia. I mean, who the hell ever does a cooking show from Nova Scotia? Newfoundland or Labrador, for that matter. And what about New Brunswick?"

"Iceland, Greenland," Christian said with a nod. "I see where you're going with this."

"But as a hook, I think something more attainable for the

typical traveler might be in order," she told them. "Which led me to Mexico."

"Yeah," Rory said. "I was headed that direction, too, but it's pretty much done."

"But not completely," she told him. "Take La Crucecita, for instance."

"Where's that?" Christian asked.

"A small town north of Bahias de Huatulco," she said. "Now that I think about it, Huatulco might be even better. It's a conglomerate of nine bays with thirty-six widely undeveloped white-sand beaches. Very 'old Mexico.' Eighty percent of the tourism is domestic because they only have a small international airport—and it's just not a hugely heard-of destination. A handful of resorts, mostly coastal, some solely occupying their own coves, with nothing but the Pacific Ocean sprawled before them. It's hot and humid year-round, but look at these views."

She handed over a few printouts.

"Nice," Christian said of the turquoise waters and tree-covered hills.

She told Rory, "I'm thinking the regional chiles will probably be a staple for your best recipes. Maybe black mole salsa—thirty different ingredients, including chiles and chocolate. Every woman in the world will tune in for that. A hot chef and chocolate. That screams *winner*!"

"Not a thought to be discounted," Christian agreed. "What else have you got?"

"My second selection is Todos Santos on the Baja Peninsula," she said. "According to Jewel, Cabo San Lucas has become quite commercialized and it's even spreading toward San José del Cabo, where a lot of celebrities have houses. But Todos Santos is more of that artsy, cobblestone-street quaint coastal village we're shooting for. Tons of local flavor there."

Rory studied some of the documentation on this town.

Bayli continued. "Finally, in the spirit of one of the last tried-

and-true sleepy seaside villages, there's Puerto Peñasco—or Rocky Point, in English. The town is on the cusp of being considered Cabo of yore, maybe in the next decade, so this would be a great time to showcase it. Shrimping is a mainstay and they have a fantastic fish market. The town is on the Sea of Cortez about an hour from the Arizona border." She distributed more photos.

Christian shot Rory a look.

He said, "These weren't on my list. But I like the views and the history. I bet we could do great things with these."

Christian's gaze slid to Bayli. "Excellent job. Tell us more."

She went into the details and nuances of each locale, proving she'd done her homework the way she had when she'd played cigar hostess the night he'd met her. Just like then, Christian was impressed. Rory appeared to be so as well. They discussed a few possibilities for where they'd physically do the demos and Christian was sold on all the preliminaries. He slid another look Rory's way, who nodded his approval.

"Well, then," Christian said. "I'd say cheers are in order." He held up his champagne glass and they did the same. They all clinked rims. "Here's to . . . Oh, fuck. We don't have a name for the show."

Bayli and Rory exchanged a look.

"Shit," she said. "That was the last thing I was thinking of."

"It'll come," Christian told them. And took a deep drink. Then said, "Now that we have destinations, I have to get back on the phone."

He kissed Bayli before heading to his study.

NINETEEN

Bayli had a series of photo shoots and then interviews lined up, some individually, most with Rory. It was next to impossible to do as Christian had asked and act professionally, like there wasn't anything going on behind the scenes between her and Rory, especially when it was so easy, so natural, for them to flirt with each other. A greater challenge was pretending there was nothing going on behind the scenes with her, Rory, *and* Christian.

But Bayli played her part.

She returned to her apartment building a couple of days before they were to leave for Huatulco so that she could collect some of the clothes she'd picked out with her personal shopper and pack up a few other items. Christian had insisted on hiring a car service for her, and Bayli got a little thrill over having her own driver, Max. Her dreams were finally starting to come true. More so than she'd ever imagined, actually. She hadn't factored into her Grand Plan two amazing lovers she couldn't get enough of—who couldn't get enough of *her*.

At that moment Bayli was feeling pretty damn lucky.

Two seconds later, however . . .

She unlocked the door and stepped into the small space. Her keys hit the floor. Along with her jaw. Her heart sank to somewhere around her knees as her gaze swept over the disaster that was now her once meticulously decorated apartment.

"Oh, my God," she said on a sharp breath.

Max peered around her, then instantly sprang into action. "Stay right here." He checked the bathroom, the tall armoire, and under the bed, to make sure the intruder was no longer inside. Then Max eyed the mess of ravaged furniture and clothing, broken vases and lamps.

Bayli's beloved books were scattered everywhere. She could barely process it all. Was in a bit of shock while her driver continued to move forward, calling the police. Then Christian.

This brought her around. "He'll be completely enraged when he sees my place trashed."

"Don't touch anything," Max instructed.

"I wouldn't even know where to start." Tears stung her eyes. Everything she owned that wasn't at Christian's apartment, of course, had been destroyed. Her CDs, the small single-disc player. Her dishes. Even her shoes.

She carefully navigated around the piles on her floor and crossed to the bed. The jewelry box she'd kept on a shelf she'd installed herself was overturned, the cheap costume pieces strewn over the rumpled comforter and sheets that had been shredded. She did a quick mental inventory. Something was missing.

Her gaze dropped to the floor again. Then her eyes squeezed shut, though tears seeped out of the corners as her heart broke.

Her lids fluttered open and she sank to her knees, her fingers sweeping the air an inch or so above the remnants of the crystal bracelet her mother had given her.

"Damn it," she choked on a sob.

She usually always wore it but had left it here after changing out the tote bag she regularly took to Christian's. She'd been doing laundry that day and had taken the bracelet off and put it away for safekeeping. Now it was nothing but microscopic shards.

"Unbelievable," she whispered in agony. Her fists clenched. "Who would do this? Who would ruin all of my stuff?"

Max was still doing a visual inspection that led him to the Roman shade covering the window. He drew it back and swore under his breath.

"Well, I can't say who," he told her, "but I can tell you they broke in through your window. They used the fire escape to get up here."

"This is insane. There's nothing in this apartment worth robbing me over. And for God's sake, why wreck everything? *Because* there's nothing here worth robbing me over? Did it piss them off that they were able to get in and then found absolutely nothing of value to anyone other than me?"

"I don't know," Max said with a shake of his head. His tone was low and full of empathy as he added, "Seems as though they'd get a few bucks by pawning those clothes and shoes. But that would leave a paper trail. Plenty of crooks get busted because they hock the things they steal."

"So best just to tear it all apart? What the hell were they expecting to find from someone in this building? You don't rob the poor, right?"

"They were likely looking for some electronics."

"I don't even have a TV!"

Bayli wanted to scream. But what good would it do?

The police eventually arrived, not looking remotely surprised by the break-in, not in this neighborhood. Nor were they overly enthused to take her statement and survey the damage. Until Christian and Rory showed up. The female officer got a little starry-eyed over Rory, and her male partner wanted a recommendation for a steak marinade.

Christian took Bayli out into the hallway and pulled her into a tight embrace. She cried on his shoulder. It was one thing to feel violated over having her private space turned upside down, her pretty new clothes destroyed. But her bracelet . . . that couldn't be replaced. It had been a tangible connection to her mother. Something Bayli could admire and touch. It had also represented a fond memory when she had so few of them from her childhood.

Now it was gone.

"I'm so sorry this happened to you," Christian said.

"Some of the things in there meant a lot to me."

"I'm sure. Again . . . I'm so sorry, sweetheart."

She felt his own agony—for her. It made her feel worse, because she'd dragged him and Rory into the bleakness she'd been trying to escape.

The police said they'd investigate; Rory provided some more information, including letting them in on the spider delivery. This intrigued the officers more than the ransacking. They exchanged contact numbers with Rory and said they'd call. Christian and Rory took Bayli back to Christian's apartment.

"I need a shower," she said as Rory helped her out of her coat. "I feel creeped out again."

She headed upstairs and stood under the spray for a while, trying to find some perspective. Bayli was usually a silver-linings kind of gal. But it was difficult to see around the glaring loss of her bracelet.

After she dried her hair, she slipped into a pair of black leggings and socks and one of Rory's vee-neck sweaters in heather gray. She joined Christian and Rory downstairs, where they had a nice fire going that helped to warm her chilled insides. Lily was also there.

Christian's assistant gave her a quick hug. "That's just terrible about your apartment, Bayli. You must be devastated."

"It's tough to swallow at the moment, but I'll survive."

"Thank God you weren't there at the time. Anything could have happened." Lily squeezed her hands. "You must be so freaked out."

"Kind of regretting that I bypassed renter's insurance," she tried to jest. But her tone was flat and hollow.

Christian put his arm around her and kissed the top of her head.

Lily looked taken aback by the show of affection and covered it up by lifting a shopper's bag from the long, glass-topped dining table in the center of the cavernous room and thrust it at Bayli, saying, "I brought some necessities, since Christian said everything was smashed."

"Thanks, that was really nice of you," Bayli said, accepting the bag. "Luckily, a lot of my personal items are here, but I'll reimburse you for all of this."

"Oh, um . . ." She shot a look toward Rory, then turned her attention back to Bayli, who'd never seen Lily Madison quite so flustered. "No worries. I'm just trying to help. I can't imagine what you're going through. Really, it must be terrifying."

Rory crossed his arms over his chest and said, "I'm sure someone in the neighborhood saw something that will give the police a lead."

"Right. In the meantime," Lily said, "I have a friend who's a Realtor, if you want to look at some different places to rent. She can find you something in your price range. In a safer part of town. And I'm more than happy to help you shop for new furniture and clothes. I'm an expert at that." She smiled eagerly.

"You're really very helpful, Lily," Bayli said. "I'm not even sure where to start, honestly. Cleaning the place out is the first order of business, I guess."

"We'll hire someone to take care of that. And you can stay here," Christian offered . . . quietly demanded? "In fact, I'd prefer it."

"I think that's a great idea," Rory agreed. "You're spending most nights here, anyway."

"I didn't know that," Lily said, looking uncomfortable again, making Bayli wonder if there'd been some sort of romantic involvement between her and Christian. Or Rory. Both? Or perhaps Lily just preferred to be "in the know" about all facets of her boss's life. "I thought you and Rory . . . ?" Lily shook her head. "Doesn't matter. None of my business. I'll be going now."

"Thanks again," Bayli told her. To Christian, she said, "And thanks for the offer. It'll be helpful not to have to worry or think about the apartment while there's still so much to do before we leave for Huatulco. I have to buy all new outfits and shoes again."

"Wait." Lily placed a hand on Christian's arm, her uncomfortable expression turning to one of grave concern. "Hold on a second. You're not seriously considering this trip right now? Launching the webcasts while Bayli's clearly under fire? Christian, that could be very dangerous for her. For all of you."

"I'd say that's true," Rory interjected, "except that whoever's trying to rattle her cage is here in New York. If we were shooting here, that might cause a problem, leave her wide open to be targeted. But we're traveling to very remote areas in Mexico. I highly doubt this person is willing to follow her from location to location. And even so, we just decided on the destinations. They're not currently public knowledge."

"These things leak, Rory. You know that," Lily insisted. "It seems a bit risky to move forward before the police even have the chance to try to find some leads."

"I want to do this," Bayli said. "We've invested too much time and effort, not to mention money, into kicking off this series. Rory's ready to turn the restaurant over to his executive chef, and we're at the perfect point to launch the show."

"She's right," Rory concurred.

"And I'll be with the two of you the whole time," Bayli added. "In fact, I'll be under your nose more while we're traveling than here in Manhattan."

"That's true." Christian raked a hand through his hair as he debated the situation. Then said, "We'll move forward. But if the police don't come up with anything concrete, I'm going to speak with a private investigator and a bodyguard when we get back."

"Fine." Bayli nodded. "I just don't think it's anything to worry about while we're in Mexico. According to Scarlet, who researched the ISPs for the stalker e-mails I've received and the worst of the hater comments related to the video, the provider is in Japan. Either in or around a prison, as best as she can tell. So, if it's him and he's trying to get me to stay away from Rory, then he can find people here in New York to carry out his dirty work. Much more difficult for him when we're in Mexico."

"Why didn't you tell us any of this?" Rory asked. "About Scarlet looking into the ISPs."

"She did it on her own, after I told her about the spiders. I didn't want you to think I was still upset about that." She kissed his cheek. "You've had enough to contend with, getting the restaurant and staff ready for your departure, dealing with the media, and plotting out chefs to meet with on our trip. Not to mention other things." She winked.

"It would probably be best if, in the future, you didn't keep things like that from us." This from Christian.

She kissed him as well. "Duly noted."

"Well, I need to get back to the office," Lily said. "Call me if there's anything I can do for you. Anything at all. I'm here to help." She whirled around on her tall heels and breezed out of the apartment, leaving her signature fragrance wafting under everyone's noses.

Bayli eyed Christian and Rory, and while wagging a finger between the two of them, asked, "Did you both . . . with Lily?" Her brow crooked.

"Just Christian," Rory told her. "She's not my type."

"It was very casual," Christian said. "And over before it was even officially over."

"Huh. Not sure I know what that means, but okay. Anyway, I need to call Joyce and tell her it's back to Barneys, Bloomingdale's, and Bergdorf's for us in the morning."

Rory's arm wound around her waist and his head lowered to hers. "Are you sure you're all right?"

"Not exactly thrilled my personal belongings have been reduced to rubble and all those outfits we bought for the show are nothing but strips of cloth and unraveled thread. And, yes, I am pretty angry. Mad as hell, to be honest. But mostly, I'm just devastated that I didn't think to put my bracelet back on. I always wear it, but I didn't want it to get caught on the rim of the washer and then I was in a hurry and didn't remember to get it from the jewelry box."

"Was the bracelet insured?" Rory asked.

She smirked at him. "Come on, Rory. This is me you're talking to. It was maybe worth twenty-five bucks. But it was a birthday present from my mom and I cherished it. Now it's nothing but fairy dust."

His jaw worked, and she could see in his eyes that he wanted to tell her he and Christian would buy her a new one. But he also understood the significance *that* particular bracelet held for her and that it truly couldn't be replaced. So he didn't say a word.

Bayli went to the foyer to retrieve her cell from her coat pocket and placed the call to Joyce. Then tried to find ways to distract herself so that she didn't dwell on the fact that some guy in a Japanese prison just might be miffed to high heaven that she had a boyfriend.

Thank God he didn't know she had *two* of them!

"This scenery is absolutely breathtaking," Bayli said as she sat in a window seat of the private jet and marathon-snapped photos of the coastline with her iPhone.

From beside her, Rory told her, "Brian's taking photos with his high-tech digital camera. I'm sure he'll be happy to share some with you."

"Sure, if I pay him royalties when I want to post his copyrighted material on my Web site or Facebook page. But beyond that, the point is that I'm here, taking these shots myself. Get it?"

"Got it." Rory chuckled. Then he said, "So that's our cove right there on the end."

"And such a beautiful resort."

"Actually, we're staying in a house in the hills," Christian chimed in. "That house, to be exact."

There was only one tucked into the tree-covered hillside and it faced the ocean. Completely out of eyeshot of the resort, where the production crew was staying. Bayli had assumed she, Rory, and Christian would stay at the hotel as well, but it was exciting to know they'd have a whole house to themselves. She took a few pictures of it, along with the cove, with one large mound of rocks rising above the water and several smaller conglomerations the waves broke against, sending whitecaps shooting into the air. Then the water smoothed out to form the semi-circular lagoon.

The beach was pristine, though she'd read in a travel magazine that the sand could be a bit rough on the feet. Not to mention hot. A heat wave rolling through the region didn't help matters, and the forecast called for high temps and humidity. She figured hotel guests would be spending most of their time in the numerous pools sprawled across the vast property, including the swim-up pools edging the bottom-floor rooms and the spas on some of the patios.

The entire area was gorgeously scenic and Bayli was racking up the photos. Even as they landed at the small airport and stepped off the plane into the blazing heat, she snapped shots of the *palapa*-topped terminal. It wasn't air-conditioned, unfortunately, but they were whisked through Customs and into an SUV with the frigid air blasting in no time. The crew followed in three vans with their equipment and luggage.

They wound through the cozy town and Bayli made dozens of notes in her book. She mostly had her logistics plotted out with the cameramen to capture the unique features of the region, but it was something altogether different to be here in person rather than home using the Internet for research.

Plus, Bayli planned to spend time interviewing locals while Rory was meeting with his chefs. They'd end up with a lot of decisions to make after a few days, but she had a feeling it was going to be a rich, fruitful endeavor.

The vans split off at one juncture to head to the resort, and the SUV continued on to a private gated drive.

They traveled to the very southern tip of the cove and passed through more gates that opened to a lush lawn with vibrantly colored flora and full palm trees. There were fountains and beautifully trimmed topiary. And an enormous two-story house that stretched before them.

Staff assisted with their luggage as Bayli, Christian, and Rory passed through the glass doors and crossed the marbled floor, taking in the open, spacious quarters. Rory inspected the gourmet kitchen. Bayli admired the ocean view from the wall of windows, and the long, narrow infinity-edge pool that flowed from one end of the house to the other.

The patio was laden with comfortable-looking rattan lounge chairs with turquoise-colored cushions. There were tables and chairs scattered everywhere. Several large hammered-bronze cauldrons served as fire pits.

"Nice little getaway?" Christian asked from behind her as his arms slipped around her waist.

"Sensational little getaway. I could live here and be a very happy girl."

He laughed. "You're easy to please."

"Are we still talking about the getaway?"

"Mm," he murmured as his lips skimmed her neck, sending a shiver along her spine. "Rory and I do enjoy how open-minded and receptive you are."

She gazed at him in the reflection of the tall glass panes. "I'm not sure what's generating the most heat. The fact that this wall of windows faces the sun . . . or you."

His erection pressed to the cleft of her ass as his hands skated upward and he palmed her breasts. Squeezed the mounds as they grew heavy with desire.

"Now's not exactly the time to get frisky with me," she chided. "There are people around."

"They're leaving. Everything's taken care of here." His tongue swirled around that sensitive spot at her nape. Then he whispered against her damp skin, "It's just you, me, and Rory."

Christian unbuttoned her blouse and slid the material down her arms.

"Starting the party without me?" Rory asked as he sexily strutted into the living room.

"I knew you'd come around shortly," Christian told him.

"Pun intended, eh?" Rory grinned mischievously. Then he reached for the material of his shirt at the back of his neck and hauled it over his head, dropping the garment on the polished floor.

Bayli sighed lustfully as she watched Rory slowly saunter toward them while Christian released the clasp of her bra, between her breasts.

"I want to lick every inch of you," she told Rory. Then let out a throaty moan as Christian's fingers and thumbs toyed with her nipples, making them hard.

Rory kissed her, hot and hard, before kneeling in front of her and shoving her short skirt up to her waist. "That's exactly what I'm going to do to you," he said. "Starting right here."

He yanked her panties down her legs. His large hands skimmed up her legs, his thumbs caressing her inner thighs, making the flesh quiver. His tongue swept over her pussy lips, licking enthusiastically, then suckling the sensitive folds with his mouth, then licking again. Purposely avoiding her throbbing clit. Teasing her. Driving her wild.

Just as Christian's kisses on her neck and his hands on her breasts did. He knew she liked him squeezing and fondling. Knew she climbed a bit higher when he pinched her nipples into tight peaks that tingled and ached for more.

She snaked an arm around Christian's flexed biceps and craned her neck to kiss him. His tongue delved deep and she could feel the erratic beats of his pulse and heart. She threaded her fingers through Rory's hair as he finally homed in on the swollen pearl between her legs and suckled deep.

Christian caught her moan in his mouth. Her knees nearly buckled. These two men were sensational together. And when Rory's fingers slid into her slick canal as his tongue fluttered over her clit she came instantly.

TWENTY

Rory's cock pulsated against the fly of his dress pants. He'd been aching for some time now to be the one to take Bayli's ass, but he'd been holding back, letting Christian top her because he possessed much more control than Rory did when it came to this woman. Rory had decided it was best for her to get used to them both fucking her, but above that, *he'd* needed to find a way to dial down his intensity so that he didn't get carried away. Didn't hurt her.

But tasting her, stroking her, making her come, had him teeming with the need to finally feel his dick buried in her small hole while Christian thrust up into her.

So Rory stood, kissed her, then murmured, "I want you to come even harder."

She gave a weak, giddy grin. "I never, ever complain about that."

Rory swept her into his arms.

"Hey," she quipped. "Don't go getting all sweet and romantic on me. I might start thinking you like me."

"You really are a sassy one."

She nuzzled his neck with her arms around him. Over Rory's shoulder, she said to Christian, "Come along. I have a feeling this is about to get naughty."

"If Rory and I have any say in the matter." He stripped off his shirt and followed them up the curving suspended staircase.

"You both have *every* say in the matter," she said in a flirtatious tone.

"Good," Rory told her. "Because we're going to try something different."

"Notice how I don't wig about that anymore. I like trying new things." She nipped his earlobe, sending a bolt of lightning straight to his groin.

"And you've become quite addictive," he admitted.

"Aw, flattery. Coming from Angsty Chef. How I'll cherish this moment."

From behind them, Christian gave a half snort. "You've tamed him," he told Bayli. "But who the hell is going to tame you?"

"I was too tame to begin with," she said. "A little sauciness is apparently just what you two need."

"You have that in spades," Rory assured her as they crossed the open mezzanine and entered the master suite. Rory dropped her in the middle of the enormous bed.

"Very caveman-like," she grumbled. "So much for taming you."

He whisked off her clothes as Christian cranked the AC to high so that he could pull back the drapes on the long wall of windows and the patio doors. The heat rolled into the room, but the crisp air pumping in from the vents kept the temperature moderate while allowing them all to enjoy the panoramic view of turquoise water for as far as the eye could see, with no other land in sight.

Both men undressed. Christian had snagged his laptop bag before coming upstairs and he pulled out a few condoms and packets of lubricant.

Rory joined Bayli on the bed, settling behind her as she sat on the edge. He hooked his hands under her thighs and coaxed her to widen her legs so that she bent them at her knees and planted her feet along the outside of his thighs. She leaned back against his chest.

Christian moved in from the front. She reached for him and kissed him as Rory filled his palms with her breasts and kneaded roughly while liquid fire rushed through his veins.

Christian's fingers eased into her pussy, massaged slowly. He dragged his mouth from Bayli's and said, "She's so damn wet."

"Good." Rory's hands slid away from her and he sheathed himself, adding extra lube. Christian innately seemed to know what Rory had in mind. He withdrew his fingers just as Rory's palms slid under Bayli's ass and he both lifted her up and spread her cheeks at the same time. He held her balancing just above the tip of his cock as she clung to Christian, her fingers coiling into his biceps.

"Slow," Christian warned.

"I know." Rory's teeth gritted. He wanted her so badly that his cock throbbed almost painfully and his muscles turned to stone. His heart thumped against his ribs and he tried to keep himself in check so that he didn't fill her with one forceful thrust.

"Rory." She tried coercing him with her sultry tone. "Don't tease me."

"This isn't teasing. This is me trying to be really, really careful."

"But I already know what to expect. Christian has—"

"Been gentle," Christian interjected.

"I've wanted you like this from the very beginning," Rory reminded her. He eased her down so that his cockhead pressed against her tight hole. "Fuck," he groaned.

"Rory," she urged again. "I want to feel you. All of you. Every inch of you."

He lowered her a tiny bit, so that his tip penetrated.

She let out a soft cry. "Yes. More."

Everything inside of Rory pulled taut. God, he wanted her like this. Wanted to feel her surrounding him, grinding against him. Wanted to fill her as Christian fucked her.

So Rory gradually eased her down, not plunging recklessly, just allowing her to take him inside her at her own pace. Until he was suddenly fully encased in her heat and she was whimpering evocatively while still clutching at Christian's muscles.

"Oh, hell," Rory murmured as emotion flowed through him to mix with the excitement burning in his gut.

Christian leaned into Bayli, and Rory experienced the solid width of him as his cock slid into her pussy, stretching her as Rory did.

She moaned, low and throaty.

Rory did everything in his power to keep his hips still, to keep his butt from clenching and pushing deeper into her. He held her legs spread wide with his hands under her thighs and let Christian set the steady pace.

"Oh, God," she said on a sliver of air. "Oh, my fucking God."

"Don't tense up," Rory whispered in her ear.

Her head fell back against his shoulder. He kissed, then nipped at her neck. Sexy, erotic sounds tumbled from her parted lips.

Rory could feel Christian increase his tempo slightly. Until they were all smoothly rocking together and Rory was half out of his mind, Bayli was murmuring almost incoherently, and Christian's mouth was on her breast, toying with her nipple.

A distinct hunger ate at Rory. Not just the need to send them all over the edge but a sense of unity gripped him—that elusive sensation he and Christian had been searching for, for well over a decade when they'd discovered their mutual penchant for sharing women and their gift for pleasuring them.

This went beyond physical stimulation. Rory was completely taken by Bayli. And knew Christian was, too. They both had been . . . from the very beginning.

That got Rory going even more.

"Christian," he said in a strained voice. "More."

"Yes," his friend agreed. And pumped with more gusto.

"Oh, yes!" Bayli wailed. "Yes!"

"Make her come," Rory demanded. "Fuck her harder."

His restraint was slipping. But the way Bayli writhed against him and loudly whimpered, completely uninhibited, spurred him on. He had to feel her come with his dick in her ass. To feel her cream seep from her wet pussy to his balls. To know he and Christian had worked her into this frenzy that took her even higher than ever before.

"This is so good," she choked out. "So amazingly good."

Christian's hips bucked and Rory kept himself stabilized as her ass wiggled against his pelvis.

And then he heard the hitch in her breath and he knew she'd reached that point of no return.

"Harder, Christian," he commanded.

Rory could feel how deep inside her Christian was. Could feel his powerful strokes. Bayli was clutching them both and letting out breathy little moans.

And then she squeezed them both tight, screamed Rory's name, followed by Christian's. Rory absorbed the quaking of her body as the climax tore through her and she milked both their cocks.

He couldn't hold on a second longer. "That's it, honey. Christ, that's so good. Bayli!" He erupted. Christian was right there with him. Their gazes locked on Bayli as she kept coming.

Later that evening, after Rory grilled mahimahi and served it with rice and steamed vegetables, Bayli lay between her two men, her arm wrapped around Rory's waist as her breasts pressed to his back and Christian curled around her from behind, holding her close to him.

Her body felt incredible. Scintillatingly searing in some places, achy in a good way in others.

It was so exhilarating to teeter on this precipice of near perfection knowing that all she, Rory, and Christian had to do was give in to the emotions and sensations that wavered amongst them, hovered over them, permeated throughout them, and they'd all achieve something great. Something substantial. Something life-long.

It was what Bayli wanted more than anything else.

More than being famous.

More than convincing herself that becoming a household name was the only way for her to feel as though her mother's sacrifices weren't in vain.

Bayli had become a part of something much bigger than herself . . . and that was the highest of highs she could ever ride.

She slept soundly with the crashing of waves hitting the shore, despite the doors being closed, because it was too damn hot to open them after they'd learned that doing so automatically shut off the air-conditioning—and Bayli simply couldn't have that. The surf surged and broke powerfully, and the house was so close to its edge that the undulation and spray lulled her into a deep sleep and kept her suspended there. So, too, did the incredible orgasms Christian and Rory had given her. And the intimate cocoon the three of them created under the light covers.

Around nine the next morning, Bayli woke to the scent of strong coffee and huevos rancheros. She sat up in the empty bed, spying the breakfast waiting for her on a table in the corner and hearing the shower running in the bathroom.

She knew Rory had several full days ahead of him, but he'd taken the time to cook for her. Christian was likely the one in the shower. He, too, had a packed schedule. Mostly conference calls and FaceTime sessions, but he was also following her around to all of her documentary shoots.

Tossing off the bedcovers, she crossed to the table and devoured breakfast. Then took her glass of OJ out to the balcony, where she reveled in the breathtaking views. Then she returned to the room just as Christian strolled in, looking devilishly handsome in a black polo shirt and dress pants.

Though she told him, "You're going to swelter in pants today."

"Won't be the heat that does the trick," he told her. "You're mostly going to be in a bikini the next two days. That'll send my temperature into the red zone."

Her first assignment was investigating the local mom-and-pop shops and eateries. Then she'd be swimming with the dolphins, snorkeling, and, finally, learning to windsurf in the resort's cove. The cooking demos would take place later in the week.

She asked Christian, "Rory's off to work with his chefs?"

Christian slipped his arms around her and said, "Yes, and he's building in the competition for favorite local recipes with four chefs going head-to-head. This ought to be interesting. The audience for the exhibition and competition will be a mix of regional residents and tourists. So I'd say the pendulum could swing any way."

"This'll be fun. But we're cramming a lot into one hour, aren't we?"

"The network and I decided we'd do two-parters for the test run. Pack as much of a punch as we can."

"Because we need to stand out," she said with a nod. "That makes sense. There are tons of cooking shows on TV." She gnawed her lower lip. Felt a sense of foreboding low in her belly.

"Hey, sweetheart." Christian kissed her temple. "You are going to shine so bright. No one doubts that for a second. So don't worry. Don't stress. Just be your radiant self."

"Hmm. Rory's always telling me that."

"Well, then, fuck. What a drag that I have to agree with him."

She laughed. "You can always be counted on to ease the tension." She kissed him. "You're really too fantastic for words."

"I know."

Bayli rolled her eyes.

He said, "Now . . . go shower. Your hair and makeup ladies are on their way."

She went about her business while Christian went about his. They met up in the foyer later and their driver took them into town, with half of the production crew trailing behind—the others had departed with Rory. They filmed Bayli's documentary with all of her tidbits gleaned from her research. There'd been numerous takes from various angles to be edited together, but Bayli had been so enthused and had been so well prepared that she could deliver commentary smoothly and easily.

By the end of the evening, though, she was exhausted. The next day was more of the same. She was in the string bikini Rory had once teased her about. Had a mask on her face and flippers on her feet, and was about to wade into a shallow cove and photograph the ocean life when one of the production crew handed over a small stack of freshly made flour tortillas.

Her brow knitted. "It's not exactly lunchtime. What am I supposed to do with these?"

He told her, "Pull off chunks and drop them in the water. The fish will swarm you. Better shots for the show."

"Yeah, no." She shoved the stack back at him. "I don't want to be swarmed. I know the new fad is to have fish nibble your feet, but huh-uh, no way. Not for this girl. Not going to happen."

"You're wearing fins," he reminded her.

"Still not interested in the swarming." She shot a look over her shoulder to Christian. He gave a half shrug. "Oh, sure," she said. "Easy for you to be so noncommittal. You're not swimming with piranhas."

"Fish, sweetheart." He grinned. "They're just fish."

"Right. Just fish." She took the tortillas and went snorkeling. And loved every second of it.

She'd expected the dolphins to be an easier scenario to work with, but having the large creatures come right up to her and get in her face—in the most adorable way—had her squealing in near terror. For all of two seconds. She smoothed her hand over the head of one and it squeaked as though content and suddenly Bayli was in love.

On the third full day, she was in the resort's cove on a

lightweight board with water socks on her feet, gloves on her hands, and a life vest buckled around her. She'd spent the entire morning learning to balance her weight on the board while it sat atop two logs spaced from tip to end. Then she'd worked on her technique in the shallow water. Now there was a sail attached to the board and as it floated in the water, the instructor yelled out directions for her to hoist the sail and let the wind catch it.

Sure. All good in theory.

But bending over to clasp the uphaul was challenging, as the light ripples of water caused the board to rock. She lost her balance and fell backward into the lagoon. Repeatedly. On her fifth or sixth try, she was actually able to lift the sail.

"Grab the boom!" her instructor directed.

She did. And fell right into the sail as it slammed into the water.

She sputtered.

Christian called out with concern, "Are you okay?"

"Dandy," she groaned. But got right back on the board and tried again. She might end up drowning, but at least she'd put some effort into it.

Eventually, she was able to keep the sail up and she did, indeed, catch the wind. Too much of a stiff breeze, because she headed straight out of the lagoon and into the rougher waters of the Pacific. Bayli screamed. Though, in truth, it was a huge rush. She just didn't know what to do now that she was seriously on the move.

She hit the choppier waves and absorbed the rise and fall with bent knees, but she had no idea how the hell she was going to get back into the lagoon. She laughed, a bit hysterically, and dropped the boom. The sail collapsed and she fell backward into the water again. When she surfaced, she climbed onto the board and waved to her instructor and his assistant as they were on their way to retrieve her.

She couldn't wait to see the footage of her actually wind-surfing . . . though the bloopers would be infinitely more entertaining, she knew. And Christian felt they'd "humanize" her for the audience.

At dinner, she told Rory all about her adventures. He, too, had experienced some entertaining moments, including one of his chefs preparing fire-roasted peppers on an outside grill that was positioned under a *palapa* top. The peppers weren't the only thing on fire. Luckily, the flames fringing the dried palm fronds were immediately doused. No harm, no foul, according to Rory, but it created some memorable shots.

The next day was reserved for taping the show. Christian and Rory were on-site mid-morning, while Bayli prepped herself mentally and her stylists spent extensive time on her appearance. Her nerves were a bit jangled, but the best part of having done the documentary-ish portion of the show in advance of the cooking demo was that she'd spent several days in front of cameras already and was feeling more comfortable with moving around, rather than simply posing.

She felt natural and liked that there had been plenty of interactions with people on the street and locals to generate a friendly, fun platform.

Now for the pièce de résistance!

Bayli was beyond excited, even if the hint of anxiety continued to linger. The girls left her to meet up with Rory on location, telling her they'd touch up Bayli once she arrived. She was happy for the respite so that she could just chill out over a light lunch and then relax before the limo came for her.

Christian had worried over leaving her alone for a few hours, but Bayli was grateful for a little solitude. Plus, she was ensconced behind two sets of heavy, coded gates. And the housekeeping staff was still downstairs, finishing their work.

So she slipped behind the closed drapes in the master suite and out the patio doors to enjoy the view for a few minutes. It was another cloudless day, the sky a perfect shade of blue and the sun blazing bright. Bayli had taken dozens of pictures from this balcony.

The scenery truly was breathtaking, especially since it was all unobstructed.

Unfortunately, she wasn't a fan of the heat and was only good for five minutes of soaking up the vitamin D and beautiful vistas. She headed back to the sliding door and tugged on the handle. It didn't give.

She tried again, panic instantly sparking.

She yanked harder. Several times.

"No!" Bayli cried out, and pounded the heel of her hand on the hot glass.

The door was locked from the inside! A member of the staff must have flipped the latch without knowing Bayli was on the balcony because they always kept the drapes closed when the sun beat down on the backside of the house this time of day.

Bayli was dressed only in her long, navy-colored, silk nightgown. She grabbed up some of the flowing skirt and wrapped it around her fist so she could make contact with the glass without burning her hand.

"Melita!" she called out to the main housekeeper. "Let me in!" She pounded harder.

Then she raced over to the railing and planted her hands on the top of it to look over the edge and see if there was anyone tending to the downstairs patio or the grounds who could help her.

But she hadn't given thought to how the metal railing would have absorbed the heat and she let out another scream at the searing pain on her palms.

With barely a breath in her body, she managed to call out for Melita again. Then Bayli hurried to one end of the balcony and yelled for help. Then the other. But there was no one in sight.

Now in a full-blown panic she grabbed the small end table between two rattan chaise longue chairs, held it by the legs, and banged on the door. It only bounced off, not even leaving the tiniest of cracks or chips.

"Fuck!" she wailed. What was this, bullet- and soundproof glass?

She kept at it with the table while begging for someone to help her. She prayed this would just be ten minutes of her own harrowing travel experience to regale Phillip and Colin with, but as her strength waned, the perspiration dripped from her, and her makeup melted under the intense heat, Bayli had the horrific feeling this was not going to be a short-lived nightmare.

She suddenly had petrifying visions of the scene from *Interview with a Vampire* when Claudia and her new "mother" were trapped in the underground cell of the theatre players with the impending dawn creeping in on them, sun rays slowly filling the grated opening above them. The two female vampires had been huddled together in their long evening gowns. But nothing could save them from incineration. Not even Louis, who'd barely grazed the ash that had once been Claudia's arm and she'd disintegrated before his very eyes.

Not a particularly comforting visual given Bayli's current predicament.

Dropping the table, she went back to the railing, cautious not to touch it or get too close to the glass panels that enclosed the deck. She screamed for help again. But there wasn't a soul on-property to save her.

Bayli had no phone with her. No way to signal for help. No water. Except . . .

"Oh, thank God!" There was a two-person Jacuzzi tub on the balcony. She crossed to it and cranked the knob for the cold water. A pathetic little stream trickled out. Then . . . nothing.

"No way," she said on a shattered breath. She cranked the other knob and got the same result. Tears stung her eyes.

No water.

None for her to sit in and cool down until someone rescued her. None to drink.

Like the two vamps, she was trapped under the relentless rays, with zero breeze and not an inch of shade for protection.

Fuck! This really couldn't be happening.

But it was.

She went back to the patio doors and banged some more. Until she had to admit that there was no one on the other side to let her in. And jumping over the railing didn't seem like such a fab idea because she'd hit the hard patio below and break every bone in her body. Probably bleed to death from compound fractures before anyone got to her.

So she needed a Plan B.

Survival mode kicked in and she surveyed the balcony. The only saving grace she could see was the chaise longue chairs. She stripped the cushion from one and spread it horizontally in the tub. Then she took the other and perched it on the ledge, creating a little bit of shelter from the sun and the hot surface of the tub. She crawled in, the sweat still pouring from her body and her breathing shallow.

She needed water. Badly. But she tried not to think of heatstroke and dehydration and just plain shriveling up and dying right there in paradise. . . .

TWENTY-ONE

Christian was with Rory when the driver he'd hired to pick up Bayli phoned.

"*No esta aqui,*" came the driver's rapid-fire Spanish.

"What do you mean she's not there?" Christian demanded.

"I've searched. There's no one here in the house. Not on the patio or the grounds."

"That's impossible! Where would she have gone? She doesn't have a car." Fear gripped Christian.

Rory gave him an insistent, imploring look, only hearing half of the conversation.

Christian said, "Keep looking."

He disconnected the call and told Rory, "She's missing."

"How?" he asked, incredulous. "That place is locked down. And like you said, she has no vehicle."

"What's going on?" Lily joined them. "You two look panicked."

"Bayli's not at the house," Rory curtly said.

"She has to be," Lily assured them, looking deeply perplexed—matching Christian's and Rory's expressions. "There's nowhere for her to go. Not even down to the beach. There's no direct access. She'd need transportation no matter where she wanted to take off to."

"She could have called a cab," Christian strove for a reasonable explanation. Not the horrifying one creeping in on him.

"No way," Rory said. "Not without telling us. And besides, she doesn't know the gate codes to let anyone in."

"Look," Lily urged, ever the problem solver. "She has to be there somewhere. Go to the house, Christian. The audience is already filing in and we're supposed to be taping in half an hour. Rory can get things rolling."

"Not a fucking chance!" the chef roared. "This is exactly what we *don't* want. Me interacting with these people. That's the very reason we tanked the first time. And it's Bayli's job."

Lily threw her hands up in the air in frustration. "We have to do something! Christian." She clasped his hands firmly. "Go get her. Worst-case scenario, I'll fill in until she arrives. I can warm up the crowd. We can stall for a half hour or so. There are margaritas to pour and I'll play hostess while Rory and his chef whip up an appetizer."

"With what excess stock? We're cooking specific items here," Rory gruffly told her.

"We'll have the resort send down ingredients. We're using their beach—I'm sure they'd love additional promo."

Rory raked a hand through his hair. Shook his head. "No. I'm not going to be able to concentrate until I know where Bayli is and that she's safe." To Christian, he said, "I'll go with you to the house. Lily, cancel today's taping. We'll do it tomorrow. Offer some sort of incentive for everyone to come back."

He was on the move, and Christian knew there was no stopping him. He was hot on Rory's heels.

Christian didn't bother with the driver, just grabbed the keys from him and slid behind the wheel. He and Rory tore out of the parking lot and wound up the hill.

Rory said, "Maybe she just got cold feet and went for a walk to clear her head."

"You didn't see her the past few days. She was perfectly at ease in front of the cameras—no cold feet there. She was laughing, making fun of herself when warranted, talking about the region as though she'd lived here her entire life. Bayli's sensational in this role."

"Then where the hell is she?" Rory demanded in an edgy voice.

Clearly, neither of them wanted to consider the possibility that her stalker might have actually followed her to Mexico. But after the break-in and the box of spiders . . . anything was possible.

They passed through both sets of gates and Christian jerked the SUV to a stop in front of the house and jumped out. He and Rory raced into the foyer, where they found the driver they had hired for Bayli.

He said, "There's no one in this house but me. I just covered the entire lawn. She's not out there, either."

That was not an acceptable answer for Christian or Rory. They took off in separate directions to comb every square foot of the house, calling out Bayli's name. Rory started downstairs. Christian took the suspended steps two at a time to the mezzanine. He checked all the nooks and crannies and then searched the bedrooms and bathrooms. No Bayli.

"Goddamn it!" he hollered just as Rory stormed in.

"No sign of her. At all," Rory said in agitation.

Christian's gaze swept the master suite where they'd met up. His eyes fixated on the closed blackout drapes that kept the powerful sun from turning the room into a sauna. Bayli wasn't a sun worshiper in this kind of heat; she'd told him so herself. But what if she'd gone out for a few minutes to work on her tan and had fallen asleep?

He strode to the doors and reached around the curtain to pull on the handle. It didn't budge. The door was locked, so that answered his question. She wasn't outside. Except . . . she wasn't anywhere else, either.

With a forceful gesture he shoved back the drapes.

"What the fuck?" Rory mumbled as he stared out the tall

windows. Toward the Jacuzzi tub. And the lounge chair cushion covering one end of it.

"The wind didn't do that," Christian said. "There is no wind today."

He flipped the latch on the handle and slid back the door. He and Rory dashed across the balcony. Rory tossed off the top cushion.

"Bayli!" Christian yelled out. She was in her nightgown, curled in the fetal position.

Her eyelids fluttered open, but she appeared to have difficulty focusing on him and Rory. She weakly said, "Finally, someone found me."

Christian scooped her into his arms and carried her inside. Rory closed the door behind them and stalked toward the thermostat.

"Wait, no," Christian said. "Don't make it any colder in here. She's going to have to acclimate as it is." To Bayli, he asked, "How long were you out there?"

"No idea." Her voice was but a mere wisp of dry, crackling air.

Christian told Rory, "Get a glass of water from the tap."

"Why not a bottle of cold water from the fridge?"

"Because it's not good for her insides when her internal temperature is so damn high."

"How would you know that?"

"I read it somewhere," Christian told him. "I think she has heatstroke. And she's sunburned." Her skin was coated in perspiration as well. "We should put her in a bath."

Rory ducked into the bathroom. Let out a harsh litany of swear words and stormed back into the suite. "There's no fucking water! That's why she didn't fill the tub when she was stuck out there."

Christian carefully placed her on the bed, propping her against the mound of pillows, as Rory went to the wet bar and grabbed several bottles of unchilled FIJI from the butler pantry. He set them on the nightstand and then returned to the bathroom for towels.

Christian twisted the cap off the water and held it to Bayli's mouth, helping her sip because her body was shaking. She attempted a deeper drink, and he eased the bottle away.

"Not so much, so fast," he told her in a quiet voice. "Little sips. Okay?"

She glared at him through eyes that danced in their sockets. Christ, for all he knew, her retinas were fried.

Rory dampened a hand towel and wiped all the makeup from her face. He tossed it aside and reached for another, moistening it as well and gliding it gently along her neck and collarbone. Christian helped her sip some more. He wished like hell he could remember precisely how to treat heatstroke. It'd been in an article in the *Wall Street Journal* when a CEO's plane had crash-landed in the tropics and the executive had only narrowly survived the extreme climate.

They needed to cool Bayli down, just not so quickly that she went into shock. So no packing her in ice.

Christian told Rory, "We have to get the water on so we can get her in the bathtub."

Rory handed over a wet towel. "I'll be back."

With Rory out of the room—because he didn't want his best friend exploding over the terrifying situation for Bayli—Christian asked her, "How'd you get locked out? It's not an automatic lock."

"Melita," she said, still hoarse and weak. "She didn't know I was out there. She locked up before leaving."

"Do you remember when that was?"

"I'd just had lunch."

Christian swore under his breath. "So about four hours with no water. Thank God you're a smart girl and created some shade for yourself." He kissed her temple. "The problem is, all that glass and metal probably adds about six to ten degrees to the temperature in that confined area. You must have felt like an ant under a magnifying glass with the sun beating down on you."

"Exactly."

"Sweetheart, I'm so sorry."

"Not your fault," she said with a feeble attempt at a smile. "Melita can't be blamed, either, Christian. She knows I don't spend any serious time out on that balcony. It was an honest mistake. Don't have her fired or anything, okay?"

"Always worried about others." He kissed her softly. Then said, "I'll have to figure out how to break it to Rory, because he *will* want her fired."

"Not when he calms down and sees the incident for what it was."

Rory returned minutes later and started the bath. He then told them, "Kind of odd that the water was turned off outside."

"Maybe because they didn't think anyone was here," Bayli offered. "They could conserve water during the day that way if they have some leaky faucets or sprinkler heads."

"Sure. That makes sense." Though Rory didn't look convinced.

Bayli pulled in a few unsteady breaths. Tried to collect herself, evidently. She closed her eyes for a couple of seconds and this time inhaled deeper.

But then her lids fluttered open. Her tawny irises were clouded and she frowned.

"What is it?" Christian asked, instantly alarmed.

Her head rolled on the pillow and she pinned him with a look. "When was Lily here?"

"You have fucking *got* to be kidding me!" Rory thundered.

After Bayli had spoken, both Rory and Christian had taken a hearty whiff of air and there it was—the faint scent of Chanel No. 5 clinging to the fabrics as it always did following Lily's departure.

Christian appeared to put a good deal of effort into keeping his jaw from clenching and his tone from being downright lethal. "She didn't have lunch with you, Bayli?"

"No."

"She had no reason to be here at all," Rory pointed out, not bothering to couch his own anger in a calmer demeanor the way Christian had. "Her assignment was keeping all the logistics flowing with the production crew. *That* was the reason you brought her along. Not to hang out with Bayli."

"I'm well aware of that," Christian said.

"I never saw her here," Bayli interjected.

"That's because she's clearly working behind the scenes to scare you off. Think about it," Rory urged. "She has access to your home address. She's seen you wear the bracelet that was destroyed. She knew you were spending time at Christian's apartment—"

"She seemed genuinely surprised when she learned I'd been spending nights there," Bayli reminded him.

"That's what she wanted you to think." Rory got rolling again. This time, his irritation was directed at Christian. "Why the hell did you need to bring her along?"

"I don't want to lose her at the office."

"She's behind all of this, Christian!"

"You don't know that for a fact," Christian said as he stood and got in Rory's face. "So just bring it down a few notches and we can figure out what's really going on."

"Seems pretty cut-and-dried to me." Rory's fury built, fueled by the very real and distressing fact that Bayli looked like hell, had actually been to hell, and it could have been so much worse. What if they hadn't found her for another couple of hours? "Lily was a bit too eager beaver to jump in and help with the show in Bayli's absence. An absence *she* orchestrated."

"She wanted to take my place?"

"Yes," Rory told Bayli. "And prior to all this, she was pissed at Christian for some time for not getting the chance to audition when we decided to change the platform for the show."

"Look, I understand that you're upset, Rory," Christian said, "but—"

"You brought her along to placate her, Christian. But it's your goddamn assistant that almost killed my girlfriend!"

"*Your* girlfriend?" Christian demanded as his gaze narrowed, his eyes turned even icier, and his chest pressed to Rory's.

"*Our* girlfriend," Rory corrected. Though he didn't back down.

"Please," Bayli admonished. "Don't fight. That won't solve anything."

That she didn't move from the bed to intervene spoke volumes. She was still suffering from the heatstroke.

"Goddamn it!" Rory exploded again.

"Stop!" she shouted, albeit raspingly. "Stop arguing with each other before you say more you'll regret later on. I'll live, okay? And, sure, our accusatory fingers can currently be pointed at Lily, but that just might be too easy. The comments on the video and the angry e-mails I received all came around the same time as the spiders, with similar messaging. And none of that was from Lily. Some guy in Japan found the means to get to me in New York, so apparently I was wrong when I said he couldn't reach me here in Mexico."

"You really think it's your online stalker wreaking all this havoc?" Christian asked, his tone still holding a razor-sharp vibe, though he spoke more softly to her.

Meanwhile, Rory was still sufficiently riled.

She said, "Chances are very good. His entire campaign has been to keep me away from Rory. Having me 'accidentally' locked out so I couldn't make it to the taping of the show plays right into that."

"But shutting off the water?" Rory shook his head. "That's downright dangerous, Bayli. Potentially deadly."

A shudder ran through her. "Yes." She reached for the FIJI and took a few more sips. Then said, "I need to get into the tub. And then I have to call Scarlet."

"You think she can help?" Christian asked.

"If I tell her everything. Rory, I'm going to need to give her the contact information for the police officers investigating the ransacking of my apartment. Scarlet has connections with the NYPD. I'm sure they'll let her in on the case. She has global connections, as well. She can get access to *federales* here in Huatulco if need be."

"Fine," Rory concurred. "Whatever we can do to put a stop to all of this." He gingerly lifted Bayli into his arms and carried her into the bathroom. He set her in the tub and turned off the water. It was moderate, just cool enough to be refreshing without sending her into shock or anything.

She sat back, immersed up to her neck, and let out a long sigh. "Oh, my God. That's so helpful."

Rory scowled. "I didn't even take off your nightgown."

"Doesn't matter. It was just as drenched as I was. Sort of used to having it plastered to me now."

Rory knelt alongside her and swept strands of damp hair from her forehead. His heart wrenched at the sight of her. Over knowing what she'd just been through.

He said, "You must have been really scared."

A light mist covered her eyes. She worked down a hard swallow. Nodded her head.

"Bayli, I'm so sorry." He pressed his lips to her cheek, then her mouth, which had chapped.

"You don't have anything to be sorry about, Rory. Other than being mad at Christian. He's not to blame for any of this. Whether it's Lily who's behind this or some crazy fan in Japan, that's not Christian's doing."

Rory shoved away from the tub and stood. "This is a lot more complicated than our relationships in the past, honey. I don't know that Christian and I were ready for this. That we can handle how wrapped up we both are in you." His shoulders bunched and his gut coiled. "Maybe we just proved that we can't."

He left her to soak while he went back to the wet bar and poured a stiff drink.

Christian was nowhere in sight.

Bayli's heart hurt.

The tension between Christian and Rory was excruciating to witness. But she understood the extenuating circumstances. Knew she must have been a fright when they'd discovered her. Knew they'd probably been half out of their minds with worry when she hadn't shown up on location.

Adding to the disastrous situation was Lily's potential involvement. Though Bayli really couldn't fathom she'd go to such extremes just to stand in for or push Bayli out of a cooking show. There had to be more—

She sat up suddenly. She recalled the notecard Rory had recovered from the lobby after the spiders had been delivered.

STAY AWAY FROM HIM

She'd assumed that warning had been for her to stay away from Rory.

But if Lily had been upset over losing Christian to Bayli, perhaps that was the actual warning. Maybe it had nothing to do with Rory—and everything to do with Christian. And the show.

Her mind working feverishly seemed to help her body come along more quickly. Bayli carefully climbed out of the tub, peeled off her nightgown, and wrapped herself in the matching satin robe. She was alone in the suite and that gave her pause, making her wonder if she should seek out Christian and Rory. She didn't actually think they'd come to blows over her, but then again, this wasn't some minor lovers' quarrel they were embroiled in. She could have been seriously injured. And both men were wound tight over that realization.

Bayli might be able to alleviate all of that and strengthen these suddenly tenuous bonds. She phoned Scarlet and spilled everything.

Christian had a dozen different thoughts running through his mind, including the very ominous and highly infuriating notion that Lily could possibly have had something to do with Bayli being trapped on the balcony.

"Should we call the doctor the resort recommended for emergencies?" Rory asked as he joined Christian on the patio.

"Already did. He's on his way over."

"Good. That's good." Rory stuffed his hands in his pockets. Hung his head.

Christian let out a long breath. "If you're here to apologize—"

Rory's head snapped up. "I'm still really pissed."

"Of course you are. That's second nature for you."

Rory smirked.

Christian said, "Be pissed all you want. For as long as you want. You have every right to be, and so do I. But the bottom line is, we need to know what's really going on here. Who's really trying to hurt Bayli."

"Agreed."

They stared at each other a few moments. Then Christian's cell rang with the specific jingle for gate access. He answered the call, confirmed it was the hired physician, and then punched in the code to let him through.

Christian said to Rory, "Maybe you can make her something easy to eat. Then she should probably sleep."

TWENTY-TWO

Bayli woke the next morning to familiar voices approaching. She opened her eyes as Christian entered the suite, followed by Rory. But she homed in on the female voice. Sat up and grinned as Scarlet stepped around the men and rushed over to the bed.

"What on earth are you doing here?" Bayli all but squealed as Scarlet sank onto the edge of the mattress and they hugged.

Scarlet said, "Christian sent a plane for me. I have tons of news. Been up most the night. But first, how are you feeling?"

"Like I could drain a lake." Bayli reached for her glass of water bedside and gulped half of it down. "And it feels like there's a marching band playing inside my head, heavy on the drums and cymbals, epic tempo, totally out of sync with each other. Not to mention my skin is fried, so I'm shivering, even though psychologically I'm still burning up on the inside."

"Sorry I asked," Scarlet deadpanned.

Bayli laughed. "Aside from all that, I'm just fine."

"That's what I like to hear. Now, here's the lowdown, if you think you can handle it before breakfast."

"Definitely before breakfast so I don't heave on you if this gets too terrifying."

"Bayli—" Rory cut in.

She raised her hand. "I can deal with this. Don't go all Superman protecting Lois Lane on me."

"More like the Beast saving Beauty," Scarlet muttered under her breath. "But anyhoo. Here's the situation: Your stalker is still locked up in Japan. He was definitely the one to send you e-mails and post the hatergrams on YouTube. He was not, however, the one to send you the creepy-crawlies via courier."

Bayli's stomach churned. "Thoughts on who did?"

"Not just thoughts. I've nailed it down. So, the officers who investigated the break-in at your apartment found a guy who saw the would-be robber on the fire escape. They had a sketch for me, which they e-mailed. I forwarded that sketch to the courier service, and they confirmed the NYPD rendering was the same guy who hired them to make the delivery."

Bayli sighed dejectedly. "Let me guess. That man was someone hired off the street. So no way to track him down."

"Wrong!" Scarlet instantly lit up like a Roman candle. "This guy isn't cloaked in shadows. See, I scanned the rendering into a digital file, uploaded it, and ran matches. That led to an actual photo. Which led to a craigslist account. When I delved deeper into that, I discovered this guy is linked to a service that's sort of like mercenaries for hire."

"I'm starting to get queasy," Bayli said. Christian and Rory moved in a little closer. She gave a slight shake of her head at them. "Don't coddle me. I have to hear this. I have to face this."

Scarlet was clearly locked in investigator mode and excitedly told them all, "I had someone from my network track down Paul Richards, our bad guy, and my pal did a little shakedown that I don't even want to know about, but we learned Richards was hired through the Internet links. And I pinpointed the ISP for where those communications to him originated."

Bayli spared a glance toward Christian and Rory. This was going to be a big reveal that would set the stage for everything that followed.

Her gaze drifted back to Scarlet. "Please tell me the ISP is from a Japanese prison server."

Scarlet frowned. "Not this time. The domain associated is in Manhattan." She peered at Christian, then Rory, and added, "More specifically, from Davila–St. James Enterprises."

"Nobody yell," Bayli quickly said. She shot both men a look. "No. Yelling. My head is killing me as it is. Just . . . process. And don't point fingers." She turned back to Scarlet to explain, "This is very sensitive. The woman I told you about is not only Christian's assistant, but they also slept together on occasion. Over the course of three years. Touchy subject."

"Bayli," Christian ground out.

"I'm setting the scene, so Scarlet knows all the players. I already gave her the four-one-one on Lily; I just didn't mention her full involvement with you."

Scarlet stood and started to pace. Bayli recognized that to be her friend's strategic planning disposition and waited patiently— as much as was humanly possible, at any rate—to learn what Scarlet came up with. Rory and Christian appeared much less tolerant with the waiting game but clearly didn't want to upset Bayli.

Finally Scarlet pulled up short and deduced, "So, Lily's feeling kicked to the curb romantically, but also professionally, since she was completely overlooked for this new show."

"That's not exactly the way it unfolded," Christian said between clenched teeth.

"That's *exactly* the way it unfolded," Bayli assured Scarlet.

Christian pinched the inner corners of his eyes with his finger and thumb.

Rory said, "She was more than interested in stepping into Bayli's role in order for us to film yesterday."

Scarlet smacked her hands together. "Perfect! So here's what we do. Rory, you go back on location today and 'convince' Lily that it's imperative she fill in for Bayli, since Bayli is under doctor's orders to stay in bed and recuperate."

"But I'm not under doctor's orders to stay in bed and recuperate," Bayli lamented, fearing her golden TV-premiere opportunity was slipping through her fingers.

"Just work with me here," Scarlet said. "We're going to push this woman up against the ropes—I've done it a million times before and it always works. Once the villain feels as though they're getting what they wanted all along—are *getting away* with their villainy—that's when they fall prey to me." She winked. "So Lily gets Bayli's stylists and everything moves forward to make Lily the heroine. She's saving the day, saving the show, whatever. Sell it hard."

Rory groaned.

Bayli grimaced. "See, the thing is, Scarlet, you're asking Rory to play nice with a woman he pretty much wants to crush under his heel at the moment."

"I don't care," Scarlet said. "Make her feel like she's God's gift to this show. Let me handle the rest."

Christian skulked about. Rory's fists clenched at his sides. Bayli told them, "I trust Scarlet. Please trust her, too."

Rory said, "Fine. I'll do my part."

Christian was the one to contact Lily to make sure everything was reset for shooting later in the afternoon. Rory arrived on location and greeted his guest chef.

Then Rory found Lily and, forcing a humble tone, asked, "Do you think you can take Bayli's place for this first show? She's still not up to it, and we can't postpone another day."

"Of course," Lily enthusiastically said. "I mean, I'm sorry Bayli's under the weather, but at least she's going to be okay. And last night I studied all of her notes that she'd sent me to print out before we left Manhattan."

"That'll be helpful. The stylists are here for you and they brought some extra outfits to try on."

She gripped his arm and said, "You won't regret this at all,

Rory. I swear. I'm completely prepared to do this. It'll be fantastic!"

Lily rushed off to get the royal treatment with hair, makeup, and wardrobe. Rory seethed. How could the woman be so happy about this when Bayli had been traumatized? It took every ounce of restraint he possessed not to confront Lily. Not to wring her neck. But he'd do as Bayli asked. He'd follow Scarlet's lead . . . and hope like hell the investigator knew what she was doing.

Bayli was a bundle of nerves as she and Scarlet stood on the fringes of the makeshift cantina erected on the beach, with a grilling area, long counter, and numerous tables and chairs that were already filled with the show's tasters/audience—all under a tall thatched cone-shaped top, the dried palm fronds rustling in a gentle breeze off the bay.

Lily was dressed in a pretty, flowy sundress in a floral print, her blond hair beautifully coiffed, her makeup perfectly done. She was a striking woman and she knew how to work the crowd. She poured margaritas and apparently told jokes, because she had everyone laughing and grinning.

Bayli's insides clenched, most notably her heart. "She's really good at this. What if it turns out that she's not our culprit and Christian and Rory decide to keep her on as hostess?"

"Come on, Bay," Scarlet said as she delicately rubbed Bayli's back to comfort her. "There's no way they'd choose Lily over you. In any capacity." Her brows wagged. "Those two men are clearly hooked on you. They are so worried about you. And when Christian contacted me to fly me out here because he thought it would help to soothe you, there was no mistaking how crazed he was over something bad happening to you. He was very intense. He wants this all to be over so that you can relax, not look over your shoulder every second of the day, and be able to do the show."

"That was before Lily had a chance to strut her stuff. Look at her. She's a natural."

"So are you. But you're much more genuine, Bay. And Christian and Rory want *you*, remember?"

Again, that was prior to them seeing Lily in action. Who eventually ducked into the privacy tent where she'd been made up, likely to do last-minute touch-ups before the taping began.

"Here's your chance, Bay," Scarlet urged her forward. "You know what to do."

Bayli drew in several deep breaths, then rounded the back of the cantina and headed toward the tent. She slipped through the opening, the material silently falling back into place, not disturbing the other woman.

Bayli quietly crept up on the vanity with a large mirror attached to it where Lily sat, dabbing red lipstick on her already perfectly painted mouth. Her signature scent filled the moderate space. It had once been a pleasant aroma to Bayli. Now it made her stomach roil.

Lily started when she caught sight of Bayli in the reflection and let out a small shriek.

"Good Lord, Bayli!" She pressed a hand to her chest. "You nearly scared the life out of me."

Serves you right.

But Bayli kept that thought to herself.

Instead, she said, "Sorry. I didn't mean to startle you. I just came to say thanks for warming up the crowd and for helping out today."

"Sure, sure. It's no problem at all. I'm happy to do what I can. But . . . why are you here?" Lily capped the tube of lipstick and stood. "Shouldn't you be in bed? Rory said you fell asleep on the sundeck at the house and suffered heatstroke. That must have been so awful."

"Yes, it was pretty terrifying."

"I'm so glad you're okay. And you look fantastic."

The stylists had secretly returned to the house to primp Bayli after they'd worked on Lily. She wore a sleeveless turquoise dress that had a bejeweled neckline and a low blouson waist that

complemented the tight skirt and short hem. Her raven hair was
sleek and angled at her collarbone, the strands currently defying
the heat and humidity with the mass quantity of products used to
keep any frizzing at bay.

Lily took her in from head to toe and said, "Wait. Why are
you all done up? I've got everything under control here. You should
be back at the house resting."

"Luckily, I've made a full recovery. So thank you very much
for agreeing to stand in if need be—that is so far above and beyond
the call of duty, Lily. I know you have other responsibilities to—"

"'If need be'?" Her brow crooked.

Bayli smiled as congenially as possible. "Yes, in the event I
couldn't make it today. You're a wonderful understudy, really."

"Understudy?" A hollow laugh fell from Lily's lips. "Rory all
but begged me to fill in today. He wants me as his hostess, Bayli.
I'm so sorry, but—"

"Actually, he doesn't," Bayli said, starting her full-court press
the way Scarlet had coached her earlier. "You were a last resort so
that we didn't have to cancel the taping again. Nothing to worry
about there, because I'm feeling much better and completely prepared to do my job."

"No, Bayli." Lily's tone held a distinct edge and her manicured
fingers curled into her palms at her sides. "*I'm* the one who's prepared to do her job. *I'm* the one who primed the crowd. I memorized
all your notes. I'm dressed and ready for this, and . . . Rory chose *me*."

"That's because he wasn't sure I'd be all right after you locked
me out of my suite and left me to fry on the balcony. I didn't fall
asleep by the way."

Lily's laugh was a sharper one this time. "*I* locked you out?
That's absurd!"

"So is trying to convince me that Rory would pick you over me
to work with him."

"You can't honestly think that I'm just going to walk away from
this opportunity?" Lily's voice dropped an octave. "Not a chance in

hell. After all I've done for the company, and for Christian, I deserved the chance to audition for this show. I *earned* the right. And just because he fell for your legs or your sugary sweetness doesn't mean shit. This is my turn to prove what I'm capable of, to be in the spotlight. Nobody's going to take that away from me."

A chill ran through Bayli at Lily's icy gaze and menacing tone.

Yet Bayli managed to say, "You've decided to usurp the lead performer, but I'm on to you, Lily. You've lost the element of surprise and—"

"If you think spiders and heatstroke are bad, trust me when I tell you I can come up with far worse, far scarier than that."

"So it *was* you."

"Yes, it was me!" she erupted. "I warned you to stay away! I even told you and Christian that it was dangerous to keep you involved with the taping when you were under fire. Did anyone listen to me, heed my warnings? No. But I can assure you, Miss Styles, that if you don't back out of the show I *will* make your life a living hell. And if you breathe one word of this to Rory or Christian you'll be checking under your bedcovers and inside your shoes every night and day in fear of what I might have waiting for you. Let's not forget . . . accidents *do* happen."

"So do kidnapping and perhaps even attempted-manslaughter charges when you intentionally trap someone in an oven and leave her for dead."

"I think the heatstroke has gone to your head. I only intended to delay you until after the show. I even sent Christian for you. Too bad Rory couldn't separate work from pleasure and had to go as well. That's clearly changed today. Whatever went on between all of you last night, he's obviously aligned himself more appropriately, concentrating on the success of this venture, not your drama."

"And here I'd thought all this time that I was the desperate one," Bayli said, a hint of sadness in her voice. "I understand your ambition, Lily. I've lived and breathed it for so long, I know it's hard to let it go."

"Great. We're on the same page. So glad to hear it, because I don't have time to continue this discussion. I have a show to star in."

"You know, I really felt bad when I slept with Christian, then Rory, while I was trying to land the hostess job at that restaurant. It didn't seem right, ethical, whatever. But I haven't stooped the way you have. I never would. Never could. I feared I was nearing the end of my rope financially and professionally, but I'd rather pack away my dreams and go home to River Cross with my tail between my legs than stab someone in the back to get what I want."

"That's why I'll be famous. You won't be. That e-mail stalker of yours really came in handy. I just piggybacked off his ominous comments and left everyone thinking he was the one threatening you. Worked like a charm. Now step aside, beauty queen. I've got this."

Bayli's teeth gritted. She squared her shoulders. "You just try to take my stage." Her pulse pounded in her ears; her skin crawled as though all those spiders Lily had sent her crept through her veins. Yet she hitched her chin. "I dare you."

Lily scoffed, "Go back to the sandbox, Bayli." She whirled around on her sandals.

Bayli's heart launched into her throat.

Lily cried out.

In the opening of the tent stood Christian and Rory. Scarlet. Along with two *federales,* automatic rifles resting in the crooks of their arms.

Bayli said, "I'm guessing a live confession in front of six people will hold up in a court of law. Hmm, Mexican prison." She made a soft *tsk*ing sound. "*You* might want to check your bedcovers and shoes, Lily. No telling what you might find . . ."

Christian was on the patio enjoying an expensive cigar and the phenomenal view—that being Bayli in her bikini as she swam in the infinity-edge pool that gave way to the scenic ocean stretching south with no barriers.

Rory plopped onto a chaise longue beside him and said, "We knocked it out of the ballpark today with the taping. Bayli was perfect."

Without taking his eyes from the object of his and Rory's desire, Christian puffed on his stogie, then told him, "You were both perfect together. The way you shift and move with each other, the banter—whether intelligently witty or comically snarky—doesn't matter. You two were extremely entertaining. We're definitely going to have a huge hit on our hands."

"Let's hope so."

"I'm not just talking about the show." Christian set aside his cigar and sipped his cognac. Then said, "I'm talking about our girl."

Rory grinned. "Yeah, she's something else."

They were quiet for a few moments.

Christian knew what Rory was contemplating as surely as Rory knew where Christian's thoughts were headed.

Rory eventually said, "I'm not the only one in love, right?"

"Right."

"Then here's to finally finding the woman we've dreamed of, personally and professionally." He lifted his cocktail and clinked rims with Christian's glass.

"Ah, playing nice, I see," Bayli teased as she ascended the steps and grabbed a towel to rub her hair. "No more fighting over little ole me?"

"Well, no guarantee there," Rory mockingly grumbled.

Bayli sank onto the cushion of Christian's chair and told them, "I was sort of hoping we could all get along, Rory."

"Maybe make this a more permanent arrangement?" Christian suggested.

With a radiant smile, Bayli said, "I did get a little thrill over the thought of staying with you after my apartment was trashed. Though I'd really like the live-in arrangement to include Rory, if you could handle that."

"Long as he keeps his hands off my dick."

Bayli snickered. "Only when I'm not around."

Both men glared at her.

"Oh, come on," she said. "If it makes me happy . . ."

Rory leaned forward and kissed her. "*Whatever* makes you happy."

She glanced at Christian. Raised her brow.

He deposited his glass on the end table and pulled her to him. "Whatever makes you happy."

Bayli smiled again. "That's easy. The two of you. The three of us. In love."

She kissed Christian.

Rory simply said, "We're going to need more condoms."

He was right, of course.

EPILOGUE

Bayli was riding another high.

"This is the best party ever," she announced, a little on the tipsy side. Luckily, it was Christian pouring the champagne for everyone and not her, so that she didn't spill.

Scarlet, Jewel, Rogen, Vin, Phillip, and Colin had joined her, Christian, and Rory at the trio's apartment—since Rory and Bayli had officially moved in. They were all on the heated terrace enjoying the light snowfall over Central Park and cocktails before dinner.

"Our cooking show is an overnight sensation!" Bayli proudly declared. "And so am I."

"Never doubted it for a second," Christian said, and kissed her temple.

"Well, *I* did," Bayli told everyone. "What with Angsty Chef and Christian's psycho assistant—and I do feel justified in calling her that because, seriously, what woman in her right mind would send eight-legged monsters to another woman? Anyway, with the dark cloud hovering over me, I was starting to fear this whole thing would never come together."

"But it did." Rory wrapped an arm around her waist and gave a squeeze. "And the excessive online streaming of the show crashed the site temporarily. Twice."

She laughed. "Who would have thought it possible?"

"It's a great show," Jewel contended.

"With a solid network behind it," Christian said, and they all raised their glasses to toast the success.

Bayli added, "I think we do owe Lily a tiny bit of thanks for creating more hype around the launch with her insanity."

"We are *not* toasting her," Rory adamantly said.

"I wasn't even suggesting it," Bayli assured him.

Pierre appeared at that moment and told them all, "Dinner is served." It was Monday night and Davila's NYC was dark. Pierre had volunteered to play host this evening, and Rory's executive chef had offered to cook, wanting to spread his own wings and give Rory some thoughts for the new menu that incorporated inventive and traditional favorites.

While Pierre ushered in their guests, Christian and Rory stayed behind with Bayli.

Christian said, "I hope this is everything you ever wanted."

Her eyes misted. "You know it is."

He took his hand in hers and lifted it to his lips. He said, "I wish I'd known you back in River Cross. Then I would have been aware of your mom's heart condition and after I'd met my college roommate, Gene Eckhart, I could have asked him to help you. To help her. He's really quite brilliant."

Tears crested her eyes and rolled down her cheeks. She told him, "Christian, we both lost our mothers because of circumstances beyond our control. We can't change that. But something all my friends keep telling me is that what I do as I progress in my life is something for my mom to be proud of. She'd appreciate my tenacity, the strength I've finally found, the huge amount of love I have in my life. The fact that I both give and receive it."

She hugged him tight. Then she turned to Rory.

"You give me all kinds of crazy fulfillment I never anticipated."

He chuckled. "I do like to keep you on your toes."

"And you're quite good at it."

Rory exchanged a quick look with Christian, then extracted a long, narrow box from the inside pocket of his suit jacket. "This is from us. For . . . everything."

He kissed her forehead.

Bayli stared at the pale blue box with TIFFANY & CO. stamped on the lid and a white satin ribbon tied in a pretty bow.

"Why do I already know this is going to be way over the top?" she asked in a breathless voice.

Christian said, "Just a little something to keep the smile on your face."

"You both do that amazingly well without jewelry."

"Open it," Rory told her.

Christian took her champagne flute so that she could accept the box from Rory. She pulled the ends of the bow and the satin unraveled. Bayli lifted the lid, peeled back the neatly folded white tissue, and gasped.

Nestled in velvety folds was a diamond tennis bracelet. And they were no small diamonds.

The gift completely took her breath away.

Rory freed the bracelet from its tiny clasps and secured it around her wrist. He said, "We know it can't replace the one your mother gave you, and we're both sorry about that. But you'll always have her in spirit, honey. And a constant reminder that Christian and I love you."

She threw her arms around him and held on tight. Then she hugged Christian again.

"I love you, too."

Bayli had two incredible men, fantastic friends, and a blossoming career. She'd paid off all the medical and credit card bills and was finally officially starting her life.

She led Christian and Rory into the apartment just as Pierre served the appetizer plates.

Phillip and Colin both shoved back their chairs, jumped to their feet, and let out girlish cries.

Phillip pointed at the prawns and wailed, "They still have the heads on them!"

Bayli laughed, boldly, loudly, wickedly.

And her friends joined in.

Read on for an excerpt from *The Billionaires: The Stepbrothers*, coming soon from Calista Fox.

Butterflies took flight in Scarlet's stomach and she felt a little giddy, which she could maybe blame on the wine but knew better what the real reason was. She was antsy over the rest of the evening. Anxious to see Michael and Sam naked and hard.

Wanting her.

Heat burst on her cheeks. This was quickly becoming the longest dinner ever.

Both men kept the conversation light and she was grateful for that. She wouldn't have been able to concentrate on anything too mentally taxing.

They had crème brulee and coffee in a separate room, in front of a tall fireplace. The drapes on the windows and patio doors were pulled back to showcase the grounds and the falling snow. It was all very lovely and even cozy, despite the enormity of every room.

When dessert was over, Michael said, "We'll take a car to the guest house. It sits on the back portion of the estate."

Anticipation could be a real bitch. It clawed at her. Hitched her enthusiasm.

Michael and Sam escorted her to the foyer, where they were handed their coats by the butler. Sam helped her into hers. They left the main house and Michael drove them down a winding pavered path carved into the trees that lined each side of the estate as well as the acreage beyond the mansion. The three-bedroom guesthouse had a gorgeous wood-accented entryway and sweeping staircase, numerous windows, and a heated swimming pool and spa.

Sam built a fire in the living room hearth as Scarlet admired the views through the glass panes along one wall.

Michael stole behind her and whisked her hair over her shoulder. He kissed her temple, then asked, "Do you want wine or water? Anything?"

She gazed at his reflection and smiled. "I want to know that the two of you are still going through with this."

"We're here, aren't we?"

She faced Michael. His mouth sealed to hers. His hands clasped her hips just as her fingers fisted the front of his shirt. The searing lip-lock went on and on. Until Scarlet was breathless.

She pulled away . . . but still wanted more.

Her gaze landed on Sam, standing alongside the fireplace, watching them. The vibrant glow in his eyes spurred her on. She crossed to him, slid her palms up his chest to his shoulders. Then downward where she clutched his bulging biceps. He kissed her slowly, teasingly, their lips and tongues twisting and tangling. He palmed her ass and squeezed before pressing her firmly against him. She felt his erection and it thrilled her even more to know how quickly he responded to her. To the sight of Michael kissing her and the wicked promise of what was to come.

Behind her, she smelled Michael's distinct scent and her excitement ratcheted as he moved in close and his lips skimmed along her neck. He nipped the skin as Sam continued his sensuous kisses. Already she was careening toward sensory overload. And they'd just started. . . .

Between kisses, Sam murmured, "Let's take this to the bedroom."

Desire flared deep within her. She was really and truly going to get her wish. Her fantasy.

Michael stepped away. Sam scooped her into his strong arms and carried her upstairs with Michael hot on their heels.

Scarlet's fingers raked through Sam's lush hair and she nibbled on his earlobe. Then whispered, "Nothing's off-limits as far as I'm concerned."

"Careful about granting carte blanche, darlin'. Michael and I will take advantage of it."

"I know what I'm doing. What I want."

She'd spent the past two days preparing herself with her toys. She'd boldly asked her friends about double penetration, and both Jewel and Bayli swore by it. Just hearing them describe how amazing it was to have both of their men inside them at the same time had gotten Scarlet's juices flowing.

They entered a room and Sam set her on her feet. Then he flipped the switch for the gas fireplace and sank into a chair next to it. Michael propped his shoulder against the doorframe and folded his arms over his chest.

Scarlet eyed one man, then the other. What were they up to?

The suspense drew out as they both stared at her. Taking her in from head to toe and back up. She wore a tight black tank dress with a caramel-colored leather jacket over it. Black thigh-high stockings and four-inch heels. Michael appeared transfixed by her legs. Sam's gaze remained on her breasts.

Eventually Michael spoke.

"Strip for us," he quietly commanded.

Scarlet's entire body went up in flames.

It was one thing to have Michael or Sam peel away her clothing. It was something altogether different to do it herself while they both watched. While they both knew the other was getting hotter and hotter with every layer removed.

Christ, *she* was getting hotter and hotter just thinking of it.

She gripped the lapels of her jacket and slid the leather slowly down her arms. Let the garment drop to the floor. Then she strolled to the end of the bed and kicked off one shoe. She planted her foot on the bench at the end of the mattress and rolled the top of her stocking along her thigh. She bent at the waist to continue rolling the nylon down her calf, knowing the short hem of her skirt had hitched up far enough to give her captive audience a glimpse of her g-string panties and bare ass cheeks.

Holding the position a few seconds longer sexually charged the air. Then she kicked off the other shoe and repeated the pro-cess. Lingering once more. Until Sam shifted in his seat, his crotch apparently too tight for comfort. Served him right.

She kept her gloating smile in check. Instead, she turned to face them and eased a thin strap over her shoulder, letting it fall to the crook of her arm. The other strap followed. She worked the mate-rial over her breasts, down her stomach, over her hips. It pooled on the hardwood floor and she flicked it away with her foot.

She stood before the men wearing nothing but her strapless bra in black satin, matching g-string, and a diamond tennis bracelet.

"The bra first," Sam instructed.

Scarlet reached behind her and unhooked the clasp. Tossed the lingerie aside.

"Now the panties," Sam said. "Slowly. And bring them to me."

Her pussy clenched. She should have known they'd turn this into a wicked game that stimulated her as much as it did them.

Crooking her thumbs in the strands at her sides, she dragged the satin downward. When she reached her knees, she bent at the waist again. Stepped out of the g-string. Took her time straighten-ing, her gaze landing first on Michael, then sliding to Sam.

She walked over to him, crisscrossing one leg in front of the other with her gradual progression. Sam's eyes were glued to her. When she reached him, she dropped the panties in his lap.

"Per your request." She smiled slyly.

He rubbed the scant material between his finger and thumb and his irises darkened with lust. "You're wet." He lifted the lingerie to his nose and inhaled deeply. "Fuck, you smell good."

"She tastes even better," Michael informed him in his deep, intimate voice.

"I'm about to find out." Sam gazed up at her and said, "Put your foot on the top of my thigh."

She did, balancing on one leg.

"Stick your finger in your pussy," Sam told her.

Scarlet slid her hand along her hip and to her apex. Her fingertip glided over her clit and then dipped into the tight canal.

Sam said, "Now brush that finger over your lips."

Her pulse jumped. She wasn't even sure anymore who was more aroused—them or her.

She followed Sam's lead.

"Kiss me," he demanded in a low, smoldering tone.

Scarlet's foot slipped from his thigh and she pressed her knee to the cushion at his hip so that she could lean over him. Her mouth swept against his. Sam's tongue darted out and swiped at her lips.

"Nice," he murmured lustily.

She engaged him in soft, playful kisses.

But it was a huge mistake to think *she* was in control.

The first two books in the
sexy new billionaire ménage
Lovers' Triangle series by
CALISTA FOX

THE BILLIONAIRES
Available April 2017

THE BILLIONAIRES:
THE BOSSES
Available September 2017
